5937208348

Pr

The OPPO⬛⬛⬛⬛RT

"*The Opposite of Art* draws the reader in a way seldom accomplished in a novel. A powerful, moving story of reconciliation and redemption. Dickson has written another page-turner."

—Eric Wiggin, author of *Blood Moon Rising*

"Masterful imagery, unforgettable characters, and a compelling journey in search of answers to the fundamental questions of life. A book to be savored, themes to be discussed with friends, and a story to treasure for years to come."

—Stephanie Grace Whitson, novelist, public speaker, and historian

"Dickson's novel shimmers on the page like a work of art itself, inviting readers to step beyond the evocative prose into the deeper truths within its pages. At once suspenseful and captivating, *The Opposite of Art* is impossible to put down and impossible to forget."

—T. L. Higley, author of *Petra: City in Stone* and *Pompeii: City on Fire*

"Athol's passionate, lyrical storytelling reminds me a bit of Salman Rushdie's *Shalimar the Clown*. Sheridan Ridler's artistic search for Glory is a journey into hope, and I'm profoundly grateful for the privilege of going along."

—Elizabeth White, author of
ACFW Carol Award–winning *Controlling Interest*

"*The Opposite of Art* is mesmerizing, intriguing, and inspiring; a story that stays with you long after the last page."

—Nancy Moser, author of *An Unlikely Suitor* and *Masquerade*

"*The Opposite of Art* pulled me in from the first page and held me captive. Characters that are richly drawn, a plot that twists and turns. What a stunning read!"

—Traci DePree, author of *Into the Wilderness*

"Athol Dickson has created an elegant and gritty masterpiece, nuanced by allegory and delivered in resplendent prose. This lyrical novel can't be rushed; it must be sipped, savored, and pondered to attain the lasting afterglow."

—Kristen Heitzmann, award-winning author of
Indivisible, Secrets, and *The Tender Vine*

"Once again Athol Dickson proves his skill as a writer as he takes his readers on a pilgrimage. The story spins through continents and characters but never leaves the reader behind. This is more than a novel. It is an experience. Once again, Dickson triumphs."

—Marcia Lee Laycock, author of *One Smooth Stone*
and devotional columnist at www.noveljourney.blogspot.com

"Athol Dickson pens an honest, gritty story of an artist tormented by love. He takes the reader into the world of art, greed, murder, and mystery. If you value art, mysteries, and a wild ride across time and around the globe, you'll enjoy *The Opposite of Art*!"

—Nora St.Laurent, founder of
The Book Club Network, www.bookfun.org

The OPPOSITE of ART

A Novel

ATHOL DICKSON

HOWARD BOOKS
A DIVISION OF SIMON & SCHUSTER, INC.
New York · Nashville · London · Toronto · Sydney · New Delhi

Howard Books
A Division of Simon & Schuster, Inc.
1230 Avenue of the Americas
New York, NY 10020

This book is a work of fiction. Names, characters, places, and incidents either are products of the author's imagination or are used fictitiously. Any resemblance to actual events or locales or persons, living or dead, is entirely coincidental.

Copyright © 2011 by Athol Dickson

All rights reserved, including the right to reproduce this book or portions thereof in any form whatsoever. For information address Howard Books Subsidiary Rights Department, 1230 Avenue of the Americas, New York, NY 10020.

First Howard Books trade paperback edition September 2011

HOWARD and colophon are trademarks of Simon & Schuster, Inc.

For information about special discounts for bulk purchases, please contact Simon & Schuster Special Sales at 1-866-506-1949 or business@simonandschuster.com.

The Simon & Schuster Speakers Bureau can bring authors to your live event. For more information or to book an event contact the Simon & Schuster Speakers Bureau at 1-866-248-3049 or visit our website at www.simonspeakers.com.

Designed by Renata Di Biase

Manufactured in the United States of America

10 9 8 7 6 5 4 3 2 1

Library of Congress Cataloging-in-Publication Data

Dickson, Athol, 1955–
    The opposite of art / Athol Dickson.
       p. cm.
    ISBN 978-1-4165-8348-6
    1. Art—Collectors and collecting—Fiction.   I. Title.
    PS3554.I3264O67 2011
    813'.54—dc22

                                        2010054499

ISBN 978-1-4165-8348-6
ISBN 978-1-4391-7760-0 (ebook)

For Brad Coleman,
who reminded me that you
cannot serve both art and money.

Whoever heard of a bad poet committing suicide?

—WALKER PERCY,
LOST IN THE COSMOS

The opposite of art is not ugliness . . .

—ELIE WIESEL,
OPENING CONVOCATION SPEECH,
CENTRE COLLEGE, DANVILLE, KENTUCKY

The OPPOSITE
of ART

PART ONE

Now I want
Spirits to enforce, art to enchant;
And my ending is despair,
Unless I be relieved by prayer,
Which pierces so that it assaults
Mercy itself and frees all faults.
As you from crimes would pardon'd be,
Let your indulgence set me free.

—WILLIAM SHAKESPEARE,
THE TEMPEST

I.

Sirens called him from his dreams. When the racket stopped, he rose and crossed the little bedroom of his hotel suite to lean out into the night, trusting his life to the freezing wrought iron railing just beyond the window so he could gaze down into the alley where a couple of New York City's finest had thrown some guy against the bricks. Even from five floors up, even in the dark, Ridler recognized the lust for violence and the fear down there, but that was nothing compared to the play of the police car's lights on the wall across the alley.

Shivering, Ridler watched the blood-and-bruises rhythm of the red and blue, red and blue, the flashes regular against the dirty masonry, worlds colliding in the patterns of lights and bricks. He saw cryptic shadows slash across the wall, carved from the flashes by a few bricks which stood out to cast empty voids across their fellows like witches conjuring a pitch-black portal to a future or a past. Lately he'd been interested in portals. He sensed a presence waiting beyond time in them, something no one else had painted. Gazing at the wall, Ridler ignored the policeman down below pummeling the screaming fellow's kidneys with methodical jabs—left, right, left, right. Although that too was a pattern in its way, there was no color in it, and certainly no transcendence.

When the guy dropped facedown in a puddle of oily rainwater, Ridler tucked his long black hair behind his ear to better consider the rotating colors rippling in the glistening pavement around the man's body. Steam arose like ectoplasm at a manhole cover, transubstantiated from ghostly grays to primary colors by the police car's flashing lights. It occurred to Ridler they would switch off the lights at any moment.

Turning from the window he ran into the sitting room, which he used as a studio, his easel standing on a paint-splattered tarp in one corner, finished paintings hanging everywhere, stacks of waiting canvases against the walls. From the dining table he gathered his sketch pad and some pastels. Seconds later he was back in the bedroom, haunch against the window jamb, half in, half out, colored chalks and charcoals on the sill beside him. While his fingers dashed back and forth over the pad, he kept his eyes mainly focused on the bricks across the alley, ignoring the cold in his desperation to memorize the image on the wall in case he couldn't get it down before they killed it off forever.

The lights went out. The brick wall was just a wall again. Ridler leaned dangerously far into the frigid air beyond the wrought iron railing, teetering five stories up to shout, "Turn your lights back on!" The policemen down below ignored him, focused as they were on dragging the inert man over to their car. Ridler's breath turned into clouds, drifting off into the night. "Give me back my lights!" The policemen drove away without bothering to look up. Pulling back in from the brink, Ridler muttered, "Pigs."

He tossed the sketch pad onto a chair cushion and went to the small table beside the bed. He switched on the reading light and poked with chalky red and blue fingertips among the pile of cigarette butts in the overflowing ashtray. He found a roach. He lit it and inhaled deeply, sucking in pastel dust and marijuana smoke, closing his eyes to savor the gentle buzz that quickly calmed his mind.

"I thought you weren't going to do that anymore."

Opening his eyes, he saw Suzanna standing in the doorway, her tall and slender figure silhouetted by the light beyond. He exhaled the calming smoke and shrugged. "Are you feeling better?"

"Would you please just put it out?"

The roach was too short to handle anyway. He dropped it back into the ashtray. "I thought I heard you throwing up."

"Must have been something I ate."

As she entered the bedroom he thought of her across the table from him at Max's Kansas City, steaks and salads between them, her skin a smooth burnt umber in the dim lights. After dinner they had headed for the Bowery and CBGB's in the hope that Patti Smith or someone good was playing down there, but it was just some cover band. Still, they had hung around awhile, her drinking a little white wine, him drinking scotch and sneaking a few hits off a joint in the men's room and trying not to think about the reason why she had been acting so distant and unhappy all evening. When the people at a table beside them started staring—the usual hassle about a white guy and a black chick being together—he had almost felt relief. It was an excuse to go someplace quiet where they could talk, his place being the obvious choice, since hers was way up in Harlem.

"So, seriously," he said. "Are you better now?"

"I guess." She sat down on the bed.

"Well, as long as you're here, how about taking off your clothes so I can paint?"

"I told you I'm not going to do that anymore."

He tried to hide the disappointment. Over the last few months, Suzanna had become his favorite model. He had painted her so often he already knew how he'd have her pose this time. Naked on the bed she'd lie almost on her belly, her left leg and left arm straight down, her right arm cocked underneath her chin, and her right leg bent so that her ankle lay upon her calf. He imagined how the open window's draft would raise goose bumps to cast tiny shadows in the oblique bedside light, her brown curves assuming surrealistic forms, a mountain range, a field of dunes. His eyes would roam across the shapes and masses as they would across a landscape, the slightly upraised shoulder as one peak, the buttocks as two others, the graceful spine curving between them like a hanging valley. The play of light would impose intriguing shades upon her dark skin. Shadows within shadows. Something beckoning, that same elusive quality he had almost seen within the streaks of black across the bricks.

"Please, baby," he said, "I really want to paint you tonight."

"That's not all you want to do to me."

He smiled. "Well, that too. But first I want to paint."

"Only if I leave my clothes on."

He sighed. "Oh, all right."

Nearly two hours later, standing at his easel in the sitting room, he said, "Hold still, why don't you?"

He only wished to keep looking at her, so beautiful in the chair, more beautiful by far than any professional model. Still lifes, landscapes, cityscapes . . . models had always fallen into the same category for him, objects to be captured. But for some reason, Ridler saw complexity beyond the sum of arms and legs and torso in Suzanna. While she held her pose fitfully, staring at a blank spot on the wall, he wondered if she thought of him, of the two of them, of their past or future moments. Or did she think of something else, someone completely different, a part of life without him? Ridler drew a dry brush across the canvas, pretending to trace out her form. He realized she had a life beyond the time they spent together—other people, other places, other things he did not know. Alone of all his models, the magnitude of Suzanna's life confronted Ridler every time he tried to paint her. She intrigued him. She challenged him. Sometimes, she frightened him.

"Seriously," said Ridler, "hold still."

She broke the pose completely. "I'm feeling sick again." She rose from the chair and walked around behind him to look at the painting. "You painted me without my clothes on."

"I think of you that way."

She sighed. "How long has it been finished?"

"I don't know."

She slapped his shoulder lightly. "How long?"

"Half an hour, I guess."

"And you just let me sit there?"

He forced himself to smile, although the fear was almost overwhelming. Everything had changed.

"Oh, Danny," she said.

Moments later, she was in the bathroom. He had followed her through the bedroom and stood outside the door. "You could spend the night," he said. "We could grab breakfast at Louie's and go to that Japanese woodcut exhibit before it gets too crowded in the morning."

Through the door he heard no reply. It opened. She walked past him in her peasant dress with the broad leather belt and matching high-heeled boots. Around her neck was the little golden cross inset with sapphires, the one she refused to take off, even during sex.

Suzanna paused to look at the canvas on the easel again. "So you just pretended you were painting?"

"Only toward the end."

"Why?"

He shrugged.

She touched his arm with the back of her fingers, lightly, and then removed her hand. "I can't stay."

He felt his jaw set with a sudden rush of anger. Turning, he strode out of the bedroom into the little sitting room. He leaned against the white enameled kitchenette and lit a Marlboro, knowing that annoyed her almost as much as marijuana. She followed him, stopping in the middle of the sitting room, one foot on the edge of the tarp beneath his easel.

"Please don't be mad," she said.

He took a deep drag on the Marlboro and stared at the ceiling. "I'm not mad."

"Of course you are."

Still looking away from her heartbreakingly beautiful face, he exhaled a cloud of smoke. "Whatever you say."

"It's not that I don't love you."

"Who said anything about love?"

"Danny, please."

The tremor in her voice broke through his resolve. He looked at her and immediately regretted it. It was hard to be angry when she stared at him all doe-eyed, but still, he had his pride. "I just don't get you. Sex is beautiful."

"It's not about the sex. That's just the way it comes out between us."

"I have no idea what you're talking about."

"It's not that hard to understand. I love you, Danny. I fell really hard for you. But I lost myself."

"Lost yourself?" Flicking the cigarette butt into the kitchenette sink he said, "What's that supposed to mean?"

"Making love and not being married . . . it isn't who I am."

"Oh, I see. It's not you. So who was that other chick?"

"I'm just trying to—"

"Seriously, who was she? I'd like to know, because she seemed like she was having a great time, and I'd like to get her back in here."

"Please, I—"

"I remember a couple of weeks ago she was over on the bed screaming, 'Yes! Yes! Yes!' and I sure got the impression she meant every word."

"It's not that we weren't—"

"In fact, I remember a few times when she couldn't seem to get enough."

She stared at him with those eyes which were the only thing he had ever doubted he could capture on canvas, and he basked in her beauty, and he longed to get down on his knees and worship her, beg her to reconsider everything, just be with him without conditions, but he knew it wouldn't work. Something in him fought all that.

He walked over to the easel and pretended to examine the painting there. It had no face. He never gave them faces, but maybe in Suzanna's case . . .

He lit another cigarette. It made him nervous, thinking what he was thinking.

After a minute he heard a rustling sound and turned to see her putting on her coat.

"Where are you going?"

She would not look at him.

"Hey, baby," he said. "Come on."

She picked up her purse, a huge macramé thing filled with the most amazing collection of unexpected objects. Whenever they went out, it seemed like she had whatever he needed, no matter how weird it might be. Slinging the bag's strap over her shoulder, she went to the door. Still she had not looked at him. She turned the latch. She put her hand on the doorknob. Everything was out of control. He wanted her the same way she wanted him. Why couldn't he find a way to explain that?

"Marry me," he said.

At first she stood motionless, gripping the door; then she released it and turned. "Why? So we can sleep together again?"

"Not just that."

"What else then, Danny?"

The words just wouldn't come. He tried, but in the end he could only wave his hand between them, the cigarette trailing smoke. "You know."

She covered her mouth with a palm. Staring at him with those amazing eyes, which had begun to well, she shook her head. She took a shuddering breath. She lowered her hand and faced him squarely. "You don't really care at all."

After the door had closed behind her, he turned back toward the painting on the easel and spoke to empty air. "That's not true."

He cocked his head, smoke drifting toward the ceiling from the cigarette between his lips. He tried to think about the painting. Something about the energy in the legs was wrong. He tried a few light pencil lines, looking for a better way to compose the legs, and then put the pencil down and began to pace the little hotel suite, back and forth between the sitting room and bedroom, thinking of Suzanna. Against his better judgment he paused to stare at the snapshot she had pinned to the wall above his bed a few weeks before, when she got him to admit he slept around a little.

"I dare you to leave it there," she had said, "while you do it with some stranger."

It had been just a guilt trip of course, so he had left the photo there to spite her. Even when he was alone he pretended to ignore the image of her smiling at the camera, but in truth he could not seem to avoid looking at it, whether he was in his bed alone or not.

Moved by a sudden impulse he leaned over, pulled down the snapshot, and stuffed it into his hip pocket.

He didn't want a snapshot.

He wanted Suzanna, even if he had to beg.

Ridler paused only long enough to pull his parka on over his T-shirt. Ten seconds later he was running down the hall. He ignored the elevators, which were ancient and notoriously slow, and took the hotel's ornate stairs, boots pounding on the treads and echoing against the plaster, brass handrails and vaguely art nouveau–patterned iron railing to the right of him, other tenants' unimportant paintings on the walls along the left. He himself had paid for three months' lodging with oils the management had not yet hung.

He descended round and round the spiraling staircase past the work of lesser talents, until he reached the ground floor hall, and then the lobby and finally he charged out through the front doors onto West 23rd. He turned first toward the synagogue on the left, but she wasn't there. He turned the other way and saw her short Afro silhouetted in the rear window of a departing cab. He turned back toward the synagogue. No taxis in that direction. He set out running after her. He didn't notice the cold, or the harsh whistle of his breath—too many cigarettes, too many joints—as he chased the cab. All he could think of was Suzanna getting away, his mind on nothing else until, half a block up the street, he ran straight out into 7th Avenue without looking.

A southbound cab locked its brakes to avoid him, horn blaring and all four tires screaming on the pavement. Its right front fender stopped an inch away. The driver rolled his window down and cursed him. Ridler ran to the rear door and opened it. The cabbie was still cussing when Ridler got into the backseat, so he yelled to make himself heard. "Twenty bucks on top of the fare if you shut up and go east on Twenty-third! Step on it!"

The driver closed his mouth and took off with a squeal of rubber.

Leaning forward, Ridler searched the traffic ahead for her cab. He saw only one, passing under the next streetlight. It had to be her.

"Where to, kid?" asked the driver, gaining on them.

"Follow that cab," said Ridler, pointing forward.

"Get outta here. Seriously?"

The taxi ahead drove steadily, passing Broadway, Madison Square Park, Park and Lexington. At the river it turned north under the South Street Viaduct. The traffic light went red.

"Run it," said Ridler.

"No way."

"Another twenty."

The driver slowed a little, glancing left, then charged on.

They paralleled the viaduct then merged onto FDR Drive, with the Brooklyn lights across the river on their right. Ridler reached into his parka's pocket, looking for a hair band. His fingers touched a dime-size baggie with some grass and papers, also an old prescription bottle which contained a few pills he had picked up at a bar, black mollies, reds and 'ludes. He found the hair band, gathered a ponytail at the nape of his neck, slipped it through the band, which he twisted with a practiced motion, and then passed back through a second time. His long black hair now hung down his back, out of his way. In the driver's rearview mirror he caught a glimpse of himself when an oncoming car's headlights illuminated the inside of the cab. From the front he looked like he had short hair. He remembered something Suzanna had said while he was painting her one time, before things went wrong.

"I like your hair that way."

"Yeah? How come?"

"It makes you look more civilized."

He remembered deep blue violet on his palette. He always painted Suzanna in blues. "Civilized? That'll be the day."

"Seriously, Danny, have you ever thought of cutting it?"

"Why do you call me Danny?"

"Sheridan's too stuffy. Sheri is a girl's name, and Dan just doesn't fit."

"You could call me Ridler, like everybody else."

"That's not who you are."

Of all the people on the planet, only Suzanna thought that.

"Hey, kid." The driver turned a little in his seat, staring back at Ridler in the mirror with a pair of large dark eyes on either side of a nose the shape and color of a Bosc pear. "Forty bucks don't buy a lot of trouble. What's the deal?"

It never crossed his mind to admit he was following Suzanna to beg her for forgiveness. "The girl in that cab stole something from me. I need to get it back."

"I could get dispatch to call the cops."

"I don't want to get her into that much trouble."

They drove for blocks, below the Queensboro Bridge, past Roosevelt Island, then under the overhang at Carl Schurz Park. After a few minutes the cabbie said, "What color is this girl of yours?"

"What kind of question is that to ask?"

"Hey, no offense, but we're gettin' into Harlem."

"Just stay with her."

He couldn't stop thinking of Suzanna. He saw how it would go in his mind. He'd catch up with her before she went into her building. He'd do the whole thing, get down on one knee, take her hand in both of his, tell her that he loved her and beg her to be his wife. He'd use his hair band for a ring, tell her they'd shop for a diamond to-morrow. He'd do it right there in her neighborhood. He'd do it even if there was a crowd of brothers around, even if it got him mugged.

They rolled under a footbridge and FDR Drive turned into Har-lem River Drive. Ahead on the right, Ridler saw a bright orange glow in the sky. The driver shifted in his seat. "I don't know where she's goin', but I ain't drivin' into Harlem. Ain't goin' into no South Bronx, either. Not this time of night."

"What's your problem, man?"

"You a tourist, kid? Don't know where we is?"

"I know." The truth was he had only been to Harlem a couple of times with Suzanna, and always in the daylight. He had never been into the Bronx. "It's no big deal."

"No big deal he says. You see the sky over there?" The driver waved the back of his hand toward the glowing sky across the river. "Like that Cosell said, the Bronx is burnin', kid. Every night a dif-ferent buildin'. This ain't no neighborhood for a white boy like you. Not this time a morning."

"I have a hundred-dollar bill here. It's yours if you just shut up and follow that cab."

"A hundred?"

"That's right."

"Lemme see it."

Ridler reached for his wallet. His hip pocket was empty. In a flash he visualized his wallet in a drawer back at the hotel.

"Come on," said the cabbie. "Lemme see the money."

Ridler smiled into the mirror. "Don't you trust me?"

With no warning, the driver stood on the brakes, throwing Ridler hard against the front seat as the car squealed to a stop. Twisting around to face Ridler, the man said, "You don't got my money?"

"Sure I do. Just not on me."

"Get outta the cab."

"Come on, man."

The cabbie leapt from the taxi and opened Ridler's door. A car roared by, the driver laying on the horn. The cabbie reached in, grabbed Ridler's coat, and yanked. "OUT!"

Moments later, Ridler stood alone on a narrow strip of dirt beside the road. The toes of his boots touched the concrete curb. The heels were against a chain-link fence. In spite of the late hour, cars rushed past him every few seconds, so close he felt the tug of their back draft. He stared up Harlem River Drive the way Suzanna's taxi had gone. He tried to remember her address, but the few times he had been to her apartment she had always given the address to the cabbie and he had not paid attention, focusing instead on her profile beside him, her earlobe, her jawline, the corner of her eye.

Ridler turned his back on the street, curled his fingers through the fence, and stared in misery at a strip of gravel on the other side where construction trucks were parked. Apparently it was a temporary staging area for work on the Madison Avenue Bridge. Beyond the construction equipment the Harlem River slipped slowly toward the right, black and silent, and beyond the river loomed the derelict brick and concrete buildings of the South Bronx. As he watched, a giant tongue of flame uncurled between a pair of empty warehouses, rising in the night to lick the bulbous belly of the clouds. The fire's reflection flickered in that pregnant sky as if the pent-up snow were radioactive. The Bronx was burning; wasn't that what the cabbie had said? He had read about it: blocks and blocks of vacant buildings, landlords risking felonies for insurance money, failure lighting up the heavens.

The flame dropped down again to hide behind a row of buildings on the far side of the river, but Ridler could make out the devil's palette through the warehouse windows, the orange and red and yellow squares, a grid of colors standing out against the black wall, much the same as what he had seen before from his hotel room, the red and blue revolving lights against the bricks, motion in the color, a still, black nothingness in the background. And in the blackness . . . what?

Staring, he refused to blink. There. It was there. The same thing again, in the blackness over there between the windows. A distance in it, something infinite around those fiery squares. As he watched, the pattern gathered. He saw as only artists see. A vibration in the air, a rhythm almost musical compressed his chest as if it were a drum, the city's sounds in strange syncopation—horns, engines, hissing tires on pavement, distant shouts and barking dogs—all of it somehow merged together, and in that merging also was the crisp scent of metal and the stench of automotive fumes and the pungency of humans far too numerous to count, and sweat, and breath, and fear and joy and tears and laughter, tongues of light, burning color and the blackness, all of it combined in one transcendent wave of everything an artist might sense or feel, beckoning to him across the Harlem River. Even time had opened up before him. He stood at the frontier of something set apart, a model worthy of his skill. He had only to believe, and go.

A panel van thundered by, mere inches behind him, furiously stirring up the frigid air. He ignored his parka's flapping at his ribs. He gripped the chain-link fence and climbed.

Dropping down on the other side, he ran toward the bridge. Normally the span would have been impossible to reach from down beside the river, but scaffolding had been erected around the columns. Ridler found a ladder and ascended. The steel bars burned with cold beneath his naked fingers.

Up on the bridge, the eastbound walkway had been blocked

off. A long section of the concrete barrier between it and the traffic lanes was gone, and the usual inward-curving fence at the outer edge of the bridge was missing. He set out across the river anyway, working his way around sacks of concrete and a portable mixer and piles of metal reinforcement bars. He shouldn't be there, but the crew was working on the westbound side and wouldn't hassle him. Cars roared by. He felt the pavement shudder underneath the weight of passing trucks. He felt the frigid winter wind above the Harlem River. He didn't care. In pursuit of something no one else had painted, he raised the parka's hood over his head, jammed his hands into the pockets like a monk within a cloister, and hurried toward the feasting flames.

2.

S louched behind the wheel of his Buick Electra, Talbot Graves ignored a beer commercial on the radio. He needed something more than liquid courage. Maybe it would help to think of all the reasons Ridler ought to die.

He decided to begin with Suzanna, his assistant for five years. He thought about her misery lately, whenever they spoke of Sheridan Ridler. The welling eyes. The quivering lips. Her obvious embarrassment.

The man must be a mesmerist. Graves would never understand how Ridler had conquered Suzanna otherwise. She was a level-headed businesswoman, and she had seen the same abuses Talbot Graves had seen, yet somehow the painter had convinced her to model for him. After that she had inhaled Ridler's lies as if they were oxygen and dined on his abusiveness as if it were the bread of life. Over the last three years Talbot had watched with growing distaste as Ridler had done the same with many other women. Talbot had warned Suzanna that the man gave no more thought to using women than he gave to eating lunch—Ridler was a Rasputin, a Svengali, a demon in the flesh—but she had kept her infatuation secret until the strange contagion was too far advanced, and in the end it had consumed her.

Talbot's own chances with Suzanna had been a long shot before, what with him a quarter century older and of course the color barrier, but now with Ridler in the picture it was completely out of the question. All the women Ridler already had, and the greedy swine took dear Suzanna too. That alone was unforgivable.

It was so cold. Even with the Electra's engine running and the heater at full blast the gallery owner shivered behind the wheel, pulling his overcoat a little tighter around himself and settling his chin lower in his scarf. He drew no warmth from the calculating rage which seemed to possess him, much as Suzanna had been possessed in her way.

It wasn't as if Ridler had confined his thoughtlessness to women, of course. Thinking back over the last three years, Talbot found it easy to recall a long string of indignities he had endured at Ridler's hands, beginning with the night the painter had missed the opening of his first exhibition at the gallery. Most of the important patrons had already left, but Ridler had walked in four hours late, as if he were a potentate instead of a nothing, a nobody from Nebraska or Ohio or some such awful backwater. After all the work Talbot had done to get the opening arranged, all the influence he had used to get the best people there, Ridler had never bothered to explain, much less apologize.

Talbot also thought about the faces. If Ridler would just paint facial features on his nudes, they would surely sell more easily.

"Why not?" he had asked. "It's not as if you shy away from details."

"I don't paint faces," had been the dilettante's response.

"You paint fingers. You paint toes. Look at *Nude 26*. You put numbers on that clock in the background. Just a pair of eyes, a nose and lips. Why not?"

"Graves," he said. (Ridler always called him Graves.) "Because it's you, I'll explain this just one time, and never again. I don't paint faces, because the paintings are about me, okay? What I'm trying to work out. What I want to understand. If I gave them faces, it would be about the models. You have to get this straight if you're going to represent me. I won't paint for other people."

"But the collectors say—"

"Enough!" the egomaniac had interrupted. "I don't care what collectors say!"

How he hated the ingratitude. He would have dropped the little poseur long ago, but he had sold five paintings that first night, and the paintings kept on selling, so he had comforted himself instead by lying about the sale prices and pocketing the difference. It had been easy to do. For all his posturing, Ridler was a fool when it came to money. Robbing him had been a simple matter of typing two different price lists, one for customers, one for Ridler. There had been great satisfaction in keeping Ridler ignorant of his own success, especially when the pompous little dolt had come to him for loans, thinking he was broke. But of course it couldn't last forever, not when Ridler's immense talent supported such high prices.

Everything had begun to fall apart three weeks ago, when Zero Mostel had purchased eight canvases. It seemed the Broadway star was also an accomplished painter and collector. Purchases by such a famous patron could not be concealed. Ridler was certain to learn of Mostel's interest, and he would probably find out what the man had really paid. That would lead to questions about the much lower prices Talbot had reported in the past, which would be the end of everything.

Talbot remembered the negotiations with Mostel, the comedian having already offered almost twice what any Ridler painting had commanded up to then, and Talbot asking for more. Mostel, thinking seriously about it, had asked the question, "How old is this guy?"

"Twenty-two or -three."

"Then that's my final offer."

Talbot Graves had understood Mostel's logic immediately, and with that understanding had come the idea. As vast as Ridler's genius was—and he was indeed a genius on the order of a Manet or Picasso—still, his work could command more, much more, if the supply was limited. The decision was inevitable after realizing that.

Even worse than losing his gallery and possibly suffering legal prosecution of some kind for swindling the artist, Talbot Graves could not endure the thought of letting Ridler have the upper hand. So he would kill the egomaniac for the women—to avoid future heartache and to preserve decorum—and for the sake of common courtesy, self-defense, and profit.

Very little argued against it. The possibility of getting caught was chief among the reasons that gave pause, and that risk could be minimized. He would simply tell no one of his plans and involve no accomplice. He would do everything himself. That was the safest way.

Still, as he shivered in the car, Graves wasn't sure that he could pull the trigger. He hadn't fired a gun since he was a child. Even then it had only been an air rifle. As far as murder was concerned, the firearm on the seat beside him was perfect, an antique Webley-Fosbery automatic revolver handed down from his grandfather to his father, a gun nobody knew he owned. But the revolver had not been fired in more than thirty years. Who knew if it was functional?

The thing might very well explode in his hand instead of putting a bullet where it belonged, in Ridler's brain.

So he had dithered, sitting in the car outside the hotel, hoping to gather up the courage to go in. He had tried to visualize success: a knock on Ridler's door, the artist opening it, seeing the revolver in his hand and smiling because he would not think Talbot capable of such a thing, and then the shocked expression when the gun went off, the smirk wiped from that handsome face, and Talbot tossing the untraceable revolver down beside the body and walking calmly to the elevators.

Several times Talbot's gloved fingers had closed around the Electra's door handle. Several times he had been half a second away from getting out and walking in and doing it, but other possibilities always came to mind. Someone in a neighboring room opening a door, a maid appearing, or a bellhop, or the revolver misfiring, or Ridler lunging for it—a struggle, heaven forbid—or his aim being off and Ridler living to tell who fired the shot.

At that moment, Suzanna emerged from Ridler's hotel. Talbot's rage swelled to a crescendo at the sight of her, knowing she had been up in the painter's rooms. Then he realized what he had almost done, how close he'd come to going up there with the gun while she was with Ridler. He passed a palm over his forehead, feeling weak at the thought of what might have happened.

She stood at the curb for quite a while before a cab rolled by. He watched her hail it and get in, and just then Ridler charged out onto the sidewalk.

Seeing him there, staring wildly left and right, Talbot Graves was almost convinced the man had somehow read his mind. The painter certainly seemed agitated, even angry. Ridler searched the street, apparently looking for the cause of his displeasure. Graves settled lower in the seat, his eyes barely level with the Buick's dashboard as he watched the artist set out running in the other direction.

Graves had the car in gear as Ridler dashed across 7th Avenue without looking, and a taxi nearly ran him down. Strangely, Graves felt himself flinching as the taxi slid toward Ridler, instinctively hoping the car would miss the man. How foolish, when an accident would so neatly solve his problems. But the near miss did inspire him. His thinking was too limited. The revolver was not his only option.

Talbot followed the taxi east on 23rd and onto FDR Drive, becoming more and more nervous as they went north. He didn't want to go to Harlem at this time of night. Still, he stayed behind the taxi.

Fortunately, when the cab stopped suddenly in the middle of the road, Talbot was just approaching a temporary construction turnout. He reacted instantly, pulling to the right and parking. He sat just off Harlem River Drive, watching Ridler on the curb ahead and thinking now would be the perfect opportunity. There wasn't that much traffic. He could get up to speed, swing to the right, hop the curb at the last second, and where could Ridler go, trapped there by that fence?

Do it. Do it now before you lose your nerve.

Talbot put the Electra into gear and glanced into his rearview mirror, waiting for a moment when the road was clear. Soon that moment came. No headlights in the mirror whatsoever. But when he looked forward, Ridler was halfway up the fence and out of reach. Talbot felt a great relief. It didn't matter. Tomorrow would be soon enough.

He rolled on, turning from the gravel construction drive into the right lane of the Harlem River Drive, looking forward to reaching his apartment and some sleep. The feeling of relief annoyed him. He did not want to think himself a coward. He told himself tension in this situation was only natural, and it was natural to feel relieved when the reason for the tension disappeared over the fence. He had the courage to do this. He would do it. Tomorrow.

As Talbot approached the Madison Avenue overpass, he glimpsed Ridler climbing a set of scaffolding beyond the chain-link fence and he realized where the painter was going. Talbot knew if Ridler was going to cross the river on the bridge, there was still a chance.

He pressed the accelerator and the Electra's eight cylinders roared. The car surged forward, speeding north as he searched for an exit. It was a long time coming, maybe four minutes, before he saw the sign for 8th Avenue. He took the off-ramp from the left-hand lane and then he was heading south again on 8th, past some projects on the right and a basketball court on the left, under the West 155th Street overpass.

The light ahead turned red. He slowed to a stop. Ten or fifteen black men stood below a streetlight on his right. He pretended to ignore them, watching from the corner of his eye. He saw movement in the periphery. He turned to see several of them stepping off the curb, heading his way. He pressed on the accelerator, running the red light. For twelve blocks after that he slowed at red lights, glancing left and right before driving on. If the police pulled him over he would just explain that he was lost and scared to stop.

Eight minutes after he had last seen Ridler, he turned left onto 135th Street, remembering it was the last exit off Harlem River Drive before the Madison Avenue Bridge. From there it was just three and a half blocks to the river. He turned left again, onto

Madison. He slowed as he climbed the ramp, allowing a pair of cars to pass him. He saw no headlights in his mirrors.

He drove onto the bridge, and there, sure enough, was Ridler walking on the right. The man had the hood of his coat pulled up, but Graves would know that swagger anywhere.

It was the perfect chance. Not only were there no vehicles behind him, but he saw no headlights coming on the other side. They were alone on that side of the bridge. Even at four in the morning it was a miracle of sorts in New York City.

Talbot swallowed back the bile that threatened to rise up.

"Do it," he whispered.

He wasn't going fast enough. He sped up to nearly fifty, the dark figure ahead rushing closer, closer, until it was just there on his right and the moment was upon him, all he had to do was pull right just a little, only a couple of feet . . . but Talbot's hands would not cooperate. He steered straight. Even before the chance was completely over, even while there was still time left to follow through, he knew that he would not. He would pass the man and drive into the Bronx, and find a place to turn around and go back home, because it seemed he was a coward after all.

Then Ridler stepped in front of him.

It was impossible to swerve away.

The impact was much louder than he had expected. The Electra shuddered with revulsion but kept rolling. With both hands on the wheel, Talbot turned his head to see the body soar as if in slow motion, Ridler hanging in midair beside the car, Ridler dropping down beyond the edge of the bridge, unencumbered by the guardrails and the fence which had been removed for repairs, dropping down into the Harlem River. Talbot would always remember that frozen moment, the way the painter's form had hovered upon a fiery background, the Bronx behind him burning up with color, the artist nothing but a black and empty silhouette against it, and in the years to come the unreality of that image would take precedence and Graves would begin to question what had happened, to feel it had been only an imaginary episode, something so greatly desired that he had built it from thin air.

3.

Silent and alone, the boy slipped through the darkness between the western shore and the caissons below the Park Avenue railroad bridge. The dim light from a waning moon had turned the bridge's spiderweb of powder-blue steel into a ghostly white. Stinking water gurgled against the tar which sealed the fabric hull of his little homemade boat. The oars in his hands, made of flattened coffee cans wired to broom handles, dipped into the river only occasionally to correct his course as the current carried him downstream. He sometimes shipped the oars in order to release them and blow into cupped palms. It was almost dawn, the coldest time of all. Although he hated for the night to end, he knew he must return the boat to its hiding place before he became too easily visible from the riverbank.

He had gone much farther that night than ever before, all the way up to the Hudson. In just over four hours he had rowed beneath ten bridges, maintaining a steady, methodical stroke upstream, warmed by the hard work, pausing often, careful to hug the shoreline lest the current farther out take hold of him. He had seen trees growing from the rusting hulks of long-abandoned barges. He had steered well clear of dark, mumbling forms seeking heat from a pile of burning garbage on a muddy bar. He had seen the larger flames across the river in the Bronx, the abandoned buildings an inferno there, as if hell had risen through the frozen sewers. He had rowed, and rowed, and dreamed of wider rivers, cleaner water, oceans, and escape.

He had timed it to arrive at about three thirty, low tide, when the slack would minimize the current. Even then, Spuyten Duyvil Creek had nearly overwhelmed him. The "devil's spout," which connected the Harlem River with the Hudson had been aptly named, for it was an evil amalgamation of eddies and swirling currents. The boy had nearly lost control rounding the point below the tenth bridge, the Henry Hudson Parkway, but with a minute or so of furious rowing he managed to maintain his headway, and then he was there, staring past the open swing bridge at the mouth of the creek, staring out across the black void of the Hudson River, toward the lights of New Jersey twinkling on the far shore.

He had worked the oars to stay in place at the mouth of the creek for almost twenty minutes, breath steaming from his nostrils. He lingered in the cold, watching that opposite shore, thinking of beds with mattresses over there, instead of blankets on the floor, and refrigerators filled with ham and cheese and chicken, and boys with fathers, and mothers who were not crack-addicted whores. Then he came about and let the current take him down again, down to Harlem and real life.

In all of that real life to which he must return, the boy cared for nothing but the river and his boat. He could barely read or write. He could not tell an elephant from a tyrannosaurus, but he could explain the difference between a schooner and a ketch, and he could instantly identify a bark or brigantine. He had one dream and one only, which was to leave his mother's stinking apartment forever, to step onto a boat, and sail away.

He had no concept of the size of oceans. He had been aboard a vessel larger than his little boat only one time, long ago, when he had crossed the harbor with his Maman on the Staten Island Ferry. It was his finest memory, his Maman in her bright head scarf beside him holding his hand, and the water all around, and the idea that the boat was not on rails or wheels, was not bound to roads or tracks, but on the contrary the ferry could turn in any direction, could carry him anywhere and never stop.

But they had returned to Manhattan and to Harlem, and his Maman had died soon after, and since her death three years ago he had not cried, he had not laughed, he had known just the one emotion, the longing for the river.

The boy had built the little boat himself. It had not been hard to do once he had the right materials. A pair of bedsheets, stolen from a neighbor's laundry line and stretched tightly over a frame he had formed from plastic pipes and wire, then thickly coated with hot tar and reinforced on the inside with pieces of corrugated fiberglass, all of which he had taken in a single night from a road construction site and from a pair of garbage bins in the alley by his building. He sat on a small wooden plank that spanned the boat. The broomstick oars worked in locks fashioned from wire coat hangers. At his feet he had a plastic milk jug with the top cut out, leaving the handle and a large opening, which he used from time to time to bail. Also in the boat was a small flashlight, stolen from the bodega on the corner of his block and very seldom used in order to preserve the batteries. He had some tap water in a plastic Coca-Cola bottle, and the remains of his dinner—half a bag of potato chips—also taken from the bodega.

Although it had required four hours of hard work to make his way upstream against the current, after merely an hour he had already returned to his starting point, a landing well downriver from the railroad bridge.

The abandoned wharf projected about thirty feet over the water, many of the pilings underneath it rotten and collapsed. Glancing over his shoulder often, the boy steered toward a pair of pilings on the upstream side. Behind them, below the overhanging wharf, a bar of mud and garbage had collected, piled up by floods and currents through the years until the top of it lay just about a foot above the high tide line. It was the perfect place to conceal his boat, completely out of sight from the Harlem side because of the rotten wharf above, and too far away and deeply shadowed to be seen from across the river in the Bronx.

He had little time remaining. With the pale glow of approaching sunrise already spreading high above the rooftops of Mott Haven, he slipped into the darker shelter of his secret place. He had to get out from under the wharf before the morning light began to glow more brightly. He could not take a chance on being seen as he emerged, lest someone become curious and discover his boat, or he himself be caught by the gang that controlled that neighborhood.

After three more dips of the oars as he drifted down among the pilings, he felt the bow shudder as it slipped across the bottom. The tide had been rising for only a few minutes, so most of the bar was still exposed. He shipped the oars and scrambled out. Gripping the bulwark of the little boat, he began to pull it up. Above the high tide line at the top of the bar where the bulkhead under the old wharf met the island of Manhattan, he tied it off securely. Giving his little boat an affectionate pat, he set out through the darkness, feeling his way toward the place where he had disguised an opening in the wharf overhead, his secret access to the hidden bar. With the concrete bulkhead at his elbow, he ducked beneath low-hanging beams until he stood below the opening. Then, in the growing light at the water's edge nearby, he saw the man.

His first instinct was to run, but where could he go? The bar extended just a few yards beyond the end of the wharf at low tide, and then there was the river. Besides, the man was lying down, most likely passed out drunk. The boy froze in place, staring. When the chest did not rise or fall, and when no steamy breath emerged from the lips or mouth, he decided it might not be a sleeping man. It might only be a corpse.

Curious, he approached the body. It lay in the mud at the waterline with its legs undulating slightly in the river's silent flow. The boy stopped about ten feet away, a little higher up on the bar, and squatted down onto his haunches. He wrapped his thin arms around his knees, propped his chin upon his arms, and watched some more. For ten minutes, he did not move. Neither did the man.

The water rose a little in that time, reaching the hem of the man's coat. The boy thought it was a very fine coat, even smeared with mud. He especially liked the furry fringe around the hood. He decided it might bring as much as five dollars. He wondered what kind of shoes the man might be wearing. He wondered what might be in his pockets.

Still squatted on his haunches, the boy moved crablike, just a little closer. The rising tide began to lift the body slightly. The boy felt no sympathy. He felt no fear. He simply worried that the rising river might wash the man away before he could get the coat.

Suddenly the body moved. The boy stood up to run, but it was just the current.

He took one step closer and squatted down again. In the growing light he realized the dead man was white. That surprised him. He knew very little about white people, but it seemed to him they didn't often end up in the Harlem River. He watched the nose and mouth very carefully. He saw no sign of breath, no steam whatsoever emerging in the cold. The eyelids never fluttered. After a full fifteen minutes, he was completely satisfied there was no life.

The boy stood up. He took the final steps down to the body. He bent and gripped the coat and pulled, but the corpse was very heavy, and he was too small to move it much. He decided to go through the pockets. Inside the coat he found a plastic bag filled with drugs. So that was probably what happened: some rich white guy thought he'd go up to Harlem and make a score, and lost his money and his life. But no, in that case why did he still have the drugs in his pocket? Who would throw him in the river while he still had drugs? It was an interesting question.

The boy put the plastic bag in his own coat pocket and resumed his search. He found nothing else, no wallet and no cash, but he did notice the man's boots, which looked like they might also go for five dollars or so. The only problem was, the legs were still floating in the water, and he didn't want to wade in after them. He put a knee in the middle of the dead man's chest and a hand on the body's upper thigh and leaned out as far as he could, reaching for the boots. Suddenly the body underneath him heaved. The boy leapt back.

Black river water spewed from the body's mouth onto the mud, then it heaved again, vomiting onto the bar, and then the boy saw thin tendrils of steam begin to rise up from its mouth. The boy ran.

With three pilings and forty feet between him and the man, the boy stopped and turned around. For two or three minutes, the man remained exactly as he was, then he rolled onto his side. Poised to leap into the icy river if necessary, the boy hid deep in the shadows farther up under the rotting wharf. The resurrected man sat up. The boy watched him lean forward and vomit more water. The man sat hunched over for another minute, and then, slowly and with what appeared to be a monumental effort of his will, he stood.

Swaying on his feet down beside the river, the man began to mumble. He staggered up the bar, moving toward the downstream end of the wharf, away from the boy.

Careful to make no sound, the boy followed.

Beyond the overhang, the river was no longer black. The rising sun had painted it with reds and purples, yellows and oranges, the colors of an African flag. The man paused beneath the edge of the overhang, swaying slightly and looking down toward his feet. He bent and picked something up. From a distance, the boy thought it was a stick. If the man intended to go up against whoever had thrown him in the river, the boy did not believe the stick would be much help.

The man stepped out of the shadows, out under the dawning sky. He stumbled along the short slab of bar remaining, following the river's waterline as it turned him toward the shore. In a few steps he reached the end of the little bar, where the mud slipped underneath the water and the river lapped against the concrete bulkhead.

The top of the bulkhead stood at about the same height as the man's head. He faced the concrete wall and began to rub the object in his hand across it. The boy heard a hollow sound as the object scraped along the concrete, and then he realized it was a metal pipe. But what was the man doing? Trying to sharpen it into a point? Make it into a better weapon?

From underneath the abandoned wharf, the boy peered around a piling, watching as the man continued his strange motions. Scratching at the coating of sludge and mire that had turned the concrete bulkhead black over the years, the man's movements were sometimes long and sweeping. At other times he beat the wall with short, staccato strokes as if tapping out the rhythm of a song.

Although the boy could not have said when the transformation started, he began to see a change. The man's posture became more erect. He stood more steadily upon his feet. He bent at the knees, putting his whole body into his strange beating and scraping on the concrete. Sweeping his outstretched arm across the bulkhead, his breathing became powerful, puffs of steam ejecting from his nostrils in time to his arm's motions. In the boy's imagination, he became an angry bull snorting as it scraped the ground, or a wizard somehow drawing out the strength of the old bulkhead, channeling it into himself through the piece of metal in his hand, becoming solid with the power of that concrete wall which held the river back from Harlem.

The boy thought of stories he had heard from his Maman before she died, stories spoken in her Haitian accent of the hidden Powers in the world, the Ancient Ones who lived within the soil beneath the streets. In thinking of those stories, the boy felt a strange attraction, as if the man might somehow take him back into that time when his Maman had been alive, a time when he could still feel joy and sadness, hate and love and—

"NO!"

The sudden shout roused the boy from foolish daydreams.

"NO! NO! NO!"

The man had stepped back from the wall, back into the river. He stood facing the bulkhead with water up to his shins. "NO!" he screamed again.

The man's protest echoed from the hulking walls of derelict apartments and abandoned warehouses, the artificial canyon through which the river flowed. He flung the piece of pipe against the bulkhead. It bounced off the concrete with a clear, loud ping, and fell into the river, and the boy thought of another story told by his Maman, of a sword cast into a lake, and a lady's hand that took it down.

The man ran straight at the wall. The boy thought he meant to crash into the substance of the bulkhead, to merge his essence with the Power in it, but at the final instant the man leapt and gripped the top of the concrete, then he pulled himself up to the ground above, and he was gone.

The boy remained behind the piling underneath the wharf.

He waited five full minutes before moving.

Finally, he stepped out onto the open bar. He crossed it quickly, unwilling to remain exposed to view for long, casting glances all along the top of the bulkhead. At any moment he might see someone up there looking down. He had never taken such a chance before. Always he had timed his river explorations to allow him to return to his own neighborhood before daylight. It would be bad enough if someone saw him coming from below the wharf and came down to investigate, bad enough if they found his boat and stole it, but above all else he must not be seen by one of the gang members who controlled that neighborhood, which was eight long blocks from where he lived. For trespassing in their territory they would surely beat him. He wasn't sure why he was taking such a chance. He only knew he had to see the wall.

Drawing near, he saw a pattern of scratch marks, just random marks, nothing meaningful or mystical. He stood close for about a minute, trying to understand, and then the danger of his situation overwhelmed his curiosity and he turned to go. But in his turning, from the corner of his eye he witnessed something.

He turned back toward the wall. He looked more carefully, and as he stared he slowly sank onto his knees. He forgot about the dangers in the city up above. Kneeling on the Harlem River bar, he forgot about the gang, and his long gone deadbeat father and the crack-addicted whore who was his mother, and his dear departed Maman. He forgot about himself. He simply stared, and stared, until more than an hour had passed and the bar beneath him had been long submerged, and the risen water almost reached his waist, and when at last the shivering boy was forced to turn away from the thing upon the bulwark, on his face were tears.

4.

The newly resurrected Ridler trembled like a drunkard at the edge of Harlem River Drive, dripping filthy water on the ground. With every passing moment he returned into himself a little more, and the more into himself he came, the more the memory within him faded. Ridler could not hold them both— both himself and the memory—and he could not seem to stop his own returning. He must hold on to . . . something. A timeless moment, an eternity, his interior landscape unfolding to reveal astonishing immensity. That resplendence had been so clear, pristine and perfect, and then his consciousness arose to sweep away the radiance and the shining Glory fled before him toward a far horizon, like a storm front chasing daylight from the sky.

Ridler longed to decrease that it might increase. He needed to possess it. Possession for him meant one thing. He required a better medium than a metal pipe and a concrete wall. He required brush and paint, sticks of charcoal, a pencil, a pen—anything with which to leave a better mark—but every thought of art was one less instant spent in contemplation of the setting Glory. What excruciating paradox! To even think of rendering the thing which had unfolded in him seemed to hasten its departure. To realize it was swiftly fading was to grieve, and the insult of grief became a kind of rage, which increased the swiftness of the Glory's fading. Thus Ridler's own arising, building in momentum, dimmed the vast surprising thing he had encountered until he knew he had to find a way to render it or else be left completely at the mercy of its absence. He must paint the Glory now, from life, before it passed away forever, leaving him with only his inadequacy.

There at the edge of six lanes of busy morning rush hour traffic, Ridler lifted his gaze toward the projects on the other side, sixteen stories of brown bricks and empty windows looming over a spindly canopy of branches. Focused on that destination, he stepped into the flow of speeding vehicles, staggering on legs like wooden stilts, limping from the forgotten blow that had knocked him off the bridge into the river, his head and body canted out above the pavement in a constant state of falling forward, his collapse avoided only by his busy feet below. Horns blared. Tires squealed. A truck burdened with water cooler bottles missed his heel by just three inches as he crawled over the barrier at the far side of the highway.

The winter air, whipped into a frenzy by the truck's turbulent passing, frisked his soaking clothes with frozen fingers. Ridler pulled his parka closer, and leaning forward for momentum once again, he stumbled into Harlem.

Like tufts of hair upon a leper's scalp, clumps of brown grass clung to the bald earth around the projects, with bits of trash among the grass like dandruff. Ignoring sidewalks, Ridler traveled straight across the property. He crossed a basketball court where a pair of men stomped their feet against the cold and stared at him from within the shadows of their hoods. Someone cursed him drunkenly as he skirted the entrance to a building. He neither heard nor paused, but stumbled on into a narrow valley of a street, which teemed with people bound for work. Ridler's was the sole white face among a hundred black ones. Early-rising residents descended chipped limestone steps from Victorian row houses which had been converted into apartments a century before. Pigeons on rusting fire escapes gazed with jaundiced eyes upon the passing throng below. Bars over ground-floor windows hinted at the midnight trials of residents and landlords, as did fences topped with coils of barbed wire.

That narrow street opened onto a wider boulevard, choked with traffic. Ridler staggered past businesses with storefronts secured behind corrugated rolling doors. Congo Hair Braiding. Rollo's Soul Food and Southern Fried Chicken. Plus Size Diva Boutique ("Eat What You Want and Then Shop Here"). His focus remained inward, on the task at hand. He must preserve the setting Glory's afterglow. What scant attention he paid to the outside world was given solely in pursuit of something he could work with, any way to capture what was fading.

Ridler paused before a vacant lot. Mounds of garbage, higher than his head, had been piled against blank walls on each side of the property. Here was great potential. Ignoring a No Trespassing sign, he dropped to his knees beside the closest pile of trash. With one hand after the other he tore into the pile, flinging refuse away like a dog digging for a bone. He found a felt-tip marker and tried it on a cardboard box. It was completely dry. Dropping the marker without another look he pulled a shattered picture frame from the pile, and many handfuls of less substantial garbage, junk mail fliers, bottles and boxes which had once contained soap and cereal and cleaning fluids. He was desperate for a ballpoint pen, a stub of pencil, anything to leave a mark. In his struggle to record the Glory and contain it, Ridler did not notice the acrid scent of smoke lofting from the alley at the rear of the vacant lot until a voice called out, "What you doin' there?"

Glancing up he saw three men warming their hands above a small fire crackling in an upturned clothes dryer.

"He be stealin'," said one of the men.

"You got any money, boy?" said another.

Ridler rose to face the men. Every sensation received from the outside world increased him and reduced the Glory. The revelation was just a pinpoint in the distance now, a single tiny star within a huge and moonless sky. It was escaping him. He was losing it. "No," he moaned as the three men began to move toward him. "No, no, no, no, no."

"Listen to this boy here," said one of the men, before blowing into his cupped hands. "He done lost his mind."

They came still closer, the one in front now cocking his head curiously. "Son, you need some help?"

Ridler looked at the trash-strewn ground, at the cracked stucco walls, the gray winter sky. "Oh, no."

"We ain't gonna hurt you, son," said the man. "We got our own problems."

Ridler backed away, his eyes up on the clouds.

"Maybe you hungry? Wanna little somethin' to eat, huh? How 'bout that?"

Ridler saw the heavens ripple as his eyes began to well. It was nearly lost. "Don't go," he whispered.

"We ain't goin' nowhere," replied the man.

Ridler fled the vacant lot. He staggered through a tide of people hurrying to work along the sidewalk beside the boulevard. He ran sometimes, colliding with a stranger now and then, focused inward as he was, desperate to preserve the afterglow. His lungs began to burn, punished by the history of cigarettes. Damp clothes steaming from the heat of his exertion, the river's stench arose and formed itself around him. He moved within that steam as if he were an altar boy whose censer had been filled with sewage, garbage, and despair. Those fragrant heralds spoke to people of his passing, but he himself became invisible, concealed within a nebula which seeped out from his pores, a cloud of self-awareness not contained within him anymore, but spreading in pursuit of the Glory's final vestige.

Never had a fog like this been seen before in Harlem. The mist of Ridler drifted down the boulevard, obscuring storefronts, signs, and citizens, only to clear instantly when he had passed. Some who saw it looked away, those whose reputations could support no further doubts about their sanity. Others stared with open mouths or rubbed their eyes and blinked and looked again, to see nothing left. Only one small boy set out in pursuit. Catching up with Ridler in front of a barbershop, the boy entered the cloud and was immediately overcome. Long afterward, when the boy awoke on the sidewalk in a barber's arms, he could only speak of light and love at war with selfishness.

Leaning out ahead of his hardworking feet, in a perpetual state of falling forward, the momentum of Ridler's struggle drove him left, into an alley. He stopped, although there was no stillness in him. He wavered. He teetered. Every sinew in him quivered like a cable stretched beyond its limits. Before him were five boys of sixteen or seventeen years, each of them hard at work upon the alley walls with cans of spray paint. Imperceptible, Ridler watched as words and images appeared. None of it intrigued him. Their graffiti might be art, but it was bad art, derivative, without a hint of deeper meaning. He had seen the like on walls and subway cars all over New York City. Only their paint itself attracted him, a cardboard box filled with spray cans on the pavement. Lost within their petty renderings, the boys did not see or hear him in his fog of silence and invisibility.

Ridler fell upon the box. He possessed it. He absorbed it. He drew the pigments deep into himself and began to paint at last. His eyes saw beyond the alley wall before him, far beyond into eternity. The paint flowed from his fingers. Driven by a cloud of aerosol, pigment joined the fog surrounding him. It swirled about him, a cyclone of color, a whirlwind flying to the bricks. Ridler's eyelids fell and rose like two sides of a spinning coin, now concealing his work to expose the subject, now concealing the subject so he could do the work. The Glory rose, approaching as if coming from beyond the surface of the field of bricks. With a can of spray paint in each hand, both of his arms moved in mighty arcs, rendering the joy with joyous-ness. Painter, paint, and painted were all one, a perfect trinity.

A blinding flash of light, a wave of pain, and Ridler was only himself again, collapsing to the alley pavement. There he lay upon his belly, arms and legs akimbo, gazing out along the asphalt as a paint can rolled away. He tried to reach for it but a shoe stomped down, pinning his arm in place. He felt a rib crack when another shoe swung hard into his side. He cried out and was kicked again and again in a strangely familiar blood-and-bruises rhythm.

One of the boys knelt down to look into his face. "Don't be comin' up in here toyin' us, ofay."

"I just want to paint," said Ridler, lips moving on the pavement.

"What he say?"

"Boy think he be a writer," said another voice. The rest of them began to laugh.

One of them stomped hard on Ridler's kidneys. He saw the Glory dim beneath another wave of pain. "Please," he said, "I'm losing it."

The kneeling boy moved his face down farther, to within six inches of Ridler's eyes. "What you losing is your mind, think you gonna come up in here, use *my* cannons to tag *my* alley."

Ridler said, "What's a cannon?"

The boy snorted. "Listen to this ofay," he said, grabbing the can of spray paint. He shook it quickly in front of Ridler's face. The metal ball within the can rattled like a snake. "This here a cannon, fool." He aimed the can at Ridler's face and sprayed. Ridler barely closed his eyes in time. "Boom!" shouted the boy. "Hear that cannon now? Boom!"

"Say, Petey," came another voice. "Come look at this here."

"Shut up. Can't you see I be taggin' me an ofay?"

Ridler tried to turn his head, but one of the boys standing over him pressed a shoe against his ear and said, "Just lie."

"Man," came the other voice again. "I'm tellin' you come look at this."

Ridler heard the scrape of Petey's feet as he shuffled across the alley. A moment later the shoe lifted from his head, and he heard that boy's footsteps cross the alley, too, along with several others. Within his mind he tried to see the Glory. Was it there? Did anything remain?

"Hey, Petey. This boy cryin' over here," said one of the graffiti crew, laughing.

When nobody answered, the boy above him spoke again. "Hey. What y'all doing?"

Still there was no answer.

Ridler rolled his head to look across the pavement in the opposite direction. There, on the far side of the alley, he saw four of the teenagers standing silently before the wall. He saw the fifth boy, the one above him, walk away to join them. He heard that boy's laughing voice trail off, his questions fade, as he too simply stood and stared.

With a grunt, Ridler pushed himself up onto all fours. His ribs were sharpened spikes that stabbed his sides, his ear a ringing heckler. His eyes stung with paint. He was completely back within the world, completely back inside himself, all hint of the Glory gone.

One of the teenagers saw him rising and ran across the alley. Ridler cringed at the impending blow, but the boy bent down instead and put a strong hand underneath his armpit, lifting. "Here you go, mister."

With the boy's help, Ridler made it to his feet. Another boy had joined them, and together they assisted him across the alley.

"Mister, we sure sorry," said the one named Petey, turning from the wall. "You think it be okay if we watch?"

Ridler did not understand. "Watch?"

"Y'all give the man some space," said Petey, stepping back. "J.J., bring them cannons here where he can reach 'em."

Most of the boys moved back from the wall while one of them brought cans of paint to Ridler reverently.

"We just gonna watch you write if that okay," said Petey.

"Write?" asked Ridler.

"Paint, mister. We just wanna watch you paint."

Slowly Ridler turned to face the wall. Before him was his handiwork. He knew it was a masterpiece, yet it was merely an outline of the limitless potential of its subject, a hint and a suggestion, nothing more. He closed his eyes again. His pupils flitted wildly to and fro behind his dripping eyelids, searching for a vestige of the Glory. All he saw was his imagination. Once it had seemed rich and endless. Now it was exposed as so much less, a shapeless emptiness composed of nothing but desire and hope and wishful thinking.

The vast unfolding had vanished, leaving a vacuum far beyond his imagination's capacity to fill. The resplendency, the Glory, had become merely an urge, the craving of an addict. "I can't paint it," he said. "I can't remember what it looks like anymore."

"Oh, mister," said one of the boys. "Please. You just got to try."

5.

He couldn't bring himself to beg for subway fare, so he made his way back to the highway, stuck out his thumb and started walking slowly, pausing often, exhausted and in pain. After a while he began to fear it would be long past dark before he got to his hotel apartment. The temperature would drop another twenty degrees, and his clothes were still not completely dry. He thought about the stories he had heard of bums who froze to death on New York City sidewalks.

A Volkswagen van stopped abruptly beside him, rocking on its axles as the side door slid open. The scent of burning marijuana and the chords of Ravi Shankar's sitar drifted out onto the sidewalk. "How, Chief," said a smiling girl inside, holding up her palm. Ridler saw his own reflection in the window of the van, his face still coated with red paint, his long black hair hanging loose and stringy. He did look something like an Indian on the warpath.

"How," he said.

The girl wore her long brown hair parted in the middle and restrained by a leather headband. The roses in her cheeks matched her bloodshot eyes. "Are you coming?"

Although his ribs still felt like daggers, he did his best to smile as he climbed in.

Brightly colored Mexican blankets covered the van's original upholstery. Brown-and-yellow batik fabric hung inside the windows. A rainbow curtain of beads separated the front two seats from the one in the middle, where Ridler settled in beside the girl. Six of his seven fellow occupants wore tie-dyed shirts and jackets in reds and greens and blues. The one exception to the riot of color was an older man in the rearmost seat who wore a plain white robe. Ridler thought he looked like Jesus, or an Arab, or maybe just Italian. His black hair was as long as Ridler's, but unlike Ridler he wore a beard down to his chest, flecked with subtle gray. He sat with his arms around the shoulders of two lovely girls, one on his left and one on his right. His eyes were closed. He held his head erect.

With a grinding of the gears the van rolled back into the endless stop-and-go of New York City traffic. The driver made an illegal U-turn through a break in the concrete barricade. Ridler said, "Hey, I need to get to Chelsea."

No one said a word as the van continued the wrong way. The girl beside him with the leather headband passed a joint. The driver turned up the sitar on the stereo. Ridler had no energy to protest. Without taking a hit he handed the joint through the beads to a young man in the passenger seat ahead of him. He stared out through the side window as they crossed the river and made their way on backstreets and up onto a highway ramp. Suddenly they were level with the second-story rooftops, speeding along an elevated freeway with pillars of black smoke rising from the city on his right, where the Bronx continued burning.

Ridler's breath condensed on the side window. He raised his index finger and began to draw on the glass. He lost himself within the art, trying again and again to capture what he had lost. After each failed effort he wiped away the image with his palm, exhaled on the glass, and tried again. It was only when a voice disturbed his

THE OPPOSITE *of* ART

reverie that he saw the forest out beyond the window and realized they had left the city. "What did you say?" he asked, gazing through the frosty image at the passing trees.

"I wondered if you are a prophet," said the man who looked like Jesus in the backseat.

Ridler turned to find the others staring at the glass. "I don't think so," he said.

"But how do you explain that?"

"What?"

"That which you have drawn on the window."

"I was just doodling."

"It's beautiful," whispered the girl beside him.

Ridler returned his attention to the window, where a few beads of condensation had dripped, tracing random parallel lines across the sketch. He wiped the image away with his palm. "It's nothing."

"Nothing is nothing," said the bearded man.

Everyone in the van repeated his words, as if committing them to memory.

Ridler tried not to draw. He clasped his hands together in his lap, right gripping the left as if they could restrain each other. He closed his eyes and let his head nod forward.

A rush of cold air awoke him. It was dark. The van had stopped. Through the open side door he saw snow on a field, and a large farmhouse shining in the moonlight. The girl beside him said, "Go on, Chief."

Ridler got out. The girl with the headband followed, as did the two other girls and the man in the robe. "Welcome, my son," said the man. Standing in the snow with open sandals over bare feet and no coat over his white robe, the man showed no sign of the cold. He spread his arms as if expecting an embrace.

Ridler hugged only himself. "Where are we?"

"This is my ashram. Here, you will find what you seek."

"Who are you?"

"My name is unimportant. You may call me teacher, or guru if you prefer."

Smiling beatifically, the man turned away and strolled through the snow toward the farmhouse with the two girls close behind.

Ridler faced the girl in the headband. "Guru? He sounds like he's from Jersey."

A smile lifted her rosy cheeks a little closer to her bloodshot eyes. "His name is Bob Feldman. He's from Hoboken, I think."

"What is this place?"

"Rip van Winkle country, baby. Our little Catskills home."

Watching the guru and the girls and the two men who had been riding in the front of the van as they approached the house, Ridler said, "All of you live here?"

"Uh-huh. You wanna hit?" She held out a joint.

He felt strangely repulsed. "Maybe later."

She stepped close and slipped her arm between his elbow and his aching ribs, moving him toward the house. "Underneath that war paint I think you might be cute, but you need a bath and some clean clothes."

"That would be cool."

"Totally. A nice hot bath, and some dinner, and then, who knows?" She bumped her hip against him playfully.

Thirty minutes later he lay in a cast iron tub, the water steaming aromatically around him with hints of rosemary and jasmine. A huge bruise covered his left thigh, which ached. He didn't think the bruise was from the mugging in the alley, but he couldn't remember what had caused it. His ribs hurt only when he moved. The pain in his jaw and head had mostly subsided after he finished scrubbing the spray paint from his face. He felt strangely at peace in spite of the fact that he had no idea where he was, or who his hosts might be, or what they wanted.

The bathroom door opened and the girl came in, carrying some folded clothes. "These should fit you pretty well."

Naked, he stared up at her. "Thanks."

She returned his stare evenly. "I'm Jean."

For some reason, he did not want to give his real name. "I'm Grant."

"Like the general."

"Not much."

She smiled again, enlarging her cheeks, and put the clothes on a wicker hamper in the corner. "Good. I'm not big on soldier boys."

"What are you big on?"

"Oh, peace and love, you know."

"Why did you people pick me up?"

"I thought you looked cute. And lost. I'm a sucker for cute, lost things."

"Bob didn't mind?"

"Why should that matter?"

"I guess I figured he was in charge."

Kneeling beside the tub she slipped a hand into the water. "Mmm. Nice and warm. Want some company in there?"

He thought about it. She was pretty enough. A broadness in her face kept her from being beautiful, but still she was all girl in all the proper places. . . .

Suddenly he thought of Suzanna. It shocked him. How could he have gone all day long without her crossing his mind? He shifted away from the girl's hand. "I don't think so."

She cocked her head. "Are you gay?"

"There's this girl."

"Ah."

Standing up, she dried her arm on a towel. Then she reached into a pocket and removed a snapshot. It was the photograph of Suzanna. "I found this before I put your stuff in the wash." She laid the snapshot down on top of the clean clothes. "Monogamy isn't my scene, but I can dig it. Come on down to the kitchen in a few minutes. We're having lasagna. Vegetarian." She cocked her head, considering him. "You don't eat meat, do you?"

"Not if you think I shouldn't."

She laughed on her way out the door.

Ridler tried to understand himself. Turning down joints. Turning down sex. Going all day without thinking of Suzanna. What was happening to him?

He lay mostly submerged and frowning until the smell of garlic from the kitchen overwhelmed the scented bathwater and his stomach grumbled to remind him he had not eaten for a day. He rose painfully and dried himself and dressed in someone else's clothes.

In the middle of the kitchen sat seven people at a round oak table. Above them was a crystal chandelier, very out of place in such a rustic room, paneled as it was in knotty pine. Along two walls were handmade cabinets and an old gas range and a curvy whirring refrigerator that looked to be from the 1950s. The guru from Hoboken smiled when Ridler entered. "Welcome, Grant. Sit and partake of our bounty."

Ridler nearly made a crack about the guy's corny language, but no one else around the table seemed to think it was funny. He took an empty chair directly across from the man. Jean, sitting to his right, smiled at him and then returned her attention to the lasagna on her plate.

The dinner scene reminded him of growing up in Omaha. Eight

kids and his mother, always harried and exhausted, alone with Ridler and his siblings most of the time because his father had been a traveling salesman with a five-state region. Like Jean and the guru and the others, Ridler's family had also gathered at a large round table in the kitchen, his mom and oldest sister doing the cooking, a couple of his middle sisters passing out the food as it came off the stove, and him, the youngest, always the last served.

His had been a family of many talents. Pianists and flautists, athletes and scholars. His father, on his occasional weekend days at home, had expected nothing less than excellence from everyone, and the children knew that good work was the only way to attract his attention.

One of Ridler's first memories was of lying on his belly in front of the Saturday-morning cartoons on television, drawing spacemen with his crayons. His father had walked through the room, paused to look down on his work, and said, "That's not really good enough, is it?"

Another boy might have given up, but Ridler had always been stubborn. He honed his craft instead, always working far above the level of his peers, but never far enough to gain the approval he craved. Always there was room for improvement. Never were there accolades. Gradually, Ridler's interests shifted, until only the love of art remained, art for his own sake and no one else's.

In the Catskills commune, the guru said, "Heidi, would you please serve our guest?"

A small brunette beside the man rose from her chair.

"I can do it," said Ridler, reaching for the pan of lasagna in the middle of the table.

"No, my son! Let Heidi be of service to you."

When the petite woman had served him, the man in the white robe said, "I sense you require healing."

"I'm okay," mumbled Ridler, his mouth full of lasagna.

"Your chakras are clearly in disharmony, perhaps even blocked completely. As soon as you have sated your physical hunger I will heal you spiritually."

Ridler had no idea what chakras were, but the lasagna was good. "Okay," he said.

"Tell us, what were you seeking when we found you?"

Ridler chewed a moment. The man's question made him uncomfortable. How was he supposed to discuss what happened at the river when he didn't even understand it? He decided to avoid the question. "What makes you think I was seeking something?"

"The guru sees our auras," said Heidi.

The man in the white robe closed his eyes and smiled. Everyone else turned to look at Ridler. He put his fork down. "I saw a fire across the river and there was something . . . Look, this is going to sound a little crazy."

"The truth often does."

"Okay. It's just, there was something strange in the shadows, right? So I started across the bridge to get a closer look. Next thing I knew, I was lying beside the river."

With his eyes still closed, still smiling, Bob from Hoboken said, "You sought fire; you found water. The elements are one."

"If you say so. But I have no idea how I got from the bridge to the riverbank."

"That is obvious," replied the guru. "You experienced astral projection."

"What's that?"

"All will be revealed, but first, what more did you experience?"

"I felt . . . I met . . ." Ridler stopped. As was the case when Suzanna started talking about love, his inability to speak his mind was maddening. He only knew there had been a perfectly pure light.

Absolute whiteness. Overwhelming peace. Love unlike anything he had dreamed possible. His urge to capture the experience in paint was nearly physical, a frustration aching to express itself in action, like a lust for sex or vengeance. Why bother trying to describe a thing like that with language? Only paint and canvas could contain what he had seen.

"You have no words?" asked the guru.

Ridler stared at his empty plate and shook his head.

"Good." The man pushed his chair back and stood. Immediately everyone else stood as well. "Silence is the beginning of wisdom."

Again, everyone repeated his words. Then the man extended his hands and gestured upward as if lifting Ridler from his chair. "Let us now begin Grant's healing."

Ridler did not think he needed any kind of healing. He simply had to find a way to remember his experience precisely, then he could get to work. He was done with nudes. He would paint an entire series focused on the Glory, a completely new period in his career. With such a subject as his inspiration, the series might easily become a movement with many imitators, something they would study in the centuries to come as people now studied the Renaissance. What he wanted wasn't healing, but instead a chance to record the experience on his own terms, to draw it, to reimage and reshape it to suit himself. No guru could help with that.

Still, it was possible the man might know a way to clear the strange obstructions in his memory, so Ridler rose and followed him.

They passed through an opening and down a very narrow hall, which led into a large room. The high ceiling was obscured by draped white material, which Ridler thought perhaps might be a silk parachute. It gave the space the feeling of a tent. This was reinforced by more fabric hanging from the walls, by many rugs upon the floor, and by the fact that there was no furniture, only pillows scattered on the rugs. Someone lit some incense. Sitar music flowed softly from hidden speakers.

"Lie here," said the man, gesturing toward a rug in the center of the room.

Ridler looked around. When Jean encouraged him with a smile and nod, he lowered himself to the floor, grimacing at the sharp pain in his ribs. The others sat around him on pillows.

"Lie on your back, close your eyes, and begin to clear your mind," said the guru.

Ridler reclined but kept his eyes open, watching as the man opened a small wooden box and removed a gemlike stone. The open box was given to Jean, who also removed a stone before handing it to the young man at her side. As the box was passed around the room, the man in the white robe waited with his eyes closed. He said, "I sense your name was once Tuta. The broken one. Does this seem correct?"

On the contrary, it seemed crazy to the painter, but he would go along with anything if it might help him remember. "I don't know," he said.

"What has so disturbed your chakras?"

"Chakras?" asked Ridler, looking at Jean.

She smiled and leaned closer. "It means energy."

"I don't know what that means."

Jean said, "He wants to know why you're upset."

"Oh. Well, like I said, I saw this thing. It was . . . I felt . . . it's really hard to talk about."

"Only fools speak of the ineffable," replied the man, and again, everyone but Ridler repeated his words. "What was the effect on you?"

"Mostly I'm confused, I guess."

"You seek clarity."

"I want to paint it."

The man opened his eyes. "You want to *paint* it?"

"Yeah. But I can't remember it anymore, you know? For some reason I must have been kind of dazed or whatever while this thing was around, then when I started to snap out of it, the thing began to leave. It was like, the more normal I began to feel, the less of it there was, you know? But I wasn't tripping or anything. It was real and it was . . . incredible. I have to paint it."

The guru lifted the stone and touched it to his own forehead. All the others did the same. "Close your eyes," he said.

Ridler glanced at Jean, who smiled again and nodded. Lying on his back at the center of the circle, he gazed up at the white parachute a moment, inhaling incense. He let his eyelids fall. He heard Bob Feldman, the guru from Hoboken say, "Let us all imprint our crystals. Focus on entering. Enter. Enter. Good. Now visualize this seeker's chakras. See them struggling to emerge. See them intertwined in conflict, the confusion in him. Find the one for your crystal. Visualize it unencumbered. You are in it. You are in it. Good. When you're ready, you may emerge. Come out. Peacefully, now. Come out. Good. Let us place them now."

Ridler heard the soft sound of fabric on fabric and opened his eyes to glance sideways and see one of them placing a stone on the rug beside him. He felt something touch his hand. He flinched.

"Calm yourself, Tuta," came the guru's voice. "Close your eyes and be at peace."

Ridler felt the man place a crystal in his hand.

"Clasp this over your heart."

He raised his hand to his chest and held the rock there.

"You must focus all of your energy on wholeness now. Do not limit yourself to seeking anything. That is far too small. Think of everything. Abandon yourself to everything. If you focus on your desire you will not find it. You must instead embrace everything. That is where your desire lies. Focus only on your unity with all."

Ridler peeked through his eyelashes, watching as they rose and left the room one by one. Alone, he closed his eyes completely. He felt warm. He felt comfortable. His nostrils flared, taking in the musky scent of sandalwood. The sitar's fluid rhythm bathed his mind. Soothed by the harmonic strings, he felt he had been lifted on a rising tide. He drifted endlessly on the melodious currents. He began to believe it might really be possible to regain contact with the Glory. He tried to follow the guru's instructions. He willed his consciousness to search along the edge of his horizons. Then he remembered the man's words and told himself he should not search. It was important not to think about the Glory, to simply open himself to everything. The Glory was in everything.

After a few minutes he began to wonder if the crystal in his hands might feel a little warmer than before, might have begun to vibrate, just a little. Then he realized merely thinking about the crystal was a barrier. He did not want to be distracted by that one thing. He wanted to focus on everything, like the guru said. He sought the Glory in it all. He sought the great unfolding. He went back in his mind to the resurfacing, or returning, or whatever it was that had happened somehow in that time he lost between the bridge and the riverside, when there was so little of himself and so much joy. He remembered the effect of it, but his memories were not it . . . no, he should not be thinking of memories or effects. Why was this so hard? Before he had not even tried, and it was there. He could have painted it easily. He wanted . . . he wanted . . . no, he must not want only that. He must want everything. The Glory was in everything. But what was being if not sensing, doing, thinking of particular things? He had no idea how

to be in everything, or not to be in himself. To be or not to be . . .
Wait a minute. Wasn't that Shakespeare? Sure it was. He was
lying in some stranger's living room, holding a rock and thinking
lines from Shakespeare.

With a grunt, Ridler opened his eyes, put the crystal on the rug
at his side, and pushed himself up painfully to a seated position.

"That was quick," came a woman's voice behind him.

He turned to find Jean still sitting where she had been all along.
"I thought you were gone," he said.

"You should go on meditating."

"What's the use?"

"Maybe it would help if you explained the problem."

He sighed and dropped his gaze to the Persian rug between his
feet. "If I understood the problem, it wouldn't be a problem anymore."

"You don't want to get high. You don't want to get it on. You
don't want to meditate, so what *do* you want?"

He thought of Suzanna, but would not use her name. Somehow,
he thought she might accept him if he could show her the Glory. "I
just want to paint."

"Cool. Do you know how?"

"I'm the best there is."

She laughed. "Why so modest, Grant?"

"It's true."

"Okay, so paint already. How about a mural? We've got lots of
empty walls."

"Even I can't paint something if I can't imagine it."

"What do you want to see? Maybe I can take you there."

"It's not a place. It's a thing. And I already saw it. I just can't remember it anymore."

"But if you don't remember it, how do you know you saw it?"

"Because it was . . . it was . . ."

He gripped his head and shut his eyes. Then she was behind him, her arms around his shoulders, her cheek against his back, saying, "It's okay, baby. It's okay."

Although she was touching him, he was all alone. He said, "I felt so light. Free. There was so much love. But that's all I can remember."

"I've had trips like that." She started rubbing his back. "I remember once I was at the flicks on a little orange sunshine—"

"I don't do acid."

"Mushrooms maybe? Peyote?"

"Cut it out."

"Okay, okay. So if you weren't tripping, what was it?"

"I don't know."

Ridler stood up and left the room.

The next morning he wanted to join the rhythm of the commune. He wanted to help Heidi prepare breakfast. He wanted to do the dishes and then do the laundry. It felt good to help, good in a way he hadn't experienced before and did not understand.

After lunch Ridler sat in on a kind of seminar led by the guru, who spoke about the wheel of becoming, the *bhavacakra*, through which all must travel, and the *ka,* or subtle body, the physical self, the vital principle, the mind-sheath and the causal body. The guru said Ridler had experienced a shift or transcendence in his *ka,* an out-of-body experience in which he journeyed on the astral plane. It was the astral projection the guru had mentioned the night before.

"This world, as we understand it, is like a dream," said the guru, speaking to the group while smiling at Ridler. "Everything is in the dream and the dream is everything. The problem is, when you're in a dream, you don't know it. Few have risen from the dream to see everything at once as Tuta has."

The others gazed upon Ridler as if he were their hero. The looks on their faces made him nervous. He had no idea what the guru was talking about.

That evening Jean returned from a shopping trip to Cooperstown with tubes of titanium white, ivory black, cadmium red, yellow and green, cobalt blue, yellow ochre, burnt sienna, and burnt umber. She also brought several sable brushes—rounds, flats, and brights in different sizes—and a can of turpentine and another of refined linseed oil. Ridler fell on these supplies as a starving man might fall upon food. Drawing back the fabric that hung before blank plaster in the tentlike room, he set to work immediately.

Weeks passed as he painted, although he did not bother to keep track of time. He didn't care about his apartment at the hotel. The paintings there were nothing compared to his work now. He never thought of Talbot Graves at all, but sometimes he thought of calling Suzanna. He tried to convince himself that she would be worried about him, but did not really believe it. Chances were she had moved on. She might not even know he'd disappeared.

He continued doing his share of the mundane chores—cleaning, cooking, even splitting firewood and shoveling snow when his ribs began to heal—but the pleasure he had felt in being helpful for the first few days after his experience with the Glory faded. He began to begrudge the time it took away from painting. He wanted to spend every moment working.

Normally when Ridler painted, the effect upon him was akin to meditation. With a paintbrush in his hand, his breathing usually became deeper and more regular than usual, his heartbeat slower than a sleeping man's. But the Glory seemed to taunt him. It offered him no peace. He strained at the distant edges of his mind for a memory of a memory, for the elusive bliss which had been piercing in its clarity while he was still unaware, only to become muted and disjointed when he sought it, like the words of a conversation only halfway heard as one awakes. Sometimes he lost his temper and attacked the blank space on the walls as if literally wrestling with the Glory. Sometimes despair overcame him and he painted only to be painting, moving his hand and arm mechanically, sketching the same pattern over and over again, desperately hoping to recall an image of the transcendental thing which had possessed him on the bridge, hoping to be lost in it again, to forget himself, to find the Glory so he could harness it, capture it, take it for his own and drag it back into his world.

After their evening meal the others often sat cross-legged on the floor behind him, watching while he painted, their hands forming a bowl on their laps, palms turned upward and thumbs touching. The object of their meditation was the object of Ridler's obsession, the image which refused to form beneath his brush.

He covered the walls with it, and when the walls were covered, he covered those images with more images, each new attempt begun with hopefulness that this time he would finally remember, each impression growing much the same before him until the inevitable moment when he could remember nothing more, when the wonder he had hoped to capture dissolved into an infinite blankness and his genius fell away into that blankness, as if he were an old-world explorer sailing off the edge of a flat earth.

One night when their time of meditation was complete and the others had dispersed throughout the house, Jean remained behind while Ridler worked, stabbing furiously with his brush as if it were a weapon. Standing close behind him she said, "Maybe you should take a break."

"I can't do that."

She ran a palm across his back, caressing him. "Sure you can. Just come away for a while."

He knew that was impossible. Like a mountaineer who could not bear the idea that a summit was beyond his reach, Ridler had to keep on climbing until he stood above the Glory. He shook his head, laying down another stroke of crimson. "I have to get this down."

"Why, baby? What makes it so important?"

"If you have to ask, you wouldn't understand."

She removed her hand. "You think I'm stupid?"

He paused to look back at her. "I didn't mean it that way. It's just you're not an artist."

"That's like refusing to talk about God because somebody's not a priest."

"It's not like that at all."

"It's exactly like that. Stop acting like your art is some kind of secret religious ritual. Give me some respect and tell me why you have to paint this thing."

Ridler shrugged and turned back toward the wall. "Because it's there."

"You know what I think? I think art is your religion. I think you're trying to paint God."

"Don't be ridiculous. I don't even believe in God."

"That's good, because you can't paint him."

Ridler's fingers tightened on the brush. He jabbed at the palette and then attacked the wall with crimson. "I can paint anything," he said.

A man's voice spoke. "But can you paint everything?"

The guru had entered the room and settled down silently onto a pillow behind Ridler and Jean while they talked. He said, "God is everything, Tuta. Everything is God. Which is just another way of saying God is not one thing, which is just another way of saying God is nothing, which is why you can't paint God, just as Jean said."

"If you heard her say that, then you also heard me say I'm not trying to paint God."

"What else could this be?" The guru gestured toward the image on the wall.

"Oh, come on. You don't seriously think it's God." Ridler laughed.

"I prefer to think of it in terms of the energy in everything," replied the guru.

"What energy in everything? That doesn't make any sense."

"Even if what I say does not make sense, nonsense is also part of God. All of these ideas you have, everything you think you see and do and feel and want is part of God. Everything in nature, everything that exists is all God, including even your idea of God."

"I don't have an idea of God."

"Unbelief is also part of God."

"That's crazy."

"Craziness is—"

"Part of God," interrupted Ridler. "Sure, I get it."

"Not yet," said the man with a smile. "But you will."

Later, as Ridler lay sleeplessly on a pile of pillows and rugs below his latest painting, his thoughts returned to Suzanna and the strange things she believed. He remembered that last night, when he had convinced her to pose one more time, a desperate ploy to make her stay a little longer. Sitting in the chair, refusing to lie on his bed again, refusing to pose nude again, she had talked of Jesus this and Jesus that, as if Jesus were another man she loved and he was standing right there in the room. It had taken Ridler completely by surprise. It had angered him.

He remembered another time before that, an awful fight about her little gold-and-sapphire cross. He had mocked her for refusing to remove it when she modeled for him, or even when they had sex.

"It's not like it covers anything," he had said.

Looking at him strangely she had replied, "It covers everything," and then she had risen and begun to dress.

"What are you doing?" he had demanded.

"I have to think."

"It's just a piece of metal. It distracts me. Is that so much to ask?"

She had faced him squarely then, an open challenge in her eyes. "Yes, it is."

Her refusal to submit had driven him to say some things he wished he could take back. At the time he had excused his behavior as understandable. The change in her had shocked him, had seemed to come from out of nowhere, but now he realized Suzanna had always given hints. He had simply missed the meaning of her words because of the way her incredibly full lips formed shapes to match the sounds she made, and the way the dimples just above her bottom moved when she walked, and the way the little girl she used to be still sometimes peeked out from beneath her surface to arouse the strangest instinct in him, the need to protect her, but from what?

From Jesus, as it turned out.

Jesus, his competition.

There had been so many women. How strange, how completely

unexpected, that he could fall so hard for someone who actually believed such nonsense. Her ideas were as foreign to him as an African religion. She might as well have worshipped sticks and stones. How could an amazing woman choose a myth, a fable, over flesh and blood?

But while the guru from Hoboken had been trying to convince him everything was God, Ridler's thoughts had wandered to the bridge, the river, and the thing which came to fill him there, and even though the details were unclear, he had to admit he wasn't sure about the difference between fact and fable anymore.

Maybe it was just a matter of semantics. Maybe the thing he had chosen to call "Glory" was the thing the guru chose to call "God." Maybe he should respect these people's beliefs a little more, give them a little credit. After all, the commune had done far more than simply take him in. They had offered him escape from the desperation which nearly drove him mad when he first lost the Glory.

But with the initial shock of that awful separation long over, Ridler wondered if they had anything left to offer. He was convinced he had encountered something in particular in the lost time between his memory of the bridge and his awaking on a Harlem River mud bar, not some vague, amorphous everything. Whatever it was, it had been more present than anything he had ever known. It was not everything, as the guru said, but on the contrary it was completely different from everything, separate and apart.

At three in the morning, lying wide-eyed on a Persian rug, Ridler realized the guru could not help him. Only someone who believed the Glory could be right there in the room would be able to show him how to find his way to it again, and Ridler knew just one person who might believe a thing like that.

Over breakfast, he explained why he had to go.

"You seek what cannot be," said Bob the guru. "But it is good to seek. We will take you to this woman."

Five hours later the VW van double-parked across from the address Ridler had found in the phone book. He emerged and stood before the van's open door to say his good-byes. All seven members of the commune had come, and each of them had given him a gift in parting. A pale pink crystal, which was said to channel spiritual clarity. An L-shaped twig to be used in dowsing. A handmade necklace with a pendant in the shape of an upside-down five-pointed star, a black candle, and a small jar filled with some kind of oil, all of which they promised would protect his health and guide him on his journey.

He carried their gifts in an army surplus backpack they had also given to him, along with a change of clothes, two sandwiches, and the painting supplies Jean had purchased. She made him one last offer of a joint, which he declined, and she leaned out of the van for a good-bye kiss. Then, with waves and laughter, they closed the door and ground the van's gears and lurched away, the sound of Ravi Shankar's sitar fading quickly, until Ridler stood alone on the sidewalk, staring across the street at the kitchen window of Suzanna's apartment, trying to summon up his courage.

It had been over two months since his encounter in the river, two months since he last saw or spoke to anyone he knew in Manhattan. He had emerged from the cloud of Glory into a kind of waking dream and the dream had morphed into a surreal life at the commune. Time became irrelevant. Without radio, television, or newspapers he had felt detached in the Catskills, as if he were on the far side of the world. But of course that sense of isolation had been false. He had been just a short distance from Manhattan all along. He could have come back anytime, could have called or written, but he had convinced himself Suzanna would not care. Now, standing across the street from her home, he could only hope he had been wrong.

On the ride into the city he had fantasized about his reunion with her, the things he would say, the questions he would ask. He had imagined her eyes going wide as he spoke of his encounter in the river. He had dreamed of her relieved embrace when he told her he now believed, if not in her God exactly, at least in something real and transcendent. He dared to hope she might take him back. In fact, he wondered if that might be his real reason for returning. Or had he come back mainly for her help in seeking the one thing on earth he could not seem to paint?

Ridler tried to separate those desires, to weigh them one against the other, but they were too completely intertwined. All he knew for certain was his pulse had quickened now that he stood just a few steps from her door.

What if she rejected him? Everything he longed for teetered in the balance. His whole life hung suspended over ruination by a thread.

He could not approach her door. Instead, he paced up and down the block, pausing now and then to watch the brownstone. Two old women emerged slowly from a yellow taxi, one of them balancing a stack of bags and boxes from Bloomingdale's as the other searched her purse for the fare. A pair of teenage boys hurtled down the middle of the street on bicycles. The mailman in a dark blue uniform climbed the brownstone's steps, entered the vestibule, and emerged a few minutes later, sorting letters as he descended to the sidewalk. A young woman approached Ridler, walking briskly at the center of a pack of dogs on tangled leashes. A row of young maple trees rising from cast iron grates showed signs of budding. The daylight began to fade. He should make a choice. He should not remain in Harlem after dark. A light came on in Suzanna's kitchen window.

Ridler stared hard at the window, hoping for a glimpse of her. He knew it was irrational, but somehow he felt if he could just lay eyes on her before he rang her doorbell, he might know how she would respond. Watching, sweat broke out on his palms. He dried them on his jeans. The moment was upon him now. Any instant he would see her and she would receive him, accept him, love and guide him . . . or not.

6.

Suzanna Halls paused in the cased opening and pressed her back against the jamb, straightening her spine. "At least there's no morning sickness," she said.

"That's the spirit," replied Talbot Graves, entering her kitchen, nondescript and businesslike in his gray suit. He removed a bottle of Beaujolais-Villages from a brown paper bag, set the wine on the tile countertop, and began opening drawers.

"It's the one on the left," she said, splaying her feet and bending her knees to slide down the jamb an inch or two as if to put more pressure on her spine.

She wore bell-bottom jeans with several patches, a peasant blouse with dark brown paisleys much the same color as her eyes, and nothing on her feet. Watching her flex her body against the jamb made Graves feel even older than his years. He opened the drawer and withdrew a wine opener. "Sure you won't indulge with me, dear?"

"Talbot, you know I can't."

"No, I suppose not, but it is a shame. This is such a good vintage." He peeled the foil back from the bottleneck and began to twist the corkscrew in. "I admire your discipline, you know. You'll be a fine mother."

"If I keep it."

He paused to look at her. "You're thinking of abortion?"

"Of course not. But I don't see how I can raise a baby on my own."

"Whyever not?"

"Kids are expensive. It might be better to give it to a rich couple."

The cork came away with a low pop. "Have you any stemware?"

"You'll have to use a water glass. In the cupboard there beside the sink."

"Oh, dear."

She slipped behind him and opened the refrigerator to remove a metal pan covered with aluminum foil. "It gets worse. Dinner's just a tuna casserole, I'm afraid."

"Fish? If only I'd known, I could have brought some Pouilly-Fuissé instead of this red."

"I'm a lousy hostess."

"I'm *kidding*, dear." She ignored him, silently opening the oven and sliding in the dish. "Suzanna? I didn't mean to offend you."

She straightened and sighed with both hands pressed against the small of her back. "It's the hormones, not you."

Graves clucked his tongue. "Listen, there's no reason why you have to go on living in poverty this way. Not when I need you so at the gallery."

"I won't take charity, Talbot."

"How can you say that? You know I've been completely lost without you all these months."

"Would you rather have lima beans or sweet peas?"

"Whatever you want, dear."

"Okay. Lima beans." She removed a green can from a cupboard. "And toast."

"That will be lovely. But what about the gallery?"

"I don't think I could spend my days looking at his paintings, Talbot."

"Ah. I hadn't thought of that."

"It wouldn't be so bad if I knew for sure. . . ." She applied a can opener to the peas, but the cutting disk slipped and the can fell sideways, trickling liquid onto the countertop.

"Let me help," said Talbot Graves, setting down his wine and taking up the can opener. "You get started on the toast."

"Toast is a stupid thing to have for dinner."

"Not at all."

They worked in silence for a moment, then Talbot Graves said, "It would be best for you to accept the court's decision, dear."

"I can't. And I don't understand why you wanted him declared dead so quickly."

"We've been all over this, dear. They searched both sides of the river for a quarter mile and found no sign that he had come to shore. It just wasn't possible for him to drift or swim any farther than that and survive the freezing water. Plus there was the distance of the fall and the strength of the current. It would have taken an extremely strong swimmer to survive all that, and Sheridan was no athlete."

"But Danny wouldn't do that to himself."

"But he did. I saw it happen."

"He still might have survived somehow."

"If he was alive he would have come to us weeks ago."

"Maybe not. I left him. He loved me, and I left him."

"Did he say he loved you?"

"He wouldn't. You know how he is."

"I know how he *was*."

"If you say so."

His efforts with the can of lima beans complete, Graves took a small sip of wine. He decided it really was an excellent vintage. "You blame yourself, I think."

"Maybe," she replied. "A little."

"Don't. We're all responsible for our own choices in affairs of the heart."

"I keep thinking, if only I'd been a little less . . . or a little more . . . something."

"Suzanna, you've got to face the facts. Lovely though you are, and you *are* a very lovely girl, Sheridan did not love you. That man loved no one but himself. I don't know why he chose to kill himself, and I'll regret to my dying day that I couldn't see it coming, but he jumped off that bridge of his own free will. I only wish I could have been a little closer and stopped him."

"I still don't understand what the two of you were doing on that bridge at four in the morning."

"Yes, you do. You've heard it a dozen times. He called me. He was acting wild. I think he was on drugs, maybe hallucinating. He insisted I drive him up there. Wouldn't tell me why. Then he made me stop on the bridge and he got out, and . . . it happened. He stood there on the edge and he looked back at me and then he just stepped off. Nobody made him do it. Not you, not me, not anyone. So there's no sense in feeling guilty."

She gave him a wan smile. "I suppose that's true."

"Of course it is. Now listen, dear. About your finances. Sheridan owed me quite a lot of money, as you know. Fortunately, he left a few canvases behind, and his family have been reasonable. They signed over ownership of all the paintings we found in his apartment, plus everything I already had at the gallery in return for my waiver of his debt. Most of the canvases he left are rather crude, I'm afraid, not worth much, but I still think I can sell them to raise what it will take to pay your medical costs."

"Oh, Talbot. That's so kind, but I don't know. . . ."

"Now, now. It's only right. The child is his, after all."

"Still, I'd feel strange taking your money."

"Well, it's really Sheridan's money in a way."

After a moment she said, "Okay. I need the help, so okay. And thank you."

"Not at all. But there is one thing you could do."

"Anything."

Talbot Graves removed a folded paper from the inside pocket of his suit coat. Pressing it flat on the kitchen countertop, he said, "This is rather silly, but my attorney insisted on it, and you know how attorneys are."

She stepped closer and cocked her head to read the paper. "It's getting dark in here."

Graves reached past her to flip a switch on the wall and an incandescent glow bathed the kitchen. "There you are. Now, this is just a simple waiver. As your baby's legal guardian, it says you agree on behalf of Sheridan's child that the paintings are my property."

"I thought you said his family has already signed them over to you."

"They have. But the attorneys tell me this little technicality is still necessary."

"I don't get it."

"Neither do I, to tell you the truth. I believe they said it has something to do with the child being his most direct descendant, you see, so without this it's possible that technically nothing could be done with the paintings until the child reaches the age of majority or some such thing. But of course you're going to have a mountain of medical bills long before then. This way I can sell the paintings with confidence that there will never be any difficulties later about Sheridan's estate, and you can be sure you won't have any problems with the hospital."

"You couldn't sell them without this?"

"I don't see how. I mean, I couldn't promise the buyers a clear provenance, could I? And how am I going to help you with the bills unless I can do that?"

She put both palms against the small of her back and rubbed. "I don't know."

He sighed and began to fold the paper. "Well, if you don't trust me . . ."

She laid a hand on his arm. "It's not that. You've been wonderful, Talbot, and I so appreciate everything."

"Then I'm afraid I don't understand, dear."

She turned away from him. "You'll think I'm just being silly. But it feels like if I sign that thing, it means I'm giving up on Danny."

"I think I understand that."

"Do you? I'm not sure I do. He never said he loved me. He never promised me a thing. I know he was with other women. And I'm not like that, Talbot. I'm not the way I behaved with him. Something just came over me. I'm old-fashioned. I was a virgin when I met him, did you know that? I was waiting for a husband when I met him. Someone to have and to hold and all. I don't understand why I slept with him. I feel so . . . so connected to him now. It's like I can feel him out there somewhere, but he won't come back to me. And even if he did, I couldn't have him. We're too different. I'm a Christian woman, did you know that? Did you know that about me, Talbot?"

"No, my dear."

"There, you see? You should have known it. Danny should have known it. But how could he know it when I didn't act like it?" Her voice broke and she wiped her eyes. "Oh, Talbot. I've been such a fool."

Talbot Graves stepped closer. Placing his hands on her shoulders, he turned her toward himself there in the center of her little kitchen. He drew her close and wrapped his arms around her. She was completely pliant in his hands.

"There," he said. "There, there."

He held her loosely at first, as a father holds a daughter. She pressed her palms against his suit coat and her cheek against his tie, and bowed her head a little. At first he thought she might try to conceal the evidence of grief from him, but the emotion in her seemed to build, as if a storm offshore had driven wave upon merciless wave across her fragile frame to crash down relentlessly, sobs rolling through her body, breaking on her spirit, the foam and spray eroding her resolve until she made no effort to defend herself, but fell against him altogether in her sorrow. She moved her hands around him, clinging to him tightly, abandoned to her tears, her body firm and supple underneath his fingers, her breasts and hips pressed tightly to him. He bent and kissed the top of her head. "There, there," he said. "It's all right now." He kissed her forehead, her cheek. He withdrew his own hips slightly, lest he be betrayed by his growing excitement. His hands roamed across her back, kneading her, exploring her. He forgot the twenty-five years between them. He forgot she was in grief, and then he did not care. Of what importance was her sorrow measured against hunger such as his? He had been famished for her for so long, but too afraid to act. Men like Sheridan Ridler seemed to conquer women without effort, but the idea of approaching a beautiful woman had always held a terror for Talbot. He might hang beauty on a wall, buy and sell it, but in real life he could only dream of moments such as this. Now here was this gorgeous woman, writhing in his arms. The temptation was irresistible. He had to try. He simply had to try.

He closed his eyes and kissed her cheek again. He remained there, lips upon her flesh, savoring the salty flavor of her tears. Still, she clung to him and sobbed. He moved his lips down to the lovely angle of her jaw, which he had so often admired from across his gallery. "There, there," he whispered, the words thick in his throat. He parted his lips and pressed the tip of his tongue ever so lightly to her skin. He thought of the fullness of her lips, inches from his. He was compelled to kiss them, compelled to drive his tongue between them. He would have done it even if it cost him everything he owned, even if it meant his life. If he could just place his lips on hers, he knew then he would have her completely. He would have all of her, whether she agreed or not. He moved closer, closer.

She stiffened. She moved her hands between them, pressing on his chest. "Talbot!" she said. "Talbot, he's out there!"

"What?" he mumbled, muddled by his lust. "Who?"

"Danny! I just saw him through the window!"

She pushed against his chest more strongly, and then she was away.

He said, "That's not possible."

"I saw him!"

She ran out of the kitchen and across her little sitting room. She threw open her apartment door. He hurried behind her along the short interior hallway to the brownstone's entry vestibule, past a row of mailboxes and outside into the gloaming. She charged down the steps and dashed across the street. On the far sidewalk she turned left, then right, then left again as pedestrians streamed by.

When Graves reached her she said, "He was standing here. He was right here, staring at me through the window."

The branches of a budding maple tree beside them clawed a sickly yellow sky. A black web of power lines crisscrossed the air above. "That's just not possible," he said.

"I tell you I saw him!" She gripped his arm, her fingers sinking into his muscle.

Her strength surprised him. He knew she could have beaten him off. He would never have her as Ridler had, not even by force. The humiliation of that quickly turned to anger. "Suzanna dear," he said. "Sheridan is dead." He saw wild hope within her eyes give way to pain and spoke the delicious words again. "He's *dead.*"

"No," she said, releasing him.

"Yes, he's dead, and it's time you stopped this foolishness. But just for the sake of argument, say you're right. This still doesn't make any sense. Why would he come here and then hide from us?"

"I don't know," she said. "Unless . . ." She covered her mouth with both of her hands. "Oh."

"What?"

She gripped his suit coat. "Do you think he saw us? In the kitchen just now? Do you think he saw us and misunderstood?"

She stood so close, her hands on his coat, right there within his reach. The hunger rose in him again, but of course it was impossible to take her on a public street. It had been impossible all along, although if she had been a little weaker he would have tried. He would certainly have tried. He smiled down at her. "Oh, my dear. You and me? I don't see how he could have misunderstood, really."

"No," she replied, accepting his statement with an irritating ease. "I don't suppose he could think that about you."

It was the cruelest blow.

He watched as she continued looking left and right for Ridler. He remembered why he'd come. He would salvage something from this humiliation. He said, "Do be practical a minute, dear. About that paper . . ."

She stared at him blankly, and then he saw remembrance come. "Let me see it."

He removed the agreement from his pocket, along with his fountain pen. She took the paper from him. "Turn around," she said. "Bend down."

She signed it on his back. He took the waiver from her, worth a million dollars if it was worth a penny, blew on her signature, refolded the paper, and slipped it back into his suit coat pocket. "Now, you just forward all your bills to me. Or better yet, bring them with you when you come to work."

"That's sweet, Talbot, but I really couldn't be around his paintings all day long. I'm sure you understand that."

He sighed, pretending disappointment. "I suppose."

Patting his arm she said, "Let's go back inside. I'll bet you're really hungry, aren't you?"

"Oh yes," he said. "I'm ravenous."

PART TWO

His colours laid so thick on every place,
As only show'd the paint, but hid the face.

—JOHN DRYDEN,
"TO SIR ROBERT HOWARD"

7.

The fat albino lumbered out into the ring, the band marking each step by a beat upon the snare drum. He stopped and turned and placed one foot forward, perpendicular to the other, and one hand on his waist. His shoes extended far before him. *"Damas y caballeros!"* he announced. "Let the show begin!" With a sweeping gesture of his other hand he bent too deeply at his waist and his courtly bow became a farce. He fell and rolled end over end across the sand until he came to rest in a sitting position with both legs sticking out in front, the travesty attended by a well-timed drumroll, the toes of his ridiculous long shoes atremble with the aftershock.

Thus began another show, perhaps the ten thousandth in a hundred years beneath the patchwork big top. There were no paying customers, just the members of the troupe scattered here and there upon the bleachers, which were otherwise unoccupied. They clapped with delight as Juan and Julio Merlo, the Flying Blackbirds, ascended to the trapeze boards in spite of the resistance of leotards stretched almost to bursting by abundant pasta. Shouting "Hep! Hep!" at every frightening moment, they soared to and fro, performing midair pirouettes and cutaways without a net.

A large egg rolled into the tent and bumped against the center ring, where it exploded in a cloud of smoke to reveal Gregorio the dwarf, who amazed the yawning audience by producing smaller eggs from out of empty air. The little eggs in turn exploded to become rabbits, which flowed like rivers from his hands until the center ring became a lake of living creatures. Isabel the wolf woman laughed uproariously, although like all the others she had seen it many times before.

Vicente the *vaquero* rode into the tent atop a pair of palominos, the skinny horses' ribs rattling like xylophones. With one foot on each animal's backbone and his hands upon his waist, Vicente thrust his chest out proudly as the steeds charged round the center ring, flinging sand and gravel skyward with their hooves and breathing smoke and sparks from flaring nostrils.

At last the Beautiful Zoraida stepped onto a revolving wheel, surrendering herself to Fate, as El Magnífico—his pure white teeth bared in a cryptic smile beneath his grand mustachio and both of his eyes tightly closed as usual—flung flashing knives at fleeting places between Zoraida's spinning arms and legs.

When the last of these amazements was complete, Esperanza stepped into the ring. Adorned in a sparkling black cape that covered her from head to toe as if she were a starry sky, she stood with only her square chin and regal cheekbones on display. In the dimness of the smoking lanterns she might have been a girl of twenty rather than a contemporary of Cortés. In spite of her countless years, every man who gazed upon her felt a longing in his heart. "Dear ones," she called in a clear and piercing voice. "Thank you for a most amazing evening, most prodigious, most stupendous, most astounding and colossal. Your skills are beyond human understanding! Who could improve on such a spectacle? Who would dare to try?"

"San Pablo can!" cried Isabel in Spanish, the black hair on her forehead, cheeks, and nose alive with yellow lantern light reflections. "Let San Pablo tell a story!"

Shouts of *"Sí! Sí! Sí!"* erupted and the company began to chant, "San-Pab-Lo! San-Pab-Lo!"

Esperanza turned her gaze to Ridler. He could not resist. He rose from the bleacher. He descended. He took up his place within the center ring, facing them without a costume, prop, or painting. As he stared into their eyes, Isabel said, "Tell the one about the birds again, San Pablo."

They had named the graying man whom she addressed not after the apostle but after the dead cubist, promoting him to sainthood in consideration of his religious eccentricities.

"You know the one," Isabel insisted. "With the tiger and the church."

"It was not a church," objected the obese albino. "As San Pablo will shortly be explaining."

"It was not a tiger, either," said the dwarf.

In the shadows of the lofty tent, forty pairs of eyes watched Ridler with eager expectation. Storytelling was an old tradition on the show, the entertainers' favorite form of entertainment. It might break out at any time. Everyone took turns. Some members of the troupe were famous for amazing fantasies; others told the truth. San Pablo's stories seemed to fit both categories, which was why he was their favorite.

Outside the big top, countless cicadas hidden in surrounding mesquites hummed mechanically, their pulsing rhythm drifting on the slow, hot Texas breeze to match the cadence of the eternal ringing in Ridler's ears. He added his voice to theirs. His Spanish was fluent if accented and oddly formal, for he had learned to speak the language as books and teachers said it must be spoken. He began where he always began, in his hut on the beach a few yards above the high tide line, eighty-eight hundred miles away and a quarter of a century in the past.

He told them he had been living on the beach for twenty-four months at that time. He had made his living wandering among the tourists, selling necklaces and bracelets made of shells and beach glass. The tourists back then had been Americans mostly, Vietnam veterans returning six years after the fall of Saigon with their wives or girlfriends, searching for a nirvana they'd glimpsed during heady days of rest and relaxation between patrols. A few Australians and Swedes also visited the beach, and a sprinkling of Brits and Germans.

Most of them arrived on Korean mopeds. Turning left at the hand-painted sign on Thailand Route 41, they were lured by the single unexpected English word nailed to a palm trunk halfway between Bangkok and Phuket. PARADISE. They followed the winding dirt road ten kilometers through dense jungle to the beach, fording small streams twice along the way to emerge blinking from the leafy shadows, burdened by their backpacks and inevitably frowning to find white people already on the pristine sand, or else simulating boredom, the usual tourist's camouflage against uneasiness and uncertainty.

It was an achingly perfect beach, like many others throughout Southeast Asia, a gentle curve of sand stretched between black granite cliffs three stories high at either end, and sloping to a sea of transparent turquoise. Here and there coconut trees draped horizontally above the swish of gently breaking surf, which competed for attention with the jungle calls of parakeets and monkeys. Suchart, the retired Thai army captain and owner of the land behind the beach, had granted Ridler the right to live there on a more or less permanent basis in return for fifty baht a day. The Thai even allowed Ridler to build a small hut just inside the tree line, a low roof of palm fronds on a spindly frame of saplings he had harvested from the encroaching jungle with a borrowed machete. The sides of Ridler's shelter were open except during the monsoon season, when he enclosed it with a blue plastic tarp he had liberated from a construction site in Bang Mak. The end result was little more than a tent, but in paradise it was all he needed.

On the nearly empty bleachers in the big top, everybody stirred and mumbled their agreement. Tents with open sides were better in warm weather.

Ignoring them, San Pablo continued to explain that his landlord Suchart's name meant "born into a good life," which the man took to be a prophecy, convinced as he was that his land would one day be purchased from him at a premium to construct a canal across the Isthmus of Kra. "You see soon," he often said. "Big ditch, right through here. Big ships gonna come and go. Big money for yours truly."

Suchart had operated a kind of resort at the far end of the beach, which consisted of five bungalows, a well-stocked bar and kitchen under a single thatched roof, and open-air dining at white plastic tables on the sand. Suchart also rented blood-red hammocks to the backpack tourists for two hundred baht per night, plus a five-hundred-baht deposit. He did not allow visitors to string their own hammocks up between the palms, but he did let them camp on the beach for free.

Most days Ridler strolled the beach, shaded by a battered straw cowboy hat, his shoulders protected from the tropical sunshine by a plaid cotton shirt, unbuttoned and flapping around his blue jean shorts. He gazed out at the idyllic setting through a pair of cheap Ray-Ban aviator knockoffs he had purchased in Bangkok. His hair had grown more than halfway to his waist, and he wore it in a single braid most of the time, thick and black.

"You had a very long ponytail back then, and you were not so gray?" asked the woman whose face was covered with black hair. The albino moaned and threw up pudgy hands at the interruption.

"That's right," said Ridler.

"Ooo," said the wolf woman. "I wish I could have seen you then."

"Isabel!" said Gregorio the dwarf. "Why do you always ask him the same questions?"

She crossed her arms, which were also thickly covered with black hair. "He doesn't mind, do you, San Pablo?"

"No," replied Ridler, smiling. On the contrary, he enjoyed that part of the tradition.

"We mind," said the dwarf from the shadows.

"Okay," said the woman. "No more interruptions, unless it is to cry."

"Promises, promises," muttered the fat albino as Ridler resumed, explaining how he had approached the tourists with jewelry made from beach debris, every one a little sculpture, a fine work of art. The backpacking tourists' first reaction was usually annoyance, but that often changed when they saw the quality of his work. He did okay, making enough to pay the rent, buy a meal from Suchart's kitchen every day, and drink a few cold Singhas with the veterans and their wives and girlfriends around sunset. Often his beers were paid for by the tourists in return for sharing local knowledge. Answers he did not have, he invented, which was how he learned to tell a story.

Each night after Suchart closed the bar, Ridler returned to his ersatz bungalow and worked by firelight until dawn. Using only tempera paint on paper because he could not afford oils or canvas, he wrestled, groaned, and strove with all his might to capture what he'd seen two years before in Harlem. He hung the paintings which seemed closest to the Glory from the sapling frame within his quarters. The more glaring failures he destroyed. The only other decoration was the photo of Suzanna. He was sometimes troubled by the fact that he had pinned her image above his bed in New York City just to prove he could ignore it. Now he kept it there above his sleeping place because he wanted to adore it.

Four times every month, early in the morning on the days of the full moon, the half moon, and the quarter moons, he arose before the sunrise, changed into long trousers out of respect for his holy destination, and left the beach to walk inland, covering the ten kilometers to the highway. There he waited as a crowd of people slowly grew, arriving on foot, on mopeds, or in automobiles, everyone gathering at that place with the same intention. Eventually there were enough of them to safely travel on together, and as a group they entered the jungle on the far side of the road.

It was unwise to follow that well-trodden footpath through the monsoon forest without the company of at least two dozen other pilgrims. Men and women, boys and girls, thirty-eight in all had perished on the jungle trail within the last five years, every one of them a victim of the evil Mara Leopard. Sometimes their remains had been discovered not far from the path. The death place of others had been marked only by blood, the proof of their demise found only in their disappearance. The manslayer had attacked more than two dozen times in daylight. It struck one group of ten, killing two men on the spot before the others drove it snarling back beyond the jungle's shroud.

No one walked that path alone. No one traveled after dark. Few who lived within the region even dared to sit outside their homes after the sunset.

As Ridler's companions moved along the path, ahead and behind them traveled the largest men. They beat at the jungle constantly with long staffs. Girls and women in the middle of the traveling group warned away the leopard with high shrieks and ugly admonitions. They remained as tightly packed together as they could. Only the youngest children laughed.

Sometimes impenetrable bamboo stands on their left and right rattled in the ocean breeze. Always beside them and overhead were jade vines, tamarinds, bananas, teaks, crotons, and elephant ears, a solid veil of green from which their death could come. Pollen layered the air like smoke within a shuttered room, illuminated only by the few bars of sunlight that managed to penetrate the jungle's canopy and understory. For twenty kilometers they traveled, the last hour on a steeply climbing path which switched back and forth across a hillside in the Tenasserim Hills, the backbone of the Malay Peninsula. Along that final climb they passed great conical granite outcroppings, some as tall as teaks. Then they reached the summit. The path opened onto a clearing. They had arrived safely at their sacred destination, Wat Bua, the temple complex holy men had hidden in that hanging valley many centuries before.

The stone walls standing between Wat Bua and the monsoon forest contained many graceful structures. Near the center was a *bot*, where men who desired to become monks were inducted. Beside that stood a sort of chapel where pilgrims celebrated feasts and listened to sermons, a small *kuti* where the monks resided, and a central courtyard paved in granite slabs.

In typical Thai fashion, the older buildings had pyramidal *prangs*, towers shaped like giant ears of corn, which rose in heavily ornamented tiers toward a central finial at the peak. Each of the buildings had been carved directly from the living granite of the hill. Grass and bushes thrived in cracks along the walls. Massive trees astride the rooftops sent roots thick as a man's thigh down around the lichen-spotted stone to flow without motion in a testament to passing time, as if poured in molten streams which had solidified into an implacable embrace.

Wrapped in saffron robes, novice monks with heads and eyebrows newly shaved attended to the compound's granite pavement, sweeping it with handmade brooms of twigs tied together. The calming whisper of their brooms upon the granite joined the bright tinkle of rusty bells along the eaves. Pilgrims knelt in prayer or strolled in attitudes of silent contemplation. Elsewhere on the earth might strife and disharmony exist, but never there. Everything about the place breathed peace.

Speaking with one voice, a pair of boys inside the tent in Texas interrupted Ridler's story. "That's all very nice, but please get to the part about the doves. We like that part best."

"We know, we know," grumbled the dwarf. "Because they fly."

"Yes," replied Juan and Julio Merlo, the Flying Blackbirds. "They are our sisters."

The dwarf extended both of his hands toward the albino as if pleading for support. "Every time," he said. "Every single time these people say exactly the same things at exactly the same moment in the story. It's as if they have no choice."

"It is very tiresome," said the fat albino, nodding. "A great burden."

It was Gregorio the dwarf and the albino fat man against Isabel and the Blackbirds, the same argument as usual. Ridler, uninterested in their debate, let his thoughts return to the past.

He remembered the inquiries which had led him to the doves.

That part of his journey had begun somewhere along the New York City Public Library's seventy-five miles of shelves, where he had retreated for solace after seeing Suzanna in Talbot Graves's embrace.

Ridler's grief at the sight of them together in her kitchen had been maddening, for he had no one but himself to blame. In fact, he would have done the same thing in Graves's place. And as for Suzanna, why shouldn't she move on? Ridler had given her no reason to expect him to compromise with her beliefs. He even understood why she had chosen Graves. The man might be older, but he was well-off, well established in the New York art community, not unattractive in a straitlaced kind of way, and although Ridler hated to admit it, Graves even had a certain kind of class.

Unable to distract himself from grief by finding fault in either of them, Ridler had considered other means. There were always drugs and alcohol and women, of course, his standard modus operandi, but he had lost his taste for those amusements. The pursuit of physical sensation had seemed sadly superficial compared to his encounter in the river.

Justified by his own genius, Ridler remained convinced of his supreme importance, but he had been confronted by a challenge, a claim that he was trivial, that something far more excellent than Ridler existed, and he could not shake the sense that it was true. He felt as if his own ego had thrown him over, much as Suzanna had done with Talbot Graves. To put things right again he must somehow reassert himself, and for Sheridan Ridler, there could be only one way. All he needed was a model.

To find it, he decided he would search the entire world if necessary.

Ridler had returned to his rooms at the hotel, only to discover everything he owned in boxes waiting to be removed, his paintings already gone, no sheets on the mattress, not even any toilet paper in the bathroom. On a label attached to one of the boxes he read Talbot Graves's name and gallery address, along with the words *Executor of the Ridler estate.* Only then did it occur to him that anyone might think him dead.

Ridler decided it was best to let that misconception stand for the time being. To avoid distractions, he would contact no one from his old life until he had conquered his nemesis.

He spent a sleepless night, gathering a few possessions and staring out the window at the brick wall across the alley. He tried not to think about Suzanna, dwelling instead on the guru's theories.

Ridler needed to know more, so he stood stomping his feet and blowing into cupped hands at the New York City Library's main entrance when it opened the next morning. Once inside he had gone directly to the religion section. There, after many hours of searching, he stumbled onto the Buddha's explanation of a world gone mad.

If a man was blinded by a freak accident, it was not actually an accident at all, but was instead the natural result of looking lustfully at images of naked women in a prior life. If a man died of starvation, the cause lay in his callous disregard of beggars, centuries before. Harelips were undoubtedly the consequence of malicious gossip in another time and place. Similarly, an untimely death was caused by violence or murder done in generations past. And as it was with evil, so it was with good, for robust health in the present was the reward of caring for sick ancestors, and many friends resulted from a past life spent in sacrificial service.

Ridler had heard of karma, of course—the word was often bandied about in marijuana smoke–filled rooms—but never had he thought of how much sense it made of everything. On the contrary, if asked he would have said the world around him was mindless and chaotic, without patterns, purposes, or logic. But that was before his confrontation with the luminosity below the Harlem River, and the guru's challenge, and the bleak prospect of life without Suzanna, which drove him deep within the stacks of that massive marble building in New York. There, he encountered Buddha's thoughts and sensed transcendence flickering at the edges of his consciousness again, the model he required coming a little closer.

Opening a moldering volume penned a century before by a long-forgotten Zen master, he had read: *"For a man can be distanced from the original consciousness because he has restrained innocence at some time in the past, and if he has restrained it in the past, surely the path to enlightenment lies in releasing innocence again."*

Turning the page, Ridler had found himself staring at five crisp hundred-dollar bills, tucked there like a bookmark. Goosebumps rose upon his flesh. Could this be karma proving karma, right before his eyes? Then his common sense kicked in. The money had probably been left there deliberately by the last person to check out the book. Probably it was just somebody's offering to the cosmos, left in hopes of tapping into the flow of karma. Certainly it was no miracle.

Still, he thought, if such things as signs existed, surely they must look like this.

Another hour's worth of research had led him to the story of Wat Bua, the Temple of the Lotus, where the doves could be encountered. Two days after that, he disembarked from a Thai Airways DC-10 into the humidity of Don Muang International Airport, exhausted and alone. Three days after that, on the evening of the half moon in October, he had first released a dove. Every month since then he had done the same four times, always hoping for another glimpse of the ineffable.

The dwarf was shouting something, the argument within the

big top returning Ridler to the present. "But every single time they interrupt San Pablo at this point in his story!"

El Magnífico rose to his feet, a most impressive sight. The dashing man wore a white silk shirt and tight black trousers, with a wide crimson sash around his waist. Add a black felt hat, a black mask like a blindfold, a rapier, and he would have looked like Zorro. But instead of a rapier, El Magnífico carried many knives, and instead of a blindfold, he simply refused to open his eyes.

Addressing the dwarf he said, "You are no different, Gregorio. It is true they interrupt San Pablo at the same moment every time, but you always complain about them in the same way at the same time. If such repetition offends you, why not refuse to play your part?"

"But these people *make* me do it!"

"Children, children," said the storyteller, the one who spoke the strangely formal Spanish of textbooks and professors, the one they called San Pablo. "This is not the time for a discussion of free will and predestination. We will get to that again one day, if Allah wills it, but this is a Buddhist story. Now, shall I continue?"

"Yes, please," replied the Blackbird twins in unison, and Isabel clapped her plump hands with delight, although the curly black hair on her palms muffled the sound.

"Very well," said Ridler. "On to the doves." He resumed his tale of Thailand.

Stacked on rows of wooden tables at one end of the courtyard were the reason Ridler had gone across the world, the reason he had remained long after his visa had expired, the reason he had ascended from the beach to Wat Bua with each phase of the moon. On the tables were many cages made of wood and wire, at least a hundred of them, each about the size of a shoebox, and each containing a single dove.

The procedure was simple. On the south end of the temple compound's central courtyard, Ridler approached a banyan tree so large it might have been a forest in itself, larger even than the greatest tree in Sai Ngam, and certainly as old as the temple. Underneath that verdant canopy he joined a line of pilgrims waiting to appear before an aged and obese personage ensconced like the Buddha on a low divan, propped up by many pillows and selling tickets from behind a small teak desk. Because of the many folds of flesh upon the ancient's face and the looseness of the flowing robes which contained the enormous body, it was impossible to distinguish that person's gender. Nor could the ticket seller's age be known, although it was certainly greater than the oldest monk or pilgrim, since no one could recall a time when the person had not been there, selling tickets and looking much the same.

A ticket cost two hundred baht, but it was customary to give a little more as a way of making merit. The androgynous personage received the money and provided the ticket with great deliberation, using only the plump thumb and index finger of its right hand. Each time when it was Ridler's turn to stand before the ticket seller, he tried to penetrate the strangely distant aura that seemed to shroud the ancient one. On one occasion he had extended the money only partway between them in the hope that the swollen and much-spotted hand would reach toward him a little farther, perhaps with some acknowledgment of the break in routine. But the thumb and index finger merely waited, well within the normal range of the ticket seller's usual gestures, until Ridler moved the money closer. Nothing in the obsidian gaze within the folds and wrinkles of that unmoving face had ever once betrayed the slightest trace of interest in humanity. Therefore, among the monks and pilgrims in that place, it was assumed the ticket seller had achieved complete enlightenment.

Taking leave of the fat mystery beneath the banyan tree, Ridler next traversed the courtyard to the northern end. There he joined one of several shorter lines, each of which terminated at a table piled with cages holding doves. Before each table stood a monk. The monk made no eye contact, but carefully observed the placement of the ticket in a small clay bowl held in both of his hands. In that way, with the pilgrims' money given to the ticket seller on the far side of the compound, and the tickets placed within the bowls instead of in their hands, the monks of Wat Bua remained sufficiently distant from the exchange of filthy lucre.

Once the ticket was within his bowl, the monk at Ridler's table solemnly observed as Ridler peered into the little wooden cages in search of a perfectly white dove. Finding one, he swung the door open on its fabric hinges and lifted the cage above his head until the creature in it flew to freedom.

Four times in each of the last twenty-four cycles of the moon Ridler had performed this sacred act, and in the current lunar cycle had already done it three times more, so this dove would be the hundredth. Although the doves had shown him nothing of the vanished Glory he so desperately longed to reencounter and subdue, they had begun an unexpected change in him. In the early days he had felt nothing as the doves flew toward the jungle canopy and disappeared, but on his fifth or sixth ascent along the pilgrim's trail he had found himself anticipating the dove's freedom with pleasure, and now as he prepared for the release, he knew his spirit would soar along with the little creature. He would return the empty cage to the monk with a sense of satisfaction, his karma healing more and more each time he released the innocence.

Unfortunately, on that one hundredth and final enactment of the sacred ritual, his satisfaction was destroyed. The creature emerged from the cage and took to wing. Titanium white against an azure sky, it climbed. Ridler watched its ascent with a simple joy he did not remember having before Thailand. But something happened as it rose. The dove faltered in midair. It fell a dozen feet or more, and then seemed to catch itself and continue on, but it was struggling, the rhythm of its wings irregular, its flight trajectory wavering. Squinting toward the sky, Ridler raised a hand to shade his eyes and watch. "Come on," he whispered.

Two years before that day he would not have dropped a nickel in a beggar's cup, but as the little creature disappeared unsteadily into the jungle, he did not hesitate to set out running to its aid. His pounding footsteps echoed from the lichen-dappled granite. His unseemly haste attracted glares from monk and pilgrim alike. He did not care. He only knew he had to help the dove.

In half a minute he was outside the temple compound. Before him lay the well-worn pathway which led down through the undergrowth toward the first switchback on the hillside's steep decline. The opaque jungle towered on the left and right. Without a pause he turned off the trail, charging into the monsoon forest near the place where the struggling dove had disappeared. After a dozen hard fought steps through tangled undergrowth, he lost sight of the temple and all other signs of humanity. Miraculously, however, in spite of the chaos of vegetation rising like a barricade between them, he soon saw the dove. Its perfect white shone like a beacon up among the greens and shady blues. It sat on a low limb with one wing slightly extended, much as a crippled man might rest with his game leg cocked at a strange angle.

Ridler struggled toward it. Like an insect in a spiderweb he shook off clinging vines and creepers. Slowly pressing through the jungle, eyes always turned upward toward the injured creature, he whispered promises. "Don't worry. I'm coming." The dove aimed its beak at a point midway between them in order to gaze down at him with its right eye. "What's the matter, little bird?" whispered Ridler. "Did you hurt your wing?"

He had it in his mind to reach up very slowly, his every motion smooth and steady, and to carefully extend his hand beside the bird while coaxing it onto his palm. Closer he approached. Every step required careful planning. With his bare hands he yanked and pulled at the stubborn vegetation, fighting against the uncaring jungle. In fifteen minutes he had moved only ten feet. In half an hour he had traveled twenty. The bird gazed down at him. It looked away. It looked down again, its round head jerking back and forth with rapid motions.

"Don't be afraid," he said, panting from the effort. "I only want to help you."

Finally he stood beneath the bird. It was the culmination of an hour's heavy labor. Soaked in sweat and bleeding from a dozen little scratches, he reached up just as he had planned, slowly, slowly, speaking sweetly as he moved. He reached ever closer to the injured bird until his fingers almost touched the gentle creature's feathers. At just that final instant it took flight again.

Ridler groaned as he watched it rise. Flopping through the air ungracefully, it barely managed to remain aloft within the space between the trunks of trees which rose like columns toward the vaulted canopy. Soon the bird was out of sight, somewhere deeper in the jungle.

Determined to assist it, Ridler set out again. After twenty minutes more of heavy going through the thicket, slowly he began to find it possible to move more easily. The vines and branches seemed to thin.

Suddenly he stepped into a mighty forest hall. Far above his head the verdant canopy spread as far as he could see, a huge profusion of greenery supported in midair by countless monumental tree trunks rising up from great roots which arched to earth like mossy flying buttresses.

He heard the shrieks of what could only be some kind of monkey, and the tweets and chirps of countless different kinds of birds, but he did not hear the gentle cooing of the dove. Perhaps because the dense canopy allowed only a trickle of life-giving sunlight to reach the ground, very little undergrowth survived. In that shadowed place below the trees were mainly ferns and crotons. Wide expanses of the jungle floor supported no plant life at all, covered only by fallen leaves and branches and perfumed by rotting fruit. Even at midday it would have been a twilight place, but Ridler sensed the sun was close to setting, and only then, only in the darkening, did he recall the leopard.

With a sharp intake of breath he glanced around and quickened his pace. How could he have forgotten? The great cat might be watching at that moment, crouched among the tangled roots of that nearby teak or hidden in the branches of that banyan. He had been a fool to enter the forest alone, a fool to put his life in danger merely for a dove.

Ridler believed the footpath which connected Wat Bua to the highway must be on his right. Abandoning his search for the wounded creature, he turned in that direction. He ran, and when his breath gave out he walked as quickly as he could, and then he ran again. He encountered many strange and lovely things. Three vines which climbed two hundred feet along a tree from ground to canopy, intertwining all the way to form a perfect braid. Innumerable small holes chewed by insects in the broad leaves overhead, through which sunlight sparkled like a starry sky. Countless bromeliads cleaving to trunk and branch, their white and red and shocking pink a foreign presence in a world otherwise completely green.

He heard a distant sound and something primal in him writhed with fear. He had never heard a leopard's call before, but surely that was what it must have been. He tried to hasten even more, telling himself he would find the pathway soon, and then reach the temple safely, but the jungle darkness became total and he tripped on something, fell, and struck his forehead. Rolling on his back, he knew he had to stop. It was mad to stumble on in that complete darkness. He must wait for morning.

On hands and knees Ridler found a mass of roots. He crawled as deeply in among them as he could, pretending he had reached a place of safety, yet in his heart he knew there was no refuge. The manslayer could follow him anywhere within the jungle, could seek him out by scent alone, or find him with night vision much superior to his.

Ridler settled in where moss had thickly padded the surrounding roots, and there he sat, trying to remain motionless. Sleep was inconceivable, cramped and sweating and worried as he was. Instead he listened carefully for the kind of telltale sounds a predator might make, the snap of a twig beneath a stalking paw, the sharp intake of breath as air was sampled for the scent of prey.

He could not gauge time's passage. Perhaps an hour went by. Perhaps it was four. He only knew it was intolerable to go on listening for the sound of death approaching in the darkness. Sanity required distraction. He thought about his quest.

One hundred times he had released innocence, and what was the result? Still he had found nothing he could paint.

On the contrary, he was lost and hunted in a foreign world where violent creatures preyed on pilgrims as they sought enlightenment. Thais called the man-eating leopard "Mara" after the demon lord who had so viciously tormented the Buddha, and Ridler thought them right to do so, but the monks at Wat Bua said a conception of the world in terms of good and evil was wrong. It was wrong even to think in terms of life and death. Death was only change, and change was life. Mountains eroded and rose. Perfect flowers wilted and bloomed. Everyone was doomed to rot within the earth one day and be reborn to live again.

But while everything must change within the never-ending stream of reincarnation, it was impossible to apply the thought of change to whatever Ridler had encountered in the Harlem River. It had been too pristine, too flawless, too complete within itself. Ridler did not remember much, but he did recall that sense of monolithic, vast apartness. Indeed, he sometimes wondered if it was that very wholeness which he could not paint, and thus that wholeness which he longed to dominate. How he hated the idea that something might exist beyond his capacity to piece it apart, examine it, and reinterpret it in his own fashion.

Ridler heard a snap.

Instantly every muscle in his body stiffened. Listening with rapt attention, he heard only his own breath and his racing heart. He dared not move. Had rage and devastation come for him? If karma truly did exist, had his karma come to this?

Through the simplicity of life on the beach, with two years to think it through, he had begun to understand what drove him so obsessively. If he truly could not paint the Glory, if he could not even control his own hand, then he was utterly at the mercy of a harsh and hostile world. By the power of his brush he had to master everything, even what he had encountered in the river. He knew no other way.

Yet Ridler felt the dead weight of all his thoughts and actions on the cosmic scales of justice, and he wondered if that weight might be the reason for the Glory's disappearance. If karma was real, if it was ever going to lead him close enough to paint what he had seen, would even one hundred doves be enough to balance out his life of selfishness in New York City? Confronted in the jungle's darkness by the prospect of a sudden death, Ridler knew he had not found a way to banish his own appetites. The monks at Wat Bua might release the doves with genuine humility, but Ridler only freed the creatures for himself. One could not balance selfishness with self-interest, but his karmic motivation was anything but selfless.

Still, for the first time in his life at least he was trying to make merit. Even if his motives weren't correct, surely actions must mean something. So he would not give up hope. With enough time, it was still possible his efforts might attract the Glory back one day so he could capture it in paint. One day, if he survived.

But listen.

Wasn't that another snap, another twig broken beneath an evil weight approaching?

Yes! There it was again.

If the thick jungle canopy admitted little sunlight, it admitted no light whatsoever from the moon or stars. Cowering within the tangled roots, Ridler stared wide-eyed at perfect blackness. Another rustling sound came closer, and then another, even closer, and then the beast was close enough for him to hear it drawing in his scent. He felt the hot brush of its exhalation on his face, mingled with the stench of rotting flesh which clung to its fangs, human flesh perhaps, soon to be joined by his own. A drop of sweat rolled into his right eye. He dared not move to wipe his forehead. He dared not even blink. That gaping maw was inches from his face—he knew it—yet he could see nothing. Could the creature see him in that total darkness? If not, if he remained perfectly still, might death pass him by?

The stench was nearly overwhelming, as was the urge to flinch with every noxious breath. One of his eyes stung from sweat, the other had begun to dry, parched by the corrupt air blowing over it.

The impulse to close his eyelids was strong, but would so slight a motion seal his doom? Oh, the awful smell . . . those bits of arms that once had held a lover, bits of loins that once had birthed a child, bits of brains that once had prayed to God, now rotting in the hellish places between tooth and gum. Surely the Wat Bua monks were wrong. Surely this was evil incarnate, death and violence come to take him in, impossible to flee.

Although he did not believe, he tried to pray amidst the stench of death. What else could he do? He tried to pray to what he could not paint, to pray of doves, of released innocence, of one hundred long treks to the temple, of two years spent in making merit. He hoped it was enough to offer for his life.

A grunt, a sense of motion, and the fetid presence seemed to back away.

Yet he did not hear it leave, so he dared not move in case it waited within harm's reach. Minutes passed, perhaps an hour, and when he could resist no longer at last he closed his eyes. He sensed the places on his body where the teeth and claws would enter. His neck torn open. His belly slashed. The contents of his torso laid upon his lap. His legs began to tremble, although he could not have said if it was cramps or fear that moved them. After perhaps another hour he slowly straightened first one leg, and then the other, and in the moments afterward he waited for his death, but still remained alive.

Daylight appeared suddenly at that latitude, but its effect was not dramatic in the jungle. Instead, Ridler sensed a subtle difference in the darkness, an area before his eyes which seemed somehow less black. For a long time he tried to decide if this impression was true, or if it was just deluded hope. Then he remembered the twenty who had been eaten alive in daylight, and realized the sunrise offered little promise to a man in his position. Night or day it did not matter; evil would be waiting.

Still, he could not remain forever motionless. When the sun was high enough to pierce the ceiling of that great cathedral forest the artist crawled out of his hiding place among the roots. He stood and gazed around, and saw no leopard about. It was little comfort, for they said it came from the air, as every demon did. All he could do was walk and hope he would find his way back to the temple before the manslayer found him.

He set out. The sun was so well hidden, the light so uniform and faint, he could not gauge his position relative to the points on a compass, but the temple stood near the top of the hill, so he knew beyond a doubt that he was walking in the right direction.

He found a fallen branch along the way and managed to snap it in two, thus equipping himself with a staff which he could use for defense should the Mara Leopard come. It was not much, but it was something.

He thought about that night, the hideous breath which had assaulted him, an awful death so close. He remembered his attempted prayer and the immediate withdrawal, and although he did not really believe in a god who heard him, he felt certain he was still alive because of his attempts to make merit.

Walking in that twilit place, on a carpet of fallen leaves and rotting fruit, he blessed the New York Public Library. He blessed the Zen master's book which he had read there. If karma could protect him from such evil, then surely someday karma would reveal what he must paint. It merely required more merit making, more release of innocence, and then he could become the unrivaled master of his world again.

It occurred to Ridler that there was no limit to the doves he could set free each time he climbed up to the temple. If he worked harder, sold more necklaces and bracelets on the beach, he could afford to free many more captives every time he made the pilgrimage. He resolved to do it. He would set five doves free on every future visit to the temple. No, ten. If one dove per visit had made him enough merit for protection from the demon leopard, surely ten times more must yield another vision of the Glory, and this time he would be prepared.

He dismissed the spiritual concerns of that terrifying night, for they had proven to be false. Apparently it did not matter if his motives were still selfish. Making merit was the thing, regardless of his reasons, and he could do it, would do it, until the Harlem River luminance surrendered to his brush at last.

Up the hill he walked. Up and up and up. While he could not use the sun to gauge time's passing, he seemed to walk for hours. Why had he not reached the temple? How was it possible? His stomach growled from hunger. His calves and thighs burned from prolonged effort. He could not be lost. His situation was quite simple. The temple stood above him, near the top of the hill. He had only to keep the hill always above him, always climbing, never descending, and he could not fail to reach the top. While the hill was tall, ascending it should not require so much time as this. He should have arrived long before, yet he had not reached the top, nor the temple, nor safety, when it seemed to him the sunlight had begun to fade again.

He could not bear another night of hiding from the manslayer. Summoning his last reserves of will, he set out trotting up the hill.

"Please," he spoke aloud, forgetting that his safety lay in silence, forgetting he did not really believe in prayer.

Then, just as he was verging on despair, Ridler saw the dove.

It flew across the space before him, high among the trees, its perfect whiteness clear against the darkness falling there. It flew to the right, on up the hill. As it had before, the dove appeared to be crippled. It dipped and rolled and barely made it through the air. Yet he felt it wanted him to follow. The call was inexplicable, but clear, and he obeyed.

How comforting it was to know he had that small companion! "Thank you." He whispered the syllables in time with every step. "Thank you, thank you, thank you." Here was more proof that his acts of merit were enough in spite of selfish motives. Evil leopards let him live. Doves appeared to guide him. Surely he had reached a state of harmony with all creation. Surely he was moving in that karmic flow of peace and fortune called the Middle Way.

Ahead and up above, the white dove rose and dipped, flying awkwardly, showing him the path. He stepped onto it, trod on hard-packed earth worn down by centuries of pilgrim feet. The dove paused often, resting on low-hanging branches, remaining within sight as if concerned that he might stray again. Joyfully he followed upward.

He heard the single solemn bong of a great bell which had been struck by a horizontally suspended log in just that way at just that moment every evening for a dozen lifetimes. He knew it meant the temple was quite near, but it also meant the day was over. The gates were closing. He had lost his chance to enter. He must risk another night within the leopard's power. Still the wounded creature led him, and he followed.

Hardly any time had passed when he saw the temple wall higher up, and a pair of granite pillars and a little wooden gate. The gate had not yet closed against the jungle for the night. He could enter. He was safe. Laughing, Ridler climbed on.

The dove had settled on a limb before the temple wall. Near the gate, Ridler paused beneath it. "Thank you," he said again with his palms pressed together at his forehead, bowing just as he had seen the Buddhist monks and pilgrims do. "Thank you, gentle dove, for saving me."

The dove flew over the stone wall. Ridler followed through the narrow gate.

He had entered a kind of service yard behind the *viharn,* the chapel where monks preached and pilgrims listened. To one side he saw a large stack of firewood and a pair of axes. Nearby he saw a huge iron kettle supported by three cut stones. Between the stones fire danced under the kettle. Beside the kettle stood a monk, stirring its contents with a bamboo staff. Just beyond the monk, saffron-colored cloths had been draped on ropes stretched level with the ground. It was the monastery laundry, apparently.

Next to attract his interest was a slender bamboo frame which stood perhaps three paces wide and waist high, a series of horizontal rods. Perched on one of the rods he saw the dove, and not his white dove only, but five other brown ones besides. Between the horizontal poles were narrow troughs formed of bamboo opened lengthwise, and in the troughs was grain. The doves were busy eating from the troughs, their small heads bobbing up and down. Suddenly a seventh dove arrived from the jungle, swooping low over Ridler's head to alight among the others.

As the shadows gathered and the flames beneath the kettle lit the service yard, Ridler saw another monk appear. Walking toward the doves, the man drew a kind of cart behind himself. He passed near to the firelight and Ridler was surprised to recognize a Radio Flyer red wagon, the kind which once had been a favorite toy of his. In the wagon were many little cages, each about the size of a shoe box, the very cages Ridler had seen so often in the courtyard. One by one the monk lifted the doves from the bamboo poles and put them in the cages. Ridler was amazed the doves allowed this, but they seemed content, as tame as pets. While the monk went about his work, several other birds alighted. He allowed them a few moments to dine and then he put them in the cages also. When at last every cage had been filled, the monk pulled his little red wagon back the way he had come, disappearing in the shadows.

Ridler pondered what he'd seen, and as he did more doves descended from the jungle. Soon the bamboo poles were filled again, the creatures side by side and busy feasting on the grain within the troughs. He watched. He wondered. He understood.

Exhausted, starving, Ridler clenched his hands into tight fists and ground his teeth. Many times he had walked alongside monks as they traversed the jungle path up to the temple, their *dek wats* at their heels. The *dek wats*, or temple boys, who carried the monks' food and provisions were always heavy laden, but now Ridler realized he had never seen the monks' servants burdened by a single dove. So where had the creatures come from all this time, high upon a hill and deep within the jungle?

How foolish he had been to never ask.

In two years of pilgrimages to that holy place, in one hundred acts of liberation, each dove he freed had merely flown back to captivity. Because he had always searched for a white dove, it was even possible he had released the same one every time.

He had released no innocence into the world. He had freed nothing. Therefore he had earned nothing, no merit, no good karma. And then he understood what lay behind the aged ticket seller's obsidian gaze. The secret of that ancient one's long life was not peace and harmony, not enlightenment. It was only greed.

"Yes!" laughed Isabel, the fat wolf woman, clapping her plump and hairy palms together with delight. "Yes! Ha! Ha! Ha! Oh, yes!"

"There really is a sucker born every minute," pronounced Gregorio the dwarf, as El Magnífico and the Flying Blackbirds and all the others smiled and nodded.

In the tent somewhere in West Texas, illuminated by the yellow flames of kerosene, Ridler stirred and looked around, emerging from the spell that he himself had cast. He had reached the end of his story, the part they all loved the most, and as usual his companions were well pleased. Once again he had confirmed theirs was a future filled with promise, for if he, the talented San Pablo, could be so completely taken in, surely there could be no end to the stream of rubes and patsies they could separate from money.

"I'm tired," he said. The ringing in his ears was louder than before.

"No!" called someone from the shadows. "Another one. Please tell us another."

"Let someone else have their turn," said Ridler.

"Please!" called other voices. "Oh please, San Pablo! Please!"

Esperanza walked into the lantern light and took his arm. "Can't you see San Pablo has no strength?" asked the old woman. "You will kill him one day with your begging."

The woman, tall for a Mexican and straight for her age, escorted Ridler out under the stars. Ridler knew she had been a great beauty in her youth. He was an artist to whom that fact was obvious, for he saw it written in her bones.

"Will you try again to paint it now?" she asked.

"I have to."

"It would be better if you would draw portraits of the customers."

"I can't."

"At least get some sleep."

"I can't."

With her hand still on his arm, she shrugged. "'What you do is not good. You and these who come to you will only exhaust yourselves. The work is too heavy for you; you cannot handle it alone.'"

"That's from Exodus, right?"

"You have learned the scriptures well."

"You've been a good teacher, my hope."

"I am not your hope."

"I only meant to say your name."

"Do try not to lie to me, San Pablo. Remember, I know who you are."

At her suggestion he did in fact remember. He thought of entering a convenience store several months before, *una siete y once,* as Esperanza called it—a 7-Eleven—where he was to serve as her translator. He remembered waiting at the counter to buy ice, for the freezer in their commissary trailer had stopped working, and he remembered Esperanza giving him a copy of the *San Antonio Express-News* and telling him in Spanish, "We will buy this also." He had been surprised at her extravagance, but it was her circus, her money, so he had purchased it for her along with the ice.

Not until they were together at a campfire that night near Uvalde had he realized why she bought the newspaper. She handed it to him without a word, and in the flicker of the flames he saw a photo of himself as he once was, long before the change into the worn-out man he had become. Beside the photograph he saw large words, "Ridler Sets New Record," and below the headline, "The price paid yesterday for a Sheridan Ridler painting at a Christie's auction in New York set a new record in the world of modern art."

"This can't be me," he had said to Esperanza.

Her all-seeing eyes had considered him from sockets in a gorgeous skull. "Why do you say such things, San Pablo?"

"It says I'm dead."

"Do you disagree?"

Ridler had tossed the newspaper into the fire and said no more.

For weeks afterward he pondered what he'd read. He thought of it when setting up the big top, standing nine abreast with roustabouts to heave and push at the long, much-mended fabric roll, trying to ignore the pattern in the patches, hoisting poles, tying them off, setting up the bleachers, and the interlocking sections of the center ring. It was on his mind as he worked inside his booth on what passed for a midway, selling tickets to the squirming children and stoic wives of sun-bleached cotton farmers who had driven in from fifty or a hundred miles across the desert. It weighed on him behind the wheel of an Apache pickup truck, towing his rust-infested trailer on dirt roads to avoid the interstate commerce scales, breathing Texas soil launched into the air by the balding tires of other trucks and trailers in the caravan ahead.

Alone in the pickup truck he had marveled that he could have lived so long in ignorance. After seeing Suzanna and Graves in each other's arms, he had lost all interest in that other life. The man he once had been was long dead, in fact if not in body. The question was, could he remain dead? He did not care about the money, but so much of it must mean he had been very famous for a long time, and such a famous person might be resurrected against his own will.

Perhaps he had managed to live in ignorance of his own renown because he had been in another world entirely, a universe where galleries and auction houses had no place, where monks and rabbis, priests and imams, dreamed far bigger dreams than any artist could imagine. It was also true that searching for the Glory had its hardships, and hardship changed a person. Even in a tabloid-selling *siete y once* no one recognized him for the hedonistic painter he once was. But so much money . . . surely one day he would be discovered. What would he do then?

Ridler had shuddered at the thought, and the sudden shaking of his hands nearly steered him off the road. Turning back into the ruts, he wiped dust from his sweating brow and tried to concentrate, but he could only think of all the damage he had done, the women he had used, his abuse of art collectors, the insults he had heaped on Graves, and most of all, his selfish disregard for Suzanna's faith.

He understood why such sums were paid for his old work. He knew he was a genius. But compared to his paintings of the Glory, even though they were all failures, everything he had done before was garbage. To return to a life of painting bowls of fruit and landscape scenes and nudes would be more than he could bear.

Having considered all of this, he had resolved very firmly to be dead as long as possible. But since Esperanza had seen the newspaper and knew his true identity, he could only remain dead at her sufferance, and she seemed to want something else from him—or for him; he could not tell the difference—yet not once had she told him what it was.

Now, after Ridler's exhausting tale of doves, they walked beneath the Texas stars, moving in and out among the tents and vehicles, the carousel and fun house, until they reached his little trailer. Electric light cascaded from the open door to form a yellow pool upon the ground. Just inside, his latest painting stood unfinished on an easel. Knowing he would work on it until the sunrise, as he had countless times before, and knowing he would fail as always, Ridler tried to put his feelings into words. "Talking about Thailand again . . . I don't know why, I've told that story a hundred times, but tonight I thought of something. A thing I did not notice until now."

"You owed nothing to the doves."

"How do you always know what I'm thinking?"

Esperanza shrugged as she so often did. "I have been waiting for this. And now?"

"Now, I think perhaps I should make reparation where it is due."

"Reparation. Ah."

"You disapprove?"

"I do not judge. How will you do it?"

"Remember San Antonio? The newspaper article? They said my work is valuable."

"I have been wondering if you would leave us for your riches."

"So you don't know everything."

She smiled, her teeth white as the moon. "There is free will, and therefore much I do not know."

"I may leave one day, but not for money." He gestured toward the painting on the easel. "It is a way to make some kind of reparation for all the harm I've done."

"You believe in karma after all?"

"It's reconciliation that I need. Call it good karma if you want."

"I do not think I will."

"No. But just now when I told that story again, for some reason I suddenly realized . . ." He closed his eyes and rubbed a hand across his face. "So much pain I caused, maybe it's been the problem since the start, and all I have to do is make it right."

"You will accomplish that with your work? Make things right with a painting for the woman?"

He frowned. Even after all the years gone by, to speak of Suzanna was painful. "Not just for her. I hurt many others."

"That was long ago."

"A thousand years are like a day."

"So San Pedro said, but the scripture you quote is true of God alone. Do you think you are God, San Pablo?"

Ridler said, "Of course not," and then he climbed into the little trailer where he set to work to make things right.

8.

To shake off two persistent yellow flies, the gelding flexed a powerful muscle. The rider felt the ripple at her thigh. When the offending insects remained, her mount stomped its hoof sharply. Leaning forward, she patted the horse's neck. "Be still," she commanded.

The shepherd standing there smiled up at her. "Fine day for a ride, *signorina*."

To her delight she understood Italian. "Indeed it is."

"Would you share our wine?" He gestured toward a large Grecian pitcher which hung from a twist of rope around his shoulder. "It is a fine Chianti *di pronta beva, signorina*. Made on my own farm. Most refreshing."

"In that case, yes, and thank you," she replied.

With a subtle motion the shepherd brought the massive pitcher swinging to his side. He poured a stream of blood-red wine into a copper cup and lifted it toward her. Bending down, she received the cup. She raised it to her lips and took a little sip. As the wine caressed her tongue, an explosion of unsolicited memories burst upon her. The scent of an oak fire. The tastes of cinnamon and cloves at Christmastime. Abandoning gentility, the rider drank deeply of the wine and finished all too soon. She gave her mouth a lusty wipe with the back of her hand, staining her sleeve blood red before bending down again to return the cup.

She smiled at the shepherd. "Ambrosia, *signore*. Pure ambrosia."

"You are too kind, *signorina*."

"Regretfully, I must now continue on my way."

"Of course. I apologize for all these foolish sheep. We will move them just as quickly as we can."

"Thank you."

The shepherd turned to one of three boys accompanying him. "You heard the lady, Dante. Clear the road!"

"Yes, Papa," replied the boy, and with his staff he tapped the ewe before him gently on her flanks. "Walk on, Dora." The animal gave a startled bleat and leapt ahead. Its cry and sudden movement frightened other sheep nearby. Soon the whole flock was in motion toward the far side of the road.

From high astride the snow-white gelding the rider watched as woolly backs swirled past her stirrups. The summer breeze bore both the scent of fresh-mown grass and the high, clear notes of a shepherd boy's flute. It stirred the diaphanous fabric of her rosy-colored shift, and with phantom fingers traced her naked shoulders. Something subtle prodded her, a sense she ought to spur the gelding on. She could not remember why. She enjoyed not knowing why. She deemed that moment far too peaceful to be spent in trying to hurry on for unknown reasons. Better simply to be lost within that pastoral Italian scene. Better to forget all else for just a little while.

"Gemma?"

The disembodied voice startled her. It seemed to come from the sky, the trees, the distant hills, another world.

"Gemma? Where do you want this one?"

She was herself again—Gemma Halls, assistant to the curator at the J. Paul Getty Museum—standing in her own world, high on a hill in Brentwood, California, in an exhibition hall at the Getty Center. On the travertine wall before her hung a little painting, *Pastoral Journey,* collection number 86.GG.573, done in 1650 by Giovanni Benedetto Castiglione. With brush and brown oil paint and touches of white, blue, and rose gouache, the old master had portrayed a young woman in a filmy gown astride a large white horse. The young woman gazed down at a shepherd standing to her left. Around her mount swirled a flock of sheep, driven by a boy with a crooked staff. Behind her stood another shepherd boy who played a flute.

Gemma gave her head a little shake. She turned to face the man who had just asked a question. He shifted the watercolor toward her so she could better see it.

"It goes next to the one you hung before lunch," she said. *"Nude 28."*

Her assistant disappeared into the adjacent exhibit hall. With a final longing glance at the peaceful Italian painting, Gemma followed.

She paused in the cased opening between the two spaces, one foot in the Italian Renaissance and the other in the world of modern art. She watched as her assistant carefully placed the watercolor on a rolling worktable and began preparing it for mounting. She worked her shoulders, one after the other. Already the tension had seeped back into her muscles. She realized her jaw was tightly clenched. She told herself to relax. Everything was going wonderfully. Three or four more hours and they'd have the last few pieces up, the lighting properly adjusted, and the descriptor cards in place beside the watercolors, oils, and charcoal sketches, the whole exhibit ready.

Everything must be exactly right for the opening tomorrow. Hers was a grave responsibility and a chance of a lifetime. Slated to attend were two board members of the Guggenheim Foundation, the director of the Kimbell Art Foundation, and Pierre Duchamp of the Louvre, not to mention the mayor of Los Angeles. Depending on their reaction to her work, she could move into the highest echelons of her profession, or be branded forever as a hack unworthy of her father's name.

Gemma walked to the center of the hall and began to slowly turn in place, examining the array of paintings which surrounded her. Never before had so many of the artist's canvases been assembled at one exhibition, works from every stage of his tragically brief life. The exhibit was the culmination of two years of negotiations with some of the world's finest museums and foremost private collectors. Only by relying heavily on her familial connections had Gemma managed to convince many of the lenders to cooperate. She had been unrelenting, and as one collector in London had exclaimed in mock protest, "It isn't fair! How could anyone refuse a Ridler to a Ridler?"

She suspected her father was the only reason she had been chosen for her position at the Getty from among the hundreds of other highly qualified applicants, but she did not mind. Although Sheridan Ridler had perished tragically before her birth she felt a strong connection to him, almost as if he were her patron saint or guardian angel. If she had not inherited his remarkable artistic ability, at least she had inherited his passion for the arts, and all her life she had sensed his presence guiding and protecting her, leading her deeper and deeper into a world of creativity and beauty, a world she dearly loved.

Gemma had heard the stories, of course. She knew her father had not lived a perfect life, but she also knew he had been worthy of her mother's love. Any man who could inspire a lifetime of devotion in her mother was indeed a saint as far as Gemma was concerned. And of course there was his work, his glorious, heavenly, beatific work.

As she turned slowly in the center of the hall she tried to take it in, image after image of genius, every one a masterpiece that any other artist might consider the crowning achievement of a lifetime. It was an odd experience to stand there and look at them that way, since the subject of so many of them was her mother in the nude. Ridler had never painted any model's face, but Gemma knew exactly which ones were her mother. She had long been familiar with them all, having become perhaps the world's foremost authority on her father's work, but never since his death had all these images been brought together, and collectively the impact was almost overwhelming. Anyone who questioned Sheridan Ridler's status as the world's preeminent modern master had only to set foot in that exhibition hall and his brilliance instantly incinerated every doubt.

"Should I tilt this one a little more?" asked Gerald, her lanky young assistant, a man with bleached blond hair who always dressed in black.

Lost in thoughts of her father much as she had been lost in the Italian countryside before, Gemma stared at him, not understanding.

"The glare," he said. "Should I tilt it some more or is it okay like this?"

She considered the watercolor he held in position. The light did hit the glass at a poor angle. "I think a little further," she said.

He inclined the painting slightly. "More," she said. "More. Just a little more. There."

"Come measure this, will you?"

Taking a tape measure from the table, she stepped up to the wall and held it to the gap behind the upper section of the frame. "One and an eighth," she said.

"Did you cut yourself?"

She looked at him. "I don't think so. Why?"

"Your sleeve. That looks like blood."

She shifted her gaze and was surprised to see red stains on the cuff at her wrist. She said, "I must have spilled some wine at lunch."

The work continued.

That night she could not sleep. At her apartment in Santa Monica she rose before the sun and showered. Standing in her underwear at the mirror in her little bathroom, she applied mascara to her eyelashes, which were already long and black. She then added just a touch of coral to her lips. She didn't usually wear makeup, but that morning she felt the need for distance, a little something she could hide behind. Staring at herself in the mirror, she saw what everybody saw: the strong resemblance to her mother, the oval face, the straight nose and full lips, the skin a few shades lighter than her mother's and darker than her father's. She leaned closer to the mirror, looking for some other sign of him within herself. She said, "Oh boy." She took two steps and threw up in the toilet.

When that was over with, she rinsed her mouth and brushed her teeth and applied a touch of lipstick again. Finished with her face, she considered the effect. If she was not beautiful, at least she was not common. People noticed Gemma Halls. "Striking" was a word they sometimes used. "Handsome" was another.

A slice of toast with butter helped to settle her stomach. She risked a cup of French roast coffee. She dressed in a black suit with a red pinstripe and a pearl-white silk blouse with the collar open and a man's red tie loosely knotted. She stepped into three-inch heels, which lifted her to one inch over six feet tall. She gathered the luxurious black ringlets of her hair loosely between her shoulders with a red ribbon to match her necktie and pinstripes, knowing that the effect of her long hair and heels was a nice contrast to the masculinity of her suit. By thirty minutes after sunrise, she was ready. She still had three hours to wait.

She took off the jacket, draped it over the back of a chair, and sat down to watch television. With the remote control in her hand she clicked through the cable channels one after the other, pausing now and then but barely noticing the programming. She took off her high heels and felt the shag carpet with her toes. She got up, toasted another piece of bread, and poured herself another cup of coffee. She still had two and a half hours to wait.

The coffee cup was at her lips when the phone rang. She flinched and nearly spilled it on her chest. That would have been a disaster, since she had no other blouse that worked as well with the suit. Setting the cup carefully on the side table, she rose and walked across the room to the phone. After saying "Hello," she heard her mother's voice.

"Can you come pick me up a little early, honey?"

Gemma felt she could have cried for joy at the chance to get out of her apartment. "Of course, Mom. What's up?"

"The strangest thing arrived in the mail yesterday. I'd like to show it to you."

"What is it?"

"That's what I'm hoping you can tell me."

"I'll be there in thirty minutes."

"Don't break the speed limit, honey."

"Yes, Mother," said Gemma with a smile.

Traffic at that hour was still light. It took her only thirty-five minutes to drive from her apartment in Santa Monica to her mother's place in San Pedro, a personal record.

"I told you not to speed," said her mother at the door.

"Good morning to you too," replied Gemma. "Is that the mystery mail?" She could see it from the door, something thin and square, leaning against her mother's sofa. She crossed the small room and realized it was a painting.

"Who's this from?"

"You tell me."

She knelt before the canvas and knew immediately that the painting was unfinished. She also saw that the painter was left-handed and had applied the paint with a brush held at a thirty-degree angle, which was just as it should be. She saw no bleeding of paint layers. The palette was correct. The signature appeared to be spontaneous, not painstakingly forged, clearly integral to the painting instead of added afterward, done in the same ultramarine blue she saw elsewhere on the canvas. Most importantly, her instincts were at peace as she examined the image. Although she had never seen the subject matter before, all of her experience, thousands of hours spent studying his work, combined to tell her this painting was a Ridler. And yet . . .

"It's an excellent forgery," she said.

"How do you know?"

"Two things. First, I've never seen another image like this. It doesn't fit with any series he painted, and he almost always worked in series, as you know. Even the few canvases he did that stand alone are visually related to a limited number of themes. And his work was always representational. This image, whatever it's supposed to be, doesn't match anything else he did."

Her mother gazed down at the painting. "But it's beautiful."

"Yes. The artist is extraordinary."

"It makes me feel . . . I don't know. Harmonious, I guess."

Until that moment, Gemma had looked at the painting with a

professional eye, but now she joined her mother in truly seeing it. She sensed tranquillity, but also something disturbing, something which spoke of isolation and distance, the incomplete, the unattained and unobtainable. "It makes me sad," she said.

"Really? I don't get that."

"Do you think it's supposed to represent something?"

Her mother nodded. "I do . . ."

Gemma waited for her mother to continue, but instead the woman said, "Have you had your breakfast?"

"A couple of pieces of toast."

"Oh, honey. No wonder you're so skinny. Let's go fix some eggs and bacon."

They worked together in the kitchen as they had so many times before. Gemma had grown up in that apartment, in the blue-collar neighborhood of San Pedro, where her mother moved three months after she was born. Her mother had been alone in New York City, but in San Pedro she had a brother and sister-in-law she could count on. The brother was a truck driver for a shipping company based in the Port of Long Beach. The sister-in-law, Gemma's aunt Carla, had three kids of her own to raise but never seemed to mind caring for a fourth while Gemma's mother worked days at a small gallery in Rancho Palos Verdes.

It had been a good life, no frills, but plenty of sun-drenched weekends at the beach, and occasional drives high into the San Gabriel Mountains for a picnic, Gemma and her mother, aunt and uncle, and three cousins who treated her like a sister. Always there had been the visits to local galleries and art museums, the contagious force of her mother's great enthusiasm for art, fueled by stories about her father and the other artists her mother had known many years before in New York City, some of them quite famous now, but none as world renowned as Sheridan Ridler.

Over the years many journalists had called or visited their home. The world was fascinated by the thought of Suzanna Halls, the great Sheridan Ridler's muse, favorite model and the mother of his child, living in a lower-middle-class neighborhood just a stone's throw from the docks. Suzanna Halls had ignored the notoriety for the most part, jealous of her privacy for Gemma's sake. Then, when it became obvious that Gemma's heart was set on some kind of a career in the arts, Suzanna had begun to give interviews. Always she was careful to mention her "talented daughter," and slowly the international art community became aware that there was indeed another Ridler in the world, even if she went by the name of Halls. When the time came for college, Gemma had her pick of scholarships to universities with excellent fine arts departments, but in the end she could not bear to leave her mother, so she had chosen UCLA.

"When do we need to be there?" asked Suzanna.

"The reception starts at eleven, then we're doing lunch at noon."

"Are you excited?"

"I threw up once already."

"Oh, honey. I'm sure it's going to be great."

"Why would someone forge a painting by my father and send it to you?"

"Well, you said there were two reasons why you think it's forged—the image and something else—but you never said what else."

"The smell. You can still smell the linseed oil very strongly. That canvas was just finished within the last month or two. What does that have to do with someone sending it to you?"

"You're so smart to notice the smell, honey."

"It's common sense. But if you know why someone would do this, please tell me. That's a very good painting, Mom. Technically and artistically the artist knows exactly what he's doing. A decent gallery could probably sell it for enough money to send us both on a nice vacation. So why sign his name to it and give it to you? Especially you, knowing you of all people would be able to tell it's a forgery?"

"You're absolutely sure it's forged?"

Gemma frowned and looked at her mother. "Well of course it's forged. How else could you explain the fresh paint?"

Suzanna rose from the table. "Come on. I need to show you something."

Gemma stood and followed her mother into the living room. There, Suzanna lifted the painting, turned it around and leaned it back against the sofa, this time with the unpainted side facing out. "Look at that."

Gemma saw something written in pencil on the raw canvas back. She moved up close, knelt before the painting and read.

S.—

I never should have asked you to take off the cross.
I was a selfish fool. Please forgive me.

—D.

She turned and stared up at her mother. "I don't understand."

"When I was with your father, you know he painted me a lot. Usually, he painted me without my clothes on. He didn't even want me wearing jewelry. But you know my little golden cross? The one my granddad gave to me? I wouldn't take it off. He always asked me to, but I never did. One day we got into a fight about it. Or not a fight exactly, since he did all the yelling, but a disagreement. That's when I knew I had to break it off with him. I knew he really didn't understand about the Lord. I knew what I'd done was wrong."

"Posing nude?"

"Of course not. But sleeping with him . . . that wasn't right."

Gemma smiled. "I'm kind of glad you did it anyway."

Suzanna stroked Gemma's hair. "It was wrong, honey. But I thank God for the result every day. A lot of life is like that."

Uncomfortable with the direction the conversation was going, Gemma asked, "How come you never told me about this cross business?"

"I don't know. It was such a private thing . . . I've never told anyone."

"But you must have. Whoever painted this obviously knows."

"That's true, isn't it?" Her mother glanced at a clock on the mantel. "Look at the time. I'd better go get ready."

Suzanna walked to her bedroom. Alone, Gemma turned the painting back around. She sat in a rocking chair across from it and stared. Why hadn't the painter finished it? Why did the image sadden her? She tried to examine it critically, tried to think of it in terms of rhythm, dominance and gesture, of theme and meaning, of class, genre and order, but she found herself distracted by a language far beyond the boundaries of typology and theory.

Startled, she pulled back. She tried to look away, but the image enchanted her, calling like the Sirens to Ulysses. With one last effort she physically withdrew an inch or two, but surrender was inevitable. In the end she just absorbed the painting, or was absorbed by it; the difference did not matter.

She drifted as if time and space were immaterial, or as if they now applied in different ways. She sensed no breath within herself, no heartbeat. Throughout the universe there was only she herself, and light. No ground to stand upon. No eyes to close. Nothing to experience except pure Self. Nothing to experience except light. It enveloped her and filled her. It was everywhere, yet it left space for her. She knew no distinctions, only goodness, jubilation, peace beyond imagination. She had expanded to the infinite, yet for the first time in her life she was completely certain of her smallness. She must be in heaven, yet she was not in a place; she was in a living thing, or something living was in her, or both, all, everything.

How this could be possible she did not know. She only knew it was an act of love. Everything inside and out was love. She had been lost before and never knew. She had been lost, but now she had found sanctuary.

"What's the matter, honey?"

Gemma looked away from the painting to find her mother staring down at her.

"Beautiful," said Gemma. "Beautiful."

Suzanna glanced from her to the painting and then back at her again. She smiled. "You'd better go do something with your face."

Gemma raised a palm to her right eye. It came away smeared with mascara. She stood and walked back to her mother's bathroom. She felt insulated, soft and cozy. She felt totally relieved from the great stress which had so weighed on her, as if nothing on the earth would ever do her harm. In the mirror she saw her cheeks awash with black. Raccoon eyes. She laughed. She applied a little cold cream and washed her face and then reapplied her makeup. Staring at herself in the mirror she felt strangely beautiful, not in an egotistic way but in the way her mother thought her beautiful, the way she thought a Renoir beautiful, beautiful with a sunset's beauty, a tulip's beauty, the kind of beauty given as a gift because of love. Staring at herself, her deepest instinct was to thank someone.

"Hon?" called her mother from outside in the hall. "I'd hate for you to be late."

"Coming," she replied.

Back out in the living room, her mother waited. "Listen," she said. "I've been meaning to give this to you, and today seems like the perfect occasion."

She extended her hand and dropped a necklace in Gemma's palm. Gemma saw a slender golden chain and a small golden cross inset with tiny sapphires. She recognized it immediately, having seen it countless times around her mother's neck, the necklace given by her great-grandfather. She said, "I can't take this."

"Sure you can. I want to pass it on to you."

Gemma felt her eyes well up again. "Are you sure?"

"Absolutely. To celebrate your first major exhibition." Suzanna cupped her cheek with a palm. "I love you so much, and I'm very proud of you. Now turn around and let me put it on."

As her mother stood behind her, draping the slender gold chain around her neck and lifting her hair to fasten the clasp, Gemma said, "It will always remind me of you."

"One day I hope it will remind you of something more important than me."

"Oh, Mom," said Gemma. She knew what her mother wanted her to believe. Sometimes she even wished she could believe it, for her mother's sake. But where was the proof? Gemma preferred to put her faith in facts. Art, for example, was a tangible thing, yet it could take her to a different plane, just like people claimed God did. So she had art, and more than that, she had her father, a high priest of art if ever there was one. And besides, her mother's regrets about her distance from the cross were nothing compared to her own regrets about her distance from her father. Gemma looked down at the painting. "It says 'Forgive me.' Did you ever? Forgive him?"

"Of course. How could I not? I love him desperately, you know."

"Who do you think painted this, really?"

"Your father, honey."

"But you can't really think he's alive."

"They never found his body."

"Mom, I don't understand. After all these years, you get this thing and suddenly you're open to the idea he's alive. Just like that?"

"I always hoped he was."

"But you always told me he was dead."

"I was never sure, and it seemed like the best thing not to get your hopes up, too."

A hint of anger flickered. Gemma felt great sadness at the loss of peace. She felt her ego coming back and much preferred the light. She said, "You should have told me."

"I'm sorry you think that, honey, but I don't believe it's true. Not when all I had to go on was a feeling. Someday when you have your own little girl you'll understand."

"Well, if you're right we ought to try to find him."

"If Danny wants me, he knows where I am."

"How can you be so . . . so passive?"

"You can't force love, honey."

"But if he's alive it means he left you! He left me!"

"There's probably a reason."

Gemma set her jaw and led her mother from the house. They set out for the Getty with the air-conditioning on and the windows up to protect their hair. Gemma took the Harbor Freeway to the 405, driving eighty, weaving in and out of traffic with one hand draped over the steering wheel and the other fingering the cross around her neck. Her fears about the exhibition had vanished in confusion. There was her father, a great man whom she idolized, and now there was this other man, who might have left her to grow up without a father. There was her mother, who had suspected it all along, but never shared her suspicions. And there was something dark below all that, something she did not want to feel. But she also sensed the afterglow of what she had experienced while gazing at the canvas. She wondered how a human being could paint such a thing. She thought it would be worth a little trouble to find out. Speeding past a panel truck she tried to put her question casually. "Mom, what do you see when you look at that painting?"

"I see Jesus," said Suzanna. "But it needs a little work."

9

Starvation stalked them, so they did likewise to jackrabbits and rattlesnakes. Like beaters on safari they kicked at the West Texas gravel, shook the yuccas and the sage and shouted Spanish curses, herding desert creatures toward the sandy roadbed. Terrified, many serpents crawled into the open and there they met their end, chopped and crushed to death by roustabouts with shovels, staffs and clubs. Standing in the midst of the assassins, El Magnífico smiled beneath his dashing mustache and kept his eyelids tightly closed while dispatching rabbits left and right with flashing knives which he drew from a pair of broad leather belts crisscrossed at his chest. Meanwhile, as protection from the plague of sunshine, the obese albino wore a sweat-soaked felt sombrero which he had inherited from Emiliano Zapata. He also wore a drapery of filthy sheets. Like a Roman senator in search of Christian martyrs he waddled along the road with a large rock in his chubby hands, hoping to drop it on a reptile. It was hot work, but necessary, for the entire company was bursting from their antique costumes with the swelling of too much rice and pasta and too little meat.

Although the sun had transformed her trailer into an oven, Isabel the wolf woman remained in hiding there, more afraid of snakes than of being cooked alive. Through the open door and windows she wailed, "We can sew bigger costumes! Why risk your lives for old rhinestones?"

Meanwhile Esperanza, she of the aging skin and pretty bones, sat serenely on a low boulder, shaded by a lacy parasol, observing everything. "San Pablo, remember," she called down. "You too could exempt yourself from labor such as this if you would only offer portraits."

"I will do no faces," proclaimed Ridler.

"Will not, or cannot?"

Ridler refused to admit he no longer knew the answer.

Among the beaters, Gregorio the dwarf wore tiny golden spurs on his sandals. They jingled like falling money with his every step. Marching proudly at Ridler's side he said, "As long as we are cursing at these creatures, why not tell the story about the genie?"

"It is El Magnífico's turn to tell a story," replied Ridler. "And there are no genies."

"Nevertheless there is a bazaar with rugs and magic lamps and it is a fine story, and we are here among these rocks and cacti with nothing much to occupy our minds. Also, that so-called El Magnífico is always the hero of his own stories, and nothing is more tiresome. You, on the other hand, are not afraid to be the fool."

"Fool, am I?"

"Speaking as a clown, I meant it as the highest of all compliments."

Ridler smiled. "Very well," he said, lapsing already into the formal Spanish he loved to use when telling stories of the past.

"Don't forget to speak up, San Pablo," called Esperanza from atop the rock. "So everyone can profit from the full example of your foolishness." Her intoxicating laughter drew the desert creatures out onto the road just as surely as San Pablo and Gregorio and the other beaters drove them there with fear.

Ridler began to shout to everyone of Istanbul, Constantine's great metropolis. "It sits astride the Bosporus," he said. "Which is like a mighty river holding back the continents of Europe and Asia. Some say the Bosporus is named after a Thracian word that means light-bearer. I, for one, believe it, because 'Lucifer' means light-bringer, and if there was a Lucifer, surely he would shine in Istanbul."

From high upon the boulder Esperanza laughed again. "'If there is a Lucifer?' *If?* Oh, San Pablo, how you do amuse me."

Squinting up at her he continued with his story, speaking very loudly to assure that everyone could hear, and to disturb the snakes.

Having learned enough of karma in Wat Bua, he signed on as a deckhand for a tramp steamer and left Thailand. Three months he was stranded in Sri Lanka, working on the docks. He spent another five months doing likewise on the docks of Madagascar. In that way he earned his passage port to port around the entire coast of Africa. For twelve hundred Ghanaian cedi a day he loaded pigs on railroad cars in Accra. In Tangier, an English-speaking son of a forklift driver told him about Abu al-Wasiti of the Turkish Sufis. Thirteen weeks after leaving Morocco he stepped off a fishing boat into Eminönü, that ancient trading center on the southern shore of the Golden Horn.

Smoke from burning charcoal drifted across the docks as the fishermen cooked their morning catches on open fires in metal boxes mounted to their stern decks. Making sandwiches of grilled fish they sold them directly from their vessels. *"Balik ekmek! Balik ekmek!"* they shouted, "Fish in bread! Fish in bread!" as a river of Turks hustled by along the docks, pushing handcarts piled with everything from iced sea bass to sacks of grain and cashews.

When Ridler stepped onto that continent, the rushing torrent of humanity captured him at once and drove him down the docks. He offered no resistance. One direction was as good as another since he knew nothing about Istanbul and had no idea where to start his search for the famous Sufi master of the Way.

Pressed on every side by hustling, shouting Turks, he was cast eventually into an intersecting street. There the current of humanity did not carry him with such unstoppable momentum, but still he found it easier to move with the flow.

On his left and right medieval buildings three floors tall flanked the street with too little space between them to allow the passage of vehicles. He saw cracked stucco and filthy stone facades, and countless coats of paint encrusting wooden doors and shutters, and a chaotic network of exposed pipes and wires climbing the walls, which reminded him of the thick vines which had ascended toward the jungle canopy in Thailand. Here and there enclosed footbridges linked the second and third stories overhead. In places the facades on both sides seemed to lean in toward each other, and Ridler thought it might be possible for a man high on the rooftops to leap across the street.

Tiny shops with their doors propped open lined the ground floors on both sides. Everywhere were signs in Turkish, a language Ridler did not know. A few were written also in English. Watch repair. Cobbler. Laundry. The pavement in front of every shop had been given over to venders. In their stalls he saw an infinite variety of wares. Multicolored cones of powdered spices displayed in five-gallon metal cans. Copper lamps and hookahs. Plucked chickens hanging upside down. Vegetables arranged in woven baskets. Row upon row of music on cassette tapes in cardboard boxes. Pickles. Olives. Plastic children's toys.

The noise was nearly deafening. Radios blared from sidewalk

stalls. Venders shouted to each other and hawked their wares at the top of their lungs. Stray dogs barked at stray dogs. Hammers beat on copper. Blades scraped on grindstones. Women called down to the street from open windows on the floors above. Gangs of children screamed and laughed as they played chase among the crowd.

Ridler felt light-headed. His senses nearly overwhelmed him. He was choking on his own imagination. He had to purge his mind.

He found an empty place on a low stone wall, sat down, removed a sketch pad and a pencil from his backpack, and began to work. His fingers gathered up the essence of that place and spread it out on paper. A little boy appeared at his elbow and remained there, fascinated. Soon many boys and girls had gathered to watch. Curious about the cause of such uncharacteristic stillness in their children, mothers and grandmothers began to come. Eventually even the men from nearby stalls and shops were drawn into his audience.

Ridler did not notice the crowd growing behind him, so intent was he upon his work. He completed a sketch of a small boy, omitting the face, of course. He ripped the page away from his sketchbook and flung it to the ground. He completed another sketch in a few minutes and flung it away as well. Works of genius fell from him like leaves from an autumn tree. The people pounced upon them, murmuring with wonder. Some began to clap their hands. Startled, Ridler looked up to find the press of dense humanity no longer traveling past him through the bazaar. It had begun to swirl in a great circle instead, and he sat at the vortex.

Like pilgrims jostling for position as they walked around the cube in Mecca, layer upon layer joined the swirling throng. Those nearest the center of the circling crowd gazed down to marvel at the sketches. Those at the outside of the spiral had been captured by the rumor of a glimpse of paradise awaiting at the center.

The call to prayer was broadcast over loudspeakers mounted on a nearby minaret. The circling instantly ceased. The women returned to their shops or their apartments, but the men prayed where they were. Turning silently toward the southern end of the street, toward Mecca, they awaited the call. When it came on the loudspeaker they all raised their hands beside their heads, everybody gesturing as one.

"Allah is the greatest," they recited. "In the name of Allah, the beneficent, the merciful, praise be to Allah, lord of the worlds, the beneficent, the merciful, master of the day of judgment. To you we worship and to you we turn for help. Show us the straight path, the path of those whom you have favored, not of those who earn your anger nor of those who go astray."

After the recitation of those ancient words the men bowed at the waist, placing palms upon their knees. Yet again they praised their maker, calling him glorious, before straightening to hold their palms outward beside their heads just as before, saying, "Allah is the greatest!" Then as one they prostrated themselves, their foreheads, palms, knees, and toes pressed to the street. They sat up, rocking back upon their heels. They prostrated themselves a second time. They sat up again. Their prayers continued. They greeted the prophets Abraham and Muhammad once to their right side, and once to their left, and finally, prayers complete, they rose and pushed back in toward Ridler, the women and the children rushing out to join them, everybody swirling, swirling.

An old man was the first to reappear beside him. Huge white sideburns hovered like a pair of storm clouds upon his jaw. He clapped a gnarled hand onto Ridler's arm to anchor himself against the passing flow. "*Deha!*" he thundered, struggling against the crowd. "*Deha!*"

Later, Ridler learned it was the word for "genius."

As the masses passed in adoration they broke the old man free. Drifting away he called back, "You have hungry?"

"Yes, sir," replied Ridler.

"Good," shouted the old man, circling. "Trade is possible. You I feed. Me you give picture of my wife."

"No, thank you."

"But why is it? A fair trade, I think."

"I don't draw portraits."

"Draw anything is good for you. You know what is good. You to draw my shop? Okay! My tools okay! Only draw!"

Thus began the years of Ridler's commerce in that nameless bazaar. Although every inch of space was precious in the crowded street, the old man, a woodcarver, begged him to display his charcoal drawings on a small section of wall outside his shop door. Although he charged nothing for the space, the woodcarver profited from Ridler's presence by selling ornate handmade picture frames to fit the drawings. Because of plates and bowls displayed by the neighboring vender, there was only room enough beside the door to display six or seven drawings at a time, but those were quickly sold each day. On a wooden chair Ridler sat outdoors near the images, sketch pad open on his knees. All day long he drew the river of humanity flowing by, hiding faces in a hundred clever ways.

In the early days, local people stopped to purchase drawings of street life in Istanbul, but word of his ability spread quickly. Soon everyone of importance in Istanbul made the pilgrimage to implore him for a portrait. This, he would not do. Although they would offer more and more money through the years he could not be swayed.

Great crowds became a daily problem in the street, people competing for a chance to purchase sketches, people who could not afford to buy anything, but only wished to watch him work, people blocking pathways through the stalls, people interfering with the shopkeepers' trade. To maintain peaceful relations with their neighbors, the woodcarver's family set up oaken barricades, each of them a fine example of their craft, with legs and crossbars carved with flowing arabesques. Sometimes when the weather was favorable, the old woodcarver moved a second chair outdoors and sat with Ridler. Basking in the sunshine and the glow of public adoration, he and Ridler worked side by side, one with knives and chisels, the other with pencils and charcoals.

Their mutual concern for craftsmanship became a bond which could not be broken, not even when twelve Germans on a bus went missing on the road to Atatürk Airport, not even when there was a detonation down the street, a fundamentalist short-circuit accidentally destroying a good Muslim chicken vender instead of the true target. Speculation about the martyr's actual intentions raced through the bazaar. Many believed he had been on his way to explode the American artist where he sat before the woodcarver's shop. Many believed he had also wished to explode the woodcarver, who had given sanctuary to an infidel. Hearing this, the woodcarver shrugged. Although his sideburns rose beside his guileless face like thunderheads, his words added nothing to the gathering tempest. Perhaps he would be killed. Perhaps not. It was in Allah's hands.

The Turkish language was difficult. Nevertheless, in the early years when Ridler sold a drawing he always asked his customer the first complete sentence he had learned.

"Do you know where I can find Abu al-Wasiti?"

No one would admit they knew the Sufi master. Few would even admit they knew who he was. The Sufi order had been banned for over fifty years, its lodges locked and left to decay or else confiscated and converted into other uses. One lodge had become an orphanage where children were taught by the secular state to believe in nothing. Another Sufi lodge had been transformed into a public library, where one could find books by almost everyone except Rumi, Sufism's most famous poet. Even the old woodcarver claimed to know nothing of the Sufis. Turkey was determined to be part of the Western world. Yet five times every day, at dawn, noon, midafternoon, sunset and nightfall, when the muezzin called through the mosque's loudspeakers, the old man and most of his neighbors rose and turned toward the south and lifted up their palms in prayer.

Ridler adapted to the rituals of life in the bazaar. Sleeping on a narrow cot in an apartment about the size of a one-car garage, he rose before the sun. Dozens of unfinished paintings covered the walls from floor to ceiling, for after sketching Istanbul each day to earn his room and board, Ridler spent each night in desperate pursuit of the long-forgotten Glory.

The first thing he did upon arising was to kiss his fingertips and touch them to the photograph of Suzanna, which he had pinned above his bed. After a visit to the communal toilet down the hall, he washed himself at the sink in his apartment's tiny kitchen, dressed, and then prepared a breakfast, usually a cup of Turkish coffee, some pan-fried fish or chicken with a little curry, and a piece of bread. This he ate while standing at a window, staring at the street below to watch another day begin in the bazaar.

Ahmet the carpet dealer usually appeared first with a rug over his shoulder. Within five minutes he would have two dozen other rugs displayed on racks, driven in his labors by his nagging wife, Haava, who believed he could do nothing properly without constant instruction.

In front of the ice cream shop to the left, old Pinar would appear behind her handcart and begin arranging herbal medicines at her tiny stall. Soon thereafter her landlord, Coskun, would emerge from his ice cream shop with a single chocolate scoop in a paper cup. This he traded to old Pinar for an extract of stinging nettle, which he took daily to relieve his difficulty in making water.

By then the sun was usually completely up, the street was filling quickly, and it was time to go to work. Food and coffee finished, Ridler grabbed the backpack hanging on a peg beside his door and left. But always before walking out he paused to stare a moment at the most recently unfinished canvas on the wall, his latest failed attempt.

Beggars were his constant companions as he walked the three blocks to the woodcutter's shop. Hakan, a young man with a name that meant "emperor," was so called because he was the unofficial leader of all beggars in the bazaar. He awaited Ridler every morning at the doorway of his building. "Is being a fine morning, yes, effendi?" was his English greeting, no matter what the weather.

"Indeed it is, my friend," replied the artist every time, in his slowly improving Turkish.

With the assistance of two or three others, usually children, Hakan went before Ridler as he navigated through the crowd, pushing people rudely on the left and right, clearing the way with calls of "Make way! Make way! Make way for the great Ridler effendi!"

Sensitive to his status as a foreigner, Ridler had asked the beggar to desist, but that had only yielded him a wounded look. Later the woodcutter had explained that Ridler's cooperation in the matter was a great honor for Hakan, which solidified his status at the top of the beggars' society, for Ridler was the most famous vender in the whole bazaar.

One day as they neared the woodshop, Ridler noticed a young man watching him with eyes of blood red where the whites should have been. The man stood leaning against a cracked stucco wall. When he realized he had Ridler's attention, he pulled his jacket aside, revealing a dagger tucked into his belt. For weeks after that, Ridler watched the crowd outside the woodcarver's shop most carefully.

Another morning as Hakan led Ridler to his stall, an old man in a ragged robe and tunic materialized from among the passing crowd. He spoke with Hakan. The young beggar paused, listened, and then cupped his hands between them. The old man tilted a small copper pot and poured many coins into Hakan's upturned palms before turning to disappear into the crowd.

This incident troubled Ridler, since the old man appeared to be more destitute even than Hakan. In a street of such prosperity it seemed wrong that one beggar should accept alms from another. Was Hakan charging other beggars for the right to seek alms in his territory? Did he have some sort of claim on the pitiful old man? Ridler's instincts warned him not to press Hakan for an explanation as they continued toward his stall, but when the day wore on the old beggar's face remained foremost in his mind. Finally, as he always did when images lingered in his memory, Ridler sketched the old man, putting shadows where his face would otherwise have been.

The following morning, the woodcarver provided a frame and Ridler hung the sketch on the wall as usual. That day for the first time since he had entered Istanbul, there was one drawing left unsold at sunset.

The woodcarver emerged from his shop to say good night. Staring at the sketch he said, "Ah. I see you have met him at last."

"Him? Who is he?" asked Ridler.

"You do not know?"

"He's just a beggar I saw in the crowd this morning."

"In that case, perhaps I am mistaken."

"Who do you think he is?"

"How can I tell?" asked the woodcarver. "You did not draw his face."

"But you just said you know him."

"I am old, and may say many things I do not remember, but perhaps you misunderstood me, my friend."

Ridler stared at the woodcarver, considering the possibility. It was true he still had much to learn of Turkish. "I wonder why nobody bought this sketch?"

The woodcarver shrugged, the clouds beside his ears offering no hint of impending storms. "Who would want a drawing of a beggar?" He turned to reenter his shop.

"Who is this man?" asked Ridler yet again.

"It is late," replied the woodcarver. "Peace be upon you."

Three days later, sitting in his stall and sketching as usual, Ridler happened to glance up at the endlessly passing throng just as the same old beggar went by.

"Effendi!" he called. "Effendi, wait!"

The old beggar did not seem to hear. Pressed on both sides by the crowd, he was out of sight within ten seconds. Ridler leapt to his feet, removed the sketch of the old man from its place on the wall, and rushed into the multitude. With constant smiles and pleas for patience and forgiveness he pushed past those ahead, holding the sketch closely to his chest with one hand while pressing people's backs with the other. For once he longed for Hakan's help.

Three blocks from his stall, he saw the man ahead. "Effendi!" he shouted. "I have something for you!" Still the old man did not seem to hear.

Finally, two blocks later, Ridler reached his side. "Effendi, would you please accept this gift?" He held the drawing toward the old man with both hands to avoid dropping it amidst the jostling arms and elbows.

Ignoring the sketch, the beggar turned his eyes toward Ridler. They were perhaps the kindest eyes the artist had ever seen. He said, "For what purpose?"

It was an unexpected question. "What do you mean?"

"Why have you made this image?"

"It is you, effendi."

"Me?" The kind eyes sparkled. "Surely not. It is nothing like me."

Ridler flushed with indignation. Never before had anyone questioned his ability to capture any likeness perfectly. "How do you know that? You haven't even looked at it."

"No need," replied the man. "No need."

"Take it anyway. Maybe you can sell it for enough to buy your dinner."

"Why do you not sell it?"

Ridler thought about the days it had hung on the woodcarver's wall, inexplicably ignored. "No one will buy it."

"You wish to give me something no one wants?"

"No. I mean, yes. But I thought *you* would want it."

"Why?"

"Because it's you!"

Again the kind eyes sparkled. "It is not."

"Look. I'm trying to do something nice and you're just laughing at me. Why don't you just . . . I don't know . . . oh, here!" Ridler tore the sketch out of the frame, wadded it up, and flung it to the pavement, where it was immediately crushed by shuffling feet. Thrusting the empty frame against the old man's chest he said, "Go on! Take it!"

The beggar's fingers closed around the frame. Ridler entered the flow of people moving in the opposite direction. He did not bother to look back.

Every day for another week Ridler worked in the sunshine before the woodcarver's door selling charcoal cityscapes and still lifes to the passing crowd. As always, his last words to everyone with whom he dealt were, "Do you know where I can find Abu al-Wasiti?" One day he asked that question of a woman who had just purchased a sketch of the Hagia Sophia. The woman shook her head, but Ridler heard a nearby voice reply, "I can take you to him."

Looking around he saw the beggar standing at the fringe of the crowd beyond the barricade. In one hand the old man held a copper pot. In the other was a wooden staff. The woman who had just purchased a sketch dropped some coins into the pot. Although they clinked loudly against the copper, the old man did not glance at her, nor did he acknowledge her act of charity. She did not seem to mind; in fact she seemed to expect no notice as she faded into the flowing multitude without another glance in his direction. Meanwhile the old man remained still, regarding Ridler with the look of laughter in his eyes.

"What do you want?" asked Ridler, remembering the beggar's rude refusal of his gift.

"Only Allah's will."

"I'm busy here. Go away."

"As you wish."

Fuming, Ridler watched the old man turn to join the passing throng. In a moment he was almost out of sight. "Wait!" shouted Ridler. "Wait for me!"

He pressed into the crush of people. As before, again it took him several blocks to catch up. Finally beside the beggar he said, "Can you really tell me where to find Abu al-Wasiti?"

The old man smiled. His teeth were brown and crooked, but the smile was strangely cordial and attractive nonetheless. "If you wish."

"I do wish. Where is he?"

"His whereabouts cannot be spoken. He must be shown."

"All right. Show me."

"Very well."

At the next intersecting street, the old man pressed past Ridler to the left. He moved through the tightly packed bodies with inexplicable ease, as if an invisible Hakan went before him to part the crowd. The going was not so easy for Ridler. Fighting to keep up, he had to push people out of his way. "Hey!" he called to the old man's fast-moving back. "Slow down!"

The beggar went serenely on as if he had not heard.

Cursing under his breath, Ridler chased the man along the street, then into another, and finally onto the broad quay beside the docks along the Golden Horn. There at last he found the beggar standing motionless at the water's edge.

"Why the hurry?" he asked, trying to catch his breath.

Without looking up, the man pointed toward the sky. "It is necessary to be here while the sun is in that portion of the heavens."

Shading his eyes, Ridler glanced up suspiciously. "What does that have to do with finding Abu al-Wasiti?"

"Brother sun becomes jealous in the afternoon and will allow no reflection but his own." As the old beggar said these words a passing man dropped more coins into his copper bowl. Neither he nor the passing man acknowledged the act of charity.

"Look," said Ridler. "Do you know where al-Wasiti is, or do you not?"

"Indeed I do. Behold!" With a sweeping gesture of his staff the beggar turned and pointed toward the Golden Horn below his sandals.

Frowning, Ridler said, "What is this? Make sense!"

The old man simply gazed down into the water. Stepping to his elbow, Ridler also looked over the edge of the dock. There he saw his own reflection, and beside it, the old man's image dancing in the ripples.

"There is al-Wasiti," said the beggar, aiming his staff at his own reflection.

"What? You?"

"Indeed not. Him."

"But that's you."

The old man smiled. "Again you make the same mistake."

"I don't understand."

"I am not an image. I am not a name."

"You? You're al-Wasiti?"

The old man shrugged elaborately beneath his robes. "You listen but you do not hear." He turned and walked away.

Determined to keep up this time, Ridler hurried to his side. "I want to hear you," he said. "I want to understand."

"In that case, perhaps one day you will."

Just then a fishing boat's engine backfired. Ridler glanced toward the explosion. When he looked back, the old man was gone.

Many more days passed with Ridler sketching in his place before the woodcarver's door, but now instead of losing himself in his work Ridler often turned his eyes toward the crowd, searching for the beggar. Frequently he thought he saw the old man. Always he was wrong. Suddenly the bazaar seemed to teem with beggars wearing torn and filthy robes. So many hungry, ragged, sick, and sorrowful people passed him by . . . had they suddenly appeared, or had they been there all along, unnoticed among the merchants and the shoppers, the healthy ones, the wealthy ones, the comfortable and fat ones?

Ridler thought of New York City, where many beggars also walked the streets. He had probably passed thousands of them in the years he had lived there. Because of his great artistic talent, Ridler had always believed no one had a better eye for detail, but he could not bring a single face to mind, not one street person like Abu al-Wasiti. The omission troubled him. Did it mean his memory was slipping, or did it mean he did not see the world as well as he pretended?

One day while a man placed many liras in Ridler's hand in payment for a drawing, the artist scanned the crowd beyond in search of the old man. Instead he saw Hakan, the emperor of beggars, standing near a food cart that sold boiled corn on the cob. Impulsively, Ridler pushed into the river of human beings flowing between them. "Are you hungry?" he asked Hakan when he reached the other side.

"Yes, effendi. Always."

"Have an ear of corn. Have two." He gave the street vender some of the liras he had just received for the drawing and waited as the man prepared two ears of boiled corn. He also bought the beggar a cold can of Cola Turka. Impulsively he pressed the rest of the money into Hakan's hands. "Effendi!" shouted Hakan at the top of his lungs. "Truly you are a good man! May Allah bless you! May Allah forgive you! May Allah protect you! May Allah reward you!" The man continued shouting blessings as Ridler fought his way back across the street.

Ridler did not understand his own motives. Hakan was a professional beggar. The man was quite talented at his work. Probably he made as much as most venders in the bazaar. Why then give him all that money?

The artist reached his little wooden chair in front of the wood-carver's shop. He sat. He took up his sketch pad and charcoal without thinking of his actions, so focused was he on his inner world. His quest to capture the Glory had long before required him to confront his selfish past. Although he did not think of it as karma, Thailand had convinced him he owed something to the cosmos. Justice was perhaps a better concept, not actions causing reactions, but eye for eye, or life for life. Justice could be reconciled with his own genius, his need to be the master of his fate. It required only that he admit a kind of mathematical balance existed, an impersonal process of cause and effect which simply was, and therefore required no submission. One compromised because justice existed, much the way one changed one's plans because of nasty weather.

But something different had driven him across the street to Hakan. Sketching aimlessly for hours, Ridler tried to understand his motivation, to put words to it. Eventually he was forced to confess he had succumbed to something long despised and mocked in others. The word that came to mind was "guilt."

"Will you forsake union with all women?"

Ridler looked up from his sketchbook to see the old beggar standing near and watching him intently. "What did you say?" he asked.

The old man said, "If you wish to know the way, you must abstain from fornication. Are you prepared for this?"

"Are you serious?" asked Ridler.

The beggar merely gazed at him with laughing eyes. In spite of the years gone by, Ridler had slept with no one since Suzanna. "Yes," he said, for chastity was easy without her.

"Will you fast?"

"For how long?" asked Ridler.

Again the old man did not answer.

"Yes," said Ridler again, who often went all day without eating while he painted.

"Will you repent of your sins?"

Having just assuaged his guilt with offerings to Hakan, Ridler replied immediately this time. "I will."

"In that case, if you still wish to understand, come."

The beggar turned and stepped into the flowing multitude. Immediately Ridler rose and followed, leaving his work behind.

Together for the rest of that day the two of them walked through the bazaar, weaving their way up and down among the vender stalls and carts and tracing out the maze of ancient streets and alleys. As they walked, men, women, boys, and girls approached the old man solemnly to drop coins in his copper bowl. Ridler thought of the Buddhist monks standing before birdcages, accepting tickets in their bowls of clay. Like them, the old man never looked at what was given. Like them, he never asked for anything.

They approached an aged woman. She sat surrounded by cloth bags stuffed to overflowing. Ridler thought she was another vender, but as they drew closer he saw that her wares were unfit for any market. Neatly arranged on the ground around her were torn rags, bits of broken plastic, twigs, and stones. Her robes flowed loosely over her slumping body. A scarf covered her bowed head. With gnarled, arthritic fingers she held a veil across her face, leaving only her eyes exposed. Ridler took note of the burnt umber and dark sienna fabric she wore, colors of the soil where she groveled, as if the old woman had been thrust up from the earth like a rock formation.

Among the pitiful merchandise before her was a red plastic cup. The old beggar paused, bent to whisper something in her ear, and poured the entire contents of his begging bowl into it. She started laughing as they walked away. Her laughter filled the street. It flowed down the alleys. It poured into the river. It wove the clouds in patterns and choreographed the flight of birds. It buoyed Ridler and the old man as an ocean lifts a ship. It was wavelike, tidal, beautiful and awful.

"What did you say to her?" asked Ridler.

"'Now it is your turn.'"

"I don't understand."

"I know."

Looking back, Ridler saw the old woman's veil had fallen to expose a laughing mouth devoid of teeth, a gaping hole which uncoiled wrinkles like kite strings toward her flying nose, her flying ears and eyes. She herself had also risen to the center of a swirling mob of filthy children. They circled her in ecstasy as one by one she reached into the plastic cup to put a coin into an outstretched hand. Her laughter lifted them as it had lifted Ridler and the beggar. Soaring round and round her, the children were a cyclone of delight. Their giggles joined her laughter. They rose above their poverty, above the twisted streets, the mindless human river, the wicked fate which had so callously assigned them to that life. They became as doves, light and without worries. The artist, who had cause to view doves with skepticism, wondered if their flight above the towers and the minarets would only lead to their beginning. Had they been truly freed, or would they return to cages?

Unlike Ridler, the old man did not look back. "Mix yourself with Allah," he said. "'Say to everything that comes and goes, "This is not my love," or else you will be like a fire left by a caravan to burn out alone beside the road.' Thus said Pir Rumi, peace be upon him." They walked on, and with the generosity of passersby, the old man's bowl began to fill again.

After that the beggar came for Ridler every afternoon, greeting him with words from the Qur'an. "'Hasten to the remembrance of Allah and cease your trading. That would be best for you, if you only knew it.'" As he recited this, the old man's eyes were always laughing.

They strolled through the bazaar, the beggar speaking of the Sufi path, of Allah, the god of love. Once, when there was an early moon in the daytime, he stopped suddenly to stand like an island in the river of commerce. Taking shelter in his lee, Ridler heard him quote the famous poet Rumi yet again. "'He comes!'" exclaimed the old man, pointing upward with his staff. "'A moon whose like the sky has never seen, be it awake or dreaming, crowned with an endless fire no water can slay. Look! In the vessel of your love, O Lord, my soul swims, but my body is a ruined house of clay!'"

The old man rarely mentioned Allah without speaking also of love. "Love must be disinterested. Love not because you fear the flames of hell. Love not because you long for paradise. Love only because Allah loves you."

Of the Qur'an's many names for God, the beggar much preferred al-Wadud, the Loving One. "I do not say Allah is love as the Christians do, for who can know what Allah is? I only say his will is love, for the Qur'an has revealed it to be so."

He blamed concern with the body for holding divine love at bay. "Your lower self is but a black dog," said the old man sometimes. "Feed it not." Following the old man's example, Ridler trained himself to eat only one small meal each day.

Ridler's doubts remained concerning the efficacy of prayer, but to please the old beggar he practiced the Islamic ritual, facing Mecca five times every day between the morning and the night. The words were not his own, which made them possible to speak without concern about hypocrisy. Sometimes he recited along with the old beggar, "There is no god but Allah, and Muhammad is his prophet," but for him it was a formula, not a confession.

"Once I was a wealthy man," said al-Wasiti as he gave alms to a richer beggar.

"Why did you choose a life of poverty?" asked Ridler, who was poor from lack of interest in anything but Suzanna and his art.

"We choose nothing. We are chosen."

"But didn't you decide to give away your wealth, as you decide to give away your alms today?"

"My wealth was taken from me, as were my wife and children, all by Allah's will, praise be to the Most Merciful."

"If Allah took your family and wealth, how can you call him merciful?"

"Although you have learned to hear, understanding still eludes you, artist. Hear then, the words of the Qur'an. 'Lo! Allah is a lord of kindness to mankind, but most of mankind gives no thanks.' Likewise it is written, 'Say: Oh my servants who have transgressed against their own souls, despair not of the mercy of Allah. Indeed, Allah forgives all sins. Truly, He is most forgiving, most merciful.'"

"You believe Allah is merciful because the Qur'an says it's so?"

"Indeed I do. Also because he has proven his great love to me, for when my wife and children were removed from life, I was not."

Ridler did not understand that kind of mercy, but in spite of his doubts, he sensed real possibility in this master of the Sufi way, who spoke of Allah's boundless love while love shone from his eyes, who went everywhere with the Qur'an's message of benevolence upon his lips. As the old man poured coins into the palms of other beggars, Ridler heard him recite, "'On those who believe and work deeds of righteousness will the Most Gracious bestow love.'" As venders left their stalls to drop coins in the beggar's copper bowl, Ridler heard him say, "Blessed be 'those who spend, whether in prosperity or adversity; who restrain anger and pardon men, for

Allah loves those who do good.'" Following in the wake of such devotion, Ridler dared to hope he might draw closer to the vast enigma which had once drawn close to him.

One day, as they strolled along an alley so narrow it was possible for a man to touch the walls on either side at once, Ridler spoke for the first time of his encounter with transcendency. When he had finished, the old beggar merely nodded.

Ridler said, "You don't believe me?"

"Did you lie?" replied the old man.

"Of course not."

"That was my opinion too."

"Then why don't you say something?"

"It is idle waste to speak of what is obvious."

"Obvious? You think that was obvious?"

"To a true believer, certainly, but not to one who hears but does not understand."

"I have followed you for years. When will you stop saying that?"

"When you understand, even if you do not hear."

Ridler had grown impatient with such riddles. "I just want to find a way to paint what I met in the river."

"Nothing could be simpler. Only paint Wajad."

"What's Wajad?"

"Watch, painter, and learn."

They had reached an intersection with a backstreet. The old man entered a shop on the corner and returned with three young men. He began to circle the middle of the intersection, calling for more space. The venders on the four corners obliged him, pulling back their wares until there was that rarest of all things in the bazaar: a place devoid of merchandise and people. The old beggar continued to walk around the edges of the clearing, but now he clapped his hands in time with every step. The young men from the shop began to clap in time as well. As their rhythm echoed from the ancient walls, the old man repositioned his leather belt to bind his robes more tightly at his waist while allowing them to billow out around his legs. He pulled back the fabric from his head to expose a small gray cap, which was shaped like an old-fashioned fez.

"Learn, artist," he called out to Ridler. "The hat is a tomb for my lower self, and the skirt about me is a shroud. But now regard my hand, as I receive love and grace from Allah the most Merciful!"

Like a waiter carrying a tray, the beggar raised his arm to the level of his shoulders and bent his elbow up to reach toward the sky. He placed his other hand upon his waist. He added a new motion to his dance, spinning as he circled around the open place. The three young men began to lift their voices, singing something in a language Ridler did not understand. The old man spun more rapidly, stepping lightly in time with the young men's clapping hands and song. Round and round he went, rhythm joining every-thing together: the clapping, the regularity of words, the pulsing breeze his flying robes created as they lifted in a circle of pure white around his waist, the dervish himself whirling in pursuit of ecstasy.

Watching him, Ridler felt the rhythm seeping in to supersede his consciousness. His own body began to sway. He sensed oneness with the motion of the sun and shadows, with the beat of pigeons' wings, with the breath within his nostrils, the beating of his heart, the ebb and flow of everything. He began to lose himself within it. He began to sense another way of being, something different in the distance. Could it be the Glory coming? Could it be at last?

Al-Wasiti might have whirled forever, and Ridler might have joined him, had the young man with blood-red eyes not stepped out from the crowd and struck the beggar down and stood above him with a dagger. "Infidel!" he shouted. "Heretic!"

Outraged, Ridler rushed to aid his master. The assailant watched him come and smiled without concern, for when Ridler was still three steps away a gang of others overtook him. Something tangled with his feet. He fell hard upon the ancient pavement. Boots attacked his ribs, his head, his back. He saw an image from the past, an alley, an assault of teenage artists, the last fragments of transcendence disappearing.

Then he could see nothing.

When Ridler awoke he saw al-Wasiti sitting just across from him, bound elbow and ankle to a chair. Ridler tried to move and found himself restrained exactly as the old man was. They faced each other in a room lit only by one window high upon the wall, too small for escape. Dry blood marked the beggar's left ear and left cheek. The old man's eyes were open, watching him. Seeing Ridler had awakened, he smiled. Several of his teeth were gone. "How do you fare?" he asked.

"What happened?" replied Ridler.

"I fear we have entered a theological debate with my Kurdish brothers in the Hizbullah."

Ridler looked around. "Nobody's here."

"Alas, they will return. In the meantime, our bonds are their argument."

"Then I guess we're losing the debate."

"That is impossible, for we are correct."

"Well, if this is winning, I would rather lose."

The old man laughed. Emboldened by the sound, the artist pushed and pulled against his bindings. "Do not struggle," said the beggar. "Allah's will is unavoidable."

"You think Allah wants us here?"

"Why else would we be here?"

After a few more fruitless minutes struggling against the cords which bound him to the chair, Ridler knew that the old man was correct. There could be no escape. Accepting this, he sat quietly.

"Good," said the beggar. "Let us use this time more profitably."

In the hour that followed, they discussed al-Qatar, the destiny of all creation as it is ordained by Allah. "He knows all things, from eternity to eternity," said the old man. "He ordained all things and caused all things to be written at the dawn of creation."

"Even this?" asked Ridler.

"Even this was written by the first created thing, which was a pen, which was commanded, 'Write down the decrees of all things until the hour begins.'"

"So these men who beat us and brought us here . . . they're only doing what Allah wills?"

"Indeed, it must be so, for it is written, 'If your Lord had so willed, they would not have done it.'"

"But you said Allah's will is love. How can this be love?"

"Ours is but a momentary trial. The love of Allah is eternal. Trust him."

Ridler stared at the old Sufi who sat bound and bloodied in the chair across the room. He marveled that anyone could say those words in that place and time. "Where do you get such faith?"

The old man sighed and looked away. "Oh, painter, even now you hear but do not understand. How you tempt me to despair."

"I tempt you to despair, but this doesn't?"

The old man sat in silence for a while, staring at the floor between them. Then he raised his kindly eyes. "The Qur'an is clear. Everything is written. Everything. Even faith." Then he closed his eyes and bowed his head. Soon he began to snore.

Amazed that the beggar could sleep at such a time, Ridler pondered his words until the dim light through the window faded. Total darkness overwhelmed him. His elbows and ankles ached from the pressure of the cord and his back ached from the rigid position forced upon it by his bindings. He began to wish their captors would return. Perhaps then they would explain why they had done this, and he could help them understand the nature of their error. For of course it must be an error. He had done no harm to anyone, at least not in Istanbul.

When the light above their heads came on and the door swung open he was startled from another state of mind, a dream perhaps, and what he woke to was a nightmare.

Three men entered the room. One held a sword, a scimitar. The other two held steel pipes. One of them walked directly to the old man. Without a word he began to beat the beggar with the pipe, swinging at his knees. Ridler opened his mouth to protest, but a scream emerged instead as another man swung a pipe against his shoulder, once, twice, three times in exactly the same spot, each blow shooting greater spikes of pain along his arm. The third man stood between him and the beggar. When the blows stopped at last, Ridler looked to that man in the middle and saw his blood-red eyes glaring in the incandescent light, the capillaries in them clearly ruptured.

"Why?" the artist asked.

"Allah is great!" shouted the man between them, and again the other man beside him swung the pipe. Ridler screamed.

"Have mercy, brother," said the beggar. "The American has no part in our dispute."

"Indeed he does not," agreed the red-eyed man. "How could a Jewish dog understand? He is fit only for the rod."

Again the pipe swung hard against Ridler's arm. Again he

screamed. Fighting back the wave of pain he shrieked, "I'm not a Jew!"

"You have the look of a Jew. The arrogance. The wicked cunning features."

Again the pipe bounced off his arm. Again he screamed. "I'm not a Jew!"

"Inspect him," said the red-eyed man, pointing his scimitar at Ridler.

The attacker pulled a knife and aimed it at Ridler's groin.

"No!" cried Ridler. "Please! God, no!"

The blade descended, but did no lasting damage. Instead his assailant merely cut away the trousers. "It is true," said the man. "This one is no Jew."

"No matter," replied the one in charge, "for he is a disciple of this infidel. Chastise him."

Leaving Ridler exposed, the man took up the pipe to resume the beating.

"Brother!" cried al-Wasiti. "This is not the way!"

The red-eyed man replied, "One of two things is true. Either you are a liar, or you are a blasphemer. For you know this is commanded by the Prophet, peace be upon him."

"How can this be commanded?" moaned Ridler. "When Allah's will is only love?"

"Only love?" With the scimitar resting on his own shoulder, the red-eyed man turned toward Abu al-Wasiti. "Is that one of the lies you teach?"

Ridler searched his memory. Words came. "'Say: If you love Allah, follow me. Allah will love you and forgive you your sins. Allah is forgiving and merciful.'"

The man addressed the beggar, his red eyes wide, his posture indicating mock surprise. "Did your instruction omit the very next *ayah*? How convenient. But the time has come to complete this infidel's education. Quote the next *ayah*, old man."

The beggar did not seem to hear the question. At a nod from the red-eyed man, the pipe swung against al-Wasiti's knee again. The old man screamed. The tormentor shouted, "Quote it!"

Al-Wasiti mumbled something.

"Louder!"

The beggar shook his head. "To recite out of context is to twist the meaning."

"Hypocrite! It is you who taught him out of context. You speak only of Allah's love for believers. You omit his righteous hatred for infidels. Recite the rest of it therefore, or I will behead this dog, and he shall learn the truth from Satan."

The old man would not look at Ridler as he spoke again. "'Say: Obey Allah and the Apostle, if they give no heed, then truly Allah does not love the infidels.'"

The red-eyed man turned to face Ridler. "Do you hear that, dog? Allah does not love an infidel like you."

"'Allah's will is love,'" insisted Ridler. "Allah loves me."

"Indeed? Old man, let us continue this stubborn dog's education. Let us quote another from the book." The tormentor began to pace between them, tapping his sword on his shoulder. "Which one shall it be? Perhaps from Repentance. Perhaps seventy-three. Recite!"

Al-Wasiti spoke, but as before, Ridler could not hear. The man beside the beggar swung his pipe again. This time the old man's cries were mixed with tears.

"Are you ashamed of the holy Qur'an?" asked the red-eyed man. "Speak so all may hear! Speak as though you were a proper son of Islam!"

"'Prophet,'" said al-Wasiti. " 'Make war on the unbelievers and the hypocrites and deal rigorously with them. Hell shall be their home, an evil fate.'"

As their tormentor paced between them, Ridler stared at the beggar, trying to reconcile these words with everything the old man had taught him through their years together.

"Excellent," said the torturer. "Now give us nine and twenty-nine."

Ridler willed the old man to look up at him, to help him understand, but al-Wasiti's head was bowed, his gaze upon the floor. He said, "'Fight those who do not believe in Allah or in the Last Day, and those who do not forbid what Allah and His Messenger have forbidden, or embrace the true religion, until they acknowledge your superiority with tribute and are completely subdued.'"

"That can't be right," said Ridler.

Their tormentor turned on him. "Do you deny the book?"

"I don't believe that's in there. It's not love, and Allah's will is love."

The man beside him swung the pipe again. This time Ridler felt the bone break.

"Why are you doing this?" he moaned. "Why?"

"I? It is not I who acts in this matter. Old man! Who truly smites this infidel? Speak! Give us eight and seventeen."

This time the beggar spoke out plainly through his tears. "'It was not you. It was Allah who killed them. It was not you who struck them when you struck them. It was Allah striking them, so he might give you a rich reward.'"

"You see?" asked the red-eyed man. "We are nothing. We are merely Allah's hands. Allah bound you to these chairs. Allah punishes. Nothing can occur outside his will, and he has no care for such as you! Give us eight and thirty-nine, old man!"

The beggar mumbled, "'Make war on them until there is no more idolatry, and all religions are for Allah.'"

The red-eyed madman stepped behind the beggar. He laid the flat edge of the sword blade on al-Wasiti's shoulder. "Good! Now let us have nine and five."

"'When the holy months have passed kill the idolaters wherever they are found. Confine them. Lay siege to them. Wait in ambush for them everywhere. If they repent and pray and pay the tax, let them go their way. Allah is forgiving and merciful.'"

The red-eyed man lifted the sword from the beggar's shoulder. Standing behind al-Wasiti, he raised the blade, holding it in both hands cocked over his shoulder like a baseball batter at home plate, poised to swing. "And do you repent, al-Wasiti? Will you pay us tribute from your foolish copper bowl? Will you abandon heresy and live?"

The old man raised his eyes to stare at Ridler. "My life is in Allah's hands. Allah is the greatest!"

Ridler screamed a useless warning in that ancient cell in Istanbul, and again he screamed a warning in the burning Texas desert, as El Magnífico's blade flashed in the pitiless sun and a rattlesnake's head lay severed from its body.

"Ah, dinner," said the dwarf, Gregorio.

El Magnífico merely smiled and crossed his arms and surveyed the horizon with closed eyes.

The dwarf bent to lift the serpent by its rattles. "Why did they let you live, San Pablo? I ask you every time, and you never answer."

"I will answer when you explain why that snake died instead of you."

Gregorio shrugged small shoulders. "Fate."

Ridler's face was ugly. "I spit on fate."

The headless serpent dangled from Gregorio's small hand. "Perhaps you lived because God loves you."

Still lost in formal Spanish, Ridler scoffed. "You merely speak of fate a different way."

"In that case, do you also spit on love?"

Gazing down on them from high upon the boulder, shaded by her parasol, the old woman with lovely bones began to laugh. As always when that happened, everybody except Ridler smiled.

He turned abruptly, abandoning the line of beaters. In spite of immense hunger, he had lost his stomach for terrorizing desert creatures. He had more apologies to paint. He set out for his trailer, where his easel and brushes awaited.

"San Pablo?" called the dwarf after him. "Why did they let you live?"

"Leave me alone," replied the artist, furious because he did not know.

10.

His man Fleming brought the package to the library. "Put it on the desk," said Talbot Graves, "and bring a glass of ginger ale."

"Yes, sir," replied Fleming, most correct in his black Gieves & Hawkes suit. "Shall I open a door?"

It was a trifle stuffy. "Yes, that will be fine. And put that ginger ale on ice."

"Of course, sir."

With one of the doors open, Vivaldi on the sound system, and a pleasant breeze coming in from the terrace, Talbot Graves returned to his reading. He was in the midst of the Holmes translation of *The Gallic War,* at the section on the siege of Avaricum. He chuckled at the story Caesar told of Gallic wives betraying cowardly husbands who tried to slip away under cover of night. *They began to scream and gesticulate, to warn the Romans of the intended flight.* Graves laughed aloud and shook his head. Imagine warning the enemy in order to keep your husband home. He congratulated himself for his wise decision to avoid a wife.

Of course, a companion would not be completely unwelcome. He set the book aside and rose and crossed the library and stepped out through the open terrace door. All around him vines and flowers flourished in cast iron pots and terra-cotta planters. Four chaise lounges beckoned from a sunny place at the far end of the terrace, and closer to him a sectional divan with five matching lounge chairs had been arranged around a fire pit. He had fought the San Remo co-op for five years to get that fire pit.

He walked to the parapet and surveyed New York City. Twenty-six floors below him sprawled the green rectangle of Central Park. To the left lay baseball diamonds, Turtle Pond, and on the far side of the park one of his many clients, the Met. On his right a hundred sunbathers dotted Sheep Meadow, and down below him was the Lake.

Talbot Graves had reached not only the top floor of that most exclusive of New York apartment buildings; he had reached the pinnacle of his profession. Few art dealers in history had attained such grand success. But while his terrace furniture was put to use by parties every week or two, and his days were full of good books, fine wine, and the best possible food, Talbot Graves did sometimes wonder if it all might be more satisfying with someone at his side.

Certainly he still had opportunities. Ambitious young ladies and divorcees of a certain age still offered themselves regularly. But at nearly eighty years old, he had no illusions. Money was their motive. That, and only that.

Staring out across the park, Talbot suddenly remembered Suzanna. Odd, that she should come to mind so often after all the years.

Unconsciously he turned toward the north, and Harlem. Somewhere over there, far beyond the mountain range of buildings, stood the little brownstone where she had lived before she left for California. What a struggle it had been to let her go untouched. How many times he had dreamed of Suzanna as Ridler had painted her: nude and waiting, the luscious, nubile, beckoning Suzanna, now perhaps the most famous muse in history. How many times had he floundered on the rocks of indecision in her presence? He had nearly proposed once, had purchased the ring, and taken her to Tavern on the Green, and been on the verge of opening his mouth to say the words when she had started speaking of the way her baby girl reminded her of Ridler.

He had listened, smiled, and ordered more champagne. He had done his best to avoid thinking of a bridge across the Harlem River, and how close to ruin he had been, and he had realized he would spend the rest of his life trying not to think of that if she became his wife.

Now of course he was thinking of it anyway, high above Manhattan, seeing Ridler in midair because he had allowed Suzanna to arise within his mind. He shook his head to clear both of them out, and once again congratulated himself for his wise decision to avoid a wife.

"Your ginger ale, sir."

Startled, Talbot turned to find Fleming standing just behind him with a glass of bubbling liquid on a silver tray. He had a sudden thought, a picture of a pair of hands upon his back, a savage push, and him falling past his neighbor's windows with five or six seconds to think about the sidewalk rushing up. He had allowed Fleming to believe he was in the will because it was convenient to leave the man with that impression—devoted servants being such a rare commodity—but it was also slightly dangerous. Talbot shuddered. "I wish you'd learn to make a little noise when you move around."

"I'm sorry, sir. Did I startle you?"

"Of course not. Just don't sneak up on me like that."

"No, sir. My apologies."

Graves's age-spotted hand shook a little when he took the ginger ale. Fleming seemed to fail to notice.

"Will there be anything else, sir?"

"Open that package you left on my desk and take the wrapping paper away."

"Very good, sir."

Graves sipped the soda and observed the endless rows of taxicabs below, crawling bumper to bumper along Central Park West like yellow caterpillars.

"All done, sir," said Fleming, standing at the open door. "If there's nothing else for the moment, I thought I'd make sure Marie has started dinner."

"Did she get that T-bone I wanted?"

"I'm sure she did."

"Tell her I'd like some asparagus with that. And a baked potato."

"Excellent choices, sir."

"Don't patronize me, Fleming."

"Of course not, sir."

Graves took another sip of ginger ale while looking his man full in the face. Fleming's eyes did not waver as he returned the stare. His eyes never wavered. Graves swallowed. "All right. Let me know five minutes before it's ready. I'll eat out here."

Talbot turned his back to dismiss Fleming and stood a few more minutes gazing eastward as the glass sweated in his hand. Life was filled with compromises. Money didn't change that. Fleming was almost as bad as a wife. He would much prefer to live alone, but who then would prepare his meals, launder his clothes, and keep the mongrel hoards of aspiring artists at bay? No, Fleming was a necessary evil, as was Marie, the cook. How he despised them both for their essentiality.

He set the glass down on the parapet for Fleming to collect and reentered the library. Across the room the contents of the package lay upon the walnut partner's desk. Talbot grimaced. Another painting. An original, no doubt. He often received them from the desperate ones and self-important ones, the ones who told themselves they had nothing to lose, or those who believed they could not fail to capture his attention if only they could somehow lay their work before his eyes. In the summertime Talbot saved the little horrors. In winter he amused himself by burning them at parties. He staged exhibitions, placing paintings one by one upon an easel for his mocking guests' assessment before tossing them into the fireplace. Everybody roared, turning thumbs down as if condemning gladiators. What fun. And what effrontery, to think that Talbot Graves could be so easily tempted.

Crossing the library, he approached the latest piece of kindling destined for his guests' amusement. Glancing down he noticed first the small size and then the subject. It appeared to be nonrepresentational, although most of these people had so little talent it was difficult to tell if one was expected to recognize their images or not.

Apparently no letter had arrived with the painting, not even a transmittal. If there had been one, Fleming would have left it beside the painting on the desk. So that at least was interesting. Usually they included return instructions. "If for any reason you decide not to represent my work, kindly deliver this painting to me at the following address. . . ." Graves smiled to think of such naivety. But at least such notes acknowledged the possibility of rejection. Could this artist in his hubris honestly believe no return address was necessary?

Slightly interested in spite of himself, Graves squinted at the canvas. In the dim library it was difficult to make out details. He reached across the desk and switched on a lamp. What he saw then took his breath away.

He hurried to the wall beside the door and switched on the overhead lights, then he returned to the desk and made a pile of books and propped the little canvas up against them. As he backed away with his eyes focused on the painting, his heart began to race much as it had recently at the Guggenheim when he nearly fainted from excitement at the Chagall retrospective. Staring at the painting, he saw something in the brushwork, something . . .

No.

It couldn't be.

With the possible exception of Suzanna and her daughter, he was the world's foremost authority, and he had never seen this canvas before. It was nothing like any of the others he had sold throughout the years. And yet . . .

He stepped close again to inspect the signature. Opening a desk drawer, he removed a magnifying glass, and with his face mere inches from the canvas he began to search it inch by inch. Thirty minutes later he was still bent over the painting when the door behind him opened and Fleming stepped into the room to say, "Sir, your dinner—"

"Get out," said Talbot Graves without looking up.

"Very good, sir."

Another hour passed. Finally, having exhausted his inspection of the painting, he turned the canvas to examine the back side. There he found the penciled words:

G.—

Sorry it didn't work out between you and Suzanna.
For all the times I let you down, forgive me.
—S.

Talbot laid the magnifying glass upon the blotter by the painting and sank into his desk chair. Who could have sent this thing to him? Why would they do it? The signature was very well done, and the palette and brush technique were nearly perfect matches for Sheridan Ridler's work, but if they intended him to think it was a Ridler, why choose a totally nonrepresentational subject, something so unlike everything the artist ever did? And this note on the back . . . what did it mean, about him and Suzanna? Since this was supposed to be a Ridler, then obviously "Suzanna" was supposed to be Suzanna Halls, but Talbot had never told a soul how he once felt about that woman. He had never even told Suzanna.

It must have been a guess, based on a little research, the superficial knowledge that he had once known the famous Suzanna Halls, muse and companion to Sheridan Ridler. Yes, it must be only a guess. And with the apology at the end the forger had made a fatal misstep.

Ridler would never have apologized for anything. Never.

Talbot felt a rush of anger. Of all the attempts to manipulate him, this was much the worst. It was one thing to send a painting unsolicited; it was quite another thing to play on his emotions so transparently, to try to leverage his own history this way. If Talbot could, he would have sliced the thing to ribbons and returned it, but of course the forger had anticipated that reaction. It explained why there was no return address, no explanation at all. So this affront would have to be merely more fuel for the fireplace. But Talbot did not think he would display this particular one to party guests. This one he would burn alone. In fact, he would do it right away.

Energized by anger, he rose quickly, grabbing the canvas. He carried it out of the library and down the marble gallery and turned left between two pairs of Ionic columns into the living room. There he tossed the canvas into the massive fireplace and went in search of matches, opening all the drawers on the pair of Biedermeier secretaries that flanked the terrace doors. "Fleming!" he shouted. "Fleming, come here!"

"Yes, sir?" said the man, appearing almost instantly.

"Where have you hidden the matches?"

"Hidden, sir? Matches, sir?"

"Yes, matches. You know what matches are."

"Yes, sir. I believe we have some in the kitchen."

"Well, bring them here and light the gas in the fireplace. Hurry up."

"Of course, sir."

As the man rushed out, Talbot paced the room. The more he thought about the effrontery of someone trying to pass a painting off as a Ridler, someone trying to do that to *him*, the more the rage within him built. This was no mere practical joke. A forgery of that quality would not come cheap. It would take very good contacts just to find a painter who could pull it off. The thing must have been commissioned by one of his enemies in the trade, one of the many he had outmaneuvered through the years. How he longed to know which of them it was. He would ruin them. He would see they never made another penny in the art world and he would take great joy in his revenge.

Oh, the sweetness of that thought! But to endure this insult without knowing who had inflicted it was insufferable. He stopped pacing and faced the fireplace. Every painting offered hints about its provenance. Until that moment his attention had been limited to critical examination. He should look once more for clues before he burned it, try not to think of it so academically, try to find something, anything to help him guess the source, even if the guess was only based on instinct.

Talbot's knees and hips were far too old to kneel to look more closely at the painting, so he dragged a chair across the room and sat. From that vantage point, he stared down at the image. As before, he was forced to admit the forger had real talent.

Also, it was clever not to make the image similar to any other Ridler in existence. Amateur forgers usually made the mistake of painting something too much like the genuine article, copying an artist's favorite scene or model or gesture, for example. By rendering something different, this painter had made it impossible to compare the forgery too closely to an authentic Ridler, and therefore impossible to say with certainty where or when Sheridan Ridler might have painted it. Thus the forger had opened the door to the prospect that this painting had been done by the artist at a unique time and place, perhaps as a study for a larger work that Ridler had decided not to do, or maybe as a lark, or as something dashed off quickly just to document an idea, but never intended for sale or exhibition. In that way the burden was shifted onto Talbot to prove that it could not have been part of some hitherto unknown phase of the artist's development, and of course it was very difficult to prove a negative.

Talbot Graves, however, was not fooled. Staring at the painting with a practiced eye, once again he ran through all the technical reasons why it could not be a Ridler and everything still added up to forgery.

Yet once he gazed more deeply down into the image instead of simply looking at the details on the surface, somehow—and he could not explain how—it became more like a Ridler. He could not point to any single feature and say, "There. That's how Sheridan Ridler would have done it," but the more Graves looked, the more he seemed to see the sensibility, the energy, the unquantifiable presence of Ridler's hand.

How could anyone forge that?

Graves cocked his head to match the angle of the painting where it lay against the fireplace andirons. He considered the enticing way the image swirled and blended with the ground, the way it seemed to be a shapeless void one moment and an emerging form the next. He saw a kind of purity in it, a perfection, and now that he allowed himself to simply enter the experience he felt a lightness rising, something inexplicable and hopeful, like a memory, a shady patio beneath a tree, the forgotten scent of rainwater evaporating from flagstones, his long-dead mother there alive and well beside him in the hammock, the only person he had ever loved giving him a pad of paper, and his hands in motion as he sketched the leaves and limbs above the two of them, the pencil large and clumsy in his little fingers as he tried to please her, and her approving gaze, and his joy at her approval, endless boundless joy, and there before the massive fireplace, staring at the painting Talbot felt his belly squirm, for hard upon the heels of joy came awful loneliness as everything that he had ever lusted for appeared within that formless image, everything portrayed there for the taking, but also in it was the knowledge that everything he'd ever wanted would not ever be enough, and with that realization Talbot Graves slipped down to his feeble, cracking knees before the painting and he whimpered, "Burn it! Burn it! Burn it!"

Late that night, long after the cook had gone home and Fleming had retired, Talbot paced the rooms of his apartment, alone. Muttering and gesturing, he strode from living room to library to dining room to kitchen, round and round in earnest conversation with himself.

He had not been satisfied when his man Fleming burned the canvas. He wished it could be burned again. He had ordered all the ashes to be collected from the fireplace and removed, not dropped down the garbage chute, but taken from the building altogether. "Go to the river and drop it in," he had commanded Fleming.

"Which river, sir?" had been the man's ridiculous response,

standing there in his expensive suit with a sackful of ashes in his hand. Speaking very slowly, spacing his words as if explaining to a mental deficient, Talbot said, "I don't care which river. Just make sure it all goes in the water. Every speck. Take a cab, find a bridge, tell the driver to stop, get out of the cab, walk to the center of the bridge, the downwind side, Fleming, remember that, the downwind side, and throw those ashes in the river."

Only after Fleming had departed did Talbot Graves consider the horrible possibility that his man might stand at the mid span on the Madison Avenue Bridge, might scatter those horrific ashes in the Harlem River at the very place where he had last seen Ridler suspended in midair above his death.

No. There was little chance of that. Why would Fleming pick that bridge, at the far end of the island? Besides, such coincidences did not really happen. And if it did, what of that? Talbot Graves was no superstitious fool. So the painter and his painting fell into the same river at the same place. So what?

Talbot Graves stopped pacing. What had he just thought? The painter and his painting. His painting? Ridler's painting? Why had he thought that? It most certainly was *not* Ridler's painting. It was a clever forgery. Only a forgery.

And yet when he had been preoccupied with other things, he had thought of it as Ridler's, and maybe, just maybe, that was his subconscious accepting what his conscious mind denied.

"No. It isn't possible," said Talbot Graves to no one as he set out pacing again. "I could smell the oil. It was fresh. It couldn't have been more than a month old."

And yet there was the energy, the presence, the sense of Sheridan Ridler's hand in every stroke.

Pausing in the kitchen, he balled his fists and shook them. It simply was not possible. He had seen Ridler fall, had leapt from his car and looked down in time to see the water rippling out from where the man had hit the river. The impact from the car, the fall, the freezing water, the current . . . it simply was not possible.

And yet.

Imagine if the man had lived.

Forget how. And never mind why he'd disappeared for all these years. Just imagine if he lived.

It would be the end of everything.

As he paced, Talbot looked around at the three de Koonings on his walls, and the Picassos, the Matisse, and the Kandinsky. He passed the plaster Rodin bas-relief in the niche in the hallway, a priceless study for *The Gates of Hell*. He paused beside a bronze Moore on a low pedestal in the entry foyer. He gazed at his many works by lesser artists, precious to him, all. Talbot Graves's career, his investments, everything he owned was built upon his unquestioned right to own and sell Sheridan Ridler's paintings, a fortune resting on a carefully laid plan, husbanding the canvases Ridler had left behind, selling only three or four a year, building up their value over time by keeping the supply limited. But if Ridler had survived the fall, then the artist could sue for all of it and he would most likely win.

Talbot had a sudden vision of himself in a one-room apartment, surviving on commission from some gallery if he was lucky, although who would hire him at his age? And every painting, every sculpture, the house in the Hamptons, the condo in Nassau, everything, all of it, gone.

"Don't be a fool," he told himself out loud. "He's dead."

But he could not free his mind of the suspicion that it was not true. The power in that freshly painted image had been undeniable, even as it burned in the fireplace.

So on and on he paced, mumbling reassurances to himself and fighting to believe them. Finally he remembered the words on the back of the canvas. *Sorry it didn't work out between you and Suzanna.* What did that mean? What did it mean? He pounded a fist into a palm. What did it *mean*?

In the library he went to his huge desk, unlocked the upper drawer, and removed his address book to look up Suzanna's telephone number. A minute later, she picked up the phone, twenty-eight hundred miles away and obviously half asleep. Once she finally understood who was on the line she said, "What's the matter?"

He forced himself to chuckle. "Nothing, dear. Nothing at all. I was just sitting here thinking about you and thought I'd call."

"Talbot, it's one in the morning."

"Is it? I'm so sorry. I completely lost track of time."

"Where are you?"

"At the apartment."

"New York? It must be four a.m. there."

"I suppose so. Listen, I just got the strangest thing in the mail, and I was wondering if you knew anything about it. It's silly of me, and I don't quite know how to ask . . ."

"Danny sent you a painting."

He stared at the de Kooning across the study. "I received a painting, yes."

"From Danny."

"Suzanna, that's not possible."

"But you think it's from him."

"It's just a very good forgery, obviously."

"That's what Gemma said too, but you wouldn't call me about a forgery, Talbot."

He had been a fool to call at all. This was tantamount to admitting he thought Ridler might be alive, and he did not believe that. He did *not*. "No, I just wanted to say hello, really. I got this thing today, and it made me think of you, and—"

"Why?"

"I beg your pardon?"

"Why did it make you think of me?"

Talbot cursed himself. This was getting worse and worse. "Well, there's an inscription, which mentions you."

"On the back, right? In pencil?"

"How did you know that?"

"I got one too."

He clenched the telephone handset tightly.

"Talbot? Are you there?"

"Yes. Uh. You mean you received a painting?"

"That's right. It has writing on the back. It mentions something only Danny would have known. That's why I'm sure it's from him."

"He's dead, Suzanna. You know that."

"I never believed it."

"Oh, Suzanna. Not that still, after all these years?"

"Never."

"I see. Well, then, what does the inscription say, exactly?"

"It talks about a fight we had, something he told me back then, when it was just the two of us alone. He apologized."

"Did he now?"

"Sounds like he apologized to you too. What does yours say?"

"It's nothing really. Just a general apology."

"Nothing specific?"

"There is one odd thing. It proves the painting can't be from him, actually. It says something like, 'I'm sorry it didn't work out with Suzanna.'"

There was silence on the line.

Talbot waited, wondering why he had made the call to Suzanna, why he had admitted what was written on the reverse side of the painting. After all the years, could a mere painting truly have aroused the forlorn hope that she might somehow want him? He had completely lost his senses to be talking to the woman in this way, yet he found he could not stop.

"Suzanna?"

"I'm here."

"You see how that can't be from him? It doesn't make any sense. I mean, there was never anything between us, was there?"

"No, of course not."

Amazing that her words could cause him pain, and yet he had to take a deep breath before going on. "No. And Sheridan never had any reason to suspect there was anything between us."

"But he did."

"What on earth do you mean?"

"Do you remember the time you came to my apartment, it was right after they declared him dead, and you came to . . . I don't know . . . to comfort me, I guess. I cooked dinner for you. You brought wine, I think. We were standing in the kitchen and I started crying, I think, and you gave me a hug. Remember?"

"No, I don't." It was a lie, of course. How could he forget the only chance he'd ever had to hold her in his arms?

"Well, you should. That was the last time I saw Danny. We were hugging and I looked over your shoulder and he was standing right outside the window."

"Oh, yes. I seem to remember now. You thought you saw him."

"I did see him, Talbot. Clear as day. And he saw us. He saw you hugging me. And by the time I got outside, he was gone."

The squirming returned to Talbot Graves's stomach. "You're saying he thought we were . . ."

"He thought we were together, yes. It has to be that. It's why he left the way he did. It's why he never called or anything."

Talbot removed the handset from his ear and stared up at the coffered ceiling. He sighed. He raised the handset up again. "If he were alive, he would have come forward a long time ago. Think of all the money."

"Danny never cared about money. You know that."

"Everybody cares about money." When she said nothing he continued, "Suzanna, you really should face facts. After all this time it's just not possible."

"That's not what Gemma says."

"Well, maybe he did your painting way back when, but the oil's hardly dry on the one I got."

"Mine is freshly painted too. That's what makes her think she can find him. He's out there painting somewhere, Talbot, and he's sending work to people from his past."

"People? You mean just you and me, right?"

"Gemma got a call from Lloyd's a few weeks ago. They wanted her to authenticate one of Danny's paintings before they insure it. She flew to Phoenix for the inspection. She said the image was very similar to the one I have. She said it even had a similar apology in pencil on the back."

Talbot balled his fist on the desktop. "Who's the owner?"

"Jennifer Killgarten."

He knew her from the old days. A longtime collector with diverse tastes, including a particular affinity for Jasper Johns, David Hockney, and Sheridan Ridler.

Suzanna continued. "It's new, Talbot. Like yours and mine. It's not one of the pieces Danny left behind. Gemma says the apology mentions something awful he called Jennifer. She told Gemma nobody else heard the insult, so there's no way anyone could have known. And there's another one. Caleb Nelson got it in the mail last Tuesday. He called me about it. Gemma's up in Vancouver with him now."

Talbot sat down heavily. Caleb Nelson was another of the original collectors, the lucky ones who had purchased Ridlers from him at very inexpensive prices before the artist's death, or else the unlucky ones who had been forced to put up with Sheridan Ridler's monumental ego, depending on how you looked at it. There was some difficulty between Ridler and Nelson . . . oh yes, Ridler had appeared at his Manhattan pied-à-terre demanding the return of a painting for some reason. The artist had threatened Nelson and refused to leave until the police arrived to haul him off. And come to think of it, Ridler had indeed insulted Jennifer Killgarten, when she complained about him smoking marijuana openly inside the gallery. Jennifer never repeated what he had said, but it must have been truly awful, because she had stormed off instantly and never bought another work of art from Talbot Graves.

So that was four paintings, all sent to people who had known Ridler in the early days, and all of whom had good reason to dislike the artist. It was time to face the facts.

Talbot said, "Assuming for the sake of discussion that you're right, would you please let me know if Sheridan contacts you?"

"You want to talk to him?"

"Of course. I mean, if he were alive I would."

"Okay. I'll tell Gemma. If anyone can find him, she will."

"She's looking for him?"

"Day and night."

After that, Talbot lay in bed with the curtains drawn against the rising sun and stared up into the space between his nose and the ceiling. If word of this got out, even the hint that Ridler might be alive and working out there somewhere would rock the art world.

Of the top thirty most expensive paintings ever purchased, eight were Picassos, seven were van Goghs, and five were Ridlers, including the most expensive of all. Only one of the top thirty had been painted by a living artist, Jasper Johns. If it turned out Ridler was still alive, auction prices for his work would plummet. The media would dig into his disappearance. Police reports would be reexamined, and some of the details in Talbot's story of that night might not withstand the added scrutiny.

At ten thirty in the morning Talbot rose and took a shower. Standing before the mirror with a razor in his hand, a plan came to him. With shaving cream still clinging to his jowls he rushed into the library, unlocked the top desk drawer again and looked up another phone number. To his great relief, the man agreed to meet him at the gallery that afternoon.

After a solitary luncheon served by Fleming on the terrace, Talbot Graves descended to the lobby, waved away the doorman, and walked around the corner before hailing a cab. He didn't want Fleming to drive him in the Bentley. He didn't want the doorman to see him take a taxi. He didn't want anyone to know where he was going.

Arriving early, he entered the gallery, a lush exhibition hall with gleaming terrazzo floors, hand-stitched white leather wall coverings, and general illumination from a riot of multicolored Chihuly fixtures sprawled across the ceiling like a glass rainbow made of jellyfish. Ordinarily Talbot paused a moment upon entering to enjoy the Chihuly's electric glow, but that afternoon he left the lights off.

Being Sunday, his staff was not at work. Walking past a Lichtenstein, a Pollock, and a Ridler, he crossed the exhibition hall, passed through the large open space where his employees worked, and entered his office in the rear. Sitting behind his desk, he waited. At last he heard an electric buzz. He rose to look at the security monitor, verified the man's identity at the door, and pushed the button to admit him. A voice called from the exhibition hall. "Hello? Talbot?"

He hurried back out front. "Emil! So good of you to come!"

Approaching with a smile and an extended hand, Talbot thought as usual that Emil Lacuna was the most handsome black man he had ever met. At slightly under six feet tall, he was impeccably dressed in a conservative navy blazer, a starched white shirt open at the collar, and a pair of gray linen slacks. He exuded energy and health, with the broad shoulders and trim waist of a tennis player, the grace in motion of a ballet dancer, and the quick eyes of a big-game hunter. He had been one of Talbot Graves's most faithful collectors over the last decade, having purchased thirteen minor Ridlers at a combined price of nearly twenty million dollars. He was also, as far as Talbot Graves had been able to determine, associated somehow with the Giordano crime syndicate, although Talbot had no idea how a man of Emil Lacuna's race had managed to ingratiate himself with the Italians.

"Talbot," said Lacuna, taking the extended hand.

"Very nice of you to come on such short notice," said Talbot.

Lacuna shrugged. "You made it sound important and I was in town. What's up? You have another Ridler for me?"

"Oh, one or two canvases might be of interest, but that's not why I called. Shall we step back to my office where we can be more comfortable?"

"All right." The man set out for the rear of Talbot's gallery, not waiting to be led. He seemed to spring forward with every step, bouncing off his toes.

Bitterly conscious of his own body's age, Talbot hurried to catch up. "Espresso?" he asked, as they entered his private office.

"No, thank you."

"Please have a seat." He gestured toward a pair of club chairs and a sofa across the room from his desk. Lacuna took one of the chairs. Talbot said, "Emil, I know you collect because you love the art, but financially you've done very well."

"I've done okay."

Talbot smiled. "Your modesty is admirable, but of course you've done much better than just okay. To prepare for this meeting, I checked your records here against the latest auctions. I'd estimate the Ridlers you've purchased from me are now worth around fifteen million dollars more than you paid for them, altogether." He paused to stare at Lacuna, letting that sink in. Lacuna returned his stare with those hunter's eyes, saying nothing. Talbot cleared his throat. "I only mention that to underscore the fact that I've never steered you wrong."

"You're a great guy, Talbot. What's the deal?"

"Well, I'm afraid I may have some bad news."

When he paused again, Lacuna said, "Let's have it."

"All right. It seems Sheridan Ridler may be alive, and it seems he might be painting again."

"What do you mean, 'may be' and 'might be'?"

"I received a painting in the mail. Others have received them too. They appear to be authentic, but you know, it's been so long since he was declared dead, and there's been no word whatsoever, so one does wonder about forgeries."

"If you thought they were forgeries we wouldn't be having this conversation."

"That's true."

"Let's see the one you got."

"I'm afraid it was destroyed."

Lacuna stared at him, unmoving.

Talbot said, "You do see the problem, Emil? I mean, your collection has almost doubled in value, but if Ridler is still alive and painting, I'm afraid the price for his work might actually decline below what you originally paid. You could lose a lot of money, especially if he's as prolific as he was in his younger years."

Lacuna said, "Supply and demand."

"Exactly."

"You told me the supply was limited. Now you're telling me it's not."

Talbot felt a subtle tightening in his abdomen. "Well, I could hardly be expected to know the man was still alive."

Lacuna's eyes examined him without wavering. Talbot had been prepared for anger, outrage, possibly even grief, but Lacuna showed no emotion whatsoever. The man said, "I spent a lot of money based on what you said."

"We're both in the same boat here, Emil. I stand to lose everything."

"Yes. I see that."

"I'm glad. To tell you the truth, I was a little worried you might be angry with me."

For the first time, Lacuna moved a little. He reached down and straightened the crease on his slacks. "Are you telling all of your clients about this?"

Talbot's eyes went wide. "Oh, no. I was hoping to keep it just between us."

"Why us? Why tell me?"

Now that they had reached the point of no return, Talbot felt a strange reluctance to proceed. He stared around the office. He swallowed. He tried to think of other options, but he had no other options. He shifted his gaze back to Lacuna, who remained exactly as he had been, motionless and staring. "I, uh, that is, I wondered if you might be able to help me with this problem."

"What kind of help did you have in mind?"

Talbot swallowed again. There were words one did not speak, yet what else could he do? He had no choice. He looked straight at Emil Lacuna. "What if it wasn't true? What if Ridler wasn't alive after all? Then your collection would still be worth fifteen million more than you paid."

For several seconds, Emil Lacuna did not speak. Then he was on his feet so quickly Talbot could not be certain he saw it happen. He said, "It's a little stuffy in here. Let's go out to your waiting room."

"If you wish."

"I do. Come on."

Talbot rose and followed him out of the office. They passed several desks where his employees worked. They reached the reception area, which was decorated as an extension of the exhibit space, with more white leather on the walls and three Ridler originals, part of Talbot's collection which were not for sale. Lacuna stopped and turned to face him.

"Hold your arms out, will you?"

Talbot did as the man asked, and Lacuna began to run his hands along his body.

"This is awkward," said Talbot.

The search was done. Lacuna said, "Thanks. You can sit down now."

In the reception area were two white leather settees, arranged to face each other. Talbot sat on one. Lacuna sat across from him on the other and said, "Sorry about the move out here and the pat down. It's important to be careful."

"I understand," said Talbot.

"Where is Ridler?"

"I don't know. But I think his daughter does, or else she's going to find out."

"Who is she?"

"Her name is Gemma Halls. She lives in Los Angeles. She works at the Getty."

Lacuna slipped a small leather-bound notebook out of a breast pocket. "Spell her first name."

Talbot spelled it for him as he wrote it down.

"Okay," said Emil Lacuna, replacing the notebook. "Now, what made you think I could help with a problem like this?"

"Oh . . ." Talbot shrugged a little. "One hears rumors."

"From whom?"

"Many people. Listen, let's not focus on that. Let's talk about the problem."

"I am talking about the problem. Tell me more about who's spreading these rumors."

Talbot began to think he might have made a mistake. "Maybe this was a bad idea. If I misunderstood, I mean, if this isn't something you'd be interested in, of course we can just forget about it. I certainly didn't wish to cause offense."

"Calm down, Talbot."

"I am calm! Why would you tell me to calm down?"

"Talbot. Look at me." Reluctantly, Talbot Graves met Lacuna's eyes. The man said, "I need you to do one thing right now. Just one thing, okay?"

"Certainly, Emil. Anything for you. You know that."

"Tell me who you talked to."

"It was just a passing comment. I'm sure it was a joke."

"Of course. Just tell me who it was."

"Well, Joseph Napoli, actually, I think. Yes, I'm sure it was Joseph."

"Good. Was anybody else around?"

"Around? It was a party. There were dozens of people." Talbot paused, but the man stared at him and said nothing, and he knew he had to answer. "You mean was anybody else listening, don't you? Let me think. No. As I recall it was just Joseph and me in the foyer. We were looking at a Ridler and I mentioned you collect them and that seemed to surprise him and he said something . . . I'm not sure what exactly, but I got the impression, you know . . ."

"Sure. I understand. Who else have you mentioned this to since then?"

"Nobody. I'm an art dealer, Emil. Discretion is essential in my business. People tell me things, but I never repeat them."

"You told Joey Naples I buy Ridlers."

Talbot swallowed. "Yes, well, that was wrong of me. I apologize for that."

"And today's meeting? Did you mention this to anyone at all?"

"Of course not. Something this sensitive, that's the last thing I would do."

"Did you write it on your calendar or anything?"

"No. I swear."

"No need to swear, Talbot. I believe you. Do you have a knife, or a pair of scissors?"

"What?"

"Anything with a sharp edge will be fine."

"What do you want it for?"

The man's sudden smile was strangely sad, filled with perfectly white teeth and overflowing with a sense of wistfulness, but Talbot had the distinct impression it was just for show. "Don't worry, Talbot. It's not for you."

Talbot found himself smiling too. His relief was almost overpowering. "Ha ha. Of course not. Let me see . . . I suppose Susan may keep some scissors in her desk."

"That desk there? No, stay seated. I'll get them." The man walked to the other side of the receptionist's desk. Suddenly there was a handkerchief in his hand. Clearly concerned about finger-prints, he used it to open drawers. "Here we go."

"Why in the world do you need scissors?"

Without answering, Lacuna returned to the reception area and drove the point of one of the two scissor blades into the upper-right-hand corner of a Ridler valued at 3.8 million dollars.

Talbot rose to his feet. "Emil! Don't!"

With quick, firm strokes, Lacuna cut along the inside edge of the painting's frame. "Sit down, Talbot."

"But what are you *doing*?"

"You asked me for help, so do what I say. Sit down."

Talbot turned and put a trembling hand on the arm of the settee and settled back onto the cushion. He watched as Lacuna finished cutting the canvas out of the frame, rolled it into a tube, laid it on the settee opposite, and then moved to a second Ridler and began to cut it from its frame as well. "Please," said Talbot. "Tell me what you're doing."

"If I'm going to handle this problem for you, it has to look like a robbery."

Talbot said, "I see," although he did not understand at all.

Lacuna moved to the third painting. "Where's the security system computer? I'll need to disable it and delete all the recordings."

"Oh. It's in my office, actually, in the cabinet behind my desk."

"What's the ID and password?"

Talbot told him. When the man had all three of the Ridlers rolled up and lying on the settee, he returned the scissors to the desk drawer and closed it. Talbot felt an overwhelming sense of relief when the scissors were out of sight.

Lacuna said, "Hang on. I'll be right back." He walked into Talbot's office. Leaning forward, Talbot could just see him doing something to the security system there. After a few minutes, the man returned and sat on the opposite settee again, exactly where he had been before. He stared at Talbot for a moment before saying, "Do you believe in God?"

"God? I . . . I don't know."

"It's a simple question to answer. Yes or no?"

"Well, yes, I suppose I do, in my fashion."

"Do you believe God cares what we do down here?"

"I hardly see what that has to do with any of this, Emil."

The man reached beneath his jacket and removed a revolver from a shoulder holster.

"No," said Talbot Graves.

Lacuna did something with the revolver, and the cylinder slipped open. He turned the weapon and gave it a tap. Five bullets fell into his hand. "I think God cares, Talbot. I think he's interested in justice. Eye for an eye, tooth for a tooth . . ." He carefully arranged the five bullets on the settee beside the rolled paintings, ensuring that they were all aligned and pointing the same direction, toward Talbot. He picked one of the bullets back up and continued, ". . . life for a life."

"Emil, please."

"Relax, Talbot. I'm just trying to explain this to you." Slipping the single bullet back into the revolver's cylinder, he gave the gun a quick flip to the right and the cylinder closed with a click. Talbot could not take his attention off the gun. He watched as Emil Lacuna spun the cylinder. He watched as Lacuna spun the cylinder again. He watched as the man said, "I think God cares very much about justice, and I would hate to make him angry, so in my heart I try to do my best to let God have his say in these situations."

With another sudden motion, as quickly as he had risen to his feet before, Lacuna turned the gun around and pressed the muzzle to the navy blazer covering his own chest. "This is where my heart is, Talbot. This is how I let God have his say."

The man pulled the trigger.

The revolver clicked, but did not fire.

"There, you see?" Emil Lacuna smiled his sad smile again and turned the revolver away from his chest. "Justice is served."

Talbot felt warm moisture on his thighs and looked down to find he had wet himself. He looked back up to see Lacuna with the revolver cylinder open again, the four bullets already replaced, the weapon fully loaded. The man snapped the cylinder shut and aimed the muzzle toward Talbot. "I can't have you spreading rumors, Talbot," said Emil Lacuna. Then he pulled the trigger.

Simultaneously with the explosion came the blow, like being struck hard by a fist, but there was little pain. Talbot Graves looked down again to see a red stain spreading quickly at his chest. He felt strangely light-headed. He felt dizzy. He thought, I don't want to die with blood on my shirt and urine on my trousers, and then that is what he did.

II.

Ridler wrapped his latest attempt in brown corrugated cardboard trimmed to size from a box which had once contained canned peas. Then he wrapped it again in many layers of a Spanish-language newspaper from Juárez, and tied it all together with green twine. His packing materials had been salvaged from a trash bin behind Two T's Grocery Store in Dell City, Texas, the only source of packaged food for ninety miles in any direction. Standing halfway between Carlsbad and El Paso, he wrote the address on a government shipping label. The ballpoint pen he used was attached by a beaded metal chain to the post office countertop, which was fastened to a wooden cabinet, which was connected to the building foundation, which clung somehow to mother earth. Ridler held the planet on a tether. The responsibility weighed heavily upon him. He wrote carefully.

"You left off the return address," said the woman behind the counter.

"I don't have one."

She pursed her lips together in a way that creased the skin on her cheeks and chin. He felt he was under suspicion but did not know his crime.

She weighed the painting on a scale. "Fourteen dollars and sixteen cents by priority mail. I ain't got nothing cheaper. Wanna insure it?"

"What does that cost?"

"Seven-seventy for coverage up to six hundred dollars. A dollar for every hundred worth of coverage over that. Most you can get is five thousand dollars' worth." She eyed the Juárez newspaper wrapping skeptically. "I'm guessin' it's not worth that much."

Ridler only smiled.

When the woman took his money and carried the painting to a back room he released the pen. The planet began to drift away. On it Ridler saw Henry Blum ascending, the name on the shipping label, a skinny painter from Philadelphia and a fellow art student who had once allowed Ridler to sleep on his sofa for more than a month. Ridler thought of how he had seduced Henry's girlfriend in Henry's own bed, and how Henry had discovered them of course, and how that good man had cried. Ridler wondered if the painting would make any difference, if Henry would receive it, understand it, and forgive him. He remembered laughing at Henry, saying no woman was worth tears. Weakened by his guilt, untethered from the earth, Ridler thought of Suzanna through a window, Suzanna in Talbot Graves's arms, and the grief which had unmanned him, years before.

The postal worker turned back toward Ridler after propping the painting against a canvas-sided bin on wheels. "Something else?"

"No," replied Ridler. "That will do it, I hope."

He emerged from the United States Postal Service building at the edge of the tiny town. Lifting a hand to shade his eyes, he looked across a vast expanse to the northeast. On the horizon rose El Capitan, a slab of solid limestone standing a mile and a half above sea level, the southernmost sentinel of the Guadalupe Mountains, blue and trembling in the superheated air. It rose above a flat desert floor populated by sand, rocks, roadrunners, horny toads, coyotes, withered brush, and giant green circles where irrigation systems spun around stationary pipes drawing water from an underground ocean to turn the desert into chili peppers. He thought of painting what he saw and hoped one day he could, but first he had to get the Glory down.

Isabel the wolf woman and Gregorio the dwarf sat baking in the Chevrolet Apache, both of them bloated in their costumes, bodies pressing out between their buttons as the rice and pasta in them swelled. Ridler walked to the driver's side and got in and turned the key. The starter whined and whined until the dwarf cursed the truck and the engine replied with a backfire. Stampeded by the explosion, rabbits fled in all directions out across the desert.

"Why are we here, San Pablo?" asked Isabel. "This town is too small for a show, and there can be no money if we cannot have a show."

Ridler ground the gears, hoping for reverse. "Ask Esperanza. It's her circus."

"She said I should ask you."

Ridler backed away from the post office. "I don't understand that woman."

"Me, either," said Isabel.

From down below Gregorio said, "I don't understand any woman."

Isabel giggled.

Three miles beyond the little crossroads which was Dell City, the road became a pair of tracks, loosely parallel but seldom on a level plane. One rose, the other sank, tilting the old pickup truck to the left and throwing Gregorio against Ridler's ribs. Then the right-hand track declined and the left ascended and the dwarf fell back the other way, against Isabel. "You are a lot of woman," he said, gazing up at her with adoration.

"You are not a lot of man," she replied.

"I am where it counts."

The wolf woman howled with laughter as the old Apache pitched and rolled and raced across the desert, stirring up a cloud of dust behind them like a comet's tail.

El Capitan's black shadow crept among the mountains as they passed, a colossal sundial marking time. In the sunshine at the edge of that encroaching darkness lay their camp, and in the center of the camp, surrounded by haphazardly parked trucks and trailers and a motley collection of antique midway rides, Esperanza had caused roustabouts to unroll the big-top tent. Tanned by dust it flowed across the earth like robes upon a prostrate Bedouin.

"Home sweet home," said Ridler, pulling to a stop.

"I love it when you speak English, San Pablo," said Isabel. "What does it mean?"

"I don't know," replied the painter.

The three of them piled out and began unloading the truck bed, carrying groceries to the commissary trailer, the only food they could afford, rice and beans in paper sacks, and pasta in paper boxes. With his eyes tightly closed El Magnífico appeared to help them. Lifting a large sack of rice he said, "Still nothing green, I see. Still nothing that bleeds."

"You can't get blood from a turnip," said Ridler, translating the cliché.

"Nor can you get turnips from Dell City, apparently," replied El Magnífico.

"You could take those knives of yours and go out to hunt rabbits," said the wolf woman, licking her lips.

"Or snakes," added Gregorio, waddling under the burden of a five-pound sack of pintos.

Isabel shuddered.

"Alas, the desert creatures all depart before me," said El Magnífico. "They seem to have no wish to die that we may live."

"Heretics," grumbled Gregorio.

"Apostates," agreed El Magnífico, nodding.

Isabel frowned. "San Pablo, what are they talking about?"

"Theology," said Ridler. "And protein."

The Apache was soon unloaded, the beans set out in pots to soften, and the people sprawled in slivers of shade beside the vehicles and trailers, waiting for El Capitan's mighty shadow to descend from the mountains and make life bearable again. Only a few women worked. Shaded by sombreros, sitting cross-legged on the sea of fabric, they repaired the ancient big top. With leather pads strapped to their palms they pushed long needles through the canvas, adding patches where the sun and wind had worn it thin.

It was said that the tent had once been entered by Pancho Villa and his famous Dorados, having recently returned from a brave expedition to San Ygnacio and desiring to feast their eyes on the lovely Esperanza, who was a young trapeze artist at that time, long before her bones became apparent. It was said that Black Jack Pershing's men surprised them there, and a great battle had ensued within the tent, the bullet holes and saber cuts requiring many patches afterward. It was said that Pancho Villa escaped only when Esperanza swooped down to carry him aloft into the ropes and cables of the trapeze. It was said they flew for miles together before they settled down in Mexico. But whenever this was said in Esperanza's hearing she denied it.

"I might have flown with Zapata," she said, "because of his soulful eyes. But that Pancho Villa was a chubby villain."

Very little of the original big-top tent remained. It was mostly patches upon patches. It was said some repairs had been made from the khaki uniforms of Americans killed in the battle. Other patches came from the skins of animals that once had been attractions: a leopard from the mountains of Jalisco, an aged zebra purchased from a zoo in Guanajuato. It was even said one part of the tent had been repaired with the tanned and wrinkled hide of an old roustabout who had known no other home for sixty years and expressed as his last wish the hope that he could be forever with the circus.

Countless hands had stitched the tent together through the generations. A tradition had begun of matching patches to the shape of perforations, a bit of circular fabric over a round hole here, a triangle to reinforce a three-sided tear there. In that way the patches had become a history of damage done. No other pattern had been followed, yet one night as Ridler sat among the audience laughing at the obese albino's antics, he had rocked back in his hilarity, and among the shadows high above the clown he thought he saw an image, vague but unmistakable, a void, a portal, a presence waiting beyond time which no one else had painted. Leaping to his feet, he had dashed down the bleachers, rudely interrupting the albino's routine in his haste to go outside to his trailer, running past the fun house and the Tilt-A-Whirl for a sketch pad, and then running back again to stand beneath the big top with a pencil at the ready, only to look up and see no transcendence there.

Each time the circus had stopped outside a town and the huge tent was unrolled for erection, the women wandered barefoot out across it, stepping gingerly in search of holes and rips and threadbare places where a sudden gust of wind might rend the fabric. Each time their mending had been completed and the big top lifted toward the sky, Ridler thought he saw the ineffable a bit more clearly, yet it came in such small stages he could never quite be sure.

Had it been only his imagination, or had the very image which so long eluded him somehow spread itself across the greater canvas overhead without an artist's hand to guide it?

That evening after the sun had settled down beyond the Guadalupe Mountains, Esperanza caused the tent to rise again. Her reasons were a mystery, for there were not customers enough to fill the bleachers for a hundred miles in all directions. Dinner was then served, and with yet another meal of rice and beans expanding in their bellies, the troupe disbursed among the camp. Some settled down to talk around small fires. Others sat at tables in the dining tent, playing ancient Aztec games of chance. As usual, Ridler retired alone to his trailer, where he took up brush and palette in another vain attempt to regain his position at the center of the universe.

As usual, the more paint he added to the image, the less it looked like what he had encountered. Against the temptation to believe himself inadequate, inept and overpowered in the presence of his subject, he mustered all his usual rejoinders. It was only a problem of memory. He was the greatest artist of his generation. Nothing was beyond the power of his brush. Anything that he could see or imagine, he could capture in paint.

Usually these defenses were adequate, but that evening was different.

Sometime after midnight his superhuman discipline betrayed him. In a sudden fit of rage he tore the canvas from the easel and flung it sailing through the trailer door. He watched the painting fly across the desert in the pale light of a crescent moon and disappear beyond the far horizon, fifty or a hundred miles away. Then, muttering objections, Ridler left the trailer for a walk around the camp.

Strolling between trucks and caravans, he waved his arms and drove his fist into his palm and cursed the fate which caused such persecution. He had circled the encampment twice before he noticed it was empty. Perhaps that was normal. Never had he left his trailer at that hour before. Always he had painted through the night until his mind and body failed him, only to collapse from exhaustion until dawn. He did not know the nocturnal habits of the troupe, but it seemed unusual to find no one wandering about the camp, or loitering in the dining tent, or sitting by a campfire.

"Hello?" he called out softly as he walked. "Is anybody here?"

At Gregorio's caravan he paused to look in through an open door. The dwarf was not at home. Listening outside the fat albino's trailer, Ridler heard no snoring. Wandering around the circus he heard no radios played quietly, no muffled conversations, no sounds of any kind beyond the sighing wind and the cries of desert creatures and the ever-present ringing in his ears.

All the trucks remained parked around the camp. El Vaquero's palominos stood sleeping in their trailer. Surely in that desolate location no outsider could have come to carry off the troupe. Could they have simply walked away?

Mystified, Ridler stood for many minutes, staring into the desert.

At last he thought of the obvious. Turning from the desolate scene which lay around the camp, he hurried to the big top. They must be there. It was the only possibility.

Along the way Ridler paused to lift a flickering kerosene lantern from a hook outside El Magnifico's trailer. He approached the tent. He entered. He lifted the lantern. Shadows danced upon the bleachers, which were empty. In the center ring, in the circle of the lantern's feeble light, he stood alone.

Ridler stared up toward the patchwork fabric. The lantern's yellow glow was far too weak to reach such heights, but he felt the image forming in the shadows up above. He sensed it hiding from him in the darkness, mocking him for casting out the painting.

He thought of the last time he had given up that way, of Tel Aviv, gleaming on the eastern shore of the Mediterranean, a city built on dunes. He thought of history, of how the Israeli town had grown, absorbing Jaffa, that ancient port where Jonah once set sail for Tarshish, fleeing God.

Because of Jonah it was only natural that the city should receive a man in search of Glory, and as the prophet once was vomited ashore, so Ridler had been disgorged there from Istanbul. The Turkish authorities' embarrassment at his Kurdish Hizbullah ordeal had been exceeded only by their displeasure upon learning he had been in their country for so many years without a visa. He was driven in a police car to the border, where, wincing from his wounds, he limped westward from a checkpoint into Greece, bearing only his backpack, a bedroll, and three hundred thousand liras, a great deal of money in those days, which he had earned from countless sketches in the old bazaar.

Convinced he was still stalked by death, Ridler fled the Greek peninsula to Rhodes, to Cyprus, and finally to Haifa. He had no difficulty in crossing borders, for money was as good as visas in those ancient lands. During idle moments as he traveled, Ridler reflected on the red-eyed man. When his thoughts were not consumed by lingering terror, sitting on a train, a bus, a ferry, he wondered what inspired such loathing of the Sufis and the Jews.

After Ridler's years of fruitless waiting in the heart of Istanbul, al-Wasiti had come, and the artist dared to think he might be nearing the resplendency again. He had sensed it in the old man's charity, in his spinning dance, and in the gorgeous words of love and mercy he so often quoted from his book. Then, with steel pipes and a scimitar and hours of torturous recitations drawn unwillingly from al-Wasiti's lips, the red-eyed man had beaten back the Glory. Al-Wasiti was no more, and Ridler had been left alone to wonder why the beggar never mentioned all those other words. It had been Allah against Allah. Peace yet anger. Love yet hate. Perhaps there was a way to reconcile such opposites, but why should reconciliation be required? Ridler had encountered no such conflict at the Harlem River. Therefore, just as the duplicity of doves had driven him from Buddha, so had he fled the gentle beggar's world with red-eyed animus in hot pursuit.

It seemed logical to escape into the midst of those most hated. The enemy of my enemy is my friend. Also Ridler took comfort from the fact that Istanbul and Tel Aviv could not have been more different. One was ancient beyond memory, the other built by men and women only recently departed. One had grown haphazardly; the other began with a master plan. One was darkened by a thousand years of human residue; the other shone pristinely in the desert's sterile light.

Encouraged by the distance he had crossed in space and time, with his many liras converted to Israeli shekels, Ridler rented two rooms in White City, a neighborhood of buildings constructed in the Bauhaus tradition, unadorned, asymmetrical and without color. After years in Istanbul, such strict geometry seemed unreal. It was too clean, too orderly, as if someone had erected a life-size model of a neighborhood. Ridler wondered if he was a masochist. What else could explain his choice to live in such a pristine place, when he himself was bent and browned and burdened by his history?

He hid within his rooms, going out only to purchase food, flinching at the friendly shouts of neighbors in the street, muttering unintelligibly and living days in dread of darkness. He spent much time in contemplation of Suzanna's image in the photograph she had given him, so many years before. He often mourned the damage to it, creased and yellowed as it was with age. And for the first time in his life, he did not try to paint.

After a month of isolation he forced himself to go out, to walk among the living. From that day on, each morning Ridler left the small apartment, timidly strolling underneath the eucalyptus and the cedars. Usually his wandering led him to the beach, where he sat for hours, alone and staring at the sea. Sometimes the screams of children playing in the surf drove him away. Intellectually he understood they were only cries of make-believe, but they still conjured al-Wasiti's final moments.

Suzanna came to him in Tel Aviv. He saw her in the way a woman walked along the high-tide line. He saw her in a lovely profile at a sidewalk café. Although he could not banish the kitchen window memory of Suzanna in Graves's arms, dreams of her still saved him from his nightmares. Maybe she had risen to the surface because there was something of New York City in the atmosphere of Tel Aviv, something of the place where they had been together, the energy, the liberality, the rampant creativity. Maybe she had become more visible because the Kurdish Hizbullah had destroyed the distraction of his art. Or maybe she had simply come because he needed her so desperately.

Sometimes in the evening he stopped to purchase groceries at a small store on the ground floor of his building. In the back were open shelves and refrigerated display cases stocked with food. In the front were sixteen men at little wooden tables playing backgammon. Ari, the store's owner, was always in the thick of things, focused on a game. It seemed to annoy the shopkeeper to pause a game to take Ridler's money, so Ridler often waited by the cashier counter, watching.

He became intrigued by the sudden bursts of motion which erupted from the players' stillness when they reached out to move the pieces. He liked the muffled rattle of the dice in the cups, and the clicks like snapping bones as they slapped the pieces into place around the boards. No one seemed to mind him watching. No one seemed to notice. It made him feel at home to stand among them unmolested. It made him feel accepted. He began to think it might be possible to forget the red-eyed man and al-Wasiti's screams and someday maybe even sweet Suzanna, whose absence summoned up a much worse kind of pain. But still, he did not paint.

One evening while he sat on the little balcony outside his apartment, someone knocked on his door. He flinched. His guts swirled in his belly as he rose and entered the small room which served for living, dining, and cooking. He stared at the hallway door. Whoever stood on the other side of it knocked again. He made himself walk to it. He peered out through the peephole. In the hallway was a young man wearing black slacks, a rumpled white shirt, and a sky-blue crocheted yarmulke. He held Ridler's backpack. Ridler stepped away from the door. His passport was in the backpack. How did the young man get his hands on it? Ridler touched the handle, paused, drew a deep breath for courage and opened the door.

The young man said something.

Ridler replied, "I don't speak Hebrew."

The visitor spoke again, this time in English with a British accent. "I believe you left this in the shop downstairs."

Taking the backpack, Ridler began to look through it for his passport.

Watching him, the young man said, "You are American?"

"I suppose so."

"That's a strange way to put it."

"I haven't been to America in a long time."

"But you haven't been here long, either."

"How would you know?" Ridler found his passport and removed it from the bag. Brandishing it he said, "Have you been looking through my things?"

The young man's brow creased. "Of course not. It's just that you said you don't speak Hebrew. And you left your rucksack by the shop door."

"From that you know I just got here? Because I forgot a back-pack? I suppose Israelis never forget things?"

"We don't, actually," snapped the man. "Not things that might explode." He turned abruptly and strode off down the hall. Just as he was about to descend the stairs he looked back and said, "By the way, you're very welcome."

Ridler said, "Hang on a second, will you?" He left the apartment door open and walked toward the man. When he had almost reached the stairs he said, "Look. I'm sorry."

"You should be."

"Yeah, well, I am, okay? I apologize."

"Why would you treat someone that way when they go to so much trouble to return your property?"

Ridler stared at him a moment. "I've been a little nervous lately. Sometimes it makes me cranky."

The young man cocked his head. "Why are you so nervous?"

Ridler rolled up his sleeve to show a row of angry little circles where the men in Istanbul had used cigarettes. He felt as if he stood before the stranger in the nude. He said, "Hizbullah," and then told his story.

Thus Ridler's friendship began with the backgammon fanatic, Oxford alumnus, and Masorti rabbi Jonathon Klein. Three evenings a week they met in the ground-floor grocery store, where Jonathon tried to teach Ridler the basics of the game. They faced each other across a small wooden table as plastic fans hummed in the back-ground, blowing stale summer air around the little shop. To their left and right a dozen deeply tanned and wrinkled pensioners com-peted at other tables. They wore undershirts and shorts and cheap plastic sandals and stared at their backgammon boards through eyeglasses with thick lenses and heavy frames. They seldom spoke. For them, play was serious business.

"You'd think they had a lot of money riding on those games," said Ridler one night as he and Jonathon parted just outside the little store.

"Some of them, maybe, but not me. The Mishnah frowns on gambling."

"What's a Mishnah?"

"You really want to know?"

"Sure."

The rabbi explained.

It was August second, the day Iraq invaded Kuwait. In the months that followed, Rabbi Klein taught Ridler much about backgammon and much about the Torah. The book made a strange kind of sense to Ridler. He grasped the symbolism and the subtext with intuitive ease, as if it had been written by a fellow artist, but although Ridler did his best, he was unable to anticipate the flow of patterns in the game. For him shapes and forms could never be merely strategic. They were also vocabulary, meaning, metaphor. He watched the circular backgammon pieces flow around the board, and saw a microcosm of existence. He could not consider it on any other level. He played, and longed to paint. He studied Torah, and felt like he was painting. He healed, and was not well.

Almost a year after he reached Israel, Ridler bought an easel and six prestretched canvases. Deciding it would be best to start with something simple, a technical exercise at most, he arranged some oranges, grapes, and avocados in a bowl and put the bowl on the dining table in his small apartment. He dabbed cobalt blue, cadmium yellow, and vermillion onto a plastic plate and sat before the easel. In the steady light from the north window he stared at the fruit. He stared at the blank white field of canvas. He picked up a brush and mixed some paint. He drew the brush across the canvas.

The brush ignored his wishes. It would not paint the still life. Instead it called him toward the old, familiar pattern. He followed down into the frigid river. Faster and faster moved his hand across the canvas. In hot pursuit of Glory once again, he rose to his feet. He melded with unfolding majesty. He was absorbed. Consumed. This time he would capture it. This time he would make it his, as all of life should be. He painted furiously, instinctively, dangerously, but just when Ridler came the closest, it withdrew again.

He flung his brush across the room. It hit the pristine wall and left a colored stain, and at that moment someone knocked on the apartment door.

Wiping his hands on a cloth, Ridler crossed the room to find a short young woman standing almost childlike in the hallway, her sleeves rolled up to compensate for an Israel Postal Company shirt which was too large, her black hair in a ponytail, freckles sprayed across her nose and cheeks. He smiled down at her, but she was strictly serious. She extended a clipboard toward him and said something in Hebrew. When she understood he did not speak her language, she rolled her eyes and said, "Name."

"What?" he asked.

She tapped the clipboard with her finger. "Name! Name!"

He signed the thing and a minute later was alone again, with the door closed and locked and a cardboard box in his hands. Pushing the useless bowl of fruit aside, he put the box on the dining table and opened it. Inside he found a black rubber gas mask, with two clear lenses for his eyes, a strap designed to stretch over the top of his head, two more straps to go above his ears and underneath his jaw, and a canister below the mouth to guard from air exposed to nuclear, biological, or chemical weapons. Also in the box were an instructional brochure and a single dose of something called atropine, which was said to be an antidote.

Ridler sat down heavily beside the table. He stared at the mask, and thought of what it meant. Intifadas. Armies. Warheads. Red-eyed hatred in a box.

He rose. He flung the canvas from the easel. He replaced it with another virgin panel. On the table he arranged the fruit around the gas mask. This, he could paint. Beneath his brush appeared the opposite of Glory.

That night at the store, only Ridler seemed distracted by the thought of Iraqi missiles. The backgammon pieces clicked like bones as usual. The dice rattled softly in the cups. Precious few words were spoken. Indeed, the only sign of Saddam Hussein's madness was the gas masks hanging from the backs of everybody's chairs.

Watching the men play, Ridler realized they were all old hands, citizen soldiers in every Jewish war since 1948. He began to understand that this unflappability was their way of fighting back, now that they were old.

Throughout Tel Aviv that January Ridler saw the same thing. Students with a backpack slung over one shoulder and a gas mask over the other. Passengers on buses chatting among themselves as usual, ignoring the masks among their packages. Businesspeople meeting over lunch at fashionable sidewalk cafés, with masks hanging from their chairs. Their casual acceptance of the circumstances seemed unreal to him. Could it be that everyone had two masks in that city? One they carried, and another, invisible upon their face? Or could it be they truly had no fear of death?

One evening he asked his friend that question.

"Of course we fear death," replied the rabbi. "But we fear our history much more."

On January 18 at two in the morning the sirens sounded. Ridler awoke and lay in bed, listening. He heard a distant roar, and then a rumble like thunder, and knew it was the first Scud missile, hitting somewhere in the city. He thought about the poison in the nose cone. He remembered the gas mask. He switched on the bedside lamp and rose and picked it up from where it lay upon the dresser. He pulled it over his head, tightening the straps according to the instructions. He stared into the mirror, and saw a locust staring back, an idol, a demon of the Canaanite variety. He decided to step outside and watch the war.

It was cold on the balcony. He was about to go in for a jacket when he saw the devil draw a slender arc of light across the sky. This time there was no roar as the missile came in, but above the screaming sirens and the hissing of his own breath through the gas mask's filter, Ridler heard the soft and gentle impact in the distance.

Looking up, he saw that the arc of evil light had disappeared. In its place the moon had donned a black disguise like his. Starlight sparkled in the lenses as it gazed down on the planet, the god of locusts watching. Ridler clasped his arms around himself. Shivering, he wondered what the moon might see. He lowered his own gaze. Through the intervening eucalyptus trees he saw a family on another balcony across the street, people familiar to him, a grandmother and grandfather, a mother, father and three children, all wearing their masks. In the incandescence of one naked lightbulb they danced a slow circle, holding hands, the cylindrical filters on their masks bobbing up and down in time with their steps. Round and round they went, slowly in and out, lifting their clasped hands as they approached the center of the circle, lowering them again as they stepped back, singing words to a lilting and familiar melody.

As long as deep within the heart
A Jewish soul still stirs,
And forward, to the ends of the East
An eye gazes towards Zion.
Our hope is not yet lost,
Hope of two thousand years,
To be a free people in our land
The land of Zion and Jerusalem.

Watching them, Ridler thought of his own family, a harried mother overwhelmed with housework, a father obsessed with perfection. He thought of watching older brothers on the football field and tennis court, triumphantly receiving his father's approbation. He thought of older sisters at recitals, Mozart and Rachmaninoff perfectly rendered, and again, his father's dearly earned approval. He thought of his art, the only thing that guarded him from ostracism. He had learned early on that there was more than one kind of mask.

The singing on the balcony across the street gave way to an inhuman scream. Ridler looked up toward the dreadful moon again. He saw another streak across the sky, and knew this time it would be close. He felt the explosion, rather than hearing it. The concrete shook beneath his feet. The sound waves compressed him. Across the street, the family rushed inward toward the center, lifting up their hands.

It turned out the masks had been unnecessary. There were only explosives in the nose cones—no gas, no bacteria, no fallout and no death. Only twenty-two Jews were injured. Only thirty more were injured in another wave of missiles the next night, and two nights after that, only eighty-four. A small cost in Jews to everyone but Jews.

Throughout January, on and on the missiles came. A woman was crushed to death at home, someone's daughter, sister, mother. Four others died of suffocation. Having improperly adjusted their gas masks, they could not breathe, yet they were too terrified of poison gas to take them off. Many others died of heart attacks, for it was a fearsome thing to see your neighbor's house explode. And through it all backgammon continued. The clicks. The rattles. Stony stares and stubborn silence.

In late February, on the day after the Americans entered Kuwait, in the instant Ridler tossed the dice onto the board between him and Jonathon Klein, the last Scud missile fell. It hit the street outside the little store at eight fifteen in the evening, raking the backgammon tables with a hurricane of glass shards and splinters from a cedar tree. The building's facade collapsed, along with the front rooms on the three floors above, dropping tons of concrete down upon the players. The eruption of sound was impossible, too vast to be accepted. The moment between the order and chaos was at once eternal and instantaneous. Except for Jonathon Klein and Sheridan Ridler, everybody died.

Ridler's first sense of himself afterward was ringing. He thought it must be some kind of alarm, then realized it was his own ears. The high-pitched, tinny sound would never leave him from that moment on.

"Anyone?" he said. "Anyone?"

He lay in nearly total darkness, repeating the word until at last Jonathon answered, "Ken."

"Anyone?"

"Ken."

Forgetting *ken* means "yes" in Hebrew, Ridler said, "I don't know you."

He flew above the city of Manhattan, looking down on rooftop cooling towers, helicopter pads, and fields of hot mopped tar. In the distance was a river, cold and black. It flowed from the freezing northern regions, parted at the island and engulfed him. He swam in it as he had flown, without effort or control. In the blackness was a light, distant, small and wavering. He fled his longing for it with a billion crackling locusts, starlight in the lenses of their eyes, falling ravenously upon a fruited plain as the light behind him called out, "Danny? Danny? Danny?" and eventually he recognized the name Suzanna had given him, the name that somehow seemed most truly his, and so he answered, "Yes?"

Somewhere in the darkness Jonathon replied, "Hashem be praised. Are you okay?"

"What happened?"

"A Scud."

"I don't understand."

"The Iraqis fired a missile at us. It's the war, remember?"

"Of course. I just don't understand what they have against backgammon."

Ridler heard the distant sound of Jonathon, laughing. It reminded him of al-Wasiti's eyes. He tried to think of that instead of missiles. Later, he said, "Can I ask you a question?"

"Of course."

"The Torah says Moses saw God."

"That is not a question."

"Do you believe it's true?"

"Not literally. No one could see Hashem."

"Are you sure?"

"Absolutely."

"How do you know?"

"Torah also says no one can see his face and live."

"Torah contradicts itself?" Ridler thought of peace and anger, love and hate, Allah against Allah.

"Not at all. It simply speaks on different levels in different places. Sometimes metaphorically, sometimes literally."

"Does it say God hates unbelievers?"

"It says Hashem hates sin."

"That's not the same thing."

"No."

Ridler pondered this, and fell asleep, and woke again to say, "Jonathon?"

"I'm here."

"What if I saw God?"

"You saw him?"

"I saw something in a river once."

"Hashem doesn't live in a river, Daniel."

Ridler said nothing.

After a while Jonathon spoke again. "What did you see, exactly?"

"I can't remember. That's the problem."

"Why a problem?"

"How am I going to paint it if I can't remember it?"

"You think you can paint Hashem?"

"I can paint anything."

After a long pause, Jonathon said, "The Creator has no body, Daniel. You know that, don't you?"

"I saw something. You can't see nothing."

"It's not possible."

"If it's God, anything is possible."

"No."

"No? No? How can you say no? You're a rabbi. Aren't you supposed to believe God is all-powerful?"

"Even Hashem can't be what Hashem is not."

"I saw something."

"'We are to believe that he is incorporeal, that his unity is physical neither potentially nor actually.'"

"Torah?"

"Maimonides."

Ridler tried to shift his position, but something pinned his legs.

"Jonathon?"

"Yes."

"Remember I told you how that guy made us quote the Qur'an while he hurt us?"

"Yes."

"I'm kind of hurting over here. Don't quote anything to me right now, okay?"

"Yes, Danny. I understand."

In the darkness Ridler pushed back with his elbows. They dug into sharp edges. He believed he was lying on a pile of concrete rubble. He ignored the pain and pressed back harder. He sat up. Bending forward he reached out and felt a slab of concrete. He felt his legs disappear beneath it. Exhausted, he fell back onto the rubble. After a few minutes he said, "Is it necessary for a Jew to believe what you said? That incorporeal business?"

"Not exactly, but if you are a Jew, you will believe it."

"But I saw something," said the painter.

"Then you cannot be a Jew."

"But I did see it," whispered Ridler, and the words continued to assert themselves within his mind as the air was filled with sirens, flashlight beams, and shouts of rescue workers pulling back the rubble. "I saw it," he repeated underneath the big top patched with uniforms and skins and hide of roustabout; "I saw it," as he stood alone inside the center ring without a costume, prop, or painting; "I saw it," in a voice reserved for great cathedrals as he gazed into the shadows overhead, searching for an image shifting there within the dancing light of kerosene, bits and pieces joined together in a hundred years of haphazard repairs. "I saw it," said the artist, as Gregorio the dwarf called out a question, or perhaps it was El Magnífico, or Isabel, or the Blackbirds, or any of the others in the missing troupe.

Ridler looked, and for a moment he believed they were all slender and resplendent in well-fitting costumes much adorned with diamonds. He looked, and it was as if he saw them for the first time as they truly were. He looked again and they expanded all around him; eyes receded into fleshy faces; diamonds became rhinestones; fabric strained at buttons.

"I saw it," he insisted. "Just like I see you."

"But are you now a Jew?" came the question once again.

"That's impossible," said the artist as he walked out of the empty tent. "Because I truly saw it."

12.

Following a glowing map built into the dashboard of the Cadillac Escalade, Emil Lacuna drove into East Islip. Stately elm trees stretched across the road above him, branches interlocked to create a verdant tunnel some people would have considered beautiful. The aesthetics didn't interest him. He pulled to the curb beside a park. A hundred feet away two girls rode up and down on a seesaw and a woman pushed a little boy on a swing. Cars passed him on the left in stately procession—BMWs, Mercedes-Benzes, Audis—shiny, sleek, and clean, the elms reflected in their windshields. All the drivers and the passengers were white. Lacuna would stand out, but that couldn't be helped.

Wearing latex gloves, he opened a stainless steel briefcase on the passenger seat. Removing a manila file folder, he uncovered two pistols, a revolver which was necessary for the sake of justice, and an automatic, which he had purchased specifically for the occasion since revolvers could not be silenced.

He opened the folder and read a typewritten address on an otherwise blank piece of paper. He entered the address in the Escalade's computer, transposing the letters and numbers according to a personal code. The map in the dashboard went black for a moment, then reappeared to show the location. He was only three blocks away.

Lacuna put the folder back into the briefcase and removed the revolver. He checked to be certain of what he already knew: there was only one cartridge in the cylinder. He spun the cylinder. He spun it again. He leaned back against the plush leather of the driver's seat and watched the children play. He tried to remember what it had been like to be alive at that age. He wished he could remember. Maybe then things would be different, but like his therapist said, you did what you could with what you had. The main thing was to keep it fair.

With a lightning-quick motion he raised the revolver, pressed the muzzle to his chest above his heart, and pulled the trigger.

The weapon clicked quietly on an empty chamber. Again, he had been spared to carry out his mission. Justice having been served, he replaced the revolver in the briefcase, closed the lid, and started the engine.

He watched his left side mirror for an opening in the procession of vehicles and then eased into the traffic. He went two blocks south, one block west, and one more to the south. He leaned forward, reading the numbers. When he found the house he drove past it slowly, giving it a good hard look. Interesting, how a person's place of residence so often didn't seem to match their personality. He saw a clean white picket fence about hip high, with a little gate below an arched entry arbor. He saw roses, red and white in neatly tended beds, and a perfectly green lawn, and impatiens, pansies, and buttercups in window boxes between dark green shutters. He saw a gabled house set well back from the street, with mossy wooden shingles and old red bricks and rocking chairs on a deep front porch . . . all of it exactly the opposite of what he would have guessed.

The problem was there were no alleys. He would have to park on the street, or else pull into the driveway, which was a mistake. You always wanted at least two ways to go, even if your options were only forward and reverse, and if he parked in the driveway all he'd have was the one way out. So it had to be the street. That meant he would have to walk in the open about two hundred feet, minimum. In the city it wouldn't matter, but in the suburbs people paid attention. A black man in East Islip, walking up to a neighbor's door? Even in his navy blazer, white button oxford shirt and khaki slacks, it was not ideal. Still, it had to be done.

He circled the block and came back the other way, planning to park the Escalade so it would be pointed toward Montauk Highway, what they called East Main there in town. It was always better to park with a straight shot at the nearest thoroughfare or highway to minimize the turns required along your means of egress. Sometimes an extra second or two made all the difference.

He passed an old woman hosing down her lawn. She looked up but he knew she couldn't see him through the heavily tinted glass. It was one of the reasons he had chosen the Escalade, another being its speed, which was considerable for such a heavy vehicle, and another being the weight, which was useful in some circumstances, such as running roadblocks. He almost always used an Escalade. In this case, it didn't hurt that it was a vehicle of choice for busy suburban housewives with children. It would blend right in.

He passed a middle-aged couple walking a pair of golden retrievers, which was a dumb breed in his opinion, but they had a nice doggish look about them. Deep in conversation, the couple didn't bother to look at him. So far so good.

The house was coming up. He slowed, looking right and left at the closest neighboring homes. Nobody in the yard. Nobody on the porches. Although there might still be someone looking out a window, you ought to count your blessings.

Here was the house, on the left. He pulled to the curb across the street. He switched off the engine. He opened the stainless steel briefcase and removed the silenced automatic. He checked to make sure there was a round in the chamber and then he checked to make sure the clip was full. It was doubtful he'd need more than the one shot, or maybe two if the wife was home, but the guy probably kept a weapon handy, so it made sense to go in with a full clip.

He put his hand on the door handle, ready to get started. His hand was sweating a little, but that was the latex gloves, not nerves. He didn't feel a thing.

Just then the guy came out of his house, Joseph Napoli to civilians like Talbot Graves, but Joey Naples to his business associates, a guy who ought to keep his mouth shut at parties.

Lacuna watched Joey pause on the porch outside the door. He watched him turn back toward the house as a woman stepped into view. They kissed. Then the guy descended the steps and walked over to a BMW 700 series parked in the driveway. He got in and gunned the engine and backed down his driveway much too quickly. What if some kid had been riding a bike on the sidewalk? Lacuna shook his head. Some people.

Joey Naples swung around and headed north, passing the Escalade without a glance. Lacuna put the automatic on the passenger seat beside the briefcase, started the engine, and pulled away from the curb. You had to be flexible with your plans.

This could actually be better, depending on how it played out. He wouldn't have to walk up to the house in that neighborhood, risk attracting attention. Plus, he wouldn't have to take care of the wife. It was always nice to avoid collateral damage if possible.

They drove through town, up onto the Southern State Parkway,

and then north on Sagtikos Parkway. When Joey got off onto the
Long Island Expressway heading west, Lacuna figured he was going
to the city. Actually, though, he took an exit at Glen Cove Road.
They followed it a couple of miles, woods on both sides with a
few smaller streets and glimpses of some nice houses, and then
the BMW slowed and turned left into a driveway. The sign beside
it read "Glen Head Country Club." There was a gate, which Joey
opened by pushing a few buttons on a keyboard. Lacuna easily
managed to follow him in before the gate slid shut again.

They wound along a driveway, trees and bushes on each side.
They reached a building with a covered portico. Lacuna supposed it
was a colonial-style building, but it didn't look too old. They passed
it and pulled into a parking lot. Joey took the handicapped space
closest to the clubhouse, the jerk. What if some little old lady with
a walker came along? Some people.

Lacuna passed behind him without looking sideways and drove
to the far end of the parking lot, moving slowly, letting the guy get
out. By the time Lacuna had circled back, Joey Naples was standing behind his car with the trunk lid open and a bag of golf clubs
slung over his shoulder. Lacuna rolled up behind him and hit the
button on the side window. It slid down just as he stopped with
Joey between him and the rear bumper of his BMW, nowhere he
could run.

"Hey, Joey?" said Lacuna quietly.

"Yeah?" said Joey, turning around.

Bam. One in the forehead.

Lacuna rolled up the window and drove on.

Back out on Glen Cove Road—they called it Cedar Swamp Road
there, actually—he made a left turn. He made another left on Sea
Cliff Avenue and then followed the built-in map in the dashboard,
a wonderful invention, until he reached Prospect Avenue, right on

Hempstead Harbor. At one spot where there was no house on the inland side, he pulled over to the right, hopped out and pitched the automatic into the water.

He drove to a parking garage at LaGuardia and pulled into a stall very close to where he had found the Escalade a couple of hours before. If everything went the way he hoped, the owner might return from Bora Bora or wherever and never notice that the vehicle had been moved. Lacuna grabbed the briefcase, opened the door, and walked off. At the first trash can he paused and threw away the gloves. Then it was over to the taxi stand and on into the city like a thousand other day-trippers with briefcases.

He had the cabby drop him at East 70th and Park, walked a couple of blocks, and picked up another cab. That one he took across the park, all the way to Riverside. From there he walked to the marina where he lived.

"Hello, Johnny," he said to the man in charge of watching the gangway, a nice guy with three kids and another coming, kind of chubby with an accent. Lithuanian or something.

"Hiya, Mr. Lacuna. How you doin' today?"

"Not bad. How's the wife?"

"Always complainin'. Backaches. Footaches. Headaches. Sometimes I am wishing I am single like you. Nothin' to come home to but a beer and a game, you know? No drama whatsoever."

"A family man like you? You'd hate it."

Johnny grinned. "Hey, I am showing you new pictures of the kids?"

"Yesterday."

"Wanna see 'em again?"

Lacuna smiled. "Maybe later, man."

"Just say the word, Mr. Lacuna. Always the kids are in my wallet. Hey, I am getting a delivery for you this morning. Wait one second please." The man went into the dockmaster's office and right back out with a slender package about three feet long wrapped in plain brown paper. Lacuna took it and tipped him with a twenty. Looking at the money, Johnny said, "Is not necessary, Mr. Lacuna."

"Don't worry about it. You have a lot of mouths to feed."

"Well, thanks a lot. Always I am telling the wife how generous you are. Nicest guy in the whole marina, I am telling her that."

Lacuna smiled again and walked away, carrying his stainless steel briefcase and the long package as Johnny called after him, "Lemme know if I can do anything else for you, Mr. Lacuna."

He waved without looking back, following the dock, and turned right onto a finger pier. From there he stepped through the stern gate onto his yacht, a raised pilothouse Alaskan, a woody made back in 1969. He noticed a few gull droppings on the cap rail and made a mental note to clean that up before dark. It was also about time to renew the cap rail varnish, which he did himself twice a year, keeping the brightwork in excellent condition. He dove the boat himself, too, wearing a wet suit, breathing with a little electric scuba system through a yellow hose, cleaning the bottom personally. He also handled most of the electrical and plumbing and diesel work, basic maintenance mostly. Something always needed doing on an old wooden boat, which was one reason he enjoyed living aboard. It kept him busy, gave him a little pride of workmanship. He could have hired everything out of course, just like he could have afforded a newer and much larger yacht, but he liked problem solving and working with his hands and he liked the classic Arthur DeFever design of the Alaskan. Plus, it wouldn't be good to let a bunch of tradesmen on his boat, maybe see his collection and get ideas.

In the saloon he put the briefcase and the brown paper package on the coffee table and stood before a wall of teak paneling. The blank wall wasn't original. He had added it after buying the boat, closing off the opening between the galley countertop and the overhead lockers. It made the boat's interior feel smaller, which was an unfortunate but necessary compromise since he needed the blank wall to display his collection.

The painting hanging on the bulkhead at the moment was one of his smaller Ridlers, *Nude Number 17.* Lacuna removed the painting from the bulkhead, picked up the brown paper package, and went forward past the galley, up three steps to the pilothouse, then descending seven more steps to the companionway. Down below, he entered the main cabin.

Normally that space would have contained a queen-size berth, a row of hanging lockers, and a small desk, but Lacuna had installed a unique storage system for his art. At first glance it appeared to be a solid bulkhead made of vertical teak slats extending from the sole to the overhead. Each of the vertical slats had a brass handle, and beside each handle was a polished brass plate which held the handwritten name of a painting. Lacuna found the nameplate he wanted, gripped the handle, and pulled. The teak slat rolled outward, revealing a shallow, rectangular compartment lined with black velvet and suspended from an overhead track. He placed the painting in the compartment—a perfect fit—and adjusted some brass clips to secure it in position. He pushed the compartment back in place, storing the painting alongside all his others, over thirty million dollars' worth of art.

Stepping into the engine room aft of the main cabin, Lacuna flipped a switch and bathed the space in bright fluorescent light. Ahead of him the twin diesels stood on either side of a central walkway. Farther aft behind the engines were the generator, pumps, a battery rack, and some other equipment. Pipes and wires ran all over the space, water hoses connecting hull fittings and the pumps and engines, fuel lines leading to and from the manifolds, cables leading up to throttles and gear shifters, wires from electrical subpanels . . . a real jungle of equipment. Lacuna had spent hundreds of hours getting it all organized. Everything was color coded and labeled and made perfect sense once you understood it.

On his left stood a small workbench, with six red metal drawers and a vise on one end and a pegboard behind the worktop. Nearly two dozen hand tools hung on the pegboard, every one of them outlined in red so he'd remember where it went. Everything in a boat should be in its place and there should be a place for everything.

He laid the package on the bench. He rolled up his sleeves. He unwrapped the package to reveal twelve precut stretcher bars of various lengths, wooden boards made especially to fit together at the corners and form a frame on which canvases were mounted for paintings. Using a small hammer taken down from the pegboard, he glued and nailed four of the boards together. When he had done this with the rest of the boards, he had three stretchers ready to go.

Back in the main cabin he slid a rack out and very carefully removed the three rolled canvases he had taken from Talbot Graves's gallery. Returning to the workbench in the engine room, he wrapped each stretcher with a painting, pulling them tight and stapling them to the soft wood. After that was done, he set to work on building three custom decorative frames to go around the paintings, using moldings he had already painted. Two hours later, all three of his new Ridlers were ready to display.

Because of the size of the bulkhead in the saloon, he only hung one painting at a time. There was room for more, but Lacuna did not want his art to be crowded. It confused things to have more than one painting in his field of view, which was why he didn't go to art museums. People moving from one painting to another, mixing the images up in their minds, it didn't make sense to him. You had something special like a Ridler there before you, you wanted to spend quality time with it, take it in without distractions.

Of the three new ones, he decided to begin with *Woman in High Heels*. He placed the other two in their new storage racks and carried the painting up to the saloon. Five minutes later, after he had hung it and adjusted the lighting and poured himself a Glenlivet on the rocks, he sat down to take it in.

Staring at *Woman in High Heels,* he didn't think of it as stolen. After all, he was not a thief by profession. Taking the painting had been more a by-product of self-defense, a necessary evil to make it look like robbery. Also, it was a way to salvage something from an unfortunate situation, which was always nice. Joey Naples had deserved what he got. That guy. He had no business running off at the mouth the way he did, talking about Lacuna's line of work at parties. He knew what it would get him in the end. But Graves . . . that was an unfortunate thing. Still, it had been necessary, so it made sense to go ahead and take the Ridlers. After all, who would appreciate them more?

A long time ago, when Emil Lacuna had first decided it might be a good idea to invest his money in art, some guy told him it was important to collect things you liked. You got to where you had a feel for your area of interest that way, plus you could enjoy your possessions instead of just sitting around counting your money. From the start he had let that principle be his guide, which was why Ridler was the only artist he collected. He didn't know much about art, but he knew there was something special about a Ridler.

Sometimes he sat for hours in the yacht's saloon, staring at whatever image he had hanging at the time, searching for that certain quality that was in all of them. Sometimes when he stared at the paintings there was a kind of tickling in his head, like a memory trying to come up, something going on inside him that he didn't understand. He felt connected to this Ridler guy somehow, in touch with things he almost remembered, things trying to emerge. He looked at the paintings and that certain quality would whisper to him, a way of being or a feeling other people seemed to have, which was missing in himself.

For example, here was this *Woman in High Heels*. Wow. The guy could really paint. But it wasn't that the woman looked real, like she was going to step off the wall or anything. It was more like he knew her, could tell things about her, just from looking at the painting. That was the thing about the Ridlers. Somehow, Lacuna looked at the people in the paintings and they weren't closed off the way everyone in real life seemed to be. Ridler's people were understandable. They made him feel like he was part of the human race, like he had the same kinds of feelings everyone was always talking about. Except, of course, he didn't.

Lacuna sipped his scotch and wondered if Ridler might really be alive. He kind of hoped not, because he'd hate to have to kill a guy like that, a guy who could make him feel connected or whatever, but that's what he'd have to do. Graves had been right. If his collection was ever going to hit a hundred million, he couldn't have Ridler out there flooding the market with new work. So if he really was alive, that would mean there was another detail to take care of, after handling Graves and Joey Naples. But before he did the thing, it might be interesting to meet this Ridler guy, talk to him a little, see if he could feel the same way around the man himself as he did around his paintings.

Lacuna leaned forward, spun the stainless steel briefcase around on the coffee table, and opened it. Inside, he found a small leather-bound notebook. Leafing through it, he stopped on a page where he had taken notes while talking to Talbot Graves. He read the words.

Gemma Halls. Daughter. Getty Center.

Yes, that was the place to start.

13.

Gemma drank in the passing landscape, gray stone walls dry-stacked in graceful curves beside the narrow road, ancient oaks, stately clapboard and redbrick houses with lichen-spotted slate roofs, most of them commanding an acre of property or more, everything so old, and so . . . colonial. The cabdriver didn't seem impressed, focused as he was on a radio announcer's running account of a Phillies baseball game, but Bucks County, Pennsylvania, made Gemma think of three-cornered hats and men in knee breeches and white stockings with buckled shoes, and Liberty Bells, and redcoats and minutemen, and "my only regret is that I have but one life to give for my country."

She glanced down at the map displayed on her cell phone and saw the little green dot moving along their route to mark her position. The Delaware River flowed just to the east, the very place where Washington made his historic crossing. She thought of Leutze's famous painting, the great general standing with one boot on the gunwale of his boat, surrounded by men with flintlocks and oars, the river choked with ice, the sky above him dark and ominous. She marveled that it had really happened, that it was possible to visit the exact spot where men had risked so much for an idea.

The cabbie slowed and turned into a driveway. He stopped before a tall gate flanked by limestone columns. Rolling down the window he pressed a button on an intercom mounted on a low pole.

"Yes?" came an electric voice.

"Lady here to see, uh . . ."

"Henry Blum," she said. "And my name is Gemma Halls."

"You hear that?" asked the cabbie.

"Drive in and bear left at the fork. Park under the porte-cochère."

"Sure," said the cabbie. As the gates swung open silently he said, "Mind if I ask a question, lady?"

"Not at all."

"You know what port koosher is?"

"It's French for 'carriage porch.' A kind of roof you drive under."

"Oh. Like they got at hotels."

"That's right."

The cabbie grunted as they passed through the gates onto the property. The driveway, barely wide enough for the taxi, wound through a stand of trees before emerging into a grassy clearing where it forked. Beyond the verdant lawn stood a three-story house in the Adam style, with four chimneys flanking a hipped roof and a central pediment over a symmetrical entry. A pair of curved staircases swept up to the front door, six or seven feet above grade. The porte-cochère extended from the left side. The cabbie followed the fork in the driveway and parked where he had been instructed.

As Gemma emerged from the taxi, a tall door opened at the top of a wide set of steps and a short man in his late fifties or early sixties descended the steps to greet her. He wore a pair of blue jeans, a light silk T-shirt, and a pair of Italian-looking loafers.

"Ms. Hall? Henry Blum. It's a pleasure to meet you."

"Thank you," said Gemma, taking his outstretched hand. "I'm glad to be here."

"Yes, it's exciting, isn't it?"

"Well . . ."

"I mean, a new Ridler. I can't get over it. Don't you think it's amazing?"

"If it really is a Ridler, yes."

"Oh, of course. Well, we're about to find out, aren't we? Please, come in."

He led her up the steps. Just inside the house they passed a young man in a polo shirt and jeans. Henry Blum said, "Peter, would you please step outside and ask Ms. Hall's driver if he'd like a refreshment?"

"Certainly, Mr. Blum," replied the man, as Blum led Gemma deeper into the building.

They followed the side hall, which was more of a gallery, with paintings on the left and right, a fabulous collection from what little she could tell while walking past so quickly. Her breath quickened as she spotted an Edward Hopper, then a Thomas Hart Benton and an Andrew Wyeth, all within ten paces.

Blum drew her to the right when they reached the entry hall. "Sorry I couldn't greet you at the front door," he said. "We had a little accident with my grandson the other day. That rascal. He scarred the flooring with his skateboard, so I'm having it refinished."

"Not at all," said Gemma. "Your collection is amazing."

"Well, those who can't paint, collect, as they say."

"They do?"

He chuckled. "I do."

"But I heard you were a painter, Mr. Blum."

"Henry, please. And may I call you Gemma?"

"Of course."

"I used to paint a little. Went to school at the Cooper Union, you know. That's where I met Sheridan."

"You knew him personally?"

"Pretty well, yeah. We roomed together for a little while. Here we go." He gestured toward a cased opening which was flanked by four Ionic columns. "I've been keeping it upstairs in our bedroom where I can look at it before I go to sleep and first thing when I wake up. If you'll wait here in the library a moment, I'll bring it down."

She stepped into a room about the size of a four-car garage. Books surrounded her from floor to ceiling on all sides. A globe in a mahogany frame as tall as Gemma dominated one end of the space. An ornate limestone fireplace so large she could have stood inside it anchored the other end. Between them was a long table surrounded by what appeared to be authentic Windsor chairs, and piled high with more books. Before the fireplace were a pair of much-used leather sofas and four wingback chairs. Only a few paintings hung on the bookcases. She looked at the nearest one and realized with a start it was a beach scene by Potthast.

Unmindful of the possibilities, she stepped closer. In spite of the passage of perhaps a hundred and forty years, the colors remained vibrant. She saw the bathers reflected in the dampness of the sand. She heard the impudent complaints of gulls and the death rattles of a million bubbles as the surf retreated to the sea. She delighted in the gritty texture of the sand between her toes. She watched her giggling sons frolic at the water's edge. She saw her laughing husband in his trunks and tank top, standing knee deep in the frothing ocean as he raised their little daughter high above his head as if to offer up the girl for celestial inspection.

"Careful, darling," she called across the beach.

He turned to her, still laughing, and with the words, "Watch her fly!" he tossed their little girl into the air.

Gemma felt her heart stop beating at the utterly incongruous sight of the child above, a cherub in the heavens. Although their daughter was indeed angelic, surely this ascension tempted God. She imagined the wet slap of that little body on the beach, the snap of breaking bones, the cries of pain. Covering her mouth she stifled a scream. Then the girl descended to her husband's hands, shrieking with delight. "Again, Daddy!" she cried. "Again!"

Gemma could not watch, so she turned toward the boardwalk, where a pair of young women loitered in risqué bathing dresses. Sailor collars, bows and ribbons fluttered in the onshore breeze, with shapely calves in stockings daringly exposed below the women's bloomers. Beyond them a brass band played John Philip Sousa at the gazebo. Gentlemen in striped coats and boaters strolled along the boardwalk arm in arm with ladies twirling parasols.

Gemma heard a boom. Beneath her feet the earth shuddered. She turned toward the sea as riotous foam attacked the beach, the angry remnants of a mighty breaker. She saw her sons flee laughingly before the chaos. And where her husband and her daughter had been before, she saw nothing but the empty ocean.

"Darling?" she called, looking right and left at strangers. "Darling?" she cried, moving toward the water. "*Darling!*" she screamed, running toward the deep.

"Here we go," replied Henry Blum.

She turned to find him at her side, his gray hair ruffled by the ocean breeze, his jeans and silken T-shirt awkward in that time and place, a painting in his hands.

"What?" she asked him. "What?"

"Here's the Ridler. At least I hope it's a Ridler."

Gemma gripped the bookcase at her side for stability. "Could we, uh . . . could you please put it in the light over by the window?"

"Sure," said Henry Blum.

As the short man walked away from her across the library, she retained her hold upon the bookshelf, willing herself to return fully, drawing the real world up into herself from the wood within her grasp, wood which had been taken from a tree, which had grown from roots sunken deeply down into the earth. She wondered if she was the only one who ever noticed it was possible to drift away. She longed to find another who would understand her occasional need for grounding. She sensed the presence of such a person out there, somewhere.

Blum propped the painting against a paneled wall beside the window. He turned toward her. She saw puzzlement in his features. She knew what he was thinking. Why was she still on the far side of the room? Why had she not moved?

"I'm having trouble tearing myself away from this Potthast," she said.

"You like his work?"

She swallowed, nodding. "There's, um, there's a sense of time-lessness. The way the people are behaving. Except for their clothes it could have been painted yesterday."

"I have another you can see in the morning room. A beach scene, like that one. I find his work very cheerful, don't you?"

"Yes," she lied.

It became possible to release her hold upon the bookcase, the wood, the tree and roots and earth. Abandoning the beach she crossed the library, moving toward the little painting framed in black. She stood before it looking down. She knew immediately. "Oh, my," she said.

Henry Blum nodded. "Quite wonderful, isn't it?"

"Jack Dunn told me it came in the mail, with no letter or return address."

"Jack Dunn?"

"The Lloyd's insurance agent who brought me in for authentication."

"Oh, Jack. Yes, it came packed in cardboard and wrapped in a Spanish-language newspaper."

Kneeling, she gave the painting a close look, although it was unnecessary. Blum watched without speaking. Several minutes passed before she rose to her feet again. She stood beside him, staring down.

Blum said, "Well?"

She turned to him. "I'm sorry?"

"Is it genuine?"

"I believe you told the people at Lloyd's the newspaper it came wrapped in was from Juárez? And the cardboard, it was cut from a carton of peas?"

"That's right. Seems books aren't the only thing you can't judge by the cover, eh?"

She smiled. "Did you happen to notice the postal mark? From where it was mailed?"

"I didn't, actually. I never think to notice postmarks. Do you?"

"And you already threw away the wrapping?"

"That's right."

She thought for a moment. "What kind of peas?"

"Sorry?"

"The cardboard it came in. What was the brand?"

"I don't remember. My assistant might. Peter is actually the one who threw it all away. Why does it matter?"

"If the canning company is a small one they probably sell to stores in a limited area. It might help me find him."

"Find him? I don't understand."

She leaned down closer to the painting. She drew in the scent of linseed oil. She felt the force of every story she had heard about her father, all her mother's memories distilled. "This was done within the last few months. Maybe a year at the outside."

"Oh." His shoulders slumped a little. "Then I guess it's not a Ridler."

"Have you looked at the back of the canvas?"

"No. . . ."

"Could I just have a peek?"

"Sure." Blum bent and turned the painting around and leaned it against the paneling again. "Huh," he said, stepping back. "Look at that."

On the rear of the canvas were the words,

H.—
I'm so sorry about the girl. You were right to cry.
Please forgive me.
—S.

Gemma asked, "Does it mean anything to you?"

He looked at her with wonder written on his face. "I think it might mean Sheridan's alive."

"Why do you say that?"

"You said this is freshly painted. I assume you know what you're talking about, and if you're right, then he *has* to be alive, because he and I are the only people on earth who knew about that." Blum pointed toward the words on the back of the canvas.

"About what, exactly?"

"Sheridan and I were kind of roommates for a while, like I told you. He was sleeping on my sofa, anyway. He didn't have much money. This was while we were both art students, you know, and my parents had me set up in this loft. I kind of took him in, and while he was there he, ah, well, he seduced my girlfriend, actually. When I found out, I'm afraid I made a fool of myself."

"It says there you cried."

"I did, yeah. Right in front of him."

"What did he do then?"

"He . . . I guess you'd say he mocked me."

"He *mocked* you?" Gemma clenched her hands into fists and turned away from the man. "How, exactly?"

"This is a little embarrassing. What does it have to do with authenticating the painting?"

"Well, it could . . . it could . . . No, you're right." She faced him again. "Please, if you don't mind, I just kind of need to know what happened."

Henry Blum returned her stare a moment, then understanding spread across his face. "I'm such an idiot. In all the excitement, I completely forgot you're his daughter."

To her embarrassment, Gemma did not trust herself to speak.

"Aw, listen," said Blum. "He wasn't such a bad guy really."

"But he broke your heart, and then he . . . he mocked you."

Blum looked at her closely, his brow wrinkled with concern. "Listen, you don't really want to hear this stuff. Why don't we change the subject?"

She sniffled and quickly wiped her eyes. "You're a kind man, Mr. Blum, but you have to understand I grew up with this image of who he was. He was my hero, I guess you could say. He's the reason I went into art criticism. I made myself an authority on his work. I built my whole career around his memory . . . my life, really."

The man reached out and touched her arm. "And here I am, talking about what a schmuck your dad was. I'm such an idiot. Ignore me. He wasn't that bad."

"No, don't do that. Just tell me the truth. I need to know the truth."

"Actually, I mean it. He really wasn't that bad. You have to understand the times. There was this song, "Love the One You're With," you know? That's how people were back then, at least in the New York art scene. Free love and all that. Sheridan was just sort of doing what everybody else was doing."

"But he betrayed you and then mocked you."

"Well, yeah. That was pretty bad, I guess. But hey, you know what? He was right."

"What? No. How could that be?"

"He said she wasn't worth it, and that was true. Otherwise she wouldn't have slept with him, right? And it wasn't long after that I met my Sara. Now we're grandparents together. We're incredibly happy. And you know what? She's the one who got me to see that painting wasn't really my thing. I went into digital technology because of Sara, and look at me now." Smiling widely, he spread his arms out in the mansion where they stood, filled with priceless works of art.

"You're not angry with him?"

"Angry? Are you kidding? If Sheridan Ridler walked into this room right now I'd kiss his feet. That girl he slept with, who knows where I'd be if I was with her now? Dead from an overdose maybe, or in prison. And I've thought many times about what a nebbish I was before I met Sheridan. He toughened me up a little, got me to see you have to be honest with yourself about how people really are. I never would have made it in business without learning that. You could say I owe him everything for what he did."

She smiled. "Now you're exaggerating."

He smiled too. "Maybe a little. But it's true I'm not angry with him. I forgave him years ago. In fact, if you find him, if he really is alive, tell him that for me, would you? Tell him I'd love to see him again. And there was certainly no need for him to make this wonderful gesture." He pointed at the painting. "That is, assuming he did make this gesture?"

"Oh, yes," she said, more certain now than ever. "It's a Ridler."

Thirty minutes later, she waved good-bye to Henry Blum through the back window of the taxicab as it rolled slowly down the long driveway. Out at the gate the cabbie made a right turn onto the road, beginning the hour-and-a-half drive to Philadelphia International Airport.

Gemma leaned back against the seat and closed her eyes, trying to come to grips with the new image of her father which had begun to emerge. She fingered the sapphires on the golden cross around her neck and thought of her mother's calm acceptance of her father's distant resurrection. She thought of the argument about that very cross, her mother refusing to remove it, her father furious, demanding the absolute abandonment of something her mother held so sacred. She wondered why her father had demanded such a thing. She wondered what there was about that little golden symbol which outweighed her mother's deep devotion to Sheridan Ridler. She thought of Henry Blum, who had forgiven her father, just as her mother had. She had no problem imagining Henry Blum in younger days, long hair and bell-bottoms, a perpetually naive and earnest expression, not so different from the way he was today if you took away the gray and wrinkles and the slight potbelly. She saw him weeping in front of her father, utterly humiliated, heartbroken. She saw her father laughing. She gripped the cross and held on tight as the shattered remnants of a little god with clay feet began to fall around a pedestal she had erected many years before.

After a few minutes, something else annoyed her. Rousing herself, she opened her eyes. She released the cross, reached down to remove a shoe, and brushed sand from her foot onto the taxi's carpet. She tipped the shoe and saw a little more sand fall. She worked her finger between her toes, rubbing away still more. After replacing the shoe, she removed the other one and did the same.

"Miss? You know anyone who drives a white Escalade?"

She glanced up at the back of the cabbie's head. "No, I don't think so. Why?"

"That guy behind us. He was there when we left the city too."

Replacing the other shoe, Gemma twisted in the seat to look through the rear window. She saw the Escalade about two hundred yards back, keeping pace. "You sure?"

"Pretty sure, yeah."

The vehicle was too far away. She couldn't see the driver. But she knew nobody in Pennsylvania, except for Henry Blum. "Must be a coincidence," she said, turning back to face the front.

The driver yawned, exposing a mouth full of silver fillings in the rearview mirror. "Yeah," he said. "Probably a coincidence."

14.

If the turnout at the circus was any indication, Prospero, New Mexico, was poorly named. The few people wandering around the midway did not ride the Crazy Wave or the Freak Out, nor did they venture into the Fun House. They merely watched as empty cars on the Tilt-A-Whirl rushed around in total chaos. Meanwhile, beneath the constantly morphing patterns of the patchwork big top, the bleachers sprawled like giant rib cages torn from the earth by paleontologists, their pale white boards unbowed by audiences. "It is not worth an artist's time," grumbled the Flying Blackbirds simultaneously, "to risk our life above such empty air."

Rice, rice, and rice they ate morning, noon, and night. Everybody swelled. Costumes burst and were replaced by simple garments crudely sewn from empty burlap bags which had contained the rice that caused the change of wardrobe in the first place. Thus it was that everyone became acquainted with the concept of a self-fulfilling prophecy.

Isabel the wolf woman refused to howl. "I don't have the energy," she said. "I need meat. Someone kill a rabbit."

Gregorio the dwarf had reached the proportions of a round balloon in danger of explosion, exactly the same width as height, while the fat albino had achieved a reversal of the usual arrangement, standing twice as wide as he was tall.

"Why do we remain in this desolate place?" asked Ridler. "We are starving in an avalanche of rice."

"Only Esperanza knows," replied El Magnífico, the dashing knife thrower.

"We could be in El Paso, or at least Alamogordo. Someplace with money."

"And groceries," said the dwarf.

"But surely there is money here in Prospero," said El Magnífico.

"Then why won't they come?"

Esperanza approached them, waving a hand before her face as if shooing off a fly. "Enough of this talk. If your stomach demands answers, go and get them."

So it was that Ridler and the knife thrower strolled side by side into Prospero.

The circus had encamped at the eastern edge of town, therefore the setting sunshine in their faces forced the painter to squint and look away. Of course El Magnífico was unaffected. He was a match for any sun, pure white teeth aglow beneath his glorious mustache, a brace of knives brilliant in the bandoliers across his outthrust chest. Gazing ahead with eyelids tightly closed he said, "This is a lonely place, but that is not what troubles you."

"How would you know if I am troubled?" said the painter. "You can't even see my face."

"Yet I know," replied El Magnífico. "And you know that I know."

"In that case, you must also know the problem."

"I know what you believe the problem is, which is a different thing."

Ridler kicked the planet underneath them. "Why don't you be quiet?"

White teeth bared and blazing, El Magnífico complied.

The main street of Prospero was in fact a boulevard, very wide, with four lanes for nonexistent traffic on each side of a central ground, where a row of dead pecan trees stood like sentries, taproots deep and withered in the earth below, branches naked and arthritic in the sky above, black bark flaking off and falling in great patches. The street was paved with cobblestones which nestled side by side like the fossilized eggs of extinct reptiles. In the awful heat Ridler expected them to hatch at any moment, a sudden plague of widemouthed lizards rising from the rocks, desperate for sustenance. The walls of his empty stomach ground against each other. Looking toward the sound of that internal collision he spoke to his abdomen, saying, "Why don't you be quiet too?" At this, El Magnífico laughed and they were once again good friends.

They led their shadows west along the lifeless boulevard. Every step on the uneven clutch of cobblestones was a dire threat to ankles. The glass in storefronts on their left and right had long before been frosted by the blowing sand. The mortar in the walls had been worn away to leave mere stacks of bricks, precariously balanced. The names and purposes of businesses, once evident in signage, had been scrubbed away, leaving little but a hint of those who once put brush to board in order to communicate notions such as "hardware," "barbershop," and "café." Ridler, familiar with the fickle nature of brushes, observed the sun-bleached signs with sympathy.

He dared not breathe in through his mouth for fear the heat would crack his tongue. On the other hand, he also feared the fiery air would singe his nostrils. It was a difficult dilemma, which could only be resolved with compromise, therefore he alternated inhalations between his nose and mouth. Conscious of the air as it flowed in and out, he thought of Glory displaced by his own return into himself, and his first awareness that one of them must yield, for compromise between them was impossible.

In the space of three more blocks they saw no living thing, no green plant, no upright animal, no human being whatsoever.

"This reminds me of a time," said Ridler, "when I went out to walk the camp and nobody was there."

"Ah," said El Magnífico.

"Where were you?"

"I myself had gone to visit heaven."

"If you don't want to tell me, why don't you just say so?" But Ridler remembered a moment when he thought he saw the entire troupe around him, slender and resplendent in well-fitting costumes much adorned with diamonds.

A tumbleweed arrived before them at an intersection, paused as if respecting laws concerning stop signs, and then continued on across the boulevard. The solitude became a threat, like poison gas, or boredom. Ridler fought a growing instinct to turn and run.

"Steady," murmured El Magnífico through his smile. "Steady, my fine friend."

"It's just like that other time. Where is everyone? Why don't they come out?"

"Perhaps they flee before my knives. It has happened many times before with timid creatures."

"In that case maybe you should take off your knives."

"I cannot," said El Magnífico, touching his bandoliers. "They are all that holds me down."

"You say things that make no sense."

"You paint things that are not things."

"What would you know about it? You've never even looked at my paintings."

"One need not look to see."

"That doesn't mean anything." Ridler kicked the planet once again. "Let's just find the people."

"No need," said El Magnífico with his magnificent smile. "They have found us."

Looking in the direction indicated by the knife thrower's closed eyes, Ridler saw a woman standing on the sidewalk. It appeared her hair had not been brushed in recent memory. Bleached by long exposure to the sun, it was further lightened by the gray of advanced age. Her soiled clothing reminded him of another old woman in another time and place, a beggar by the Golden Horn, with robes stained by colors from the earth, folds propped up by knees and elbows like the poles beneath a Bedouin tent. "Hello," he called. "Where is everybody?"

"You got a quarter?" she asked, indeed a beggar after all.

Remembering al-Wasiti's unfailing generosity, he replied, "If I do, it's yours."

"Ah," said El Magnífico.

The woman stepped down off the curb and came rolling and pitching across the cobblestones. It was a marvel that her bent and twisted body could support such motions. Her right shoulder arched high in the air above her ear, which belonged to an unsteady head cocked at a desperate angle. Her left elbow dug into her belly. Her left forearm waved before her to and fro. Her hips also preceded her by several inches, her feet pointing first this way and then that way, her knees crashing together as if doing battle over every step. Slurring the words, she said, "I need money awful bad."

"Here you are," said Ridler, placing his last coin in her outstretched hand, which was black beneath the fingernails and grimy in the creases. "Can you tell us where everybody is?"

"Around," she replied, gazing down at the coin with an expression bordering on adoration. "Just got more sense than to be out in this heat."

"Could you take us to some of them?"

Standing with the coin in her open palm, staring down at it, the old woman did not seem to hear his words.

"Ma'am?" said Ridler. "Ma'am? Could you take us to see your friends? We have a question to ask."

"She requires another coin," said El Magnífico.

"How do you know? You don't even speak English."

"Neither will I look at this wicked world, yet even I can see she needs another coin."

"Well, I don't have another coin."

"Yes, you do."

Snorting, Ridler dug into his pockets. To his surprise, he found a quarter there. "Here, ma'am," he said, adding it to the other in her outstretched palm.

"Bless you," she said, never looking up from the shining silver. "Bless you."

Were her words less slurred? And did she stand a little straighter? Or was it only Ridler's imagination? "Give her another," said El Magnífico.

"Do it yourself. I've already given everything I have."

"You have more."

Knowing he did not, yet also knowing the maddening smile beneath that grand mustache would never let him rest until he proved that it was so, Ridler reached again into his pockets. To his great frustration, he found yet another coin. He placed the third quarter in her palm with a sidelong glance at El Magnífico.

"Do not look at me," said the man with the closed eyes. "Behold the woman."

This he did, and it seemed to Ridler that she was indeed a little taller, a little straighter, a little younger.

With no further encouragement from El Magnífico, Ridler reached again into his pocket, and of course he found a fourth coin there. When it too had touched the woman's palm he watched her very closely. This time he saw the transformation happening before his very eyes, the straightening, the strengthening. Eagerly he reached again into his pocket, and again, and again, piling silver coins upon her palm until the number had reached thirty.

She stood before him like a goddess. She turned away. With graceful strides she led them east along the boulevard. A pair of broken men emerged from a doorway to fall in behind them. Although bent beneath invisible burdens, three women also joined the little band. Others appeared, and then others, all of them the color of the dust of that infernal place, brown and dry and bent into inhuman shapes.

Every eye was focused on the thirty silver pieces in the woman's palm, every tongue licked lustfully at cracked lips. Their hands reached toward the coins, then drew back, then reached out again. They begged with groans and pleas. They offered many promises. If she would only give them just one of her coins they would not spend it on alcohol, they would use it to begin a new life, to change their wicked ways.

Stopping at an intersection, the woman put one quarter in an old man's palm. She gave another quarter to a different man, and another to a woman, and so on and on she gave. As each piece of money left her palm Ridler saw her shoulders twist a little more, her head cock slightly further to the side, her legs bow as she sank beneath the missing weight of what she had surrendered. Meanwhile, those who took her charity rose a little with each coin, just as she had risen while receiving alms from Ridler. They rose above their poverty, high above the dusty street, above the wicked fate which had so callously assigned them to that life. They became as doves, light and without worries.

When the woman had nothing left to give, when she had been reduced completely to her previous condition, she moved among the others, her grimy palm outstretched, begging them with words slurred by a drunkard's tongue. Some of those who had received coins from her were pleased to give them back, and in so doing, they grew weak again, and she again was strengthened. Thus Prospero's beggars begat beggars as alms were passed from hand to hand and back again, each citizen ascending with an act of charity received and diminishing again as charity was given.

"Come away," said Ridler to the knife thrower, and their shadows led them to the edge of town, to the place where the last sand-burnished buildings on their left and right gave way to open desert. There El Magnífico shook his head, remarking, "A closed system of beggary, which we have upset by offering our services for pay. Who has seen a wonder to equal it?"

"I have," said Ridler. "I see something more wonderful each time the troupe performs."

El Magnífico clicked his heels together with a little bow. "It is most gratifying when one's art is appreciated."

"That's not what I meant," replied the painter.

"In that case, you must be speaking of the big top."

"I thought I was the only one who noticed it."

"I see all, my friend."

Eagerly, Ridler turned to him. He dared to hope he had found a fellow pilgrim, another who had encountered the Glory. "Have you ever seen such a thing before?"

"Indeed not. Who could make that claim?"

Ridler replied, "I can."

Then, perhaps because Prospero, New Mexico, was so hot and dry, he described how water from the Tiber once competed with the ceaseless ringing in his ears, gurgling and hissing through the hollows in a five-hundred-year-old Roman wall. He spoke of the water emerging on the far side of the stones, only inches from his head, to splash from a perpetually inclined amphora into an ancient marble basin, one of the Eternal City's countless fountains. Perhaps Prospero's awful heat explained why Ridler spoke of lying cool and perfectly relaxed on an iron bed, of staring at Suzanna's creased and fading image on the photograph which was the only remnant of another life which might have been, and of the groan of springs beneath a cotton mattress as he shifted his position to watch sunlight filter through the grape leaves hanging in his window, sunlight tinting linen curtains green as they wafted in the cooling breeze. Perhaps because he was so sick of rice he spoke of the delicious scent of bread and garlic and tomatoes from the café three doors down. Perhaps because he did not care for the Chihuahuan desert's silence he mentioned the incessant honks of automobiles, and the beeps of scooter horns, and profuse masculine excuses given in Italian followed by a woman's silver laughter. Perhaps instead of answering El Magnífico's question in the negative, Ridler began his answer in that way for all those reasons, or perhaps it was only to postpone his story even as he told it, for in that moment he remained uncertain of the meaning of the patches in the big top.

In Tel Aviv while trapped beneath the result of a Muslim missile, Rabbi Klein had patiently explained the obvious as if to a child: only Christians dared believe mere man could paint the Glory, therefore anyone insane enough to try such things should probably attach himself to them.

"I've never met a Christian painter," protested Ridler.

The rabbi answered him from somewhere in the darkness. "Me

either, but there used to be a lot of them. You should seek them out. There's nothing for you here."

Thus banished from the company of Jews, Ridler had departed Israel immediately upon their rescue, choosing Rome as his destination because it once had been the center of the Christian world where art was concerned. Michelangelo, da Vinci, Titian, Caravaggio, Velázquez, Bernini, Brueghel, Raphael . . . the list of geniuses who left their mark on Rome was endless, all of them attempting to paint God or something like him. Surely some of them had seen the subject of their work. Surely some of them could show the way.

Arriving on a nonstop El Al flight from Tel Aviv, two hours and forty-five minutes removed from the chosen ones who claimed the Glory had no form of any kind, Ridler could not understand why he had never thought of this before.

It is not possible to count the images of God in the Eternal City. It took years for Ridler to search all the Roman churches. He visited la Chiesa del Gesù, where Ignatius rested in the care of Jesuits, and there immersed himself for weeks in il Baciccio's explosive revelation of the heavens, which seemed to peel away the ceiling and burst into the church with triumphant beams of light. He gazed for a month at Domenichino's similar fresco on the ceiling of the church of San Luigi dei Francesi, barely noticing Caravaggio's majestic renditions of Matthew on the nearby walls because of his all-consuming hope. In the Church of Santa Maria del Popolo, beneath the Chigi Chapel dome he had been transfixed by God and cherubs staring down from heaven. And of course because it was a short walk from his rooms he had plunged himself into Perino del Vaga's frescos of the heavenlies beneath the dome of the Trinità dei Monti, a church owned by the French above the Spanish Steps. In these and many other ancient places throughout Rome he sought the Glory, or a rendition of the Glory, or at least some sign or hint that others too had seen what he had seen, some image to guide him past the barricade of memory at last.

In spite of such a long investigation of the masterpieces, in spite of his wholehearted commitment, in the end he had learned two things only. Technically, he knew himself to be the equal of them all. He also knew those other painters had not seen what he had seen, or if they had seen it then they were unequal to the task which he had set himself. Even his worst failures drew much closer to the Glory than the best renditions painted by the so-called masters. Yet there was one master remaining, one whose work he had not seen, the best of all or so they said, Michelangelo, who in his own lifetime had been called *Il Divino*, the divine one, because of his transcendent art.

Of course Ridler had seen photographs and prints of the Sistine Chapel ceiling, the creation of Adam, that iconic almost-touch transferring life. Of course he knew nothing in those photographs or prints conveyed the sense of Glory. But Ridler also knew that no copy of a work of art could be completely true to its source. So in spite of the flight of faithless doves, in spite of Islam's savage rejection, in spite of the rabbi's airy doctrine, and in spite of years wasted searching all the walls and ceilings of Rome's most holy places, Ridler clung to hope, for Michelangelo remained.

On that last morning Ridler rose from the narrow bed just as he always had, on the right side, for the left side stood against the wall shared with the five-hundred-year-old courtyard fountain. After a breakfast of bread and cheese and coffee he gathered up his kit—pastels, charcoals, and a large pad of textured paper—and he resumed his quest. The sky hung gray and pregnant with capacity for weeping as he set out along the narrow Via Margutta. Walking against the flow of traffic, his shoes beat out an optimistic rhythm on the crazy patterns of the cobblestones, his footsteps echoing against the stucco walls of buildings which had harbored artisans and artists in their attics for two hundred years. Ocher, umber, burnt sienna, everywhere around him were rich tones of the earth.

Following the street's bend to the left he reached Via del Babuino and turned right. Far ahead he saw the Flaminio Obelisk, built by a pharaoh and stolen by a Caesar. His view of the obelisk was framed between the building facades on each side of the road. He walked three blocks toward it and emerged onto the Piazza del Popolo, savoring the sudden contrast between the narrow streets behind him, pressed in as they were by looming buildings, and the piazza's grand unencumbered oval.

On the corner to his left stood the columned portico of Santa Maria di Montesanto, one of a pair of nearly identical churches guarding that side of the piazza. In the center of the great open space ahead the obelisk aimed like an arrow toward the threatening sky. Shunning a nearby taxi stand he set out at an angle across the broad expanse of pavement, surrounded on every side by other pedestrians. At the west end of the piazza he skirted the Neptune Fountain and set out along Via Ferdinando di Savoia, toward the Tiber.

Soon he stood on the Ponte Regina Margherita, a stone bridge with three arches. The olive-green water flowed slowly thirty or forty feet below him. At a river bend on the left he saw another arched stone bridge, much like the one where he stood. Half a dozen houseboats lay against the shore below him. It should have been a peaceful scene. The Piazza del Popolo behind him, the Vatican ahead, the Tiber flowing through the city as it had for three thousand years. Everywhere he looked was permanence, stability, and certainty. Why then did he feel a strange unease on that bridge? Why a sudden sense of danger?

He lifted his gaze to the far side of the river, where a modern building towered just beyond the trees. Sunlight flashed in rows of windows. He imagined flames were dancing there. Could that building really be on fire? A delivery van roared past. It took a conscious exercise of will to remain standing. Everything within him longed to run, or to collapse. The bridge. The river. The traffic. The flashing windows of the building on the other side. Why this overwhelming sense that he had seen such things before, somewhere in a moment of grave danger? Where? When? He closed his eyes and fought against the brutish loss of memory. He must remember, yet something in his mind resisted: a ghoul, a lump of clay which dammed the flow. The moment passed and he was just himself again, a stranger alone above the Tiber.

On he walked. Eleven or twelve more blocks west he reached the little Piazza del Risorgimento, with its strange equestrian statue of a man whose horse stared down curiously at a dog. The inscription carved into the marble base seemed to say it was dedicated to the police, or *carabinieri*, but what could this mounted man in a Napoleonic hat have to do with the police? Why erect it in a place called Renaissance Plaza? And why record that strange exchange between the horse and dog? Again Ridler had the feeling he should understand more than he did. He sensed something just behind a veil he could not see, something gathering around him, strange, awesome and terrifying.

After all the years, could this be the day?

Ignoring the buses and the pale green trolleys waiting by the little piazza, he watched for a break in traffic and dashed through the confusion. He continued west with a smile and a shake of his head. Where else but Rome could four streets with four different names come together at a simple four-way intersection?

Now the street he had been following was renamed after the little piazza on his left. Glancing again in that direction he caught his first glimpse of St. Peter's dome, and to the south, down Via del Mascherino, he could just make out the Passetto, a tall freestanding stone wall from the medieval period with crenellations like a castle along the top. According to his guidebook the Passetto contained a long gallery connecting the papal residence with the Castel Sant'Angelo, a fortress on the Tiber. More than once when under siege by Saracens or Christian rivals, popes had used it to escape the Vatican. Having fled from so many holy places himself, this was something Ridler understood.

Another wall came into view beyond the Piazza del Risorgimento. The massive rampart which contained the Vatican stood at least fifty feet tall, the tan bricks leaning slightly inward as it rose. Beyond the wall many tiled roofs in the compound sloped at different heights and angles. To his dismay, Ridler also saw a lengthy line of tourists standing along the base of the wall. Could they all be waiting to enter the museum?

Crossing the piazza he approached a blond man in the line and asked. When the man did not speak Italian, Ridler tried again in English. "Ja," replied the man. "But it is not necessary to worry. They are saying it is only a small time to go inside."

Ridler checked the map in his guidebook. He was at least three blocks from the Vatican Museum's entrance. He doubted if such a long line would get him inside in less than two or three hours, but having failed to buy a ticket in advance he had no choice.

The line began to move. Surrounded by citizens of every country on the planet, Ridler passed west alongside the Vatican, then north, then west again. Always on his left towered the wall. On his right across a street called Viale Vaticano stood a row of more modern buildings, perhaps only two or three hundred years old. On the sidewalk at their base were many café umbrellas, and many Romans seated there enjoying espresso or cappuccino along with a little something sweet, perhaps brioches, or *bomboloni,* the typical Italian breakfast.

In Ridler's mind the looming wall beside him somehow merged with the vague sense of destiny which had arisen when he crossed the Tiber bridge. The permanence, the incalculable weight, gave a foreboding substance to his premonitions. But the little canvas umbrellas across the street, so fleeting by comparison, weighed upon him even more. Standing among a crowd of tourists, imprisoned by his quest, he watched a man and woman in front of a café, chatting at a breakfast table. A sudden sense of loss descended, and all the years he'd spent searching for the Glory came to rest upon his shoulders, the hardships and the deprivation, the days and nights of futile painting, alone in foreign lands. The uncomplicated pleasure of coffee and a pastry with a friend or lover—just to be with someone—seemed to him the grandest and most distant thing upon the earth. How he longed to simply cross the street and find release, yet the habit of pursuing Glory could not be resisted. When the museum entrance came into view, he turned his back upon that other life and entered.

The museum was a blur. So much work so close together. Masterpieces, masterpieces. Marble busts by the thousands. Friezes and mosaics. Monumental sculptures in the round. Paintings, paintings, paintings. Ridler felt the call of every single one. Who were all these ancient artists? Hundreds of them. Thousands, who had not left their names behind. And the moderns, van Gogh, Chagall, Mirko, Pirandello. He could have spent a lifetime in that place. He could have forgone food and drink, sleep and air, and lived on nothing but the art. How could anybody leave? How did one escape?

He might have lost himself forever had he not come upon the spiral stairway of Bramante. It slapped him to his senses with a past almost forgotten, a time and place before the Glory, a hotel in New

York, another winding staircase lined with art, and racing down those stairs in hot pursuit of . . . something. Was it Suzanna? Yes, Suzanna, whose beauty was the living equal of a million Vatican Museums. He tried to let the memories run through his mind, but the staircase only brought them back in bits and pieces. He saw himself chasing something in the darkness between reds and oranges of some kind of light, and after that he saw . . . nothing.

Ridler slapped his forehead with his palm. Why couldn't he remember anything between the bridge and river? It was as if the Glory, in retreating, had drawn with it all he was.

It didn't matter. In recalling Suzanna, he had remembered Michelangelo.

Consulting the brochure they gave him with his ticket, he realized he had somehow reached the corner of that enormous museum which was farthest from his destination. He steeled himself to ignore everything. Eyes lowered toward the marble floor, he hurried past the Roman busts observing him from shelves along a four-hundred-foot-long corridor which was the Chiaramonti Museum. He crossed the barrel-vaulted new wing and entered a series of galleries, the Museum of Christian Art, the Sistine Rooms, the Gallery of Urban VIII. Through many solitary years he had developed the habit of discipline. He conquered the temptation of art and kept moving.

Rooms became more crowded. In spite of Ridler's English, Turkish, Hebrew, and Italian, voices spoke in tongues he did not recognize. Elbows touched him. Shoulders moved him. Up he went along a narrow stairway, handrail in the center, plain white stucco on the walls, a blur of color on the vaulted ceiling, more art up there, more art to be avoided.

Finally he saw a sign. Driven by the crowd, unable to do otherwise, he turned and climbed another set of stairs more narrow still. Some-one spoke in wonder, "This is it." He stepped into the Sistine Chapel.

Pausing, he became a problem. Complaints arose in many languages. Someone pressed a hand into his back. "Move along," came words in Italian. "Move along, please." He walked toward the center, staring up with everybody else. Here was Noah, drunk and in disgrace, a flood, and sacrifices, temptation and ejection from the garden, a woman drawn from man, and finally what he had come to see, the quintessential image of divinity in Rome, the end of all his searching, which would at last unleash remem-brances of Glory, there, reaching down to Adam, God reclining in the heavens . . .

"No," whispered the painter, gazing up. "No."

How could this be all?

"No, that isn't right," he said more loudly. "It's wrong! That isn't how it is!"

Desperate he looked farther. He saw the same anemic so-called god dividing waters, the same feeble human image creating the sun and separating light from darkness. "No!" he muttered, striding to and fro beneath the mockery. "No! No! No!" he shouted, pacing like a man within a cell, pushing past astonished tourists. This was no miracle, no masterpiece, and certainly no mystic vision. This was worse than nothing. He had seen what he had seen. Compared to that, these scribbles were mere hollow symbolism, mere fable, merely flesh for Glory.

He stopped. He planted his feet wide. He shook both fists up at the ceiling and he shouted, "SHOW YOURSELF!"

Before his protest had ceased echoing through the chapel they were on him. Four men in blue suits, two at either side. They spoke words he did not hear, soft words which gave the lie to hard hands gripping him like vises. Gaping Swedes and Japanese and Greeks and Brazilians stood back as he was walked toward a door. "You don't understand!" he said to them, and it was true.

Through the door, down some steps and out another door, and they stood him on St. Peter's Square beneath a glowering sky, gray and turbulent and filled with threats. They held him there until a car arrived. They pushed him into it and drove him to a little courtyard where they pulled him out and compelled him through yet another door. In fluorescent lights between white walls and underneath low ceilings they questioned him for hours. His pockets were searched. His backpack emptied. Everything examined once, twice and again. Questions about lodgings, visas, citizenship, and profession. The same questions many times. Finally convinced he was a harmless lunatic, they let him go, ejecting him through yet another door, plain and made of steel, which opened through the massive ramparts of the Vatican.

Thrust into the Italian State beyond, he stood, backpack in his hand, alone and well aware that he would always be alone, that he alone had seen what he had seen, that all these so-called masters had been liars, had deluded everyone with counterfeits and propaganda. Standing underneath the warlike sky he cursed them for the sons of unmarried mothers that they were, the female dogs, the excrement, the practitioners of incestuous fornication. He spoke the names of Botticelli, Raphael, and Michelangelo, and then he spat. How he hated and disdained them for their fraud!

What could he do? What could he do?

As he had beneath the Sistine ceiling, Ridler paced the sidewalk. Back and forth beside the looming ramparts, he paced. All the years swirled through his mind, the cost of jungles, beaches, filthy alleys and bazaars, tortured and exploded, hungry, parched, lonely and

alone, and of course Suzanna. Suzanna lost forever. He had surrendered everything to paint the Glory, trying it a thousand times,
a thousand ways, miles of paint, gallons of it flowing across canvas
by the acre. What were these imposters' feeble efforts compared to
sacrifice like his?

"I'll show them," he muttered, dropping to his knees and opening his backpack. "I'll show them."

Removing his kit he spilled his pastels out onto the sidewalk.
Still muttering, he selected a piece of chalk and began to sketch.
His arm swung broadly over the pavement, a giant motion from
the shoulder. Line after sweeping, monumental line arched across
the slates around him. He was no mere artist. He was an athlete, a
zealot and a warrior. He was no propagandist. He was a partisan, a
dogmatist in possession of all truth. He alone could show the Glory
to the world, and he alone would do it.

Driven by his rage and his disdain, Ridler lost all consciousness
of his surroundings. He did not see the crowd gathering about him
as his colors rose from the pavement to the ancient ramparts of the
Holy See. He did not hear their whispers, nor their gasps and excla-
mations as the image swelled and spread. He climbed the wall with
only fingertips and the narrow edges of his boots, clinging to the
bricks stacked earthy and steadfast for generations. Halfway up he
released his hold and drifted. Gripping colored chalk in both of his
hands, he drew with unerring beauty and precision on his left and
right at once, a whirlwind of pristine intention, filling empty voids
as if he was a witch conjuring a portal to a future or a past. He
almost had it now. This time he would hold it fast. He would draw
back the veil. He would reveal the Glory. He would not let it go. He
would master everything.

Ridler drew among a cloud of witnesses. No *carabinieri* stepped forward from that growing crowd to protest on behalf of public property. On the contrary, the police in their white belts and chest straps stood entranced along with bankers and tourists, priests and beggars. Dozens of them turned to hundreds; hundreds turned to thousands. From the street and sidewalk, from the windows, balconies, and rooftops, all of Rome observed in breathless silence.

It never crossed the artist's mind that he might run out of colors. Again and again he pulled more pastels from his pack, never realizing it had become a cornucopia, endlessly fertile, providing everything required. Nothing was withheld. The sun itself beyond the angry clouds did not betray him. On the contrary, it remained aloft long past the normal hour, granting the suspension of time. Even gravity and space surrendered, all created things in all directions bowing in submission to his genius.

In the end it seemed the only limit was himself, for when he stopped it was his own decision. Hands and arms and clothing choked with color, Ridler sat back on his haunches. At that very moment the sun began to move again above the clouds, but it took a while to regain its usual velocity. And like the fading of the day, Ridler's own return was gradual, a slow recognition of the image spread out all around him. Shadows gathering, he gazed upon the work.

It covered half a block along the sidewalk. It climbed forty feet up the wall. It was of course his grandest effort, superior to anything that Rome had ever seen. Thousands knelt around the fringes, hands clasped at their chins, palms turned up toward heaven. Their whispered prayers combined and interlaced in midair, flowing hot across his face. Their adoration of the image plucked him to his feet as if he were a puppet pulled by strings. He disappeared into them, staggering with painful joints, fleeing yet another failure, for he was well aware that this was merely one more flawed beginning.

As he had so many times before, he had reached the end of Ridler without capturing the Glory.

At last the heavens made good on their long-standing threat, but the downpour, when it came, came meekly. Tiny raindrops arrived as fine particles of moisture on the hair and shoulders. They quivered on eyelashes, tickled cheeks and noses and coalesced on upraised hands. Because the rainfall was so gentle, it remained possible to stare at the huge image without blinking. So complete was the devotion of those who had immersed themselves most thoroughly, they did not know the clouds were weeping, therefore the effect of heaven's timid tears upon the image remained imperceptible until the moment when it first began to sparkle with the flash of tourists' cameras.

From within the Vatican came a man in a red cardinal's cassock and biretta. He moved at a stately pace among the faithful, surrounded by priests in black, blessing on his left and right. *"Chi ha fatto questo?"* he called to them. Who has made this?

No one could reply, for in their fascination with the art, none recalled the artist.

"Esso muove!" cried a female voice, and standing unnoticed in the midst of them Ridler saw that it was true. The colors had indeed begun to move. They quivered in the photo flashes. They shifted subtly. It was the rain, only the rain, yet the faithful crowd began to fall facedown to the ground, so great was their ecstatic adoration. And as the colors ran and shifted, as the tears of heaven drove them down, for a fleeting instant Ridler glimpsed an image of the Glory.

He was felled where he stood. He sighed within himself, his forehead to the earth, but when he dared to raise his eyes, determined to remember so he could record it later, what he saw was nothing but a blood-and-bruises mess of pigment dripping down the wall, nothing more than what he had once seen on other bricks and sketched while leaning out above an act of violence in an alley, nothing but chalk becoming mud, oozing from that holy instant down into the profane, across the sidewalk, into the gutter, onto the street, dispersing through the crowd, not in electric currents of transcendence, but in the filthy little channels separating cobblestones.

At that moment El Magnífico interrupted Ridler's story. "But this is excellent news," said he. "For it means you have succeeded in your quest, if only for a moment."

"Don't you understand?" replied the painter. "It wasn't me. It was the rain. The rain changed everything I did."

"Surely those were insignificant revisions, minor adjustments, which you could duplicate yourself at any time."

Ridler shook his head. "From that moment until this one here with you, I've known it is hopeless."

"But you still paint that image every night."

"Bah! I try, but those are only images of images. It's hopeless. It's always been hopeless."

"In that case why do you go on painting it?"

"Why do drunkards go on drinking? Why do old men dream of sex? I'm in the clutches of a habit. An addiction."

Dust rose from their footsteps as they approached the circus. It hung suspended in the air behind them, unmoving, as if the cosmos wished to draw attention to their progress. "I am interested," said El Magnífico, "in the fact that you chose to tell me this only after I asked if you had seen a wonder like the big top, yonder."

Gazing at the tent which shivered in the distant waves of heat, Ridler said, "Don't you understand anything?"

"I understand the patchwork there reminds you of your masterpiece."

"No," replied the artist. "It reminds me of the mess in the gutter."

"In that case, I understand your anger."

"I'm not angry! And if I was, it would only be because you think a century of accidental patches could be a match for my ability."

"On the contrary," said the knife thrower with his devastating smile. "You are angry because you know your ability is no match for accidents."

Ridler kicked the planet yet again, but that did not stop the dust from hovering, and while the dashing El Magnífico's eyes were always closed, his mouth would not be silenced.

"Moreover," said that vexing man, "your guilt compounds your anger. But all those little nothings you are painting for the people in your past will earn no audience with what you seek."

"When *will* you shut up?"

"I only say apologies are nothing if they are made from a distance. You should go to them, these ones you think you harmed."

"Knives or no knives, I'm warning you. Change the subject or prepare to defend yourself."

With a flashing smile the man replied, "In that case, for your sake I will change the subject. Are you aware the Romans were the first to have a circus? There was the Circus Maximus, Flaminius, and of course the Neronis."

"That's what I've been told."

"And are you aware performers in those days often lost their lives to animals and to the blades of swords?"

"Everyone knows that."

"Ah," said El Magnífico. "But do you know the reason why?"

"I'm so sick of 'ah'! Always you say 'ah' as if everything unfolds exactly as you planned."

The knife thrower's smile remained. "It does unfold, although the plan is never mine."

"There is no plan."

"Indeed? Are we not a circus? Do we not have blades?"

"What does that mean?"

"You asked why we remain in the desert. I merely say the purpose of a circus has not changed from Roman days till now. For some it merely offers entertainment, but for others who have eyes to see, it demonstrates the facts of life and death."

"Why be so dramatic? No one dies in Esperanza's circus."

"Go and ask the failed painters of Rome, the beggars of Prospero," said El Magnífico, "if death is necessary in order to be dead."

PART THREE

Signs are taken for wonders. "We would see a sign!"
The word within a word, unable to speak a word,
Swaddled with darkness. In the juvescence of the year
Came Christ the tiger

—T. S. ELIOT, "GERONTION"

15.

In Loving, New Mexico, Gemma Halls sipped from a cup of watery coffee and stared at nothing through a filthy diner window. A week had passed since she flew to El Paso to rent a compact car and drive into the desert. Distant mountains had loomed on the horizon with tans and browns and dry straw colors, weathered, worn and unrelieved by any hint of green, silent witnesses observing each stage of her journey across the level plain. Utterly alone on the desert highway, she had thought of *Ram's Head White Hollyhock and Little Hills,* and Georgia O'Keeffe, and antlers and white petals in the sky.

Four towns even smaller than Loving had received her, towns united across great distances by what they did not have in common. None had anything to offer to a traveler except a lumpy mattress in a motor inn and the most mundane kind of meal. None possessed an opera, ballet, or symphony of course, but there was also no art of any kind, no bookstore or library, not even a cinema. Indeed, except for bad American beer and saccharine jukebox music in one town's smoke-filled roadhouse, there was no entertainment. To hear the locals tell it, those dry and desolate communities had no springtime or autumn either, only broiling summers without rain, and Arctic winters without anything to break the merciless assault of northern winds. On the Texas side of the state line, what little money there was came from hard work in the oil and cotton fields. In southeastern New Mexico everything depended on two holes in the ground, one containing bats and tourists, the other a man-made repository for nuclear waste which would be lethal for ten thousand years.

In spite of the absence of beauty, culture, comfort, and prosperity, each of the four desert towns had drawn Gemma Halls like a parched traveler to a watery oasis, for each possessed a post office. Each of those four post offices had applied its postmark to a package received by someone from her father's past, a package containing a masterpiece quite similar to all the others. So that was eight in all, those four paintings and the first one which had been received by her mother, and the paintings reported by Jennifer Killgarten in Phoenix, and Caleb Nelson, and the one sent to Henry Blum. There might even have been nine so far, since Talbot Graves had mentioned one to Gemma's mother on the night before he was murdered, the poor man, but presumably that painting had been stolen along with three others at his gallery. All of the remaining eight were freshly painted, and on the back of all had been apologies containing details only Sheridan Ridler could have known.

While taking a last bite of her breakfast in the Loving diner, it occurred to Gemma that a better analogy for her journey might be a parched traveler drawn to a mirage, for in spite of asking questions at every business in each of the tiny towns, she had found no one who recalled her father. Even in the four post offices where she was certain someone had mailed the paintings, only one woman in an isolated place called Dell City, Texas, remembered a stranger bringing in a package—a man of average height and average build—and the woman could not identify the customer as the man in Gemma's photograph of her father.

Perhaps that was understandable, since the photo was more than two decades old, but surely the residents of those tiny towns knew everyone for many miles in all directions. Was it really possible that none of them remembered anything useful about a total stranger who came into their communities, mailed a package, and then left town again? Could it really be true that not one of them had noticed his vehicle, for example, or his clothing, or the way he spoke, or any unique identifying feature whatsoever?

Gemma suspected a conspiracy. Try as she might, however, she could not think of anything the citizens of such far-flung places might have to gain from misleading her.

Chewing and thinking, she stared through the diner's window. A faded red pickup truck rolled to a stop in front of a metal building across the street. A lean woman in a plaid shirt and blue jeans got out of the truck, adjusted her black cowboy hat, and reached into the cab to remove a white bundle. It looked like an overstuffed pillowcase. The woman entered the building.

A few minutes later another pickup truck arrived, this one faded blue. From it emerged a haggard man and a small child. Carrying a plastic basket overflowing with what appeared to be clothes, the man entered the building. Gemma decided the place must be a Laundromat, although there was no sign that she could see.

The child who had arrived with the haggard man, a girl about five years of age, wore a pretty sundress and white sandals. Her outfit reminded Gemma of one she herself had worn when she was just about that age. The little girl began to play in the gravel parking lot. She had a red plastic ball and a yellow plastic bat. She threw the ball into the air and tried to hit it with the bat. She missed. She picked up the ball and tried again to no avail. On her third try, the little girl managed to hit the ball. She ran into the street after it. She did not pause to check for traffic.

Gemma leaned closer to the glass, looking left and right to see if the child was safe. A block away she saw a white truck, an SUV, coming much too fast. Shiny and new, chrome grill and chrome wheels flashing in the sun, it would surely strike the girl. Although there was no way the child could hear her warning and understand in time, Gemma called, "Watch out!"

Trying to rise up, her legs struck the edge of the table and she fell back against the booth seat. She rapped on the window with her knuckles, desperate to get the girl's attention. "Watch out!" she called again. "Watch out!"

"What's the matter, miss?"

Gemma glanced away from the impending tragedy. A pregnant young woman stood beside her table, holding a glass coffeepot in her hand. Gemma said, "That little girl's about to be killed!"

The woman looked out toward the street, then back at Gemma. "Excuse me?"

"That little girl! Her father just left her there in the street!"

"What little girl?"

Gemma turned back toward the window. The white truck had pulled into the parking lot beside the Laundromat. Unlike the two pickups already there, it looked brand-new and expensive. In the street she saw no girl. Gemma blinked and looked again.

"But she was right there just a second ago. She couldn't have moved that fast. She must have . . ." Gemma looked back at the waitress. "She was four or five, with long black hair, and white shoes, and she came with a man in that blue truck."

The waitress gazed outside again. "I believe that's Jim Littlefoot's pickup. He ain't got no girl."

"Maybe she's his niece or something."

"Don't expect so, miss. Old Jim, he's kind of a loner."

"Then maybe that's someone else's truck."

The waitress shook her head. "Them bumper stickers? That dent in the tailgate? That's Jim's truck for sure."

Gemma shook her head. "I know what I saw."

"Uh-huh. Would you like some more coffee?"

"I don't . . ." Gemma looked back outside at the empty street.

"Miss?"

"Oh, all right."

As the woman filled her cup, Gemma tried to understand how the little girl could have disappeared so quickly.

The woman asked, "Would you like me to take your plate?"

Gemma turned away from the window and said, "Thanks," doing her best to smile. Something was wrong, but she did not know what it was. She needed time. She had to think. She looked around for something normal, a connection to the earth that could be trusted. The waitress's distended stomach drew her attention, the navel reversed and poking conspicuously through the tightly stretched fabric of her shirt. Gemma said, "When are you due?"

"Any minute now." The woman set the coffeepot down on Gemma's table and placed her palms against the small of her back. "Day before yesterday, actually."

"It's amazing you're still working."

"Got to eat."

"But it must be awfully hard."

"I hear stories about them Mexican pickers down in the Rio Grande valley. They just have their babies in the field and go on working."

"No one could do that."

The woman shrugged. "It's what I hear."

For the first time Gemma noticed how pale she was, not with the naturally light complexion of someone who spent most of her life indoors, but with the tint of pain or illness. "How much time off will you take?"

"A few days if I got to, I guess."

"You have a sitter lined up?"

"No need. I ain't gonna keep it."

Suddenly immersed in the tragedy of a parent giving up a child, Gemma tried to think of something to say. "Oh," was all that came.

The woman picked up the coffeepot and Gemma's empty breakfast plate and walked away. Gemma watched her go. When she disappeared into the kitchen, Gemma turned back toward the window and took another sip of coffee. In her mind's eye she saw that little girl at play, and then running out in front of the white truck. How could the child have disappeared so quickly? She had been in that very spot, right out there in the road, and then Gemma had turned, and then turned back and the girl was gone.

How was that possible? Where was her little yellow bat? Her little red ball?

Gemma felt the room around her shift a little. At first she thought it was a tremor, but of course this was New Mexico, and they didn't have earthquakes in New Mexico, did they? But something had changed. Something was different. Something . . .

With a sudden sense of disorientation, Gemma realized she herself had once played with a yellow bat and a red ball. When was that? She remembered pitching the ball into the air and trying to hit it. She remembered trying over and over again without success but never giving up because she was convinced it was the kind of thing boys did, hitting balls with bats, and if she had been a boy then maybe her father would not have left, and if she could only learn to hit the ball then maybe he would come home. So she stood in the patch of front yard at the house in San Pedro—this was a memory and no fantasy; she was certain of it—the house on a hill above the cranes and mountainous piles of shipping containers that was Los Angeles Harbor, swinging at the ball and missing, hitting only air for hours, until finally the bat connected and the ball went soaring bloody red against an azure California sky. With wonder she had watched it fly. It hit the street and rolled away. She made no effort to follow. She was too excited. Surely now her father would come home.

She ran inside to tell her mother, but her mother was talking on the telephone and would not listen. Then she remembered the red ball in the street and went outside again to find it, but they lived on a hillside, and the ball had not stopped rolling.

"Anything else?"

It was the waitress, back again with the bill.

"No, thanks," said Gemma. She remembered she had been wearing a pretty sundress on that day, the day she realized her father would never come to find her. She had been wearing a sundress and white sandals.

The woman bent to put the piece of paper on the table, and in bending, nearly fell. She gripped the edge of the tabletop with both hands. "Mercy," she said.

"Why don't you sit down a minute?"

"Thanks." The woman lowered herself onto the booth seat opposite Gemma. Her stomach barely fit.

"You shouldn't be working."

"I know it. But my landlady, she don't care."

"What about the father?"

"Him." The woman bowed her head. "He left town the second he found out."

Gemma stared across the table at the part in the waitress's hair. "I'm sorry."

The woman started to stand up.

"Stay awhile," said Gemma. "There's nobody else here."

"You don't mind?"

"I could use the company."

The woman sighed and settled back. "Where you from?"

"Los Angeles."

"Really? California?"

"That's right."

"I figured it was somewhere like that. You're so beautiful and well-dressed and all."

Gemma didn't understand the connection, but said, "Thank you," all the same.

"We was gonna move to California, me and Donnie. Until this." The woman laid a palm on her massive belly.

"Boy or girl?"

"It's a boy, God help me."

Gemma smiled. "You don't care for boys?"

"Boys is heartbreakers. I nearly killed myself when Donnie left."

"Not really?"

"Uh-huh. I was gonna do it with aspirin or something."

"Will that work? Aspirin?"

She looked up. "You don't think so?"

"I don't know. I just . . . I'm glad you didn't do it."

"Well, I almost did."

"What stopped you?"

The woman rubbed her stomach. "It wasn't just me anymore."

"But you said you're going to give away your baby."

"Oh, I say things . . . but I really was gonna do it before this baby started kicking. After that I couldn't. So I'm living for him now, but what if he turns out like Donnie? I couldn't stand that. I think about it all the time. If he turns out that way, I won't have anybody left. Then what's the use?"

Gemma frowned. "Couldn't you live just for yourself?"

"Is that what you do? Live just for yourself?"

"When you say it that way it sounds kind of selfish."

"I don't know about selfish." Pushing on the table with her palms, the woman struggled to her feet. "But it does sound awful lonely."

The woman walked away, and Gemma returned her attention to the street outside the window. The shiny white truck remained parked beside the two old pickups in front of the Laundromat, but the little girl with her bat and ball had returned to a small yard above the cranes and containers of San Pedro, where she belonged.

After months of chasing paintings, and a week of searching desert towns, it was time to go, time to give up on her father once and for all.

Gemma's hand trembled as she took a sip of lukewarm coffee. She put the cup down on the table and clasped her fingers together tightly. She must not allow the tremors of her dying dreams to find expression in the real world. She willed the passing to remain within her mind, or her heart, or whatever one called the place where she had shaped and molded a father out of fairy tales. If she could restrict his vanishing to her interior, then she might be able to survive it. To the outside world she could still be Sheridan Ridler's daughter, even if the artist idolized by all the world had never been—and now would never be—her real father. No one else would know about his passing in her heart, not if she could keep the evidence inside, and if no part of his passing found its way into the real world, then she would have no real thing to mourn.

Gemma did not fear the death of fantasies. Only earthly

evidence could do actual damage, the canvases in her mother's living room and in Henry Blum's library, and these shaking hands before her. That was what she told herself, in hopes she would one day believe it.

Leaving money on the table, Gemma stood to go. She walked through haze and hollowness and distance. If her father was not inside her heart, it seemed neither was she. All her years of foolish supplication . . . who was she to live for now?

"Have a good day," said the pregnant waitress.

"You too," Gemma replied, pretending it was possible.

She pushed open a glass door and stepped into the vestibule. Two paces from the outside doors the sadness swelled again. She made a desperate attempt to find some kind of grounding, something to hold her down. She forced herself to think of the mundane. She glanced right at the gumball machine, and then left, at the picture on the wall. She had expected an old print, something bought ready-framed at a discount store. But the painting was an abstract swirl, a cloud of colors, which somehow seemed collectively to become a perfect, blinding light. The sight of it transfixed her. She immediately lost everything. No part of her remained. It was as if the ground and sky and very air had all been sucked away to leave her alone and drifting in a vacuum. The light . . . the light, the dazzling and perfect light surrounded and absorbed her. It lifted her and pressed her down and filled her up and emptied her and removed all sense of her and yet fulfilled the "her" that she had always longed to be.

She returned into the world among an avalanche of gumballs. The machine had toppled alongside her, the glass front broken, a galaxy of multicolored planets orbiting around her on the floor. Lying there she gazed up at the image, begging. Let the light remain. Oh, God, let it stay. She still felt it just a little. She felt it going as she herself returned, she, coming in and pushing out the Other, but not because it was what she desired. No, she was willing—more than willing, desperate—to never be herself again if that was what it took to stay within that perfect light. "Please," she whispered, writhing in an agony of separation. "Please."

"You okay?" came the waitress's question as she opened the inside vestibule door. "What happened?"

An impossible question.

The painting melted there above her, as if a gentle rain had come to wash the colors down, and then she realized it was just her eyes, welling as they were, which caused the downward motion. She used a palm she had forgotten she possessed to wipe her eyes, and then the painting was restored. "I'm fine," she said.

Careful of tripping on the gumballs, the waitress stepped closer. "I told Kelly she oughta replace them floor mats in here. I told her and I told her. I said, 'Somebody's gonna fall one of these days, and then where will you be?' But she don't listen to nobody, Kelly don't."

"I'm fine," said Gemma again, still staring up at the painting.

"Lemme help you up."

"No, you might hurt yourself. Just give me a minute."

"Sure. I'm awful sorry."

"That painting."

The waitress looked at it. "Yeah?"

"Where did it come from?"

"Some guy gave it to Kelly. She's the owner. She swapped this fella a bunch of eggs and bacon for it. He didn't have no cash. Didn't even have enough gas to make it to Carlsbad for his groceries."

"When was this?"

"Let's see. Maybe a week ago? No, wait. It was the day before yesterday."

Gemma got to her feet. "Do you know where he went from here?"

"I guess prob'ly he's out there north of town, with that Mexican circus comes through every now and then. That's who he said he wanted the eggs and bacon for."

Without a word in parting, Gemma was outside and almost to her rental car before she realized her mistake. Returning to the diner, she opened the front door and peered into the vestibule, where the waitress remained standing at the center of the galaxy of gumballs. It crossed Gemma's mind to ask how anyone could stand so close to the painting without disappearing, but when she spoke a different set of words emerged instead. "I'm sorry to bother you again," she said. "But could you tell me which way is north?"

16.

Emil Lacuna's eyes snapped open. He had not been dreaming—he never dreamed—but he felt disoriented. He stared through the windshield at a corrugated metal wall just ahead, an alternating vertical pattern of deep purple shadows and powdery green. It reminded him of something . . . oh yeah, the wallpaper background in *Nude 14*, one of the first ones he bought from Talbot Graves. Lacuna tried to work things in his mind, adding the woman from the painting to the scene in front of him, laying her across the hood in front of the stripes, little breasts and big hips, face smudged out so you couldn't tell if she was happy or whatever. Sheridan Ridler always smudged the faces or turned them away. It was one of the things Lacuna liked about his art. It made it easier for Lacuna to imagine things about the models in real life, like they were real people he could get to know. In his mind he put the woman against the wall, seeing the painting there, but then he woke up a little more and it was too hard to keep holding her in his head. Anyway, he had work to do.

He blinked and looked around. Glancing in the mirror, he saw the woman's car was gone. He twisted to look back through the rear window. Yeah, definitely gone.

What an idiot he was, going to sleep. There was a time he never would have done it, not in a million years. He must be getting old.

Lacuna opened the door and stepped out onto the gravel and crossed the street, heading for the diner, thinking maybe someone in there could tell him where she went, or at least which direction she drove off in.

A bad feeling came as he walked closer. The place looked empty. He reached the door and tried it. Locked. A little sign said they served breakfast and lunch and closed at two o'clock. Man. How long had he slept? He checked his wristwatch. Could that be right? Nearly three in the afternoon? He must have sat over there sleeping for, what, five or six hours? It didn't seem possible, but looking at the sun, yeah, it probably was.

He was lucky the cops hadn't rousted him for vagrancy. Of course, it helped that he was sitting in a new white Escalade. People didn't usually associate a ride like that with vagrants. Then again, it was a stolen vehicle, a week ago in El Paso, so that was also an issue. A black man sleeping in a stolen Escalade in broad daylight in a hick town like that. Man, he must be losing it. Maybe he should go home. But no, he had his investment to protect. If Talbot Graves was right, if the painter really was alive, it could cost him millions.

Lacuna glanced through the diner door one last time. A painting on the wall inside caught his eye. Like a kid at a candy store, he pressed his nose up against the glass. The painting didn't look like anything he had ever seen, but something about it was familiar. Standing there, all of a sudden he had the same feeling he always got when he looked at Ridler's art. The only feeling he ever got.

Yeah, it had to be.

Imagine something like that hanging on the wall in a place like this. Probably worth more than the whole town. It made Lacuna feel better about himself, his instincts. He had been right to believe Graves, and it justified following the girl all the way down there, clear across the desert, one hick town to another, doing his best to stay out of sight while she went around asking everybody questions.

It also changed his opinion of the girl, just a little. After following her for so long, Lacuna had begun to think she might be stupid. Certainly she had no street smarts whatsoever. These tiny towns and wide-open highways with hardly any traffic, how could she not notice him? But here was a Ridler where it shouldn't be, where no one would think to look for it in a million years, and she had obviously found it, so maybe she wasn't so stupid after all.

After a last look at the painting, he turned around and crossed the street and got back into the white Escalade, which he had been lucky to find in El Paso that first night. Stealing it had been an extra risk, and it kind of called attention to itself in those little towns, but he had a thing for Escalades. Sometimes you just went with what seemed right. Besides, if he was going to start falling asleep in broad daylight his ride would be the least of his problems. His real problem was he hadn't been sleeping very well at night, not since the day on the boat when he decided he had to deal with this Ridler possibility, make sure his collection kept its value.

It was dangerous to be so tired all the time. In fact, just that morning he had overslept, woke up, and looked out onto the motor inn parking lot and the girl's little rental car was already gone. He had to throw on a shirt and some slacks without ironing them, grab his bag, and go. Didn't even have a chance to brush his teeth. He had to race all over that little town looking for her car, hoping she was still around. So then what did he do? He found her and went to sleep again. That was twice in one day he lost her due to sleeping on the job. Man. What was going on?

He wasn't worried about anything. That wasn't what kept him up at night. He never worried. He just lay there with his eyes closed, trying to sleep. It was like his mind was this big black space, silent and empty. He could have slept if it wasn't so quiet in his head, or if there were some kind of pictures in it. He was used to noise and action, like being on the boat, the rocking and the passing vessels blowing horns and whatnot, plus the city right there by the marina, all the traffic. Or like sleeping on a bench at Central Park. He took naps there now and then, sitting up like some old guy dozing off while feeding pigeons, kids screaming, people talking, horns and sirens in the distance. It was nice to wake up in the sunshine, look around, see everything going on and be right there in the middle of it without a worry in the world. Maybe a few worries would do him good, give him something to think about instead of lying in bed with nothing but that silence in his head. But how did you worry when you had no idea how to be afraid?

Lacuna started the engine and backed straight up, right across the Laundromat parking lot and the street and the diner parking lot, until the Escalade's rear bumper was about three feet away from the diner's front door. Leaving the engine running and the driver's side door open, he got out and walked back with the gun in his hand, the revolver he had picked up from a guy in El Paso, it being so much trouble to fly with a firearm.

The little bell inside the Escalade tinged while he stood with his back to the diner door, glancing up and down the street. Nobody was watching. He swung the handgun back as hard as he could. A spiderweb of cracks spread across the door, but the glass must have been tempered because it did not fall. He raised his knee and kicked back several times. Finally the glass fell inside the vestibule. Turning, he knocked out a last jagged piece that stubbornly remained within the aluminum doorframe. He bent down and slipped below the door's metal push bar. Inside the vestibule, he lifted the painting off the wall. Twenty seconds later he was rolling down the street in the Escalade, with the painting beside him on the passenger seat.

He passed the motor inn and saw the woman's car was there, so that was good. At least she hadn't left town. He parked half a block away because he figured even this ignorant woman he was following would figure it out eventually if she kept seeing the same new Cadillac at every motel. He really ought to think about using a different kind of vehicle sometimes. His Escalade habit was a lot of trouble.

When Lacuna checked back into the motel, the old man behind the counter didn't seem to remember him, or else he wasn't curious one way or the other. Back at the Escalade, he slipped out of his sport coat—a Ralph Lauren Black Label jacket he had picked up at Neiman's—and he wrapped it around the painting. It only took a couple of minutes to reach the door of his room. He stood there a few seconds, looking around. He heard a couple of crows, but no sirens, nobody rushing across town to the scene of the crime. Probably nobody would notice the broken door until they came to open the diner in the morning. Probably they didn't have any cops, a little place like Loving, New Mexico. Probably they called in the sheriff's guys when there was a problem.

Inside the room he draped his jacket over a chair back and propped the painting up on top of the dresser, beside the television set. The place stank of cleaning chemicals. He opened the only window, but he didn't want to pull the drapes back and sit there like a fish in a bowl, so the open window didn't do much about the smell.

He sat on the foot of the bed and stared at the painting. It seemed familiar—the energy and boldness of the brushstrokes, the confidence in the color choices—but now that he had time to really look the image over, he wasn't sure it was a Ridler after all. The subject matter was completely different. It didn't seem to be anything; that was the problem. Everything else he'd seen by Sheridan

Ridler was representational. That was a word he'd picked up in a gallery or a magazine or somewhere. It meant Ridler painted items you could recognize. Mostly naked women, although some of his very early stuff had other subjects. But this painting from the diner on the other hand, it was just a whirlpool of colors, everything all run together.

Then, for a second he thought he did see an image, or not an image exactly, more a sense of an image coming together in the painting. He stared a little harder, concentrating, but just when it started to stand out from those swirling shapes and colors, the thing faded back again, leaving Lacuna with the kind of feeling he got when a familiar memory wouldn't come, like forgetting someone's name when he knew them pretty well, or trying to recall the name of a street in his neighborhood.

He hated that feeling, not being in control of his own mind. He had to identify the thing behind the chaos in the painting. He blinked. He tried looking away a moment, then looking back. It wouldn't come.

Maybe he needed a break.

Emil Lacuna rose and pushed the drapes aside, peering out at the motor inn parking lot. The sun was going down. The woman's car was still in front of her room. He let the drapes fall into place and returned to the bed. He kicked off his loafers and plumped up a couple of pillows and sat with his back against the headboard. He thought about what Talbot Graves had told him, about receiving a Ridler in the mail. A new Ridler. It had not crossed Lacuna's mind that Graves might be mistaken. If an authority like that said he got a new Ridler, then it made sense to believe him. But what if the old man had been wrong? What if Ridler's daughter was also wrong? What if she came all the way out here to the desert looking for her father and all she found was a forger?

Lacuna didn't want to kill a forger. He thought of putting the re-volver to his own chest unnecessarily. He didn't have a death wish. He never liked to take a chance on justice unless it was required. So he returned his attention to the painting. It was important to decide if it was real.

This time he tried to do more than simply stare at it. He tried to stare into its past, to see it as a thing growing in time, to imagine the glistening paint on sable bristles slipping across canvas. He tried to visualize the hand holding that brush, and then the arm, the shoul-ders, the face, the man who had created all the masterpieces on his boat. He stared, and stared, and sure enough he sensed something, a memory from out of nowhere, but not what he expected.

He remembered heading downtown with some guys from his old neighborhood. Who were they? He couldn't remember their faces, but that didn't matter. He didn't remember any faces from back then. In fact, it was unusual that he even saw himself stand-ing on the subway, sixteen, maybe seventeen years old, a tough kid looking cool with his hand resting on a steel bar overhead, rocking with the motion of the train and staring down the front of some white woman's dress. He remembered how she wasn't wearing a bra, some hippie chick, and he could see it all, and he stood there looking down and she didn't notice and he didn't feel a thing. He remembered being curious about not feeling anything, knowing it was different for his friends and wondering why. He remembered her standing up at a stop and saying, "Excuse me, please," being especially nice to him, the black kid, and him stepping back to let her pass, her and the man with her, a guy with a long ponytail, and then he followed them, his friends behind him griping, "What you doin', fool? This ain't the stop."

"Y'all go on," he said. "I got to check on something."

The man and woman climbed a set of stairs and emerged onto

a street, maybe somewhere near Times Square because they must have passed a dozen hookers in the two blocks he followed them to the movies, and Times Square was full of hookers back then.

They went inside the theater. He stopped at the ticket booth. "Gimme one," he said.

"Which show?" asked the gum-chewing girl beyond the glass.

"Same as them last two people."

"Five-fifty."

Inside the doors some Puerto Rican kid in a red jacket took his ticket, tore it in two and gave him back half. Lacuna said, "Which one is it for?"

"What?" The guy looked at him through horn-rim glasses, like Buddy Holly wasn't dead.

"Which show is this ticket for?"

"Why would you buy a ticket if you don't know what it's for?" Saying "you" like "jew," the way they did.

"Answer the question, fool."

"It's *Silver Streak*. That one over there." He pointed to a pair of doors on the other side of the lobby. Lacuna crossed the carpet and went in.

It took a minute to get his eyes right, coming into the darkness, then he started down the aisle, looking around. The theater was pretty full. He saw them, about halfway down in the center. "Look out," he said to the old guy sitting in the first chair on that row. The old guy tried to pull his knees back as Lacuna passed, stepping on his feet.

He took the seat next to the woman. She smelled like reefer, and sure enough, the guy with the ponytail passed her a roach. She took a hit and passed it back. Right then they started showing commercials on the screen. She hardly even glanced his way.

The thing about movies was, he never understood them. He

followed the action all right, and he usually knew why the actors were doing what they were doing, but he couldn't figure out why anybody cared to watch that nonsense. For example, the *Silver Streak* movie was supposed to be funny. He knew that because it had those guys, the Jew with the bad hair and that brother, Richard Pryor. Those guys were supposed to be comedians, so he knew it was a comedy. That, and the fact that everybody laughed a lot. The girl especially. He tried to understand it, what was so funny, but it made no sense to him, those guys climbing around on a train, stealing cop cars. Even when they were just talking, which was when the audience laughed the most, he still didn't get it.

After a while he ignored the movie. He watched the woman instead, sitting there beside her, looking at her from a foot away. She never even noticed him staring. She laughed almost the whole time. She had an ugly laugh, high and squeaky. It got on his nerves after a while. Finally he leaned close to her ear and said, "Hey."

She looked at him, surprised.

"Shut your mouth," he said.

Her eyes went wide for just a second, then she turned toward the movie screen. For the rest of the show, she just sat there, no more laughing. That was something he wanted to understand, that look in her eyes. He felt unsatisfied.

At the end the Jew kissed the girl and the brother drove away and the lights came on and the hippie chick and the guy with the ponytail got up to go. He followed them outside. He wanted to see that look again, get a sense of satisfaction, know he understood what she was feeling, something that made sense.

On the sidewalk, he caught up with them. He noticed the man was much bigger than he was, maybe six inches taller and forty pounds heavier. He didn't care. He walked up right behind them and said, "Hey, man."

The guy turned and Lacuna caught him in the throat with one quick punch, very hard.

He was ready to follow up, but the guy fell back against a wall, gasping for air the way they usually did. "Jimmy?" said the woman. Stupid woman. "Jimmy?"

The guy slipped down the wall until he was sitting on the sidewalk with his legs sticking straight out and his hands clutching at his neck, turning kind of purple. The woman started screaming.

"Hey," said Lacuna. "Shut up."

She just screamed louder.

He laid hands on her, spun her around, pushed her back against the wall beside the guy on the sidewalk and covered her mouth with his palm. "Shut up or I'll hurt you even more."

That was when her eyes went wide again. He could feel her body go stiff. He lowered his palm from her mouth. She didn't scream. She just stood there, staring at him. He put his hands on each side of her face, holding it, aiming it at his face. He moved very close, maybe six inches away. He stared into her eyes. He tried to absorb it, the terror inside her. It made perfect sense to him. She was right to be afraid. It was logical. But how did it feel? He tried to drink it in, to get a sense of it. Pressing against her cheeks with his palms, squeezing fear out of her like toothpaste from a tube, he said, "What does that feel like? Tell me what it's like and I'll let you go."

The woman couldn't speak, or wouldn't speak, either way it was the same.

"Tell me!" he said again.

"I don't know what you want," she said.

He thought maybe he'd use his knife, get it out of her that way, but then the guy down on the sidewalk punched him in the crotch. The pain doubled him over. It was a surprise.

"Run!" said the guy on the ground, his voice kind of wheezy.

The woman took off screaming toward the movie theater. There was no way he could follow her, not right then. He just stood there, bent over with his hands between his legs, waiting for the pain to pass and staring down at the guy on the sidewalk. The guy seemed to feel better. He had to work at it, but he managed to get to his feet. Lacuna tried to walk away, but it just hurt too much. The guy came over—man, he was big—and he slammed a fist into Lacuna's nose. Two more punches and Lacuna was on the sidewalk. The guy started kicking him then, and after that, there was only pain, which was something else that made perfect sense.

Sitting on the bed in the Loving, New Mexico, motor inn, Emil Lacuna stared at the painting and tried to figure out why that particular memory had come to him just then. He didn't often think about the past. He didn't remember much about his youth, and his early childhood was a total blank. In fact, he probably hadn't thought about that pounding outside the theater for twenty years. So why now? What was it about the painting that had brought it back?

He thought about the look in the hippie woman's eyes, one of the only times he had almost understood what someone else was feeling. He stared at the painting. Yes. Something was in there. Maybe he would get it if he just kept staring.

17.

Wrapped in a robe as black as outer space and sparkling with stars, Esperanza sank onto the folding lawn chair beside Ridler. In spite of her age, she did not touch the arms as she descended. "Here is something," she said, looking up.

Following the old woman's gaze, Ridler saw a million diamonds glittering above them in the velvet blackness, and a trillion more besides within the powder of the Milky Way. Considering that inconceivably vast helix, he said, "Yes."

"Thank you for the eggs and bacon."

He shrugged in the flickering light of the campfire at their feet. "It was nothing."

"Not so," said she. "I myself have eaten seven hundred and fifty-three tortillas in a row, interspaced only by rice. Compared to such a menu, eggs and bacon are definitely something."

Ridler remained silent, knowing what she wanted.

"Still," she said, "in this situation even the welcome sacrifice of hens and pigs cannot compare to offerings of citrus."

The aluminum tubes and fabric straps beneath him moaned as he shifted position.

"Scurvy is regrettable," she continued. "A disease best left to ancient sailors, don't you agree?"

"I suppose."

"It bends the bones and rots the gums."

He sighed.

"Here is an old wound." Turning toward the woman with reluctance, Ridler saw a pale forearm extended from the starry sky surrounding her. On her wrist a deep gash glistened with fresh blood. "For now let us say it is a saber cut," she said, "which I sustained alongside Villa in the attack on Ciudad Juárez."

"That was a hundred years ago."

"Approximately."

Ridler sighed again, and again he shifted his position to the accompaniment of metallic moans.

She continued. "It is the scurvy, you see, which reopens these old wounds."

"I've heard it can do that."

"Indeed? Then you must know the solution."

"Oranges. Grapefruit."

"Lemons," she said, nodding. "Limes."

"Such things cost money."

"Which I do not have."

"Because you keep us out here in the desert."

Ridler felt her eyes upon him, but he refused to respond. Leaning forward with a stick he stirred the fire. Rising sparks combined with diamonds overhead, yellow points of light among the white.

"It is difficult to believe," said the old woman, "that you are completely ignorant of the reason for my actions since the moment we met."

"Sometimes I do wonder."

"In that case, let us travel back in memory together."

"No, thank you. I have had enough of the past."

"In what sense? Do you mean to say you understand the present?"

Ridler laughed. "It is futile to refuse you."

"Unwise, perhaps."

"Very well," he said. "What do you want, exactly?"

"Only what you wish to give."

"I can't paint for money."

"But can you paint for us?" The old woman waved a hand toward the caravans and trailers parked around them. "For them? For me?"

"Not until I finish what was started."

"In that case, we await your next step on the journey."

"Good luck with that. I have no idea where to go from here."

"To know where you are going, you must know how you arrived."

"Oh, I know how I got here. It's only the beginning I've forgotten."

"It might improve your memory if you spoke about your quest."

"Back to that again?" Ridler sighed a third time. "All right. Where shall I begin?"

"It is your history. I leave such things to you."

So it was that, sitting in a folding chair beside a rusting trailer in the desert of Chihuahua, the artist spoke of desperation, and as he did a diamond streaked across the velvet canopy above, a reminder of his status as a plaything, the punch line in a cosmic joke, his genius merely mud among the Roman gutters.

The Harlem River had ensnared him with a hopeless commission, but the Vatican had destroyed him, stripping him of faith in his own talent, revealing his ineptitude before the vastness of his model. A kinder god might have remained aloof. It might have let him live his final years within the delusion that he could not paint his subject because it was not really there. But the Glory had no mercy. It had revealed its own reality with nonchalant disdain, appearing in the random rearrangement of his colors in the drizzle, like finger paint smeared by the impish hand of Fate.

Ridler had descended into grave depression, lying in his narrow bed for hours, listening to water from the Tiber flow through ancient channels in the stone beside his ear, watching shadows trace the passage of the days across the stucco wall, pondering a life without his quest. Surely art could not survive the death of confidence.

Still, as a dying man continues breathing out of habit to the last, he continued painting. The product of his brush had no relation to his will. He tried a still life, arranging pears within a bowl, only to watch as if from a great distance while the same anemic memory of Glory formed before him on the canvas. He tried *en plein air* painting of the street outside his door, but his muscles overruled his mind and sketched that same half-remembered swirling vision once again. He even considered a self-portrait, but just as he could not overcome his dread of faces, so he could not stop himself from painting the pitifully inadequate image which had long obsessed him.

When lethargy restrained him from the effort necessary to obtain a new canvas, he began again on those he had already painted, adding brushstroke over identical brushstroke, image over image, Glory over Glory in a hollow liturgy of paint and palette until the pigment on the surface reached an unsupportable thickness, the painting almost a cube as deep as it was wide and tall, and the wooden easel cracked and failed and all went crashing to the earth.

Devastating though this was, to his very great surprise the source of sorrow foremost in his mind was not the loss of art. It was instead his distance from his model. Somehow his desire to master what he had encountered in the river had become a longing for the Glory, pure and simple. Half his lifetime had been squandered by the thought that he would one day capture it on canvas. With that quest unmasked at last as hopeless vanity, he looked into the future and saw, not a world without the Glory, but the true alternative, which was nothing but himself.

Days passed. Weeks and months of inactivity in his Roman apartment. He ate only occasionally, always alone in a café across the narrow Via Margutta, not thirty steps away from bed. He slept more hours than he lived awake. His beard grew to his chest. His hair became a hopeless tangle. He stank from the sweat of torment and the negligent hygiene of solitude. His ears rang with the aftermath of old explosions.

Then one night at the café, while feeding carelessly on *tonnarelli,* he heard half a dozen tourists speaking English. He had not listened to the language since he stood among the crowd of tourists at the Vatican disaster. It reminded him of Suzanna, the hope of happiness, whom he had surrendered far too easily. Although her memory oppressed him, his ear could not resist eavesdropping. In that way he learned about the Shroud of Turin, which Cardinal Saldarini had recently exposed to public view for the first time in twenty years.

Ridler spent a sleepless night upon his narrow bed, overwhelmed by his stupidity. Having seen transcendence draw itself in pastels and rain, how could he have failed to guess there might be other such self-portraits in the world? To witness that figure seared into a burial cloth, the blinding consequence of resurrection, to stand before an image of the Glory rendered by the Glory . . . the possibility alone awoke him from his desperation.

Early the next morning he arose to go. For six and a half hours he drove a rented Fiat nonstop north from Rome, rising toward the Italian Alps and Turin. He passed into that great center of industry with no idea how to reach the chapel of the holy shroud.

Reasoning first that it would be in the oldest part of town, and second that the old quarter would be somewhere on the Po, he fought rush hour traffic farther north along the western riverbank. As the sun began to set beyond the looming peaks outside the city he entered a neighborhood of narrow streets and baroque facades. There he saw the first sign, *Santa Sindone*, the Holy Shroud.

Following the arrows, he saw another sign, and then another, and at last he found a parking lot established just for pilgrims who were driving there from all over Europe to witness the miracle. He paid five thousand lire for a space and received a ticket which would grant him entrance to the chapel the following day. At a nearby takeaway restaurant he bought two pieces of grilled chicken, a small loaf of bread, a wedge of cheese and a bottle of Levissima mineral water. Returning to the Fiat he ate some of the food, adjusted the seat back to recline as far as it would go, crossed his arms over his chest and fell asleep.

The next morning after a short bus ride from the parking lot to the Piazzetta Reale, disheveled and unwashed, he joined a queue at least as lengthy as the one which had led him into the Vatican Museum. Vague misgivings came from that comparison. Ridler tried to keep his spirits up by whistling tunelessly. His windy notes echoed from the lofty vaults of the palace portico which formed the first portion of the queue. An elderly woman in the line ahead turned back to stare at him. Only then did Ridler notice the strange silence of the pilgrims as they stepped out from the portico into the royal gardens behind the Cathedral of Turin.

Beneath ancient trees and beside lovely hedges they passed along a gravel walkway through the open air. They reached a sidewalk sheltered by a canopy of white fabric. Winding along below the canopy they passed three life-size photographs, Ridler's first sight of the shroud. His misgivings grew.

Finally he entered the cathedral through the door on the left side. Three choices lay before him, each leading to a viewing area on a different level. Ridler chose the uppermost. Fifteen steps, and there it was, the shroud on which he hoped to view the Glory rendered by the Glory in a radiant burst of resurrection.

It hovered in the darkened space before the altar, the figure horizontal, the front view on the left, the rear view on the right. Even from Ridler's vantage point, which was very close, all was vague and indistinct: a hint of bearded face, of shoulders, arms, of hands clasped modestly above the groin, a darker place upon the wrist, another at the side and at the feet.

This was not the Glory. Yet unlike his reaction to the effervescent lies told on the Sistine Chapel ceiling, while gazing at the shroud he felt no outrage. In Rome he had found nothing but Renaissance trickery. In this brooding face he sensed the work not of a charlatan, but of a fellow witness. There was true power in the image, inspiration for uncounted icons, for Georges Rouault, for Gauguin's *Yellow Christ,* for the deco *Redeemer* with open arms above Rio de Janeiro's slums. For all its forcefulness, however, nothing in it was beyond Ridler. Given a few hours, he could match it—better it in fact—with artistic power of his own.

Ridler felt his shoulders slump as desperation's weight returned. He left Turin Cathedral in contemplative silence, stricken by the similarity between the shroud and his own mind. There might have been a moment countless years before when the cloth had pressed against the Glory, but if so, nothing had been captured. Nothing was remembered. It was only an aftereffect, as Ridler was himself.

He wandered without thinking, and arrived on the cobbled sidewalk which separated the exterior cathedral steps from the passing cars on Via XX Settembre.

"My son, are you troubled?"

Looking up from the stones beneath his feet, Ridler found a young man, barely half his age, facing him in a black cassock and clerical collar. On the man's face was a frank expression of concern.

"Have you eaten?" asked the priest. "Do you have a place to sleep?"

Surprised, Ridler said, "Of course."

"My apologies. It is just that I saw you, the way you are dressed, the condition of your . . . well, no matter. I only thought perhaps I could be of assistance."

Ridler's hands went to his matted hair. Patting it down, he said, "I'm sorry."

"There is no shame in poverty, my son. Our Lord himself had no place to lay his head."

"I'm not homeless," replied Ridler. "I'm just . . . I . . ." He stopped, realizing he had no words for what he was.

"Come." The young priest extended a hand toward the cathedral. "Let us have a meal together, my son."

My son.

Ridler's father had died many years before, having never once admitted that his youngest child had talent. Ridler had not gone to the funeral. Long before he had decided he would never again paint for anyone's approval. He would be nobody's son. But he followed the priest around the building anyway, through a small opening in a courtyard wall which was guarded by a gate with iron bars, along a narrow gravel path and up some steps to a carved wooden door. Inside a building behind the cathedral they entered a small kitchen where the priest said, "Please. Sit and let me serve you."

Ridler settled onto a wooden chair beside a long pine table and watched as the man opened a refrigerator and a cupboard, removing bread, cheese, salami, lettuce, peppers, tomatoes, and onions.

With practiced movements he prepared two sandwiches. After placing one before Ridler and the other at a place across the table, he brought two glasses and a bottle of water.

Sitting down, he said, "Let us pray."

Ridler watched the top of the man's head while he spoke the words. When his blessing was concluded the priest began to eat. Soon they were both finished with the meal.

"Now, my son," said the priest, fixing him with a direct stare. "If it is permitted, may I ask how you came to be here?"

"Excuse me, but do you have to call me your son?" asked Ridler. "I'm at least twice as old as you are."

"My apologies, sir. It has become a habit."

"You don't have to apologize. You've been very nice. It's just . . . I'm feeling a little useless at the moment, and it doesn't help to have a kid like you calling me your son."

"Maybe if you told me your name . . ."

He thought of it upon Suzanna's lips. Sheridan was too stuffy, Sheri was a girl's name, and Dan just didn't fit. "You can call me Danny."

The priest half stood and bent over the table between them, extending his hand. "It is my pleasure to meet you, Danny. I am Luigi." Ridler shook his hand, and the priest sat back down. "You are American, I think, but your Italian is very good. Have you been long in Italy?"

"Several years."

"What did you come here to find?"

"What makes you think I came to find something?"

Luigi shrugged in the exaggerated way of all Italian men. "You stood in front of the cathedral, having just witnessed the holy shroud, yes?" Ridler nodded, and the priest continued. "You stood there, having seen that, and you could only stare down at your feet. This, it seems to me, is the posture of disappointment, and disappointment implies a dream unfulfilled. Am I wrong?"

"No," said Ridler. "You're not wrong."

"In that case, if you would like to talk about it—what is that American expression?—I am completely ears."

For the first time in many months Ridler smiled, and having smiled, he found it possible to speak of failure.

The priest said nothing as he listened very closely, nodding often, making noises of assent from time to time to show he understood. When all had been recounted, from Harlem to the Catskills, to Thailand, Istanbul, Tel Aviv, and Rome, Luigi said, "Having learned no man can paint this Glory, as you call it, you still try?"

"It's my hands. No matter what I tell them to do, they can't seem to paint anything else."

"And having sacrificed your creativity in this fruitless quest, you still long to see it?"

"With all my heart."

"In that case, I will help you."

Ridler leaned forward and asked, "How, Father?"

Smiling, perhaps at Ridler's unconscious use of the priestly appellation, Luigi spoke of the *acheiropoieta*, the icons not made by hand, which exist throughout the earth. "The shroud of course is the foremost," he said, "but Divinity unveils itself in many others." He spoke of the *Mandylion*, the Image of Edessa, a portrait of the Son revealed miraculously to King Abgar. He spoke of the *Volto Santo di Lucca*, Veronica's Veil, on which the Holy Image had been affixed when that saintly woman dared to wipe the Savior's brow along the Via Dolorosa. He spoke of the *Uronica*, begun by the apostle Luke and impossibly completed by the angels.

Sitting at that wooden table, Ridler was unmanned. He bowed

his head and covered his welling eyes, the joy within him overwhelming. Here was renewed hope. Here was purpose. Here, his quest revived upon the brink of oblivion. "Thank you," he whispered. "Thank you."

That same afternoon he left the city of the shroud and traveled northwest, to La Sainte-Chapelle on the Île de la Cité in Paris, where the Image of Edessa had last been seen in 1792 when seized by revolutionary masses. Filled with a determination equaling the most passionate of pilgrims, Ridler spent weeks among the paperwork of the revolution at the oldest libraries and halls of records. His search for the Glory there was doomed of course, as were his efforts later at the Spanish Monasterio de la Santa Faz, on the outskirts of Alicante, where he hoped to find the fabled Veil of Veronica, but was instead confronted merely by a copy. Undaunted, he traversed the European continent in search of beatific self-portraits, from the famous *Feridas Santamente* in the ancient cathedral in Lisbon, to half a dozen reliquaries in the Balkans, each purported to contain an image given from the heavens. He gazed upon the Russian *Mandylion* at Novlenskoye and another one at Dormition Cathedral in Moscow. In spite of his remaining terror of the red-eyed man, he reentered the Middle East, climbing to the Sacred and Imperial Monastery of the God-Trodden Mount of Sinai, St. Catherine's Monastery, where he was allowed to view the world's most ancient Christ Pantocrator, said to have been sketched in gold and royal purple by the very Finger which had twice inscribed the stone tablets of the ten words on that selfsame mountaintop.

It was there, in conversation with a fellow pilgrim from Latin America, that he first heard the story of Juan Diego's robe. Thus the Guadalupe Virgin returned him at long last to his mother hemisphere.

Following the inscrutably circuitous routes so often imposed on airline travelers, Ridler flew from Cairo to Amsterdam, and thence back down to earth in Mexico City. Even with the assistance of long moving sidewalks it took him thirty minutes to make his way across that endless airport to the nearest taxi stand. There, in spite of his exhaustion, he hired a cab to transport him directly to the Virgin's famed basilica.

The driver shot across the city as if fired by a cannon, darting in and out of traffic with a constant stream of profane comments which Ridler understood in part because of his Italian. The smog and thin air at that altitude oppressed his lungs. Vehicles careened around him madly. Seven times in the first five minutes he believed he was about to die. He closed his eyes and went to sleep.

"Señor, hemos llegado," came the cabdriver's attempt to awaken him. Opening his eyes, he saw they were at a sharp bend in the road, where the furious traffic was forced to slow in order to make the turn. On the inside of the bend stood a small two-story building with red awnings and a large sign that read *Zapatería*. He had no idea what that meant. On the outside of the bend a long concrete ramp rose up beside the cab.

"Where is the basilica?" asked Ridler, speaking English.

"La rampa," replied the driver, pointing toward a set of stairs beside the long and gently climbing ramp.

With all of his possessions in a pack on his back and a valise in each hand, Ridler climbed the stairs and joined a crowd of pilgrims, passing through a set of metal barricades to reach the famous Plaza Mariana. The great expanse of marble pavement swarmed with faithful persons. Many of them waddled toward the basilica upon their knees. Some cried as they crawled. Others shouted prayers in ecstasy, their petitions soaring through an atmosphere allegedly once breathed by God's own mother.

On the far side of the plaza Ridler saw a structure which he first mistook for a sports stadium. The green copper roof rose to form an eccentrically positioned cone, held aloft by hulking concrete columns which crouched beneath it like a tribe of troglodytes huddled round a fire. When he realized it was the Virgin's basilica, the artist in him shuddered. It was no shelter for a woman. On the contrary, the building evoked a churlish masculinity. If not for the many pilgrims who approached it with such obvious devotion, Ridler's only clue to its true function would have been the cross so grudgingly presented to the heavens as if in fulfillment of a distasteful obligation.

After his other failures, Ridler approached the Basilica de Nuestra Señora de Guadalupe with the knowledge that there was nothing left. This was the last of the world's images not made by hand on his list, his final chance to see the Glory's own self-portrait. If asked, he would still have said prayer was pointless, yet as he stepped into the shadows underneath that lofty copper roof, he dared to whisper, "Please."

Within the basilica he stood on the same marble as the plaza just outside. The closed door of a confessional booth beside him bore a paper card, sealed in plastic and printed with the words *Padre Fernando. Confiesa. De jueves a martes. De 12:00 a 14:00 Hrs.* On the raised stage far across the immense space before him stood a tiny figure dressed in white. Spanish words assailed him from loudspeakers. Again, his Italian helped. He understood one phrase, "In the name of the Father, the Son, and the Holy Spirit," and realized that the distant man was praying.

Arrayed across an acre or two before him, ten thousand pilgrims sat on concentrically curved wooden pews, celebrating mass. To his surprise, many other people milled around them, whispering among themselves and ignoring the sacred ritual. He had not expected such chaos. He had expected to find focus, the Virgin at the center, but the view from where he stood included no serenity, no kind of miracle.

Many people waited in a line along one wall. Still wearing his backpack and carrying the two valises, he approached an old woman, the last person in the queue, a farmer's wife perhaps, who had come to the city in a pair of worn huaraches and a clean but threadbare cotton shirt and dress. Ridler gestured toward the line and whispered, *"La Señora?"*

"Yes," replied the elderly woman in Spanish, while holding a sweat-stained straw hat in her hands. "This is where you should be."

Since he was only just beginning to learn the language, Ridler could not be certain of the old woman's meaning, but he replied, *"Gracias,"* and joined the line behind her.

The wall beside them was three stories tall. Following its arc, the queue approached the left end of the stage, or altar as he supposed a Catholic might describe it. As they drew closer, he realized there was an opening below the stage, which the people in the queue ahead of him were entering. Apparently the miracle was kept there, out of sight.

Always when he had approached the other images not made by hands, Ridler felt a vague misgiving, wondering if the thing he was about to see would be yet another disappointment. But this time it was different. This time he imagined it was he who was observed, and he who disappointed. The old woman ahead of him looked neither left, nor right, nor up, nor down, yet as the vague sensation of surveillance arose within him, he suspected it was she who did the watching.

Such a notion was beneath ridicule of course. She was only a poor old woman from the country, piously attending to her faith. He decided to expel the strange mood from his thoughts, but the scene ahead did nothing to relieve him from that growing sense of

the bizarre, for as he approached the side of the great altar he realized those in line before him rode on a moving sidewalk exactly like
the ones he had just used at the airport.

When their moment came, the old woman stepped upon the rubber belt. With the pack still on his back and the bags still in his hands,
Ridler followed her. The moving walkway transported him between
the rear wall of that cavernous space and the back of the tall altar.
Confusion nearly overwhelmed him. In his exhaustion, having traveled directly there from Cairo, he wondered for a moment if this
whole experience existed only in his mind, if the airport and basilica
might be merging in his psyche, might be nothing but a dream.

Everyone stood silently as the mechanism moved them forward. Ahead of Ridler, the old woman's strong and upright back
remained perfectly straight, her head completely level and unmoving like a Swiss Guard at the Vatican, looking neither left nor right.
Following her example, he would have missed the image had it
not been for a young boy on another walkway moving parallel to
theirs. The boy asked a loud question. His mother shushed him and
then pointed up, saying, *"Mira,* Antonio!"

Because of the woman's gesture, Ridler gazed aloft. The wall
beside him stood perhaps one hundred feet tall and curved slightly
inward, clad in brass or gold. He saw gilded blocks protruding from
its surface, and suddenly remembered a blood-and-bruises rhythm
of red and blue, red and blue, flashing on a brick wall in his distant
past, his world colliding with another, earthy and unchanged for
generations outside his New York City hotel window, and police
brutality below, and a mystery within deep shadows on that other
wall, a presence which revealed itself again within the voids and
portals of a burning warehouse, tempting him to cross the Harlem
River in pursuit of something waiting beyond time, something no
one else had painted.

He had traveled for a lifetime to find that presence, only to arrive beside another wall. There was no mystery in the shadows cast by the gilded blocks above him. They merely merged in the most obvious way to form a cross, and above that all the roof beams came together, the space between the beams aglow with small squares of colored glass, and lower down, framed by concentric bands of gold and silver, the Guadalupe Virgin's image wore a hooded turquoise robe over a gown of gold lamé, while rays of light or tongues of flames shot out around her posture of complete composure.

She gazed slightly to her right with hands clasped in the attitude of prayer. As the rubber belt beneath Ridler's feet transported him and his baggage across her field of view, she did not notice him. Her eyes did not follow him. Her expression changed in no way whatsoever. She was merely one more thing he could have painted much more perfectly.

Turning to his neighbors to confirm the fraud, Ridler saw instead their lips moving in prayer, their fingers touching foreheads, breasts and shoulders in the blessed sign. A young woman swooned, supported at the armpits by two men.

"But," protested Ridler. "But . . ."

Their adoration silenced his protests. He was surrounded but untouched by devotion. An overwhelming envy rose within him. He understood the ancient instinct for human sacrifice, the Aztec priests atop their bloody pyramids near that very place, splitting sternums with obsidian and jade, seizing beating human hearts and sinking teeth into the living muscle. If possible, he would have done the same. He would have stolen almost anything, violated anything but art to possess what he saw around him on the moving walkways.

Another half a minute and the ride was over. Thrust alone upon the marble pavement, once again under his own power, the waste was overwhelming. So many miles to see so little.

He allowed the crowd to guide him on around the huge seating area to one of the many pairs of doors which opened onto the plaza. Outside the basilica he paused, set his two valises down by his feet, and stood blinking in the sun, completely unable to decide what to do next.

"You are fortunate."

Shading his eyes, he looked around to find the old woman standing at his elbow. She had donned the straw hat. It cast her face in shadow, but her eyes flashed like starlight from the darkness.

"Are you speaking to me?" he replied.

"If you had come a few years later they would not have let you carry your bags inside."

"Why not?"

"There will be fear of hidden bombs."

Knowing much about the consequence of great explosions, Ridler considered her words for a moment. "In that case, I suppose such a policy will be wise."

"Were you satisfied with that thing on the wall?"

He realized she was crazy, with her talk of bombs and satisfaction. She had ridden on the walkway past the famous Virgin without a glance in its direction. Probably she was no farmer's wife from out of town, but a homeless soul with schizophrenia, or perhaps only an alcoholic. He reached into his pocket, seeking pesos to buy her silence.

"Well?" she said. "Are you satisfied with the famous Virgin, or not?"

Even as his fingers touched the money, he realized she was speaking Spanish, and he understood her every word. Indeed, he had been replying in that same language, which he did not know. He removed his hand from his pocket, empty. "I'm not sure what you mean."

"I came here to find a painter. Are you he?"

"I am an artist."

"Does the image in that place impress you?"

"It is not much of a miracle."

"As an artist, you can do better?"

"Certainly."

She erupted with one short burst of laughter. It flowed across the giant plaza like a ripple from a pebble dropped in water, wavelike, tidal, beautiful and awful, catching pilgrims by surprise and causing moments of disorientation, the way an unexpected scent can bring a fraction of a memory to mind and leave a person wondering what else has been forgotten. It wove the clouds in patterns and choreographed the flight of birds. It buoyed Ridler as an ocean lifts a ship.

"Oh," she said. "You are certainly the one I came to find. I have work for you, if you are interested."

In years to come Ridler would not be able to explain his lack of hesitation. He said, "I am interested."

Without bothering to tell him to follow, she set out across the plaza, the long length of her stride a brusque contradiction to the wrinkles on her face. Unprepared for this abrupt departure, Ridler stood and watched her go for several seconds before awakening enough to bend and lift his bags and set out in pursuit.

Past the barricades they went, out into the giant city. She led him down the long concrete ramp and south along the promenade which parallels the street called de Guadalupe. He followed her between open stalls on either side, metal frames covered by blue plastic tarps, the hawkers shouting, "Votive candles! Relics! Crucifixes! Rosaries of every kind!" Commerce stretched ahead of them as far as he could see, thousands of pilgrims buying photographs of popes, and medal necklaces with likenesses of patron saints, and paintings of the Virgin Mother, and carvings of the Virgin Mother, and plaster casts of the Virgin Mother, and charcoal sketches of the Virgin Mother, and cups and plates and candles and T-shirts, all adorned by the Virgin Mother of Guadalupe, who stood untouched by flames or rays of sunshine.

The scene reminded Ridler of the bazaar in Istanbul, of Muslims swirling round him while he sketched in ignorance of coming hatred. He saw an Indian woman in a brightly colored skirt, her straight black hair restrained by a leather headband, and he thought of tie-dyed hippies in the Catskills and the theologic lethargy of self-appointed gurus. At every stall he observed customers exchanging money for religion, the Catholic reflection of Thai pilgrims paying to put prayers into the clutches of deceitful doves. The ringing which had never ceased since Tel Aviv was almost drowned out by the furious Mexico City traffic behind the stalls on the left, the protest of horns, the bellow of diesels, the popping of impertinent motorcycles, and he thought of holy ground quaking from the rage of Scuds. He saw men and women struggling toward the basilica on their knees with passion glowing in their faces, and he remembered crawling on pavement outside the Vatican, colored chalk in both of his hands, dispensing imitation glory.

It seemed to him these memories had come to speak a message if he could only pause to understand, but the old woman led him in a different direction, between a pair of stalls and away from all religion.

She paused at the curb to wait for a break in the traffic. When it came she dashed across the street as quickly as a girl. Back and arms aching from the weight of his bags, Ridler felt each of his own many years as he followed. Two blocks farther up a side street called Cuauhtémoc, she led him into a bus station. At the ticket window she told the man, "Two, please. One way for Monterrey." She turned to Ridler. "Pay him."

"But why?"

"Because you are the one with money."

He did not question her knowledge of this, but only asked, "I mean, why are we going to Monterrey?"

"Because the work you need to do begins there."

He gave the man the required pesos.

The bus surprised him with its luxury, wide soft seats, televisions, curtains at the windows, and a toilet room in back with a mirror and a lavatory and the scent of pine and lemons. The old woman sat beside him at the window. As the bus pulled away from the station, he said, "How do you know about the bombs?"

"The same way I know you are a painter," she said, and then she looked away from him, out the window, declining further conversation.

Exhausted from the fruitless decades, Ridler slept. He awoke, and it was dark.

She was there, and watching. He slept again.

"What is your name?" he asked her as the sun arose beyond her window.

"It depends," she replied. "What do you need most?"

He thought for a moment. "Hope," he said.

"In that case, I am Esperanza."

"You can't just invent a name for yourself like that."

"Are you sure?"

"You have to be the same person from one moment to the next."

"I am who God wants me to be."

"Which god? There are so many."

"Indeed? In the river did you meet a crowd?"

"How do you know about the river?"

"The same way I know about the bombs."

"Are you some kind of psychic?"

She laughed again, and everyone asleep upon the bus began to smile.

"So many questions," she said. "So little seeking."

In Ciudad Valles they alighted from the bus. It was necessary to wait three hours for another. He bought them both a meal from a street vendor, two "fatties," or *gorditas*, a kind of cornmeal pastry filled with pork which had already been cooked shepherd-style, plus two cans of pear juice. As they ate, he watched her surreptitiously. It was not possible to tell her age.

"Listen," said Ridler when their second bus began moving, "I need to know who you are, and where we're going, and why we're going there."

"This is becoming tiresome. I have already told you who I am. You already know we are traveling to Monterrey. Now I will answer one last question and no more. We go to see the marvel you have sought for many years."

"I've seen enough of these so-called images not made by hands."

"You prefer a different kind of miracle? Perhaps a dwarf? An albino? A woman covered head to toe in fur?"

"Certainly not. I have no interest in freak shows."

"You are in no position to disdain them."

The bus had traveled ten miles and the old woman had lost interest before Ridler could bring himself to whisper, "That's true."

Many hours later at the Monterrey bus station they descended. While they waited by the bus for Ridler's twin valises, a filthy man in rags approached them.

"Was your trip successful?" he asked Esperanza.

"Behold, the newest member of our troupe," she replied, gesturing toward Ridler.

"Him?" The filthy man looked Ridler up and down as if inspecting a horse. "I hope he is less stubborn than your last undertaking."

One of many things Ridler would learn in the years to come was this: the stench of a roustabout's unwashed body could be endured only with open windows. Therefore, he was grateful for the turbulent air within the antique truck as the filthy man drove them deep into the rugged country outside Monterrey. Upon arriving at the winter quarters of Esperanza's circus, among the tents and caravans, Ridler said, "First you promised work; then you said you brought me here to see the marvel I've been looking for. Which is it to be?"

Her eyes went wide as if surprised, and from the disposition of her bones Ridler knew she had recently been very beautiful. "Perhaps I made a mistake," she said. "I thought you were a great artist."

"Indeed, I am."

"And did you not claim you can create an image more perfect than the Guadalupe Virgin?"

"I did. I can."

"Then kindly do not waste my time by pretending to believe that work and marvels are different things."

Years later, outside Ridler's trailer with the campfire dancing at their feet and the velvet space above them glittering with diamonds, Esperanza laughed at that memory. Their long association had prepared Ridler to be engulfed by the euphoric wave unleashed by her merriment. He smiled and settled down into the folding chair more deeply.

"Ah, yes," she said. " 'Faith without deeds is dead.' "

"So said the apostle James," replied the artist, for she had taught him well.

"He did indeed. And speaking of deeds and marvels, do you think your apologies are working?"

"I only send the paintings. I don't know how they are received."

"You could contact the ones you have offended."

He looked into the fire. "I need to remain dead."

She waved a bony hand between them. "Don't speak to me of death. You know no more about the word than a fish knows of air. With only one exception you have always been alive, unfortunately."

"Unfortunately? Exception? What do you mean?"

"One day I hope you will find out. In the meantime, they will surely know you are alive, having received the paintings."

"There are other explanations. They cannot know for sure."

"You traded a painting for the eggs and bacon to feed us. I had hoped it was a start."

"A momentary weakness," he replied. "I am not made of stone."

"You sent paintings to old friends. You confessed mistakes and indiscretions. Surely some part of you wishes pride to die."

"I painted nothing for their sake. The paintings are about the Glory, what I'm trying to work out, what I want to understand. I only gave them away to make reparation, so it would reveal itself again. But if I contact those people, none of that will matter. The work will be about them instead."

"You say you paint to work things out, to understand? And you expect me to believe the paintings are about the Glory?"

His eyes flashed as brightly as the fire. "You would have me prostitute my art."

"There are far worse things than prostitution."

"Not for me."

"Ah. The great Ridler sacrifices everything for art." Esperanza arose. "Thank you for the eggs and bacon, anyway."

As she walked into the night she laughed again, but Ridler resisted.

18.

The money in Gemma's hand trembled as she passed it to an obese albino ticket seller sitting in the little kiosk. Because of many folds of flesh upon the albino's face, and the looseness of the flowing robes which contained the enormous body, it was impossible to distinguish that person's sex. Nor could the ticket seller's age be known, although it was certainly greater than that of anyone she had ever met. The androgynous personage received her money and provided twelve paper tickets with great deliberation, using only the plump thumb and index finger of the right hand. Gemma said, "Do you speak English?" Nothing in the obsidian gaze within the folds and wrinkles of that unmoving face betrayed the slightest trace of interest in her question.

A grimy man whose corpulence had nearly burst the seams of his tuxedo stood below a banner which announced the circus. Speaking Spanish underneath a top hat, he held up one finger. Gemma handed him a paper ticket. *"Bienvenidos,"* he said, indicating the circus behind him with a bow and a grand sweep of his arm and a smiling exposure of yellow, gold, and silver teeth.

"Do you speak English?" replied Gemma.

"I have one hundred thirty-seven years of working in your country every summer, so of course I learn the language."

Assuming the man's mastery of numbers was imperfect, Gemma said, "Is Sheridan Ridler here?"

"Oh certainly. He is just inside. Also Diego Rivera, Pablo Picasso, and El Greco. Ha ha ha!" Then, to prove he was in possession of the facts, the man began to recite pi.

His numbers followed Gemma as she entered a promenade, perhaps thirty feet wide and two hundred yards long, which terminated at the entrance to a large tent. Clutching the rest of her tickets, she passed between swirling carnival rides which creaked and moaned, and smaller tents containing freaks and curiosities, and booths which offered games of skill and chance. Everywhere she saw signs and panels bearing faded and peeled paint applied in antique styles, gilded words in Spanish, the meanings far from clear. Barkers called down from small platforms in front of the tents, aiming their remarks at Gemma since she was the only customer. But she was far from alone. Pressing her on every side were jugglers, men on stilts, sword eaters, fire swallowers, clowns, and acrobats. Bells rang as she passed. Whistles blew. Horns blared. Everybody laughed, as if they knew of her ridiculous pursuit. Staring straight ahead for fear of what she might see otherwise, Gemma slipped her long purse strap over her head and wore it diagonally across her chest, the better to deter thievery.

It had taken twenty-four hours to summon the courage to enter the circus. The day before, after learning of it from the pregnant waitress at the diner, she had driven north into the desert and parked beside the highway and gripped the door handle and gone no farther. Sitting in the car, she had stared out through the windshield at the faded tents, the motley collection of trailers and trucks huddling among the cactus, the ragged big top emulating barren hills on the horizon. She had been incapable of going on.

Sometimes as a very small girl Gemma had dreamed of life with a normal father. She had seen the possibilities within her uncle and the fathers of her friends, the strength they offered to their daughters, the infinite loyalty and faithful provision. Then she grew a little older, and the sweet words never spoken and the absent embraces weighed too heavily in her imagination. It became impossible to ignore the amputation which had been performed upon her life before her birth. In defense against that phantom pain, she had learned to distract herself from one kind of loss by visualizing a different kind instead, replacing a missing father with the absence of the world's most celebrated artist.

The fantasy had offered comfort in a hundred different settings. In her mind she had designed a clifftop house where her famous father offered panoramic ocean views through bedroom walls of glass. She saw them living in a Paris apartment in the springtime. She dreamed of Christmases in London. Gallery openings in Manhattan. Taking bows together from a private box at all the most important Broadway openings. Dinners in a silk gown at the White House. It was all so glamorous, and therefore so much safer than an ordinary loss. If Sheridan Ridler's death had left her aching for a common father, at least his fame had given her permission to escape into uncommon reveries.

Even when the little paintings started coming, even as an adult, her illusions had persisted. When she finally accepted the possibility that he might be alive, she had promptly moved him from the pinnacle of culture into self-sacrificial isolation. She had envisioned him at work in a high mountain cabin somewhere, everything forsaken for his art. She had seen a lonely farmhouse standing on the Great Plains, or a shingled cottage on the rocky shore of Maine, covered porches with long and empty views, potbellied stoves against the cold, a secret paradise of perfect creativity. Faced with the possibility of betrayal which had been presented by new canvases, Gemma had refashioned her father into the painterly equivalent of Salinger, a man who compromised for nothing, not for fame, not for money, not even for a daughter. The vestige of the little girl within her might still yearn for something less—or something much, much more—but at least a man like that could be admired for purity.

Then had come that view of the circus through her windshield, the squalor, the insignificance, the life devoted to mere *entertainment*. It was as unlike her ideal as anything on earth could be. It stripped her of everything.

That night she had lain awake, wrestling with ugliness. One moment she chastised herself for superficiality. What did it matter if her father chose to work at such a place instead of living the important life she had imagined? Was she really the kind of person who measured a man by his occupation? The next moment she accused him of abandonment and selfishness. The moment after that, she felt her stomach roil with anxious speculation. How might he respond to a daughter who appeared from out of nowhere? Might he deny her identity? Might he deny his own?

Beneath the sheets, she had curled into the tightest ball, knees against her chest, nose between her knees, searching everywhere in her imagination for another place of safety.

In the end, a vision had compelled her to return to the circus, a prophecy of arriving home at LAX with nothing changed, of life stretched out after that, unresolved, unanswered, and untried. She knew the weight of such a path could never be supported. Yet still that morning she had hesitated, paralyzed by fear. She had almost accepted that bleak future. She had risen, bathed and dressed, intending to leave for El Paso. Then, strangely, when she slipped her mother's little gold and sapphire cross around her neck and saw it in the mirror, suddenly she found she had the necessary courage.

"Guess your age and weight, miss?" asked a clown beside her, a jaunty dwarf shaped like a ball, with golden spurs.

"Oh, good," she replied. "You speak English."

"I learned it from Houdini."

Humoring his nonsense, Gemma tried to smile. "Can you take me to Sheridan Ridler?"

"Never met the man. I heard he died."

"So did Houdini, a long time before you were born."

"How could anyone know that? He escaped from that same casket many times."

"Then what makes you so sure Sheridan Ridler is dead?"

"Did I say I was sure?"

"Look, I know he's here. Why won't you take me to him?" Reaching into her little purse, Gemma removed the photograph of her father as a young man. She showed it to the dwarf, but was careful not to let him take it from her fingers. She said, "Please?"

Although it was difficult to read the little man's expression through his crinkling makeup, she believed a hint of interest flashed behind his eyes. If so, it was immediately replaced by suspicion. "Who is that?"

"Sheridan Ridler, a long time ago. He's probably changed."

"Well, I wish you luck."

"You still don't know him?"

"Good luck, I say. And now, *adiós.*"

With an exaggerated sweep of his arm across his prodigious belly, the little clown bowed before her. He continued to dip lower and lower until he rolled head over heels, and like a little ball he rolled again, then he rolled back up to his feet some distance away, and from there he kept on going with a curious side-to-side gait. The golden spurs at his heels jingled as he disappeared from sight between a pair of booths.

Gemma felt certain she should follow. Muttering, "No, thank you," to a hawker who insisted on distracting her with offers of four throws for one dollar, and "Very nice," to a tumbler who stepped in front of her and performed a standing backflip, she made her way to the opening between the booths. From there, she entered a maze of travel trailers, animal cages, flatbed trucks, and panel vans. On one side antique fenders flared over cracked and balding tires. On the other side, running boards projected below doors, and hoods folded back on hinges over engines, strapped in place with leather and metal buckles. Turning right and left and right again, led deeper and deeper in by the dwarf's jingling golden heels, she was soon disoriented in the labyrinth, and uncertain if she could find her way back out. Even so, she kept her distance from the little man, never moving around a corner unless he had already turned around another farther down. Once she thought she had lost him, a possibility she feared far more than being lost herself, but she rushed ahead and caught sight of the dwarf just as he paused outside a trailer door. She backed up behind a truck and peeked at him around the headlight.

The little person cast a surreptitious glance back the way he had come, and then he knocked on the door. Almost immediately it swung open. The occupant remained out of sight inside the trailer. Gemma could not hear their words, but she saw the little man gesturing toward the midway with his curiously stubby fingers and she felt certain he was talking about her.

"Why do you hesitate?"

Spinning with a cry Gemma found an old woman standing impossibly close behind her. How could she have approached so near without a sound? "I—I'm sorry?" said Gemma.

"Go on," replied the woman with a nod of her strong chin toward the trailer. "Do what you came here for."

Gemma saw the woman's great age, and her upright stature, and the beauty of the bones beneath her flesh. "I don't know what you mean."

The old woman softly laughed. Gemma felt her fears dissolve as something similar to peace arose. "Eh! You, Gregorio!" called the old woman with a smile. "Stop interfering!"

Gemma glanced around to see the dwarf waddling away. She looked back to find the old woman had somehow disappeared. "Please," she called to the thin air. "Please don't go."

Without returning the old woman replied, "I am not what you want."

Gemma faced the trailer again. Standing there beside the open door she saw a terrible mistake. Ever since her childhood she had visualized him as the man in her mother's photographs, a hippie, young and handsome. She had known he would be older now of course, but who was this man so aged beyond his years, so gray and ragged at the edges? He was supposed to be her universe. This was supposed to be the vital moment of her life, the focal point of everything. Within her were a quarter century of questions, emotions beyond penetration, yet that little man, that travel-trailer-dwelling roustabout, was the antithesis of everything she had imagined. She had to look away. She longed to run.

"What do you want?"

His question brought her to her senses.

"I, uh, I wanted to meet you."

The suspicion in his features only deepened. "So?" he said at last.

"So, I, uh, I'm a curator at the Getty, and—"

"What's a getty?"

Astonished, she replied, "You don't know about the Getty?"

"I wouldn't ask the question if I did. Just tell me what you want."

She took a few steps closer. "Okay. I'm sorry to bother you, Mr. Ridler, but I've been looking everywhere—"

"My name isn't Ridler. It's San Pablo."

"What? No, don't say that. I know who you are."

He backed toward the open trailer door. "You've made a mistake."

She saw him step up into the trailer, saw him turn and reach to close the door. A sudden rage arose within her. How dare that wretched little man presume to shut her out? She said, "Please don't lie to me."

He stopped, hand on the doorknob. "What did you say?"

"I've come a very long way to find you. I've made a lot of sacrifices. I've visited everyone you sent a painting to. Henry Blum. Jennifer Killgarten. Caleb Nelson." He stood there staring at her, not denying anything. She spoke another name, watching very closely. "And Suzanna Halls." Something changed behind his eyes, but he said nothing. It was the moment, if she desired to take it, the obvious point at which she should reveal herself. Instead she said, "I'm a curator at the Getty, which is an art museum in Los Angeles, and I just wondered if I could speak with you a little while, Mr. Ridler. About . . . about your work."

He said, "I don't know what you're talking about," and the door began to close.

Rushing forward, she reached out and gripped it with both hands. "Stop!" she said. "Just hold on a minute." She saw his eyes flash at her effrontery, and beyond him saw an easel in the trailer, and upon the easel was the proof she sought, a masterpiece like all the others. "There," she said, releasing the door with one hand to point at the painting. "There, you see?"

Shifting his position to block her view of the interior, hand still on the doorknob, her father said, "Whatever it is you want, I can't help you."

"I don't need your help. I just want to talk."

"Why?"

"Well, for one thing, the people you sent paintings to, they all asked me to tell you something."

He stared down at her. She clung to the door. "Get on with it," he said at last. "These people, whoever they are, what do they want?"

"They all said your apologies weren't necessary."

"What?"

He seemed to shrink before her eyes, gathering into himself. The intensity of his reaction confused her. She forgot to hold the door. She dropped her arms and fell back. She said, "They all wanted you to know they forgave you a long time ago. They all said whatever you did, it worked out for the best and you shouldn't feel like you owed them a painting, or . . . anything."

He passed his free hand over his face, covering his eyes, stretching his flesh out of its proper shape. A sigh escaped him. It wilted everything. With weary eyes he gazed above her and beyond her. As if seeing more trouble in the world than he could bear, he said, "Please just go away," and then he closed the door.

Alone below the desert sky, Gemma put both of her palms against the outside of the door. She leaned forward, pressing on the trailer as if she could pass through its metal skin. Her shoulders heaved as she inhaled raggedly. She whispered, "No." She longed to go; she longed to stay, hating herself equally for both desires. Her tears fell to the sandy soil, establishing the small oasis which remains there to this day.

Gemma did not know how long she stood in that hopeless posture. She was not aware of leaving. She somehow made her way back through the maze, and found her car, and started the engine, and shifted into gear, and pulled onto the highway. She turned south, both hands on the steering wheel, gazing through the windshield at a dead and empty landscape. In the awful solitude of her condition, she did not see the only other vehicle parked beside the highway. She did not see the large white truck with tinted glass and gleaming chrome, the Cadillac, the Escalade. She did not see the man sitting there behind the wheel, the man who watched her go but did not follow. She did not see him shift his eyes toward Ridler's trailer. She did not see him smiling his sad smile.

19.

Long into that fatal night, Sheridan Ridler painted. The images which grew beneath his brush were nothing more and nothing less than what he had already painted countless times before. In spite of Esperanza's chosen name, he painted without hope.

After all the years of searching, he had been found out. The woman from Los Angeles would report his presence to the world, and after that he could no longer seek the Glory undistracted. In a day, or maybe two, she would return with others. When his presence was confirmed, more would come from every continent. Esperanza could not hold them back with her delicious laughter, nor could El Magnífico defeat them with his glistening knives. On the contrary, the entire troupe would be overwhelmed.

He must go. He had known it in the instant that he saw the beautiful black woman standing by the truck. Even after all the years in isolation he still recognized a gallery owner when he saw one, or a museum curator, or—heaven forbid—possibly even an art broker. At a glance he knew she belonged to the greedy ones, the needy ones, the parasites and bloodsuckers. Commerce had been written large upon her face and had been confirmed by her first words about the Getty, as if he should care about the self-important indus-try which backed her up, the money and prestige.

Dipping a brush into cobalt blue, Ridler shook his head at the arrogance of it, the falsehood. Everything of beauty became petty in those people's hands. They would rather live with theories than delight. Therefore, early in the morning he would ask someone to drive him to El Paso. Although his heart ached to think of resuming the solitary life, although he longed to remain among friends, he would take a bus from there to Mexico, alone. He would continue south, through Guatemala and Honduras, and he would go on until he reached a village somewhere with no telephones or news-papers, somewhere beyond superficial questions, a place to paint where only shelter, food, and clothing were important to his neigh-bors, where each man's failure could remain his own.

Possibly the Amazon could shelter him a few more years before they found him out again. If not, he would go farther. He did not know if the whole world was large enough, or if he would run out of hiding places before he died, but he knew he had to try. And in the meantime, there would be the art.

He had brought this on himself of course, with his dreams of recompense to tempt the Glory, sending paintings as his emissaries, his calculated risk. The woman from the museum had spoken of forgiveness as a thing already given, something independent of the only currency he had to offer. He had spent a lifetime vainly strug-gling to capture the transcendent with his work. Rome had taught him the futility of that. Now it seemed his work, his sacrifice, would not even serve as reparation.

A lesser artist might have given up. If art could not capture the Glory, or reconcile him to the Glory, if even art could make no merit and could not create mercy, then why continue making art? But Ridler would continue painting even in the face of nothingness.

His virtuosity drove him to the canvas, even on that final night. He knew no other way to wait until the morning, until his escape to El Paso; therefore he worked, and the image spread across the canvas just like all the others, incompetent and incoherent in comparison to his subject matter, a suggestion offered by a genius, who was also an idiot.

Someone knocked on the door.

He ignored it, and the person knocked again.

"Leave me alone!" he shouted, jabbing at the canvas as if committing murder.

The knock came again.

Ridler slammed the brush down and stalked to the door, throwing it open. "What do you want?"

Somehow, even in that first instant, Ridler recognized the demise which stood before him. Black as the night, the visitor held both hands at his side. When the man raised one of those hands a little, in it was a revolver. He dropped the hand again, pointing death down toward the earth. Ridler backed away.

The man climbed into the trailer and closed the door behind them. He held the revolver carelessly, never aimed at Ridler, but never more than a flick of the wrist removed from pointing at his chest. Perhaps it was a vestige of the anger Ridler had felt before he opened the door, or perhaps it was the depression which had come with knowing that his days of seeking Glory at the circus had been ended, but for some reason he was not afraid at first. Instead, he had a strange sensation of removal from that place and time.

The man smiled beautifully. "How you doing?"

"What do you want?"

Death glanced at the unfinished painting on the easel, then moved to a stack of others leaning against the wall beside the door. He stared at the first one, then using his free hand he leaned it forward against his leg. He stared at the next one, then he flipped it forward too, and looked down at the third. "These are all the same."

"I don't have any money."

Still looking down, the man smiled again. "I look like I need money?"

For the first time Ridler noticed his fine clothing, his large wristwatch, and his polished shoes, the trappings of success. And why not? In the end, death never failed.

"No," answered Ridler. "I guess you don't."

"You figure a brother with a gun, he's got to be a thief." The man had not yet looked away from the paintings. "It's okay. We're all products of our environment. And no, money's not a problem. You're Sheridan Ridler."

"Yes." The revolver inspired honesty even if he wasn't yet afraid. "Is that some kind of problem?"

"Afraid so, yeah."

"In that case, I apologize for being me."

"Funny." He gestured with the gun toward the threadbare sofa. "Have a seat."

Ridler moved to the sofa and sat down. The man then eased onto the little wooden chair Ridler used when working at his easel. He sat in Ridler's place, staring at the unfinished painting, saying nothing.

Ridler observed him in silence. After a long while, he realized he was witnessing a kindred spirit. He saw it in the interplay between the man and painting. Most people simply looked at art. This man watched it. This man understood.

"It's not finished," said the man.

"No," replied Ridler.

"None of them are."

"That's true."

"Why not?"

"I don't know how to finish."

Without turning away from the work in progress the man said, "You're not afraid of me."

"I don't think so, no."

"Why not?"

"What's the worst you can do? Kill me?"

"I can do worse than that."

"But you're not going to, are you?"

For the first time, the man looked directly at him. "It would be good if you explained why you don't care."

"Tell me who you are."

The revolver stirred in his hand. "Just answer the question."

The threat relieved the artist of responsibility. He felt he was not speaking to a man; he was speaking to his destiny. It allowed him to pretend he had no choice about revealing his lifelong futility, although after he began, it seemed he had been waiting many years to do exactly that. He wanted to explain himself. He wanted to be honest. "Like you said, it's not finished. None of them are. I'm a failure. A fraud. I've been hiding from it most of my life, but earlier today they found me. I can't hide from it anymore. I'm not even sure I want to." And as he had with Esperanza, Gregorio, Isabel, and El Magnífico, he started at the first memory, the Harlem River mud bar. However, unlike the many stories he had told to entertain the troupe, this time he portrayed himself not as a holy priest of art, but rather as a victim. Even worse, a fool.

He spoke of awakening from a strange sleep, of his being and his consciousness driving out the Glory, of his desperate first attempts to restrain it, to capture it with brutish scrapes against a concrete bulkhead. He spoke next of the Catskills, his pursuit of the energy in everything, which in the end meant nothing. He spoke of Wat Bua, the duplicity of doves and the futility of making merit, and of the Golden Horn, a god who loved his people and hated unbelievers, and he spoke of the Scuds, of yet another god who refused to reveal himself even in the rubble of the faithful. He spoke of his masterpiece becoming mud in Roman gutters and his fruitless quest for images not made by human hands. But he did not speak of his last rejection, the futility of reparations, for he had suffered it too recently and still felt it far too deeply.

Death remained before the painting. Gazing deep into the art, he said, "Tell me the rest."

Ridler remained quiet.

Death stirred himself again, casually seeking a trajectory which ended at the artist's heart. "After all those years you started mailing paintings to people," said the man. "I want to know why."

The artist was an unwilling penitent in a confessional who, having begun his sacred duty, found it taking on its own awful momentum. Until that moment Ridler had not realized he no longer cared whose hand revealed the Glory. Then, having confessed it to himself, he did the same to death.

"Do you understand?" he asked, but Death acknowledged nothing, so he was forced to go further. He shamefully revealed the iniquitous compulsion which had displaced his reverence for art. "Once I realized there were no images of it on the earth," he said, "I thought if I could get people to forgive me, then maybe it would come again."

"You tried to bribe people with your art."

Confronted by that bold description of his heresy, Ridler hung his head.

"Did it work?"

"It was hopeless," replied Ridler. "I was already forgiven. Now there's nothing left for me to do."

"Hopeless," repeated the man, who had risen and begun to move around the tiny trailer, the revolver held limply in one hand while the other hand reached out to touch a mug on the countertop, a sketch pinned to the wall. Death felt the curtains by the open window, rubbing the fabric between his thumb and fingers. He paused before the photograph beside the mirror, creased and yellowed by the years. He said, "Suzanna Halls."

And finally, a proper fear of death arose in Ridler. "You're mistaken."

"Everybody knows her."

"Please don't. . . ." Ridler could not say the words.

The man turned to look at him. Ridler saw no compassion whatsoever in his eyes, but he also saw no malice or deception. "I won't," he said. "There's no need."

Believing him, the artist replied, "Thank you."

"They say she was your muse. Isn't that the word?"

"She was . . . she is the woman I love."

"Why aren't you together?"

"I ruined it."

"How?"

Ridler shrugged disconsolately and drew a shaky breath. "Self-indulgence."

"Did that hurt?"

"It still hurts."

"Then why keep the picture?"

"I think it might hurt worse to let it go."

The man cocked his head. He did not look at Ridler; he watched him like a painting. "At least you can feel something."

Ridler stared at the worn linoleum below his boots. He could no longer speak.

The man moved back to the little wooden chair and sat again in Ridler's place before the easel. Just as Ridler had lost himself in something down below, so it seemed the man had lost himself in Ridler's painting. Time became irrelevant as Death and the artist sat together, balanced and unmoving and completely silent.

Finally, the man said, "What would you give for the pain to stop?"

"I've tried everything," whispered Ridler. "Nothing is enough."

"Would you trade your feelings for some peace? Would you give up love?"

Ridler's imagination was peerless. He saw too well a life without his yearning for the Glory, without his longing for Suzanna. "No," he said. "I couldn't live that way."

"Not even for no pain at all? Just a kind of numbness?"

"No," replied the artist. "That's worse than being dead."

The man nodded. With a motion almost too fast for Ridler to see, he flipped the revolver's cylinder open. One by one, he removed four of the bullets and set them on the easel's tray below the painting. Ridler saw one more bullet in the cylinder. The man flipped it closed again. Death spun the cylinder. He spun it again. He said, "This glory you've been chasing, it sounds like God to me. Do you believe in God, Mr. Ridler?"

The question startled him. "I believe there's something . . . I know there is. I've seen it."

"Do you believe God cares what we do down here?"

Ridler thought of his years of struggle, the half-completed paintings, the inadequacy of images by others and images not made by hands, and through it all the stubborn absence of the Glory. "No," he said. "I don't think so."

"If I promise to let you live, will you finish this painting?"

Thus at last confronted unavoidably by his greatest temptation, Ridler drew in a deep breath. He longed to live. He let it out. The artist made his full confession. "I'm not good enough."

The man nodded again, absently. He spun the cylinder again, and again, and while that cold blue metal spun, the voice of Death recited automatic words, the kind of words which must be said to cast a spell, a liturgy, an incantation. "I think God cares about justice . . . eye for an eye, tooth for a tooth . . . I would hate to make him angry . . . in my heart I try to do my best . . . to let God have his say in these situations . . . ." Still looking into the painting, watching it the way a person watched a living thing, his voice trailed away.

Ridler saw the image take him. The revolver sagged, the other hand stopped twirling the cylinder and rested on his knee. The eyes no longer searched the painting, the body remained present but the animation in him vanished. Ridler watched, and waited. He heard coyotes bark outside the trailer, heard the rustle of some kind of creature down below the floorboards, heard the ringing in his ears and his own breath and heartbeat. Trembling with terror, Ridler stood.

Slowly, inch by precious inch, he passed behind the man.

He opened the trailer door and fled into the night, running as fast as his aging body would allow, weaving through the labyrinth of cages, tents, and caravans, searching for a place to hide, or for someone else to stand against the death. He longed to shout for help, but feared it might call down his doom. "Gregorio!" he hissed as he ran. "El Magnífico! Esperanza! Isabel! Someone!"

He found no one wandering about the camp, no one loitering in the dining tent or sitting by a fire. He heard no snoring, no radios played quietly, no muffled conversations, no sounds of any kind beyond the sighing wind and the cries of desert creatures and the ever-present ringing in his ears. All the trucks remained. El Vaquero's palominos stood sleeping in their trailer. Surely in that desolate location no outsider could have come to carry off the troupe. Where then had they gone? Could everyone have simply walked away? Or had Death already rid the earth of them?

Rounding the flatbed truck, where an aged bear observed him from its cage, Ridler was confronted by the smallest trailer in the circus, Esperanza's, which was not a trailer in the modern sense at all, but rather an old-fashioned Gypsy wagon. Its tires had wooden spokes. Its sides were painted in the antique style which covered all the signs along the midway, the edges and the corners traced with laurel garlands and gilded olive branches, the sides and ends blood red at the bottom, and then deep purple as they rose, and then the darkest blue and finally pitch-black where the top merged with the night sky's countless sparkling stars. A tendril of smoke trailed from a little chimney, disbursing the musky scent of incense. The one small window at the rear, crisscrossed by wooden mullions, danced and flickered with a mellow glow which fell upon the steps.

He climbed those steps with trepidation, for he had never entered Esperanza's home before. Standing on the upper step, he knocked. The impact of his knuckles echoed far too loudly from the wooden panel. He looked around for Death.

"Esperanza?" he whispered, his lips only an inch from the door. "Esperanza!"

He thought he heard something inside. A voice? What was it saying?

Again he knocked. Again he whispered her name. Again he heard the sound within.

Something snapped behind him in the night. He spun to look and nearly fell from the steps. Death had certainly pursued him.

"Esperanza!" he called loudly, abandoning all caution. "Esperanza! I need you!"

Before him the bronze doorknob had been fashioned in the shape of an unknown planet. He covered it with his hand. He turned it. To his very great surprise, the paneled door swung open. With a final glance around, he stepped into Esperanza's little wagon.

Inside on his left and right rose mighty columns of cut stone, many pairs of them marching off into the distance. They arched together across the lofty space above him, supporting a massive groin-vaulted ceiling, also made of beautifully carved stone. In the walls between the graceful pairs of columns stood gothic windows of stained glass. In the windows, cosmic secrets had been darkly drawn in blues and reds and purples, and then traced in lead of lacy black. Tapestries beside the windows revealed other designs, unseen upon the earth since the fall of man. Massive iron chandeliers hung from long chains above, each supporting perhaps a thousand pure white candles. The perfection of that light was painful. In imitation of humility, Ridler bowed his head.

"Come," came Esperanza's voice from somewhere in the distance.

"Where are you?" he asked.

"Come and see," was her reply.

He began to walk. Underneath his feet was something like a pavement made of lapis lazuli. Each footfall echoed against it in the vastness of that space. His breaths were also heard. His heartbeat, the digestion in his bowels, even the coursing of his blood within his veins was amplified. Nothing was covert. Everything was known. When he finally arrived at the far end of the space, he was completely naked.

Esperanza moved before a crowd of kneeling people there.

Among them he saw Isabel the wolf woman, and Vicente the
vaquero, and the Beautiful Zoraida, who submitted to the knives,
and of course El Magnífico, and little Gregorio, and the Flying
Blackbirds. In the best of health, slender, without any sign of life's
travails, they knelt. Before them the stone walls and stained glass
and mysterious tapestries had all surrendered to the very thing they
represented, the universe displayed, constellations instead of walls,
galaxies instead of ceilings, the pavement underneath his feet flowing like a river, rising like a waterfall which had been freed of gravity, becoming earth, a setting for a gem, a rock, a massive skull on
which everything around him seemed to start and end.

At the foot of all of that, Esperanza, robed in stars, placed a
wafer on a waiting tongue.

"Where am I?" whispered Ridler.

"Why are you here?" replied Esperanza. "That is a much better
question."

"There's a man, he has a gun. . . ." Even as he spoke the words he
sensed a falseness in them, a corruption.

"What is he to us?"

"He's crazy! He wants to kill me!" When Esperanza continued
her ministrations, moving peacefully among the kneeling people
as if he had said nothing, Ridler tried again. "He could be here any
minute! We have to do something!"

She paused, a wafer in midair. "Do you think we fear madmen?
We, who have accepted *you?*"

He stared at her, and was stricken by her beauty. She was ancient. She was new.

"San Pablo," she continued. "It is time to stop this travesty. You
claim you are an artist, when of course you are no such thing.
Artists will brave anything to see. Your preconceptions make you
blind."

"But, he has a gun," protested Ridler.

"That is not the thing you fear."

Standing naked there among the kneeling multitude, Ridler clenched his fists. "Who are you to say that?"

"*SILENCE!*"

Ridler quaked before the power of her voice. He looked away as she approached. He trembled.

"If you ever truly wished to see the Glory," she said, "you had only to think. Where were you when it appeared?"

"I was . . . I was . . ."

"Think!"

"I was at the river."

"*At* the river? Only that?"

"I was . . . I was *in* the river? I was under . . ." The river. He had been under it. Beneath it. In it. He looked at her, amazed. "I was dead."

"At last," said Esperanza. "The so-called artist starts to see."

"But how does this help?" he asked. "You say I've been blind. Aren't the dead more blind than me?"

"Most are," she replied. "But a very few have died and seen much more than you. What a monumental fool you are. What a boundless waste of love. Billions have begged for the chance to see what you have seen, only to receive the answer of silence. You, however, were most highly honored, yet when you died what did you do?"

He remembered the first desperate moments, the agonizing sense of his own returning, his displacement of perfect peace. "I tried not to let it go," he said. "I did my best to keep it."

She laughed, and continents and oceans produced new forms of life. She spread her arms and Ridler saw the evidence of scurvy he had caused, the reopened wounds upon her wrists encompassing the universe in signs and symbols and reality, encompassing the troupe on bended knees before the skull which rose up from the earth, encompassing humanity's purest desire. "You think the one who made all things is something you can keep?"

"What can I do?" he asked in desperation.

"You are an artist," she replied, "yet you do not know these things? Even if I spoke the truth plainly you would not accept it. Go back where you came from, San Pablo. Miracles are not enough for you. Go back and truly die, and this time remain dead when you arise or you will never live to see the Glory."

20.

Ridler returned then through the maze. Seeking Death, he climbed another set of steps. He opened another door. He entered a different trailer, his own. He shut the door behind himself, as a man might seal a coffin. The air was close with dread. "Hello?" he said, looking around. "Are you here?" But the chair stood empty before the easel. Ridler groaned. Even that assistance had been kept from him.

He could not bear to view the painting on the easel. Aware that he was fleeing from the very thing he had so long desired, he began to move around the little trailer. He reached out to touch a mug on the countertop, a sketch pinned to the wall. He felt the curtains by the open window, rubbing the fabric between his thumb and fingers. He paused before the photograph beside the mirror, creased and yellowed by the years, and on Suzanna's breast a cross of gold, and on the cross, sapphires embedded.

Only then did he realize he had failed to ask the young woman from the Getty how Suzanna was when they had met, how she looked, how she felt, if she had seemed well and happy. Ridler pressed his forehead to the mirror by the photograph. How could he have been so caught up in his fear?

He pushed back from the mirror, grieving the lost opportunity to hear about Suzanna, and in admitting that one grief, he opened himself to a million other chances missed. He thought of his masterpiece in Rome, the best work of his existence, completely inadequate until it shifted in the random drops of rain. What he had struggled for a lifetime to accomplish had been done as casually as if by accident. Staring into the mirror, Suzanna and that shifting Roman image flowed together in his mind. Staring into the mirror, at last he saw his insignificance for what it truly was. He could not even give himself to love. Who was he to paint the Glory?

Hating what he saw, still he did not flinch. He gazed into his own eyes, seeing how his pride had ravaged them, deceived them, blinded them. That vision flayed him to the core but he was determined to become an artist. He would not look away, not until he had seen everything. He searched his eyes without excuses or ambitions. His so-called quest had not been a pursuit. It had been a desperate retreat. He made another great confession then, yet it amounted only to admitting what was obvious. He was a believer, and the focus of belief was all that mattered. He wanted nothing of himself anymore, nothing of his genius, nothing of the forgery that he called art, not one speck of anything which stank of the great Sheridan Ridler.

In that moment something in the mirror moved. With his own eyes he saw it. He shifted his attention to Suzanna's photograph and saw it there, as well. He looked back at his reflection, then back to the photograph, and then back to the reflection, which was no longer his alone. And that sapphire cross around Suzanna's neck . . . he had seen it on another breast, that young woman from the museum, that beautiful young woman of color, who had the golden skin and fascinating features often seen in children of mixed race.

He looked, and where he had seen only one reflection in the mirror before, now he realized there were three in one, and he saw the life-giving bonds he had abandoned, and the deadly indifference he had refused to abandon, and he knew what he must do.

Beautiful beneath ancient skin, hope began to laugh. In the sky outside, a bleeding hand sewed a patch. A pattern came together perfectly in the darkness high above the desert, a presence waiting beyond time, something no one else had painted. One white diamond appeared in the east, and the locust moon behind its mask observed that single light which arced across the sky, that Scud of love, that perfect dove descending to the trailer.

In the desert just beyond the circus, at a point well seen above Golgotha by everyone who knelt before the altar, the air produced a whirlwind, the embodiment of truth, the antithesis of falsehood, a dervish spinning in pursuit of ecstasy, the one source of sun and shadows, the beating wings of righteous prayer, the breath of life, the blood of hearts, the ebb and flow of time outside the trailer, not an image, not a name, but a manslayer, come to pace upon the earth.

It tracked its prey by evidence of faith alone and fixed it with a vision much superior to any artist's. With a sharp intake of breath, the air was sampled for the scent of justice. With a hot rush of satisfaction, it expelled the stench of rotting human flesh, bits of arms that once had held a lover, bits of loins that once had birthed a child, bits of brains that once had prayed to God, bits of lies, of betrayal, hate and murder, bits of pride once rotting in the places between tooth and gum but now completely taken deep within that leopard messiah, that guardian of heaven.

Meanwhile, inside a little ark adrift across the universe, Sheridan Ridler removed an unfinished canvas from an easel. He put a blank canvas in its place. He picked up a brush. He dipped it into paint. He stared into the perfect whiteness waiting for him. And abandoning the opposite of art at last, the greatest artist in the world began to die.

21.

At five thirty in the morning, Gemma sat on the bed in her motel room, trying to understand the damage she had done. Again and again throughout the night she had replayed the conversation in her head: what she had said, what her father had said. In the end, she decided it must have been a kind of shock that made her mention she was with the Getty, a temporary form of insanity, talking about work as if that was the reason she had searched him out, mentioning all those strangers with his paintings, mentioning her mother almost as an afterthought, never admitting she was his daughter. Never *admitting*. The word that said it all.

So many times throughout her life she had fantasized what it would be like to find him suddenly alive, imagining it like a Cinderella moment, something magical, a kind of coronation. Gemma Halls the nobody becoming Gemma Ridler, rescued from obscurity. Then the impossible happened, the moment came, but her prince had been the one in need of rescue.

For some reason, that thought reminded her of the pregnant waitress at the diner, the one stuck there in Loving with a baby in her belly while her hopes drove off to Los Angeles. Surely in her wildest dreams the woman never expected such a loss. What had she said when they were talking? Something about living for your-self? *I don't know about selfish, but it does sound awful lonely.* Gemma looked around her motel room, her bags already packed, about to drive off to El Paso and then fly to L.A., and she knew it was true. Being home wouldn't make any difference. She'd still be alone.

Closing her eyes she shuddered at the way one mistake could ruin everything. She should have pounded on his door, called to him through that thin metal wall, told him who she was and what she wanted. But the radical disparity between the man as he was in the real world and her own lifelong fantasy had shocked her into silence.

Now what was done was done, and she could not imagine any way to repair the damage. All night she had sat there trying to think of something, but in the end she had decided it was hopeless. If she returned to him and told him plainly who she was, he would surely ask why she had not said so in the first place. That would leave her just two choices. She would have to tell the truth and that would be the end of that. Or she could lie, which she would gladly do, but she had never been much good at lies, and could not think of one that sounded plausible.

Gemma tried to remind herself she wasn't really alone. Her mother waited at home of course, and of course her mother loved her. Why wasn't that enough? Why did she always want what she couldn't have? Why did just the two of them feel so incomplete?

She shook her head quickly, like a dog shaking off water.

It didn't matter why. Life was what it was. Move on.

Gemma rose. She gathered her things and crossed the small room to the door. Glancing around to make certain she had forgotten nothing, she flipped off the light and stepped outside, leaving for L.A. She looked across the parking lot. On the other side of the highway, behind the low hills at the distant edge of a vast desert valley, the sun had just begun to glow below the horizon. Staring at the unfolding colors, she thought about her mother, always talking about sunrises and God as if one proved the other. She wanted to believe that. Then she might not feel so lonely. But where was the proof, really? She so desperately wanted proof.

"If you're really there," she whispered, "show me."

As the sunrise lavenders and purples arose, she waited for an answer, but heard nothing.

She turned to close the door, and in so doing, saw the painting leaning there against the stucco wall. Being caught up in her thoughts, it took her a moment to realize what it was. She bent and picked it up. The paint was wet. She got a little on her thumb. She tried to make out the image, but the sun was not yet high enough. She stepped back into the room and flipped on the light.

Gazing at the canvas, she instantly forgot everything else. She moved woodenly to the bed and sat. Holding it in both hands, she looked down into the painting, trying to believe. All the indications were there. She saw the painter was left-handed and had applied the paint with a brush held at a thirty-degree angle, which was just as it should be. She saw no bleeding of paint layers. The palette was correct, the colors common in his other work. The signature appeared to be spontaneous, not painstakingly forged, clearly integral to the painting instead of added afterward, done in the same ultramarine blue she saw elsewhere on the canvas.

Most important, her instincts were at peace as she examined the image. All of her experience, thousands of hours spent studying his work, combined to tell her this painting was a Ridler. Yet this time the subject was not simply something he had never painted before; it was a portrait, her mother's, and to Gemma's knowledge, the one and only face Sheridan Ridler had ever painted.

Yet as she looked more carefully, she saw it was not only that, but also something else. She stared, and the image seemed to shift and coalesce and she thought perhaps it was . . . it was . . .

A sudden bark of laughter escaped her. She slapped a hand over her mouth. She cried from the effort of containing what arose within. Surrendering, laughing as she wept, she wiped her eyes in order to better see that painting, that image of her mother, and of her father, and of herself . . . that image not only of a face, but of three faces, somehow rendered all together as if one.

Realizing what she held, Gemma leapt to her feet. She ran from the room past her suitcase. She reached her car. With the painting still in her hand, she fumbled for her keys. One minute later, she was driving toward the circus north of town.

She rolled slowly through the dawn, searching shadows on her left and right, careful not to miss him. Soon the buildings gave way to the desert. She sped up a little. She saw a vehicle stopped ahead, and slowed, and there he was, leaning against a pickup truck along the shoulder, a black silhouette against the blazing sun which at that exact moment crested the distant hills beyond. She passed the truck and pulled off the road and got out and walked back toward him.

"Did you see the sunrise?" he asked as she came near. He remained leaning against the side of the old pickup truck, looking toward the horizon. "It was a really good one."

"Yes."

"All those colors in the clouds . . . I could never get that right."

"You? You could paint anything."

"No. Not anything."

"But that portrait. It's incredible. How did you do that?"

Still not looking at her, still with his eyes on the horizon, he said, "You like it?"

"I don't have the words."

"Do you . . . do you think your mother might like it too?"

"Why don't you come home with me and find out?"

He glanced at her quickly, and then away, as if afraid of what he saw. He opened his mouth, and then he closed it. He said nothing.

After a minute, she turned toward the sunrise and leaned against the truck. They stood side by side like that, only a little space still separating them. The sun was fully up, round and red and promising a new day in which anything could happen. Finally he spoke.

"They're all gone."

"I don't understand."

"The circus. It was right here when I left an hour ago."

"How is that possible?"

He turned toward her suddenly, urgently. "Listen. My father didn't set a very good example. He never told me how he felt, or hugged me, or whatever, so I don't know much about that kind of thing. But I'd really like . . . do you think we could maybe. . . ."

They reached out at the same time, and became awkwardly entangled. They backed up a little, then they tried again, and again they failed to get it right. She laughed. He smiled and stood still with open arms, and she stepped into them.

He held her tentatively at first, then fiercely, as if he feared she might want to let him go, but she did not want that. On the contrary, within his arms she felt a mad compulsion to thank someone, for surely here was the proof she had so desperately desired. And as that instinct of raw gratitude consumed her, Gemma felt her father's lungs expand as if he were a drowning victim taking his first gasp of air, and she heard him whisper, "Glory."

22.

When the woman pulled over and parked on the shoulder of the road, Emil Lacuna switched off his headlights and did the same about two hundred yards back. On the passenger seat beside him was a stainless steel briefcase and the canvas he had stolen from the diner, rolled up tight. He had kept the painting with him in the Escalade and in his motel room ever since he took it from the diner, carrying it around, a constant temptation to waste his time, looking at it whenever he got a chance. He reached over and touched it, thought about taking a quick peek, and then made himself tend to business instead.

He opened the briefcase. Among the other things inside it was a small pair of binoculars. Lifting them to his eyes, he focused on the scene ahead.

He saw the woman emerge from the little car and walk up to a truck beside the road. The sun was barely up. It was hard to make out details, but he saw the artist standing by the truck. He lowered the binoculars.

So. They were together, and all alone on a desert highway. It was a good opportunity. Better than if he had done the man in his trailer. He still couldn't understand how that had happened. Had he fallen asleep again, just sitting there? It didn't seem possible, but somehow he had let the guy get away. At first he had been unhappy with himself for losing focus, but now he was glad he had not shot the man the night before. This would be much better.

He played it out in his mind, the way it should go. He would roll up on them slowly, get close and hop out, try to be ten or twelve feet away at most when he pulled the gun. They were civilians. They'd probably freeze for a second when they saw the gun. He'd pop the guy first, then she'd get hysterical. It might take some effort to manage, but he should be able to get his hands on her before she ran. If she got away from him and took off into the desert, that would be bad. Frightened people could be hard to outrun, and he didn't want to have to shoot her in the back. He needed to put one in her temple real quick, make sure there was muzzle contact, and then put the gun in her hand, aim it off into the desert, and squeeze a round off with her finger, get some cordite on her skin. Lay her on the ground just right, and there you go. A murder-suicide, no problem.

She was standing beside the artist now. It looked like they were watching the sunrise together. That was nice. He decided to wait, give them a moment before it happened. He tried to be as kind as possible in these situations. Plus, he needed to think a little more about how to keep her from running off into the desert.

While he waited, he unrolled the canvas. He held the painting up above the steering wheel to catch the growing light of the rising sun. He had looked at the image so much he almost had it memorized, but he still couldn't figure out why it seemed so familiar.

The paintings back on his yacht appealed to him because he felt like he could almost understand the women in them, maybe even feel something about them if he stared hard enough. But this one was different. This one seemed more personal, almost like it had something to do with him.

Lacuna had always felt a connection with the artist, Ridler. He figured that was normal. A lot of people had their favorites. But he couldn't understand how Ridler had captured that strange sense of déjà vu. It was there, undeniable and stronger every time he looked into the image, something calling to him, as if the painting had a secret, something he had forgotten, or something important he ought to know.

The sunlight had a reddish quality. Coming almost sideways through the window from the far horizon, falling on the painting, it gave Lacuna a new perspective. Or was it an old perspective? The chaotic form on the canvas seemed to come together in a single swirling pattern when he tried to take it in, something infinitely organized, not chaotic after all, just too big, too complex to understand, a giant thing beyond his comprehension, a wildness he could never tame, which wanted to tame him. The horizontal light illuminated all of that, and suddenly he had a certainty about the merger of the light and image. There was a simple reason for the déjà vu. He had seen it before, in another place, another sunrise. The canvas in his hands began to shake. He put it down.

It was important to keep his mind on business. He picked up the binoculars. At first it was hard to focus with the image so unsteady through the lenses, but eventually his hands stopped shaking and he could see the woman hugging Ridler. A nice father-daughter moment. He wondered; if he could have felt anything, watching them, what would it be? Maybe envy? Jealousy? Anger that he never had such a moment? Or maybe he'd feel something positive. A lot of people did, apparently, when they saw that kind of thing. He didn't understand any of it. He lowered the binoculars and looked down at his hands. When he got back to Manhattan he'd go see a doctor, find out why they kept shaking.

He returned the binoculars to the briefcase and took out the revolver. It was time. He'd never get a better opportunity and couldn't afford to sit around staring at paintings. He swung the cylinder out and removed four of the bullets, leaving only one. He closed the cylinder. He looked up. In the strengthening glow he saw them there, still hugging probably, although they were so far away he could not be sure. Why was everyone so far away all the time?

What had he just thought?

Emil Lacuna closed his eyes, counted to ten, and opened them. What had he just thought? Everyone so far away? What kind of thing was that to go through a person's mind? It didn't make any sense.

He spun the cylinder. He heard the familiar clicking as it went around. Everything as usual. He thought about his beating heart, and those people's hearts out there beside the road. Keeping it fair. Justice. Everything balanced and correct, the way it had to be. He lifted the revolver. He pressed the muzzle to his chest, precisely over the place where he had been told his heart would be, if he had a heart.

If he had a heart?

He let the hand holding the revolver fall away, down to his lap. This wasn't right. These things going through his head had to be dealt with. He couldn't do this properly until he had himself under control. Of course he had a heart. It was about the size of his fist, slightly off center to the left of his sternum, exactly where everybody else's heart was, too. He had a heart; they had a heart. Everybody had a heart.

Okay. Get this done before they broke it up and drove off and the opportunity was lost. It might be messier for everyone if he had to do it somewhere else. Harder for him. Harder for them. This was about as good as it got. So take advantage. Be professional.

He raised the revolver to his chest again. He closed his eyes. He took one last deep breath, and in breathing realized suddenly he did not want that breath to be his last. He opened his eyes. He saw the sunshine slope into the truck from a slightly steeper angle, falling uninvited on the painting which lay open on the seat beside him. The image fluttered in the light, which was definitely something he had seen before. And suddenly, he remembered.

On the river, the Harlem River, on the concrete, a bulkhead, scraped into the sludge and marine growth by a dripping man, a frantic man, and he had seen it all from underneath a wharf, hiding from his mother, who beat him, who let her boyfriends beat him, who let her boyfriends rape him, who fornicated with them right in front of him, who laughed at him . . . and . . . and he was rowing his first boat, trying to get away, and he was kneeling on the Harlem River bar again, something he had done and then forgotten, like he forgot about his long-gone deadbeat father and the crack-addicted whore who was his mother, and his dear departed Maman. He had forgotten about himself. He had simply stared, and stared, until more than an hour had passed and the bar beneath him had been long submerged, and the risen water almost reached his waist, and when at last the shivering boy was forced to turn away from the thing upon the bulwark, on his face were tears, and . . . and . . . where was all this coming from? Who had seen these things? What was rising up around him? Was it fear? Was it awe? Was it in the painting? Was it in himself? Was this him? Was this what it meant to feel?

The cocked revolver in Emil Lacuna's hand beat a staccato rhythm on his chest.

The painting on the seat beside him swirled within the strangeness of the first tears he remembered shedding, and the colors shifted subtly.

He told himself the painting wasn't really moving. It was the tears, only tears, yet he felt an overwhelming instinct to fall face-down to the ground, so great was his ecstatic adoration. And as the colors ran and shifted, as the tears of heaven drove them down, for a fleeting instant Emil disappeared within eternity.

Countless moments after that, in spite of everything that he could do to stop it, he began to reappear. He looked up from the painting and saw the man and woman out there still in their embrace, and he turned the key in the ignition and pulled onto the road with the revolver lying in his lap, driving toward them, getting closer, closer, feeling emptiness returning back into himself and sensing joy and peace retreating as it came, and when he was beside the man and woman he knew he must remember . . . something.

A timeless moment. His interior landscape unfolding to reveal an unexpected vastness. All had been so clear, so pristine and perfect, but then his consciousness returned to sweep away the joy, and heaven fled before him toward a far horizon, like a storm front chasing daylight from the sky. How he hated his own appearing. How he feared the Glory would not rise again. Oh, the poverty of self-awareness! Compared to such resplendency nothing mattered anymore, nothing but recapturing that joy. So the little boy from Harlem blessed the artist and his daughter as he passed them by, and Emil embarked upon a quest to find what he had lost.

The Opposite of Art

Discussion Questions

1. Why does Ridler so desperately want to paint "the Glory"? Why does he find it so difficult? When does he first begin to truly understand the answer to these questions himself?

2. What is Gemma's motivation throughout most of the story? How is it similar to Ridler's motivation? What do the similarities imply about human nature?

3. Given the events that shaped Lacuna in his childhood and the nature of his crimes, what do you think of his situation in the end?

4. Was Suzanna right to break it off with Ridler? Was she right to wait for him so long, and so passively?

5. Who is Esperanza?

6. What does the novel have to say about religion?

7. What does the novel have to say about the nature of God and our relationship with God?

8. What does the novel have to say about the nature of art? The purpose of art? The source of art?

9. What are some of the novel's most powerful symbols, what gives them their power, what do they stand for, and what do they imply about the things they stand for?

10. What do the words *lacuna, esperanza,* and *graves* mean? What does the word reflect in the character and the novel's symbolism?

Author Q & A

What inspired you to write *The Opposite of Art*?

At its most fundamental level, all great art is an attempt to communicate truths beyond words. Even the classic novels are considered great because of something deeper than mere words. God is the most fundamental ineffable truth, yet very few artists have tried to communicate their impression of God directly in their work. We usually address ourselves to God's glory instead; the evidence and attributes God leaves behind as he moves across the universe. Only a few have addressed themselves to God directly, and they almost universally anthropomorphize their conception of the divine, usually rendering God as an old man with a long beard. It seems strange to me that more artists don't try to render God himself, directly, and in thinking about that I began to wonder what might happen if a great artist—perhaps the greatest artist of his generation—were to devote a lifetime to capturing the spirit of God in his work.

How was the process of writing this book different from your previous books?

Actually, it was much the same process as all the others. I began with the idea of a great painter who wants to capture God on canvas, and then began to think in terms of settings, characters, and events that might support that idea. I asked questions. What motivates this person? What stands in his way? Why is he the way he is? What are his strengths and weaknesses? What do I like about him? What do I hate about him? As I asked these questions, the decisions I had to make to answer them began to fill in all the blanks, until eventually I had a story.

There are several people that help Ridler along the way and shape his faith and religious experience, including Bob Feldman, al-Wasiti, the rabbi Jonathon Klein, and Esperanza. How have others helped you to develop and further your own faith?

Some have helped me on my spiritual journey by the positive or negative example of how they lived their lives, some by making demands that forced me to look to God for strength or courage or patience or forgiveness, and some by granting those same things to me and, in so doing, giving me a glimpse of God's own love.

Of the characters you created in *The Opposite of Art*, who do you sympathize with most?

It's not possible to pick just one. I am all of them at different times. Sometimes I share Talbot Graves's greed and lust for what he knows he should not have, and sometimes I share Emil Lacuna's emotional and spiritual emptiness. I have great sympathy for Abu al-Wasiti, whose religion has been hijacked by evil, because my own has often suffered the same fate. I sometimes long for a different history, as Gemma does, and I sometimes demand access to the secrets of the universe on my own terms, as Ridler does.

Your writing incorporates inspirational themes into plot-driven stories of intrigue, suspense, and mystery. On your website, you write that your bookcase is full of suspense and mystery novels. Which authors have influenced your work the most?

Another difficult answer to narrow down. The list is very long. I learned most of what I know about writing dialogue from Ross Thomas and Elmore Leonard. From Flannery O'Connor I learned not to be afraid to write characters who feel larger than life, and not to try to make sense of everything. Thornton Wilder gave me permission to inject myself into the story now and then. Caleb Carr, E. L. Doctorow, and Umberto Eco taught me to appreciate the power of history in forming mysteries. I gained an appreciation for unexpected miracles from Gabriel García Marquez and Toni Morrison.

As one of the most celebrated artists of his day, Ridler seems to experience the world more intensely than other people: the colors are brighter and an everyday phenomenon like rain can become a transformative event. In your experience as a classically trained artist and architect, do you think artists really do experience the world differently than others?

An artist is different only in his ability to communicate part of his experience in ways that speak to others at a level beyond words. That doesn't mean he experiences anything more powerfully. In fact, it may be that some people are too deeply involved in the richness of their lives to bother taking time to communicate what they're living. For example, I think tourists at the Grand Canyon come in three basic types. First, there are those who aren't really present because they're too into themselves. We can ignore them. Second, there are those who are present in the moment to some extent, but feel a need to document the experience (usually with a snapshot). Finally, some are so completely present they lose track of themselves within the experience. So who really sees the canyon most intensely? The one who wants to take it in, or the one who's willing to be taken in? Ridler may be a great artist, but he's in the snapshot crowd. He would see the Grand Canyon as a challenge, something to be captured. He does see something almost everybody else misses, but what good does that do when he's too prideful and cowardly to simply let it be?

The Opposite of Art required a very extensive knowledge of Buddhism, Islam, Judaism, and Christianity, and their religious texts. How did you prepare to write about each of these? Did you do your research before writing, or did it happen along the way?

Over the years I've read the Bible and Qur'an pretty extensively. I love Rumi's poetry, I spent several years studying with rabbis at a Reform temple, and I practiced Zen Buddhism before I became a Christian. So I approached this story with all of those experiences in mind.

Ridler searches for the Glory in Turkey and in Israel in the face of hostile situations. With the ongoing conflict in the Middle East, why do you think it is important to continue to grow one's faith during tumultuous times?

I wouldn't put it quite that way—"it is important to continue to grow one's faith during tumultuous times"—because that makes it sound like growing one's faith is a proper goal in life. I don't think faith is a goal; I think it's a side effect. There's an old Scottish saying: "Man's chief end is to glorify God, and to enjoy him forever." I believe that's the true goal, and I believe it's equally true at all times, regardless of one's circumstances. Faith grows automatically when we focus on enjoying God, because that focus puts life in proper harmony. Faith grows even faster when we focus on enjoying God in the midst of adversity, because then we value the resulting harmony even more.

Ridler experiences God and finds hope in other people, while Gemma sees God in art. How do you personally find faith in everyday experiences?

I already mentioned several ways people have helped me along in my journey, but art has definitely also played a role. For example, I remember one time I was at the Kimbell Art Museum staring at a landscape by Monet, and I had the most extraordinary sense of being drawn into the scene. I was in a crowded room, and then suddenly I wasn't. I was completely outside myself, much as Gemma is outside herself in a few scenes in The Opposite of Art. When I returned to self-awareness, the hairs on my neck and arms were standing on end. It was an utterly visceral reaction to the sense of communion I had experienced. Communion with Monet, and communion with Monet's creation. I remember longing in that moment to enter real landscapes in that way, not just painted reproductions, and a sudden sense of joy that came immediately, because I remembered I could indeed experience the real world like that, in communion with Jesus. It was one of the most spiritually powerful moments I've ever experienced.

What are you working on next?

I'm trying to make sense of a crazy story called Digger in a Potter's Field. It's about a boy who somehow becomes lost in a world of magic and horror, and a father who refuses to believe his son has gone too far to save.

Look for

Lost Mission

a Christy Award–winning novel by
Athol Dickson

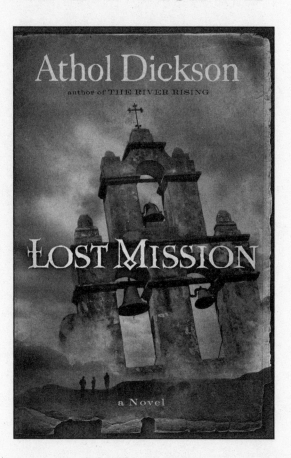

Available wherever books are sold or at www.simonandschuster.com

HOWARD BOOKS
A Division of Simon & Schuster
A CBS COMPANY